The Delight of Being Ordinary

The Delight
of
Being Ordinary

A ROAD TRIP WITH THE POPE AND

THE DALAI LAMA

Roland Merullo

༈

DOUBLEDAY

NEW YORK LONDON TORONTO

SYDNEY AUCKLAND

This is a work of fiction. Names, characters, places, and
incidents either are the product of the author's imagination
or are used fictitiously. Any resemblance to actual persons,
living or dead, events, or locales is entirely coincidental.

Copyright © 2017 by Roland Merullo

All rights reserved. Published in the United States by
Doubleday, a division of Penguin Random House LLC,
New York, and distributed in Canada by Random House
of Canada, a division of Penguin Random House Canada
Limited, Toronto.

www.doubleday.com

DOUBLEDAY and the portrayal of an anchor with a dolphin
are registered trademarks of Penguin Random House LLC.

Book design by Pei Loi Koay
Jacket illustration by Shout
Jacket design by John Fontana

LIBRARY OF CONGRESS CATALOGING-IN-PUBLICATION DATA
Names: Merullo, Roland, author.
Title: The delight of being ordinary : a road trip with
the Pope and the Dalai Lama / Roland Merullo.
Description: New York : Doubleday, [2017]
Identifiers: LCCN 2016027621 | ISBN 9780385540919 (hardcover) |
ISBN 9780385540926 (ebook) | ISBN 9780385542470 (open market)
Subjects: LCSH: Self-actualization (Psychology)—Fiction. |
Self-realization—Fiction. | BISAC: FICTION / Humorous. |
FICTION / Literary. | FICTION / Religious. |
GSAFD: Road fiction.
Classification: LCC PS.E748 D45 2017 |
DDC 813/.54—DC23 LC record
available at https://lccn.loc.gov/2016027621

MANUFACTURED IN THE UNITED STATES OF AMERICA

First Edition

For my Exeter friends

Bob Braile, Joanie Pratt,

Wick Sloane, and David Weber

and

for Jason Kaufman,

with thanks

Let us ask ourselves today: Are we open to "God's surprises"?

—POPE FRANCIS

It is my belief, for the world in general, that compassion is more important than religion.

—THE DALAI LAMA

God made so many different kinds of people. Why would he allow only one way to serve him?

—MARTIN BUBER

The gods, too, are fond of a joke.

—ARISTOTLE

ACKNOWLEDGMENTS

First thanks, as always, to my wife, Amanda, for her loving support, optimism, and steady compass in the sometimes difficult journey that is the creative life. My special thanks, also, to our daughters, Alexandra and Juliana, who brighten our home like sunlight and who inspire me every hour with their grace and wisdom.

I would also like to express my gratitude to my good friend Peter Sarno, whose Revere sense of honor and humor buoys me; to Craig Nova, a fine writer, who lives the creative life with great dignity; to Jessica Lipnack, for many kind favors; to Dennis Holahan, for his support and wise counsel; to my fine editor, Jason Kaufman, who put so much extra effort into the development of this novel; to Zanny Merullo and Simone Gugliotta, for their invaluable help with the Italian language (any mistakes are my own); and to the other good people at Doubleday— Bill Thomas, Rob Bloom, Lauren Weber, Victoria Chow, Carolyn Williams, Patrick Dillon, Chris Jerome, Pei Loi Koay, Kevin Bourke—for their help in bringing this story into print.

I am inclined to put my trust in spiritual figures who show a sense of humor, rather than those who take everything—including themselves—with a miserable seriousness. Life can be harsh, yes. The struggle to live a meaningful life, however we define that, can be rich with problems and challenges. But humor exists to soften the sharp edges of things. And so Pope Francis and the Dalai Lama, both of whom laugh a lot, seem to me like wise teachers, extraordinary men in the difficult position of guiding billions of followers, of steering vessels with a heavy cargo of good and bad history, in the same general direction, across the rough seas of modern life.

It was in a spirit of respect and gratitude that I made them the central characters in this odd parable. They are human, and in order to make the story work I felt I had to show them as people, not figureheads. In doing so, I made use of various interviews, articles, and biographies. While trying to stay close to actual Christian and Buddhist doctrines I have taken a few small liberties. For instance, I don't know that Pope Francis is actually afraid of heights, or that the Dalai Lama is actually afraid of water. My hope is that the reader accepts these fictional details in the spirit in which they were intended: respect-

ful, well-meaning, provocative in the best sense, berib-
boned with strips of humor and the big life-and-death
questions that are central to the lives of those men, and
that have fascinated me since I was old enough to write
a complete sentence.

The Delight of Being Ordinary

Day One

1

My name is Paolo dePadova—son of an Italian mother and an American infantryman father, and thanks to a peculiar combination of loyalty and luck I served, for a time, as First Assistant to my beloved cousin His Holiness the Pope of Rome. My tenure didn't last long. In fact, my duties came to an end as a direct result of the story I'm about to tell here, a story the Pope himself asked me to make public when I felt the time was right. Parts of it will be familiar from headlines in the international news, but, as you might expect, those parts were sensationalized, tarnished by rumor, stained with misinformation. The heart of it, the essence, the real, full story, remains known only to a handful of people, myself included. I share it now in a spirit of reverence and compassion, but also in service to the truth. As my cousin liked to say, *"Anche i papi sono uomini."* Which might be translated as "Popes are people, too."

2

My odd story begins, oddly enough, with a Buddhist. Or, at least, with the visit of a famous Buddhist to the most sacred halls of Roman Catholicism. It's common, of course, for a pope to receive visiting heads of state—presidents, prime ministers, first secretaries. Catholics have a great deal of clout in the world's voting booths, and politicians, even the least religious politicians, like to make a papal pilgrimage. They sit for a photo op with the Pontiff, pretend to exchange ideas, make promises they never intend to keep, then fly back to their luxurious lives and seats of power.

Popes, in my experience, handle these visits with an admirable patience. Disappointed again and again, they nevertheless always seem to hope that the leaders of the world will actually behave in ways that reduce the chance of war and give comfort to their poor.

In the case of the Dalai Lama's visit, however, the Holy Father had good reason for optimism. Here was a man whose responsibilities were similar to his own, and whose devotion to his faith and his people was beyond question. It was the second year of our joint tenure—the Pope's and mine—and probably the three hundredth official visit. I was used to the frenzied preparations: security precautions, press conferences, interviews. But when I went to see the Pope that morning I could sense, almost immediately, that the Dalai Lama's visit would not be typical.

My cousin liked to rise at four, spend three hours in prayer, and then take a light morning meal. On Tuesdays, Thursdays, and Saturdays when he was in Rome, Giorgio—as my parents and I had always called him—asked that I have breakfast with him in his relatively humble accommodations: a three-room suite at the Domus Sanctae Marthae hotel in Vatican City. Seven a.m. sharp.

This wasn't easy for me. At seven in the morning

I'm not yet at my best—not that my best is very good at any hour—but out of devotion to the famous man and in deference to his inhumanly busy schedule, I always showed up on time. In order to reach the papal chambers, even with my top-secret Vatican credentials, I had to run a gauntlet of security officials and various secretaries. After doing so on that morning I went, at last, along a familiar, carpeted corridor and tapped on a set of wooden doors twice my height.

"Entra, cugino!" the Pope always yelled joyfully. Come in, cousin! That day it was no different.

The velour curtains hanging from the windows of his dining area had been pulled aside and, even at that early hour, a golden sunlight poured through the glass. The Pope was dressed casually in dark pants and a white T-shirt, a medal of the Blessed Mother looped on a thin chain around his neck. As was his custom and preference, he was barefoot (he liked to say it linked him, however subtly, with the poor of this world). The sunlight fell on one side of his face, catching a smile so sincere and sparkling it would have caused the most devoted atheist to convert. He gave me the warmest of embraces. Another minute and we were sitting opposite each other at a small, marble-topped table. An aide brought a typical breakfast—pear slices, pots of herbal tea, two pieces of Belgian chocolate the size of bottle caps. (The Pope is famous for his sweet tooth.) We prayed over the food and began to eat, but, knowing him so well, I could see a rising tide of trouble, a splash of anxiety on the skin of his face.

"What's wrong, Your Holiness?"

"Oh, stop it," he said in his fake-gruff voice. "For the

one thousandth time, Paolo, please and kindly call me 'Giorgio' or 'Pope,' anything but 'Your Holiness.' I'm not worthy of that title, and it's like a wall between me and the cousin I love."

"Impossible, Your Holiness," I said. "I'm a simple man. If I start calling you Giorgio in private, I'll slip someday and say it in public."

"Sì, e poi?" Yes, and then?

"And then my enemies will attack me, and attack you for hiring me."

"Yes, and then?"

"Your judgment will come into question . . . and I'll be out on the street."

It was all a joke, a comic routine. "You keep me sane, cousin," the Pope liked to say. "Joke with me. Make me laugh. Remind me that I am, in fact, a human being, not a figurehead."

"Something's bothering you, Pope," I said.

He smirked, looked sideways, chewed meditatively on a slice of pear. "I can no more hide my thoughts from you than I can hide my sins from God."

"What is it?"

"How's Rosa?"

"Beautiful, intelligent, stubborn, rich, impossible to live with—which is why I no longer live with her. In short, the same as always. Don't change the subject. What's wrong?"

"And your miraculous daughter, Anna Lisa?"

"Fine, also, though I haven't seen her in four months. She misses you. Rosa, for some reason, thinks Anna Lisa has a serious boyfriend. Now, tell me, what's wrong?"

More pensive chewing. A sip of tea. As was his habit—

part of his ongoing battle with the demon of sugar—he broke one of the coins of dark chocolate in two and handed the larger piece to me. Another moment and out came the truth. "I have a confession to make."

"I'll call Cardinal Forgereau, your confessor. Let me finish the meal and I'll—"

"Not that kind of confession, Paolo. You're right. I'm troubled. I feel . . . lately I've been feeling, I don't know . . . *soffocato*. Stifled. Constrained."

"Emotionally or spiritually?"

"Both."

"Details, please."

He shook his head, frustrated. "I can't describe it."

"Should we cancel today's events? Say you're not feeling well? The Dalai Lama and his entourage are here until tomorrow, we can still—"

More headshaking. "It's not that. I'm anxious to see him. I feel so badly about not meeting him when he was in Rome with the Nobel laureates. That was shameful and foolish of me. I listened to bad advice—a terrible weakness of mine—and now I want to make it up to him." The Pope paused again, shook his head in small movements. For a moment he couldn't seem to make eye contact, an exceedingly rare occurrence with this man. At last he looked up. "Could you do me a favor, cousin?"

"Anything."

The Pope is from Argentina—everyone knows that—and his first language is Spanish, of course. But his parents—like my mother—were Italian-born, and so, in honor of our shared heritage and in deference to the traditions of the Church, we usually spoke Italian with each other. This had the added advantage of not arousing suspicion among my numerous enemies in the Vatican bureaucracy. With most of the Pope's visitors, English was the preferred tongue. I'm fluent, thanks to my parents, but the Holy Father sometimes struggles, and he hesitated so long then, spent so much time placing another pear slice between his lips, chewing, swallowing, that I worried he couldn't find the words in either of those two languages and would revert to Spanish, a tongue I habitually mangle and wreck. Another pause, and then, in an embarrassed way, he said, "I've been having very odd dreams, cousin. *Ho avuto stranissimi sogni, cugino.* I sense that God might be sending me messages, in a kind of code." He paused again. His embarrassment—so rare—embarrassed me. I wanted to ask about the dreams, but I held my tongue. He looked away, looked back. He said, *"Potresti creare un piano d'azione, cugino?"* Could you put together a plan, cousin?

"*Certo,* Holy Father. Of course. What kind of plan?"

Another smirk of displeasure. More hesitation. Then: "If I wanted to, say ... take an unofficial vacation ... three days, four at the most ... could you work out the logistics?"

"Of course, Your Holiness. But anyone here could do that. Your travel office. One of the administrative assistants. People say John Paul used to slip away to Cortina d'Ampezzo to ski. It's not hard to arrange such a thing, even with the security—"

"But I would want it arranged in secret ... to disappear for a few days," the Pope surprised me by saying. He was still having eye-contact issues. Unprecedented. "I don't want to go anywhere in that foolish bubble of a vehicle. It's a cage. It separates me from my people. And I don't want the bodyguards or the travel office to know about this. I don't want anyone to know. You and I. Rosa, if she wants to come along. We could make a side trip to see Anna Lisa, go to certain other places I have in mind. Three or four days . . . You're staring at me."

"I'm looking for signs of dementia, Your Holiness . . . with all due respect. Your face is probably the most famous face on earth. Certainly the most famous in Italy. And you and I are going to sneak away? And what? Ride the Autostrada, have lunch with my daughter, take a swim? This isn't Buenos Aires. We're not nine and fourteen anymore."

"It's absurd," he admitted. "You're right, as usual."

A veil of sadness fell across his face. To cheer him, and really only to cheer him, I said (and I will forever take responsibility for this remark), "Maybe the Dalai Lama could come along. I'll give some kind of knockout pill to the two security details, then spirit you both away."

The Pope's smile illuminated the room like light from a second sun. He took a sip of tea, washed it around in his mouth, swallowed, flashed the magnificent smile again, and then seemed to slip into the garment of his papal authority. I'd seen this before, hundreds of times, a magical transformation. He'd told me once that it was fine and good to be humble, but at some point, if you were, in fact, going to lead, you had to be comfortable using power. *"Un piano d'azione, per favore."* A plan, please, he said, as if he hadn't agreed, a few seconds earlier, that the whole idea was ridiculous. "Hypothetical but detailed. By dinnertime, if you would."

I went along with our little game. "I'll have it on your desk by lunch, Holy Father," I said.

"No, no. Nothing in writing."

And even after hearing those words, even after registering the stern expression on his face, I was sure my cousin the Pope must be joking.

3

A year or so earlier, the Pope had declined to meet with the Dalai Lama, who'd been in Rome with the other Nobel laureates. That decision—thrust upon the Holy Father by advisors who were not cousins—was intended, it seemed, to placate the Chinese government. What, exactly, Chinese leaders have to do with international Catholicism I doubt any of those advisors could have said. Clearly they were afraid of some imaginary backlash that might damage their careers, and clearly it had been a mistake to listen to them, a mistake born of inexperience. The Pope himself admitted as much to me. Since then, however, he'd grown bolder and more sure of his own judgment. In fact, as time passed, he seemed to care less and less what anyone thought of him. His global warming encyclical; his dressing down of the Curia at the annual Christmas address; his comments about not wanting Catholics to "breed like rabbits"; his secret diplomacy in the interest of rehabilitating U.S.-Cuba relations; his critique of what might be called "supercapitalism," an evil mutation of a good system—as he grew into his role, the Holy Father became as fearless and provocative as Christ. Though he still sometimes fell prey to manipulative advisors, he'd recently made a big show of publicly praising the Dalai Lama, and then inviting him to visit. Almost as if he were doing penance.

Everything went smoothly with the official aspects of the Buddhist's arrival. The Pope's staff had been through these high-profile visits many times; they were professionals, experts. The photo opportunity on the steps of St. Peter's, the tour there—no translator needed: the Dalai Lama seemed to understand all languages intuitively, and the men conversed in accented but capable English, with a few words of Italian and Spanish thrown in for good measure. A press conference, a sumptuous lunch, then some private time for the two of them before another lavish meal. Even with all their decades of experience, however, the staff never seemed to understand that this pope—unlike some of his predecessors—had no need for extravagant meals. He ate very little, in fact. I assume the Dalai Lama was the same way, a monk, after all. They were men of discipline and asceticism; and yet the staff prepared them dinners fit for a gluttonous prime minister and his coterie of overweight aides: five courses, from gourmet soup to flaming desserts. It was the equivalent of hiring an interior designer to decorate a nun's cell.

Before the second of these inappropriate meals, during their precious hour of private time, the Pope called and asked me to pay him a visit. He was with the Dalai Lama, he said, in the Room of the Blessed Mother, one of the most hidden-away places in the vast architectural maze that is Vatican City.

Another gauntlet of security types, more signing in, checkpoints, and so on. Loyal and unthreatening though I am, I had, as mentioned, a number of enemies in the

Vatican bureaucracy. First Assistant to the Pope is a job that carries a great deal of prestige, and my unexpected appointment had lit the fires of jealousy in certain quarters and earned my cousin few friends among the Church's hierarchy. DePadova isn't ordained—the first charge against me. Not experienced—charge number two. A Catholic of dubious standing, not living with his wife, not even, as far as anyone could be sure, a regular communicant at Sunday Mass—charge number three.

Filled though it is with holy souls, the Vatican has its factions and treachery. I sometimes think of the bureaucracy there as a long, heavy, slow-moving train, with the Pope in the engineer's seat. In the lavish cars behind him sit the members of the Curia—an old Latin word for "court"—and behind them, priests, deacons, and one-point-two billion ordinary Catholics. Yours truly occupied a seat somewhere near the caboose, so imagine the robes that were ruffled when I was called forward. Imagine the fits of jealousy. The Pope paid my detractors little mind. He told me he wanted a friend he could turn to in difficult times, someone he could trust absolutely. "On this earth," he said more than once, in public, "no one is closer to me than my cousin Paolo."

And so, while I worked harder and with more devotion than most of my predecessors, rumors about my reliability and loyalty wafted through the halls of Vatican City like a sour smell that occasionally reached my nose. Certain of my colleagues "forgot" to invite me to important meetings. My somewhat nervous nature and lack of political skill resulted in a few embarrassing faux pas. Because of these kinds of things—rumors, missed meetings, small lapses in etiquette—a pall of suspicion was cast across my name in some circles; and so, on that afternoon, as always, even my rather special credentials couldn't protect me from the stares of the security types. At last I entered the Room of the Blessed Mother, and I have to say that, as accustomed as I was to being in the presence of the Pope and his important visitors, there was something special in the air around those two men. They sat near each other at the ends of a matching pair of sofas, only a few feet separating them, paintings and icons of the Virgin Mary on the walls. All their various aides had been chased away. I walked across the carpet and bowed to the Pope first, and then to the world's most famous living Tibetan. My cousin motioned for me to sit in an upholstered armchair, facing them. "My beloved friend," he said, in English.

"My Pope."

He smiled, turned to his guest, and went on in a surprisingly informal tone, "Dalai—as you've asked me to call you—this is my cousin, closest friend, and key advisor, Paolo dePadova, an American Italian, son of artists. As you may know, my parents fled to South America to escape the horror of Mussolini's fascism. Paolo's mother—a brave woman who gave aid to the resistance fighters during the war—married an American soldier. Our families stayed in contact and visited each other often, and Paolo and I have been close since our youngest days."

The Dalai Lama's famous glasses, his famous shaved head, his famous smile and excellent posture. He nodded, said, rather generously, "What fine man you must be! Very great pleasure to meet you!" and made a small bow in my direction with the palms of his hands pressed

together. It was all very polite, the epitome of courtesy—
I felt truly blessed to be in their presence, truly part of
history on that day. A quiet, half-invisible part, but a part
all the same.

All was well, in other words . . . until my cousin turned
to his guest and spoke this disturbing sentence: "Paolo is
the one who's going to help us make our escape."

For a few seconds I held a plastic smile on my cheeks.
The Dalai Lama was looking at me with his thin eyebrows raised, expectantly, pleasantly. Overestimating me,
it seemed. We were all enjoying a light moment, breaking
the tension that came from the difference in our faiths,
the various stresses involved in our holy work.

"My cousin likes to joke," was the only reply I could
manage.

The Pope made a little fake cough. "Your cousin isn't
joking," he said, bluntly. "Have you come up with a plan?"

"You can't be serious."

The Pope pressed his lips together. "We've talked it
over," he said, "my new friend and I. He's having dreams
as well. Messages. Strange signals. Plus, we're both feeling
constrained. We're both men of adventure—the Dalai
escaped the Chinese, as you may know, on the back of a
donkey, no less, crossing the Himalayas dressed as a soldier
and then as a peasant!"

"I know, yes. I'd heard. We—"

"And, in our youth, you and I . . . we had some enjoyable times, yes?"

"Absolutely, Your Holiness."

"Then please do as I suggested earlier. We've decided
on a four-day trip. An escape, yes, but also a mysterious
search of sorts. I want him to see this beautiful country,

and I want to try to understand what God is whispering in my ear."

"Where? How? The security people, the schedule . . ."

Though he more often takes on the persona of the kindly follower of Jesus, when he wants to my cousin can make his face into a stern mask, a reflection of the wrathful Lord we grew up reading about in certain biblical passages. "Don't make me ask you a third time, Paolo," he said quietly. "We'll have our official dinner, and then, after dinner, please present me with a thoroughly thought-out plan. Our only window of opportunity is tonight, or very early tomorrow morning. Begin with this: His Holiness the Dalai Lama and I will say we want some time together for meditation. We'll meet in the St. Francis Chapel, no guards, no other attendants. A two-hour Buddhist-Christian meditation. Please take things from there. I'll sleep in my office tonight, not at the hotel."

I studied my cousin's face, guessing this was just his idea of a prank. Among his closest aides, the Holy Father was well known for that kind of thing: he had a reputation as a joker, a man who laughed as much as he prayed.

I turned my eyes to the Dalai Lama, hoping I might see him burst into his familiar chuckle, but the Buddhist only held his steady gaze on me for a few seconds and then said, in his lovely accent, "Tank you."

4

As long as I am on this earth I will remember the feeling of walking out of that room, down the long corridor, and

back to the main office building. I moved like a hypnotized man. I wrestled with the stark and shocking reality
of our conversation, going back over the Pope's words
again and again, as if I'd get the joke only by repetition.
He can't mean it, I thought. He can't be serious. The
dreams are just dreams—stress-related, perhaps. No doubt
the Dalai Lama is only pretending to have had these messages, too, out of politeness, hoping to get through the
formal meal, have some time for prayer, and enjoy a solid
sleep before leaving in the morning for wherever his
schedule draws him.

What operated against this line of logic was a bank
account of happy memories. In his youth, my cousin the
Pope had been known to do things just like this. "Pulling stunts," my parents had called it, as in "I wonder what
kind of stunt Giorgio's going to pull on this visit. Last
time we were here the two of you 'borrowed' bicycles,
rode to the next village, and spent half the night dancing
and singing in the barrio. The year before that you hitch-
hiked two hours to the beach without telling anyone."

Those words were spoken in a tone closer to admiration than censure. By then, the war years far behind them,
my parents were fairly settled bourgeois artists, if such a
thing exists. They had a car, a home, bills, a child to raise.
Still, they lived with creative flair, educating me themselves rather than sending me to the local school, setting
off by train to Berlin or Barcelona on an hour's notice.
My father painted our old Fiat in red, green, and white
swirls, with two small American flags near the headlights.
My mother grew her hair to her waist and was fond of
swimming in the lake as late as the first week of December, jumping off the stone wall in Mezzegra: I have a vivid

memory of her striding up the hill to our house, her hair wrapped in a towel turban and her teeth chattering. They were, in a word, eccentrics, and Cousin Giorgio's happy eccentricity amused and pleased them. I only wished they had lived to see him sitting on the papal throne.

So it was the memory of the way my cousin had behaved as a boy that convinced me, as I made that walk and ascended the familiar flights of marble stairs to my office, that he was, in fact, serious. My task, should I choose to accept it, was to make both of them disappear. The Pope and the Dalai Lama. Two of the most recognizable men on earth. Disappear, not for a few hours or an afternoon, but for four days! Surely, I thought, even if I somehow managed that Houdini trick, nothing good would come of it. The security forces, the entire world, would mount a frantic search. If anything went wrong—if one of them was hurt or, God forbid, killed—a certain Paolo dePadova would pay a brutally heavy price.

But, back in my neat third-floor office, as I stood at the window and looked out on an austere gray building known as the Office of the Doctrine of the Faith, the place where the Church's laws were made and enforced, the fingers of another emotion began to take hold of me. I recalled my mother telling me how it felt to leap from the fifteen-foot wall into the icy waters of Como, with a few bundled-up locals watching, aghast. "There's a freedom in it like nothing you've ever known, Paolo," she said. *Un senso di libertà.* "It's a victory over fear, over the constant need for physical comfort, over the urge to polish one's social reputation. Someday, when you're a little older, I want you to try it with me."

I never had the courage. On that July afternoon in

my Vatican City office, however, I did have an inkling of what a freedom like that might feel like. I understood why my cousin would want to break the bonds of tradition and duty—if only for a few days. By nature I'm a nervous and overly cautious man, but beneath my hypnotic dread, and, really, against my better judgment, I began to sense the first awakenings of a new possibility. That possibility—one wildflower sprouting in a bland lawn—carried the sweet fragrance of youth.

Soon, however, a logical, middle-aged sobriety choked the excitement into silence. The wildflower was crushed under a plain brown shoe. I sat at my desk, staring blankly out the window. It was one thing to escape the Chinese as a teenager—the Dalai Lama had been safeguarding his faith and traditions, fleeing a vicious enemy. It was one thing to borrow a couple of old bikes and ride to the next town for an evening of singing and innocent fun. It was something else entirely to shake off the heavy cloak of papal responsibility and make an unauthorized, four-day trip. It would be the equivalent of an American president sneaking away with the First Lady for a romantic weekend—not to Camp David, not with a Secret Service detail, not after notifying the press, but like an ordinary couple jumping on a bus, refugees from the world of status and propriety. That world—so fixed, inflexible, and proud—could exact vengeance in terrible ways. And the physical dangers were obvious.

Still, I'd been given an assignment—by the Pope of Rome, no less, the Vicar of Christ on earth. What kind of cousin, what kind of neurotic First Assistant, what kind of Catholic, would be foolish enough to disobey?

After considering the logistics for the better part of

an hour, I came to see, with a sudden clarity, that only a mind far more calculating than my own could hope to be successful with such an escapade. For another few minutes I sat and pondered, but it was as if I could feel time ticking by, as if I could hear the tone of my cousin's voice, see the look—"mischievous" isn't the correct word, but it's in the right general area of the thesaurus—on the Dalai Lama's face. I pulled my phone from my pocket and sat there, looking at the screen. My thumb moved to the phone icon. To Contacts. I saw the name ROSA there and a tendril of doubt took hold of me. I'd worked so hard to keep a blanket of peace between me and my estranged wife, to preserve a sort of demilitarized zone, to minimize any joint involvement in potentially troublesome activities. Ten seconds. Twenty. I thought of my mother, leaping from the stone wall into a cold lake.

I tapped Rosa's number and listened for her voice.

5

My wife (I would say "ex-wife," but the truth is, Catholics don't accept divorce, and so we were technically still married) has, among many other fine qualities, a beautiful speaking voice. In our more tender days, I'd often told her she should have been a singer, or a radio announcer. In actual fact, just after turning forty, she started a new career as a hairdresser, discovered a knack for it, widened her scope to makeup and nails, happened to do some work for a famous director—who was probably half in love with her—and by age forty-six she owned a chain of haircutting and makeup shops from the Dolomites to Sicily and was on a first-name basis with many of the great Italian film stars of our era.

Let me admit before going any further that her success, especially compared to my own business failure, was a bruise to my ego. I tried my best to fight this. I supported her in every possible way. But the fact was, in front of our daughter and our friends, I was the failed travel agent, my business crushed by the advent of online commerce, and Rosa was the spectacularly successful hair-and-makeup artist. In her defense, she never threw this in my face. Our arguments took a different shape, small firefights bred of stubbornness and the need to be right. Even so, with the benefit of hindsight I see now that a sense of my own inadequacy (why do we judge ourselves by professional success? Is there no more accurate gauge for the worth of a human life?) lay beneath most of my foolish stubbornness. If I could go back and rewrite our history, I would. Maybe Rosa would, too. But marriage is an intricate dance. Each partner is moving, moving, constantly moving; you hold your love—a precious vase—between your bodies. A single clumsy step and the vase crashes to the floor in a hundred pieces.

In the end, despite our troubles, Rosa and I had remained friends. The love of our daughter united us. Twenty-one years of living together united us. A lively physical connection, or the memory of that, united us. Every week or two we got together for coffee, lunch, or a walk in the Borghese Gardens, and while there was no talk of actually living under the same roof again, we enjoyed each other's company. As far as I knew, at least, there had been no infidelity, during or after our time together. We suffered from no deep scars like that. Still, Rosa Pesca and I were like chemical elements that can coexist in harmony if kept at a distance, but when placed together in a test tube boil over into a poisonous mess.

So it required a certain amount of swallowed pride for me to dial Rosa's number on that afternoon. I half-hoped she wouldn't answer, but she did. *"Ciao, amore mio,"* she said, the usual greeting. This "my love" was a blade in my heart, though I don't think she meant it that way. "I was thinking of you just now."

"Ciao, Rosa, listen," I said, and without wasting time on preliminaries I gave her a description of the impossible task. When I finished, there was a pause, and then a peal of the most joyous laughter.

"You're in a spot, aren't you," she declared happily.

"Yes, I need help. Advice at the very least. Where can I buy a couple of wigs, a fake mustache, some kind of enormous sunglasses?"

"Sei proprio pazzo," she said. You're truly nuts.

"Yes, I know, but the Holy Father asked—"

"I mean, you're nuts to think you can buy a couple of fake mustaches and get away with this. These are the two most recognizable men on earth."

"I know, I know. I was thinking the same thing a few minutes ago."

"I'll have to do them," she said.

"Do them? Do them how?"

"The full treatment," she said. "Hair, makeup, clothes. The works."

"Bene," I said, soaking the word in sarcasm. *"Molto bene!* Very good! I'll bring them in tomorrow morning. Do you have any availability in the shop near the Spanish

Steps? Can you cancel the appointment of some famous star and squeeze us in?"

Rosa was laughing. At me, it seemed. This was a situation with which I was familiar, and one I did not particularly enjoy. "It'll be fun," she said. "Bring them out to me and I'll make some calls, set everything up. How much time do we have?"

"Tonight. The Dalai Lama is scheduled to leave tomorrow after breakfast."

"And the Pope wants him along?"

"He seems to, yes. The conversation was brief. I was given my orders and dismissed, but I have to say the Dalai Lama seemed excited . . . in a Buddhist way."

More laughter. "Can you sneak them out?"

"No, of course I can't sneak them out," I said, but at that moment I had an epiphany, a small enlightenment. It occurred to me that the Pope's choice of the Chapel of St. Francis for their private prayer was not accidental. "Wait," I said to Rosa, recalling something my cousin had told me after his initial orientation. "There's supposed to be a tunnel. From the Middle Ages. When they had to get popes out of the way of marauding heathens. I think it comes out near Castel Sant'Angelo."

"Good. I'll meet you there. Pick a time."

"Four a.m.," I said, though God alone knows why I chose that hour.

"Done," Rosa said, and then, just before she hung up, "I've always loved this side of you."

"What side?" I wanted to ask. "The fool? The person who rises to a certain level and then sabotages himself?"

But by then it was too late.

6

I'd been invited to the formal dinner, but of course I couldn't go. I spent those hours locked in my office, pondering the crazy idea. The Pope had provided me with a first step: he and the Dalai Lama would say they wanted some time alone for early-morning meditation. This was somewhat believable, because both of them were known to rise before dawn and begin the day with prayer. But the security forces—Vatican and Tibetan both—would surely insist on remaining close by, and that presented a problem. The Pope received a death threat every other day. And I was quite sure, given the Chinese government's violent occupation of Tibet and hatred for all things religious, that the Dalai Lama was in at least as much danger. Somehow I'd have to convince their security details—teams of hard-faced karate experts and sharpshooters, the most suspicious men on earth—that the religious leaders wanted complete solitude for those two hours, and that there was zero risk of them being harmed in the bowels of the Vatican. And somehow I'd have to get these same two religious leaders from the Chapel of St. Francis to the streets of Rome without anyone knowing about it.

Impossible as this might have seemed, I realized, after thinking about it for a few minutes, that history was working in my favor. The papal escape wasn't exactly a modern notion. Popes had been the object of death threats since the time of St. Peter, and wise assistants and aides of old had developed various strategies to protect them. There was a famous aboveground escape route, the Passetto di Borgo, which linked St. Peter's Basilica and the

Castel Sant'Angelo, but that wouldn't work for us: too hard to access in secret; too well-known; and it was probably impossible, even at four a.m., to hide men in robes scurrying across an elevated walkway. But, according to what my cousin had told me after his orientation, there was another route, subterranean, top secret. "I was given two keys," he'd said, in an amused voice. "They look like they're a thousand years old. I use them as paperweights."

The Holy Father wasn't sure he remembered correctly—he hadn't taken the idea of escape seriously then—but he seemed to think there was a door at the back of the Chapel of St. Francis that led down a set of stairs to a tunnel. The tunnel ran beneath Vatican City all the way to the Castel Sant'Angelo, a famous landmark near the river, and a place that was supposed to be impregnable. Even the Mongol hordes would have had a difficult time assaulting the Castel Sant' Angelo. It was a circular building with eighty-foot stone walls and an elevated walkway from which the Pope's defenders could fire arrows, shoot bullets, and throw heavy stones down on the crazed invaders below.

There wouldn't be any crazed invaders chasing the Pope this time, no Goths or Visigoths, only the aforementioned karate experts. Simple, then: I'd get the Pope and the Dalai Lama into the private chapel, sneak them down the back stairs, lead them along the tunnel to the Castel Sant'Angelo, meet my estranged wife, and we'd all have a nice trip to the hairdresser's. A brilliant plan . . . with approximately the same chance of success as a helicopter trip to Saturn.

Not to mention other likely possibilities: that the Pope had remembered wrong, or the door to the stairway was rusted shut, or the old keys didn't work, or the tunnel—if there actually was a tunnel—had been blocked by a cave-in three hundred years ago, or one of the security men followed us, or Rosa slept through her alarm for the thousandth time.

Yes, yes, yes, there was no shortage of potential obstacles; but didn't every dream in life, every ambitious notion—a happy marriage, successful fatherhood, eternal salvation—require a kind of crazy faith? Didn't one have to go forward, always, fueled by a mystical optimism, hoping for the best? I stepped over to the cupboard, poured myself a glass of limoncello, sent up a prayer to the Blessed Mother, and went off to catch a few hours' sleep.

Day Two

7

At three-forty-five on a morning I shall always remember, I went to the Pope's office, found him asleep on the couch, and awakened him. He dressed quickly—in plain black clothes, as I suggested—handed me two heavy, rusty keys that looked like factory seconds from the Iron Age, and put a toothbrush into his pants pocket. Taking more than that—even a small shaving kit—would have tipped off the security forces. Together, we went to the guest quarters to awaken the Dalai Lama (though in fact he was already awake and sitting in meditation). Passing through a series of checkpoints and using our flimsy excuse on a series of bodyguards, we then made our way to the private chapel. In the pews of that room, while the two holy men sat side by side in prayer, I locked the door to the hallway as quietly as possible. That part was easy. I'd thought to bring along a flashlight, hidden in the sleeve of my sweater, but had rejected the idea of a change of clothes for any of us. How was one to explain a suitcase carried into the Chapel of St. Francis at four a.m.?

I cleared my throat to get their attention, then waved the two men toward the locked metal door at the back of the room. I tried the first of the two keys. No luck. The second key fit. I turned it in the lock, gingerly, worried it would snap in half as easily as a piece of Belgian chocolate. The lock clicked—a miracle. Through the door and down the extremely narrow stairs we went, three no-longer-young men guided by a single beam of light and spurred on by what can only be described as the spirit of the little boys within us. The stairway was only a meter wide, with uneven stone steps that had borne the shoes, boots, and sandals of escaping popes and pursuing heathens a thousand years ago. Cobwebs, loose gravel, air so musty it was like breathing the dust of dust. My cousin and the Dalai Lama were spry for their age, but even so, I led the way, heart thundering, hoping against hope that one of them didn't trip and fall forward, sending all three of us tumbling down in a bone-cracking heap.

"*Coraggio, coraggio, cugino!*" the Pope said behind me, as if he could read my mind. But it wasn't only encouragement that I heard in his voice. What I heard was the tone of the teenage Giorgio as we slipped through the alleys of the barrio toward the sound of faint guitar music and song. Then and now it was the tone of a person who felt absolutely beloved and protected—in the midst of a world bathed in hatred, anger, and every imaginable danger. According to Catholic legend, popes were actually chosen by the mysterious workings of the Holy Spirit. Over the centuries there had been a number of pontiffs who made you wonder about that idea. My cousin wasn't one of them.

We made it safely down the stairs—at the pace of an ant—to the stony floor. There we came upon an ancient oak door, slightly ajar. I yanked on it and it made a hideous creaking sound, its bottom scraping across stone in what seemed to me the voice of Fatherly warning. There, just at the mouth of the tunnel, I turned and faced my companions, shone the flashlight at their ankles so as not to blind them, and said, "Are we sure, Your Holinesses? From this point it will be difficult to turn back."

I looked from face to face, anxiously, humbly. They were old men, they'd risen at an ungodly hour, and the grayish light accentuated the age and tiredness around their eyes and mouths. Beneath those thin masks, however—and even before they spoke I could see this clearly—an impish electricity sparked. "Unless you become as little children," Jesus had said, "you shall not enter the kingdom of heaven." The faces I looked at then weren't the faces of little children, but something of the child had survived in both men, some lively spirit, some thrill at not being able to control the world around them. It shamed me, I have to admit. And it made me wonder, just for a few seconds, how a person like me, son of adventurers, progeny of artists and warriors, had become so maddeningly dull.

As if bestowing a benediction, the Pope reached out a hand and placed it on my shoulder. "My dear cousin," he said, and though he spoke very quietly I could hear his words echoing into the tunnel and up the narrow stairs, "of all the kind favors you have done me in my life, this stands at the summit, do you realize that? The apex. This is the ultimate good deed."

I looked at the Dalai Lama, who was nodding, his clean-shaven cheeks stretched by a long, thin smile. "What good man you are!" he said, in his singsong, delighted, fearless way. "What wonderful karma you bringing on yourself in this moment!"

"Your Holiness," I said to him, "promise me this: if

something goes wrong, promise me I won't be torn to pieces by your security detail. Cousin, promise me I won't be charged with kidnapping."

"Ignore the cold wind of fear," the Dalai Lama said, and, this coming from a man who had lived the life he'd lived, I have to say that those words carried a certain weight.

"Trust in God's protection," the Pope added.

We stepped into a narrow, dark, low-ceilinged passageway that I suspected would lead us in one of two directions: toward a grim, lonely death or the adventure of a lifetime.

8

Ignore the cold wind of fear.

Trust in God's protection.

I tried to imagine what it would be like to live every minute of every day according to advice like that! I was two steps into the dark, dusty tunnel and filled with spiritual envy. To be free of fear! To believe—to really believe—that you were always watched over and protected by a kind and all-powerful spirit. That death opened a door onto something better than this eighty-year marathon of disappointment and decay!

In my own life I tried, really I did. I believed there had to be some kind of God presiding over the millions of universes, the "Father" Jesus was always referring to. But my faith in his absolute kindness flickered like a candle on a dinner table with the windows open in summer. The Syrian slaughter, North Korean torture, ISIS, Boko

Haram, rape, addiction, murder, vitriol and violence—on some days doubt swelled up over my faith like a dirty flood.

And doubt, it seemed to me, had its own propaganda apparatus in the modern world. The hourly news reports from every corner of the map seemed designed to breed an ongoing paranoia, a sense that we had to cling to this body in desperation because there were still pleasures to be had, at any age, and beyond them only darkness. We could shoot chemicals into our face to pretend we weren't aging; we could transplant organs and, not defeat death, but at least hold it at bay. In our time, the flimsy notion of Trust in God could be placed far back in line behind more tangible allies like Novocain, morphine, penicillin, and NATO's tanks. But my two companions had some-how learned to keep that candle from going out. And look where they'd come from! Tibet and Argentina, two places where the memory of atrocity was fresh. How did they manage it?

We went forward on pure faith and the light from flashlight batteries, feeling our way along the uneven floor with the toes of our shoes, step by cautious step, the Pope's hand on my shoulder, the Dalai Lama's hand on the Pope's shoulder, the tunnel winding, twisting, steadily descending. "In life," the Pope mused at one point, "we can see only a short distance in front of us, eh, cousin? We never really know what awaits."

This was his idea of a good-humored parable—taking a legitimate worry and making a lesson out of it. The Dalai Lama laughed. I said nothing, in silent protest. On and on we shuffled, down and down in a gentle descent, a quarter of an hour, twenty-five minutes, half an hour.

At last the floor of the tunnel flattened out. One final turn, a dozen steps, and ahead of us I could see another round-topped door, wooden, with metal bracing. In front of it hung a massive cobweb. I stood still and stared. I could feel the men close behind me, and my terror of spiders like a cold steel rod in my spine. And then the good Pope—who knew of my fear—stepped in front of me and, with one straight arm extended, swept away the silken fibers as if he were a sacred knight sweeping sin from the world. He did a thorough job, spent a moment removing the gluey threads from his sleeve, then stood aside and let me approach the door first.

At that point our flashlight died.

One second after the world went dark, I heard the Dalai Lama's laughter echoing along the tunnel. Another lesson. More worry crushed under the boot of faith. It was chuckle more than guffaw, almost a giggle, and, it seemed to me, given the circumstances, completely out of place.

The laughing went on and on, a string of sunny notes, an unself-conscious symphony echoing back on itself like the sound track from a documentary on joy.

What a time for the flashlight to die—ha, ha!

The longer it lasted, the more irritating I found it. We stood there in absolute darkness, in the musty air, ten or a hundred or a thousand feet belowground—who knew?—so close together I could smell the Pope's body wash and a hint of what must have been incense from the robe of the Dalai Lama. When the merriment finally ceased, the Dalai Lama said, "Ah," in a voice that was still lit with the shine of amusement. For another half-minute we stood there in the dark, in a terrible silence. "I know little bit about other traditions," the Buddhist said quietly.

"For Hindu people, goddess Kali is symbol of blackness, of death sometimes. And in Bengali Tantric tradition she doesn't give you what you expect!" He chuckled. "Here we have blackness and not what we expect! Here we have Kali!"

Right, I thought. All we need to complete the picture is death.

I reached forward and felt for the door handle, found it, found the opening below it, inserted the second key, turned it, yanked hard on the handle. Nothing. A bolt of pain from an old shoulder injury. Another of Kali's bad jokes, apparently. I tried again. Different key. Same result. The door seemed to be cemented in place, and I wondered if the entranceway had been sealed off from the Castel Sant'Angelo side as protection against people sneaking into the Vatican. I yanked at the handle one more time and the shoulder pain sliced up into my neck and left ear. From my lips slipped a word one probably shouldn't say in the presence of the holy ones. The Dalai Lama touched me on the arm. "What means this 'shit'?" he whispered across the darkness.

I couldn't see his face, couldn't tell if he was making a joke.

"An American curse word," the Pope explained. "Paolo's upset because the door won't open. He's worried we're going to be stuck down here for all eternity."

The Dalai Lama laughed again. Stuck for all eternity— what an amusing idea!

"'Scuse me, 'scuse me," he said. He squeezed past, and just then I remembered that my new phone had, among other miraculous properties, a flashlight accessory. I turned it on. The Buddhist Holiness was manipulating the doorknob, turning it this way and that, working the key, tenderly, the way a safecracker works the dial on a bank vault. I remembered someone telling me that the Dalai Lama liked to take apart and repair antique watches. A nice hobby, for sure, but this was a hundred-kilo door, not a timepiece. I could feel the irritation puffing up inside me like smoke from a fire. What we needed now, I wanted to tell him, was a small explosive device, not tenderness. What we needed was someone who took apart aircraft carriers, not watches. He tugged the handle up a centimeter, down a centimeter, pushed it forward, tapped the door a few times with his knuckles, touched it once with the tips of his fingers. Then he stepped back in what I assumed was a pose of surrender. "Now try," he said.

I did. The door opened.

Strange as this might seem, it was only then that I started to take the man seriously. I don't mean to sound irreverent—I'm not at all—but there was, by Western standards, something a bit goofy about him. He found material for humor in places most people would not. He talked funny, his voice rising every few seconds into a high squeak, his sentences full of drawn-out vowels and exclamation points. He shaved his head. He wore a robe. He put on the caps of American baseball teams and let his picture be taken and splashed all over Facebook. What holy man did things like that?

But when he opened the old door that way—after keys and yanking hadn't worked—I started to watch him surreptitiously, to look beyond his goofiness. I started—just started—to wonder if my Western conceit was blinding me to something important, and I made a mental note to discuss it with the Pope.

We stepped across a knee-high pile of debris and found ourselves in a windowless room with stone walls and a stone staircase, half-hidden in shadow, that led upward into blackness.

"The basement of Castel Sant'Angelo," my cousin said hopefully.

"What is?" the Dalai Lama wanted to know.

"A castle, a fortress, a prison—it's been many things over the centuries," the Pope told him, as I moved the thin beam of light here and there along the walls. "It was built for an emperor of Rome—Hadrian, he was called. He wanted a mausoleum that would hold his ashes, and those of his wife and child."

"Very big place to hold ashes," the Dalai Lama said, and even in that simple comment I sensed a nugget of spiritual wisdom: didn't death trump even the largest egos?

"I don't like it," I whispered. "I've never liked this place, never even liked driving past it."

"Many terrible hours were endured here," my cousin said. "Popes hid in terror, conquerors ransacked and slaughtered, heretics were imprisoned, no doubt tortured."

"Spiders bred."

"Legend has it that the archangel Michael was seen sheathing his sword at the top of this building, five hundred and ninety years after Christ. It signaled the end of the plague. Imagine!"

"I don't want to."

The Pope put his hand on my shoulder. "Onward, my friend. Let us not dwell upon the errors and horrors of the past."

Right, I thought, because we have so many present errors and horrors to dwell upon.

Guided only by the light of my phone, we climbed that first flight of stairs, then another, and at last, all of us breathing heavily, came into a massive, circular room with one window and one door on each side, an enormously high ceiling, and a flotsam of litter—stones, old tools, and scraps of cloth—against the base of the walls. I shone the light there. A shovel, a shard of pottery, a pair of iron cuffs attached to a short chain, worm-eaten lengths of firewood, one black boot, mostly eaten through by rats or mice. It was a museum of the useless and damaged, a menagerie of the out-of-date. The windows admitted a frail light from the street, so I thought it prudent to switch off my phone and save the battery. We tried each door in turn—all locked tight.

"Now we are in need of divine assistance," the Pope quipped. And then he added, mysteriously, "Paolo, when we're free of this place, remind me to go into more detail about the bizarre dreams I've been having."

"*Certo*," I told him. Of course. But, at that moment, the Pope's dreams were the last thing I cared about.

Though I tried and retried the keys, and the Dalai Lama tried his gentle, safecracker's magic, we couldn't make either of the doors budge. The Dalai Lama started to chuckle again, and despite my newfound respect for the man, may God forgive me, I didn't think I could bear it. I went over to one of the junk piles, grabbed the heavy iron cuff, and slammed it against the door handle until we heard a noise like the cracking of bone. I kicked the door with the sole of my shoe, twice, and it opened.

We caught the scent of the nearby Tiber. We heard the throaty growl of a bus engine. The three of us stepped across the threshold into a cement-and-brick oblong box.

Twenty or thirty meters beyond the doorway we were able to look up and see a sliver of the star-strewn sky, and I understood that we were in a stone enclosure, ten meters below street level. Ingenious, really, because the way the walls of the enclosure had been built, the way the stone ceiling mostly covered it, the entranceway was hidden from the street. A few more steps and the circular bulk of the castle came into view behind us, streetlights along the Tiber raking it in a soft yellowish light.

At that point the Dalai offered this memorable line: "Now we are escaped."

We crept along like soldiers in defilade, staying in the shadows. A grassy area separated us from the nearest road. I ran my eyes back and forth across the sparse traffic there, looking for a parked van, my wife in silhouette, but seeing nothing besides two pesky *motorini* buzzing along, carrying couples away from late-night discothèques. A delivery truck, the occasional car. A police vehicle, blue light flashing, scooted away from us. I wondered if the alarm had already been sounded at the Vatican, but no, it couldn't be. We'd been gone only a little over an hour. The security detail would still be standing outside the door, respectfully, dutifully, waiting for the holy men to finish their prayers. Soon enough, though, they'd grow impatient. They'd knock, timidly at first, then more anxiously. Someone would have the courage to try the door; they'd find it locked. They'd summon the necessary equipment, a crowbar, a heavy pole, a battering ram, an old iron prisoner's cuff, and at that point a surge of panic would be washing over the twin security details. Once the door was smashed open, they'd rush into the empty chapel, see the door there at the back—we'd forgotten to close and lock it! They'd descend the stairs, make their way along the same tunnel but much faster than we'd traveled, running, tripping, pushing past each other.

We had, I guessed, roughly another hour.

"Now what?" the Pope said at my right shoulder.

"Now either Rosa appears out of the blackness or we take a taxi back up to the Vatican and turn ourselves in."

"There—I see her! *Eccola!*"

The Pope's arm stretched over my shoulder. A woman who bore some resemblance to my wife was standing on the sidewalk a hundred meters from us. I whistled two notes, an old signal. She turned, waved both hands above her shoulders. We hurried toward her.

9

From twenty-one years of wedded bliss, I recognized the signs of excitement in my wife: she was making small hops in her fashionable high heels, waving happily, her long, dark hair swinging left and right. This was, it occurred to me as we approached, exactly the type of escapade Rosa had always loved. I realized, too, that it was the kind of somewhat risky fun that had leaked out of our marriage, mysteriously, sadly, as time passed. When we were dating, when we were just married and still young, even after our child was born, some blessed spirit of adventure had lived in us. Early on, we'd drive all the way to the beach at Agrigento and make love on the sand at two a.m. On our wedding night we danced with friends until the sun came up, then ran a made-up jogging race around the Colosseum in our fancy clothes. We ate midnight meals by candlelight on our apartment's tiny balcony. We kissed for no reason, in clothing stores, outside church after Mass. Later, in a way similar to what my parents had done with me, we'd pack up Anna Lisa and jump on a slow train to Calabria, no reservations, just trusting that it would work out. And it always did. We had very little money then, but that didn't matter. We'd find a room in a small *agriturismo* or inexpensive hotel, buy food in the town markets, and make ourselves simple meals. We'd hike through the dry Calabrian hills and have midday picnics of fruit and cheese and bread and wine, propping our little girl up between us and feeding her bits of peach and sips of water, teaching her words, changing her diaper, swinging her in happy circles, singing songs. We'd ride a bus to the beach in summer and play in the waves; we'd take a train to Trento in winter and sled down the slopes. Once, after I'd made a bit of extra money, we took our ten-year-old daughter to Ancona and booked passage on a ferry to Croatia for a long weekend.

And then, somehow, we began to forget to do those things. Anna Lisa grew. There were school functions, doctors' visits, dance recitals, meetings with friends, all of it scheduled, programmed, predictable. With the increasing popularity of online travel arrangements, I began to have to struggle to keep my business afloat, which meant working more hours. Rosa started a simple haircutting shop and within a month it was thriving. Within a year she'd opened another shop; the business grew and grew and we were now a constantly busy, two-career couple who did nothing more adventurous than going out for dinner, having a glass of wine or two, then staggering home to sleep.

Some of that was natural—life changes, responsibilities intrude, passion cools: long-married couples don't spend a lot of time kissing in clothing stores. But Rosa and I had clearly failed to water the garden of our love, and it had withered.

This bit of sorrowful musing was soon replaced by something else: a familiar wash of irritation. As the three of us approached her, I saw that my wife, an otherwise intelligent woman, had not come in a plain van as I'd suggested, hadn't driven her rather ordinary Fiat SUV, but was standing beside a Quattroporte, the largest Maserati sedan. An elegant racecar. Something more suitable for a rich young bachelor than a pair of holy men. I couldn't be sure, but in the streetlight the car appeared to be lime green, with swooping, sensuous fenders and silvery stripes along each side. I'd asked for something inconspicuous, so what had Rosa done? Arrived, stubbornness intact, with the most inappropriate vehicle in all of central Italy!

Instead of a grateful greeting, a harsh whisper escaped my lips. "Rosa! *Ma che stavi pensando?*" But what were you thinking?

"Not now, love," she said calmly. Too calmly, I thought. Her excitement at seeing us had given way to a meditative efficiency. I wondered if, like so many of her wealthy clients, she was under the influence of medication. She hugged me, warmly, quickly, and said, "Please introduce me to your handsome friends."

"You know the Holy Father."

Rosa made a half curtsy and held out her hand. The

Pope hugged her hard against him, as if she were his sister and he were returning from war.

"And this is His Holiness the Dalai Lama."

Rosa put her palms together and bowed from the waist. The Dalai Lama bowed back.

"Give me your phone, Paolo," she said, when the introductions were complete. She'd taken a small plastic bag from her purse.

"What for?"

"Because it has a GPS chip in it. I'm hiding it right here." She slid my phone into the bag and pushed it in against the roots of a bush at the edge of the sidewalk.

"It'll be ruined. How can I call anybody if—"

"Think, sweetheart," she said.

I thought. I said, "Okay," and then, "Now let's go! In a car that is absolutely unforgettable. Silver stripes! A Maserati! What were you thinking? What kind of craziness is this?! Your Holiness, get in, please, quickly!"

"I like this car very much!" the Dalai Lama said, which only made it worse.

The holy men in back, yours truly muttering in the passenger seat. "Unbelievable! I wanted a van, something—"

"My sweet man." Rosa turned to me with an exaggerated patience, and in the wash of a streetlight I could see the beauty in her still, a refined, middle-aged, imperfect beauty—large nose, dark eyes, sensuous mouth—but it was there all the same and it took my heart, as it always had, and twisted it up. She had not yet put the Maserati in gear. "My sweet, innocent, naive man, who has been kept apart from the world by his new position, let me ask you this: Which one of us, you or I, knows more about disguise?"

"You, by a factor of one thousand."

"Exactly. And if two famous men, ascetic, simple, humble, holy men, were making an escape, what is one of the very last vehicles they would choose?"

"A sexy Maserati Quattroporte," I said, "which costs a hundred thousand euro."

"A hundred and fifty thousand," she said proudly. "And in case you're wondering, it's borrowed, not mine. From a good friend, also famous, but in a very different arena. I have it for a week." She produced two golf caps from between the seats. "*Ecco,*" she said, passing them back to the holy men. "Please, each of you, put one on. For now. Soon we will have some better way to hide you."

"Hats keep the head warm!" the Dalai Lama exclaimed. I couldn't look at him.

Rosa waited until first the Pope and then the Dalai Lama had turned themselves into golfers—it struck me as vaguely sacrilegious—then, casting her glorious smile across the top of the leather seat, she said, "And now, Your Holinesses? What is your pleasure?"

"Escape," the Dalai Lama said, as if repeating a word he'd just learned.

"Yes, a small vacation," the Pope added. "Four days. I want my guest to see the beautiful Italian countryside. I want to see it myself. We desire only to be normal for a while. Ordinary men. I have some ideas about where we must go, but please, no aides, guards, photographers, or reporters. And no formality!"

"No formality!" the Dalai Lama chimed in.

"Excellent!" Rosa said in an excited voice. "May I come along?"

"Rosa!"

"Of course, of course," the Pope said. "Without question. In fact, when Paolo first suggested this idea to me I knew he was secretly thinking of taking you with us. Beneath his disguise of pious humility, he's a sly man."

Rosa shot a smirk across the front seat and in the next second was zooming out of the parking space and through the streets of Rome like a woman intent on attracting the attention of hordes of traffic police.

I was running the Pope's words through my mind: "when Paolo first suggested this idea," . . . "disguise of pious humility," . . . "sly man." . . . Honest soul that he was, honest and good, I had the sinful thought then that the Holy Father might be hedging his bets. If things turned sour, really, brutally sour—if, for instance, the Curia decided that because of this irresponsible vacation or his crazy dreams, their pontiff was no longer quite sane, and if they then took some kind of unprecedented impeachment vote—the Pope could always claim he'd simply had a moment of weakness and had given in to his cousin's irreverent suggestion. And then his aide, the soon-to-be-notorious Paolo dePadova, would appear on the cover of tabloids around the world, wrists cuffed in front of him as he was hauled out of Vatican City under police guard.

We raced along the Lungotevere, the Tiber just to our left. There was little traffic at that hour, but, for reasons known only to her, Rosa felt obliged to show off for the holy men, switching lanes as if dodging cars and motor-cycles on all sides, pumping the clutch and shifting gears with a vengeance. She went through traffic lights just as they turned red, zoomed past delivery trucks parked at the curb as if there were no chance a driver would throw open his door, smash it through the windshield, and slice my head off as we passed.

I should explain at this point that my Rosa was the product of Neapolitan parents. She'd come to Rome to study history, fallen in love with me after her junior year in college, and never left, never finished her education, never looked back. At home, she wanted to speak English. "It will be good for Anna Lisa to be bilingual," she argued. I agreed. In fact, I wanted to keep my own American English sharp. But despite the calming influence of that utterly logical tongue, she remained Italian to the core. Or Neapolitan, I should say.

For those who don't know Italy well, Neapolitans are almost another species. They bear as much resemblance to Romans as Romans do to Berliners. That is, they are a wild people. Even their cuisine is wild—spicy, saucy, a mix of culinary traditions from Greek to Middle Eastern to African, everything thrown into the pot and eaten with warm bread and unsubtle red wine. They speak too loudly and are prone to bursting into song at inappropriate moments. Their dialect, filled as it is with *schs* and *wahhs* and words whose endings have been chopped off and dropped down the funnel of Vesuvius, makes them sound as if they're speaking with mouths full of food . . . which is often the case. Neapolitans are a happy people, yes, but it's a happiness that dances along the border of chaos. Having known you for three minutes, they'll invite you to sleep in their home, eat their food, drink their wine, act as godfather to their new grandchild. They will, literally, give you the shirt off their back. But try getting them to make a train run on time, or stand in line in some kind of orderly fashion, or avoid parking in no-parking zones, or show up for a one o'clock meeting before a quarter past two!

This Neapolitan side of her was part of the trouble between Rosa and me, part of our bad history. I was raised in northern Italy and, like many northerners, I was punctual, orderly, semi-Germanic, mostly soft-spoken and sober, and my wife, with her hot southern blood, was chronically late, messy in a beautiful way, owner of the first voice you heard when you walked into a crowded room, and a woman who enjoyed wine with lunch and dinner and had been known, on occasion, to overdo.

She was also a woman who, in the great Italian tradition, believed that the rules of the road existed only for the purpose of being broken.

"Are we going to Naples?" I asked, noticing that we were headed south and hoping the question, drenched in sarcasm, might encourage her to ease back on the accelerator.

"Naples!" she practically shouted. "Hah! My parents would tell everyone about their special guests. Half the city would be in their living room."

"Where, then? Monte Carlo for the Formula One races?"

"Nowhere, Paolo! Nowhere—at least until we make the two Holinesses invisible!"

The Dalai Lama leaned his head forward between the bucket seats and said, "Is very interesting to me, this idea to not be visible."

"Egoless!" Rosa shouted.

"Yes, yes, wonderful. Very good!" the Dalai Lama said, and another peal of laughter escaped him. Satisfied, he sat back in his seat, hands folded in his lap. I watched him out of the corner of my eye. He reached forward again and patted me on the left shoulder. "Your wife is a very advanced spirit," he said. "Almost enlightened."

"I've always known that," I said.

"A stream entrant."

"Yes, Your Holiness," I said, though I hadn't the faintest idea which stream he was speaking of. I turned my head further and met the Pope's eyes. He wrinkled the corners of his mouth at me, winked, showed the thumbs-up. It occurred to me then that both of them might have been pushed a short distance beyond the boundary of sanity by the weight of their responsibilities. Maybe there was such a thing as too much prayer.

"We're going to one of my shops," Rosa announced. "My most skilled associate is waiting there. Mario. There's a secret entrance, a hidden room in the back where we do big stars. It's perfect for this."

"What does the *doing* entail?"

"You'll see, *amore mio,*" she said, as we careened around a corner on what felt like two wheels. "Trust me."

10

Near the southernmost edge of the city Rosa made a sharp right turn into a narrow residential street, then, half-way along it, a not-as-sharp left turn into an alley choked with parked cars. At the far end the alley widened out like the head of a mushroom, offering a three-space parking area. My nearly enlightened wife pulled the Maserati into one of these spaces, led us to the rear of an apartment building, unlocked a door there, and motioned us inside. The back hallway opened into a room with large mirrors, two hairdressing chairs, and a trio of comfortable-looking red leather sofas along one wall. Above the sofas hung framed posters of Italy's most famous film stars: Sophia Loren and Marcello Mastroianni and Carlo Mancini and Alessandra and Giuliana Sardegni—saints of a very different faith, and faces every Italian knew and loved. For a moment my cousin and his guest stood in the center of the room, golf caps forgotten on their heads, and ran their eyes over the airbrushed portraits.

The Pope was wearing his plain black priest's pants and a black sweater to which a few spidery filaments still clung. The toothbrush poked its bristly head out of his pants pocket. Close beside him, in a dust-smudged maroon robe, stood the other great holy figure of our era. For a few seconds, as they studied the framed faces, I had the sense of time standing still. It was as if we'd been caught in a surreal photograph—the two of them looked so out of place there, in a room dedicated to superficialities. And yet it occurred to me that, in a way similar to what had been done to the people on the walls, we'd overlaid the humanity of the holy ones with a garment of fame. We looked at each of them and saw something more than a human being: a reflection of our own potential for greatness, maybe, spiritual greatness. We made them larger than life in order to remind ourselves that some part of us existed beyond the petty meanness of the ordinary day.

I turned my eyes to Rosa. You could see the tiredness on her face—she hadn't slept at all—but she was happy. She offered me a smile I didn't deserve. Old love, it was. Scarred and imperfect and fine, not airbrushed at all.

The place smelled of coffee and chemicals. I'd been in Rosa's salons before, of course, many times. Generally speaking, the men who worked there fell into a certain category—sensitive, creative, slim, dressed in a style all their own. But the man who walked toward us from a front room might have played rugby or American football, or been a star of the Bulgarian national weight lifting team. Rosa introduced him as Mario. He bowed to the holy men and gave my hand a crushing shake. Mario looked like one of the Pope's bodyguards—a head taller than I am, forty or fifty pounds heavier, with enormous shoulders and biceps pushing against the sleeves of a blue T-shirt. His head had been shaved, the skin of his face was as tanned as Berlusconi's, though more natural looking. Everything about him was big—big eyes, big nose, big mouth, big neck. "I thought you were maybe gonna be tired," he said in a deep bass voice and butchered Italian that did not betray a vast intelligence, "so I made the espresso."

Before I could tell him that neither the Pope nor the Dalai Lama indulged in caffeine, he'd handed out four cups on saucers. I gulped mine. The Pope and the Dalai Lama took a polite sip, then another polite sip, then another. All dietary rules, apparently, had been suspended.

"Who first?" he asked Rosa. *Chi va per primo?*

She pointed to the Pope. Arm muscles jumping like the thick tails of excited baby alligators, Mario motioned for the Holy Father to sit in one of the chairs, removed the golf hat, then stood behind him, hands on the papal shoulders in a posture that seemed to me less than perfectly respectful, his head tilting this way and that as he decided what kind of magic to work. *"Biondo, penso,"* he said, apparently to my wife. Blond, I think. "Blond wig wovened in with his hair. A blond goatee and mustache, maybe some sideburn. I want him to look like some kind of a tourist, maybe coming down from Belgium or Swedish, on the hunt for the young Italian girls."

"Mario," I said, "this is His Holiness the Pope of Rome. Kindly steer clear of the sacrilegious."

Mario pinched his eyebrows together; he hadn't understood the word.

"It's fine, it's fine, Paolo," the Pope said. "It's all in the spirit of our adventure. I know what he means ... And besides, he carries the name of my own father. Mario. It must be a good omen."

"And for the other one," Mario went on, unfazed, "I think he needs a brown wig, maybe, you know, a little on the shaggy side. Or long, anyways. He should look like a rich guy who's trying not to show his fat wallet, you know? Rock star, maybe. Maybe we can do something with the skin colorating, so if you go south he'll blend in, right?" He laughed at his own bad joke. "You going south, boss?"

"We don't know yet."

"Well, in any cases, we have to lose the cool glasses. Too unrecognizable. We're gonna have to fluff out the lips a little, work the cheekbones down. Round out those eyes."

"No glasses means I cannot see," the Dalai Lama said. But he said it in a pleased way, the way of a man who wanted to take a little break from seeing, who'd seen enough.

The Dalai Lama took the second chair. Mario squeezed his shoulders warmly then moved back to the Pope and set to work. I retreated to one of the leather couches. After a while, Rosa came and sat beside me.

"He's a master," she said happily. "Watch."

"Smart, too," I muttered.

She hit me with an elbow, smirked. "And we have tons of stuff here. Tons. Makeup, wigs, clothes, shoes, you name it. All the costume people come here and leave their props, sometimes for years. Sometimes they forget them entirely. That's where I got the golfers' hats."

After a few seconds she leapt up, made us each another espresso, and carried them back with her.

Mario had a blond wig in his hands and was setting it gently on the Pontiff's bald spot. He moved it this way and that, combed through it. "We have to dye the white hairs around in the edges, Your Holiness. Do I have some permission?"

"Of course, Mario. Anything you want."

The Pope was spun around, his chair tilted back, what was left of his real hair washed in the sink and then colored to match the wig. Beside him the Dalai Lama watched, entranced, his fingers working a loop of brown beads he'd pulled from the pocket of his robe. The blond wig was glued on, a goatee and mustache applied, combed, trimmed so that they fit naturally on the famous face. While the glue set, Mario went to work on the Buddhist half of the escaping duo. "We can leave the glasses, I guess, if we cover over them with these here," he said. He lifted into view a ridiculously oversized pair of sunglasses engraved with the name of a famous designer. The Dalai Lama's shaved head was then covered with a salt-and-mostly-pepper wig, rock-star-length, his medium-brown skin powdered so that it looked like my own after a month at the beach. Mario worked on the hands and forearms to match the skin color there. He put a clip-on earring in one ear, then changed his mind and took it off. "A little could be over the top," he said.

Within ninety minutes the mirror showed what appeared to be a happy pair of traveling friends, one from Northern Europe, one from the sunnier climates, both past their physical prime, but healthy-looking, ready for the discos and the beaches.

"Unbelievable," I said to Rosa.

"Isn't it?" She was on her feet again, one hand on Mario's broad shoulder. I wondered—may God forgive me—if they were lovers. "I have several changes of clothing set out in the other room," my wife said. "I threw some outfits together last night after you called me, Paolo. I guessed at the sizes but they should be more or less okay. The two of them will be in the car a lot of the time, we'll try to keep them out of view. But we should all have some changes of clothes, too."

"Bathing suits," I suggested, because I love to swim outdoors. "Shaving supplies."

Rosa nodded and ducked into an adjoining room.

The Pope and the Dalai Lama got up out of the chairs, gazed at themselves in the mirror and erupted in laughter. They stood side by side, smiling beatifically, arms around each other's shoulders. Rosa reappeared and took a photo with Mario's phone. "Now you," she said, turning to me.

"Yes, yes!" the Pope said. "Paolo, get up here!"

"Why? Why can't I just stay as me?"

"Because someone might recognize you," Rosa said. "Once the Pope is declared missing, and you're missing, they'll put two and two together and figure you spirited him off someplace, looking for ransom money. Your enemies in the Vatican will target you. Your picture will be on the TV, in the papers: 'Kidnapper dePadova Sought by Authorities in Pope's Disappearance.'"

She was grinning as she said this, but my empty stomach was coated with espresso, and the joke did not sit well there.

"We'll have to do you, too, *amore*. Mario will work on you and I'll take the holy ones into the other room and see what we can do in the way of clothing and shaving supplies and so on. Mario will give me some extra makeup because I'm going to have to do touch-up work on all of you after you shave. Your Holiness, do you mind wearing pants?"

"Since when I was a boy, I never tried it once," the Dalai Lama confessed.

"Well, the robe would be a dead giveaway."

"Lose some of the beads, too," Mario said.

More laughter. The three of them disappeared. I sat and looked at my face in the mirror—gray hair, the bent nose, the eyes that seemed either very tired or very kind. I liked things well enough the way they were. But Mario took up position behind me, his massive hands on my shoulders, contemplating, pondering. It seemed either that his voluminous mental energies had been exhausted by that late hour or that something about my face presented an unsolvable disguise puzzle.

At last he spoke: "You mind being turned into a boat-people?"

What Mario referred to as "boat people" were the poor suffering souls who were fleeing starvation and war and risking a hazardous trip across the Mediterranean in the hopes of finding, in Europe, something that resembled a decent life. Those who did not perish in the crossing came ashore in southern Italy to something less than a hero's welcome. They arrived in open boats from Libya, often enough; sometimes Tunisia or Morocco or Syria, sometimes from the Sub-Sahara, and they wandered the streets looking skeletal and terrified.

"I'm not really comfortable with that idea," I said, as soon as it was raised. "It feels vaguely disrespectful, as if we're using the poorest of the world's poor for our own lighthearted purposes."

Mario gave me a blank look in the mirror.

"Just exactly the opposite!" Rosa said, as I somehow knew she would. "You'll be getting a sense of how those people are treated, hour by hour. It will make you more compassionate, *amore.*"

"I'm already compassionate. So are a lot of Italians. I buy them food whenever I see them on the streets. I give them money. Just the other day I bought—"

"I think, cousin," the Pope weighed in, "you could use such a disguise as a spiritual lesson."

"Yes," the Dalai Lama put in. "Yes, very much. A lesson!"

"But I'll be stared at, mocked. Some people will hate me on sight, for no reason other than the way I look!"

"Exactly," the Holy Father said. He nodded at Mario, and the muscleman set to work.

11

By 6:45 a.m., after a ninety-minute ordeal of washing, cutting, curling, coloring, and having some kind of mysterious lotion rubbed onto the skin of my face, neck, arms, and hands, I was a sleepy and slightly nicer-looking Muammar Gaddafi doppelgänger, my hair all black for the first time in decades, my skin a natural-looking almond brown. Somehow, though, Mario had made me look thinner and weaker than the notorious dictator, pitiable rather than fearsome. Powerless. Frail. Staring in the mirror at my new self, I did, in fact, feel a wave of compassion. For once in my life, I would stand out from the crowd ... and not in a good way. I'd be a magnet for anger, an easy target. There were few good jobs to be had in the *bel paese* in those days; our beautiful standard of living was slipping away by the month. People would blame me and the people who looked like me, instead of blaming Silvio Berlusconi and his corrupt and decadent Parliament pals. Thinking about it was enough to wrap me in a blanket of fear.

By then the Pope, his famous chin and famously high forehead hidden behind swatches of blond hair, had been dressed elegantly in a lightweight blue suit and sparkling gold tie, with expensive-looking black loafers polished and shining like gems. Rather than a happy Dane, he now looked like nothing so much as a businessman down from Frankfurt, ready to work a deal. I wondered how he felt about all these strange goings-on, about being transformed this way, and I wanted to ask him, but it seemed to me he was caught up in a rushing stream of happiness. It had started with a thought, and the thought had somehow, magically, produced an idea, and the idea had produced a river, and he was contentedly riding the river now, down the narrow stairs, through the tunnel, into this back room of a hairdressing shop in the south of Rome. For once, his hours weren't scripted and scheduled; and strangely, now that he didn't have to worry about what he said, he was saying very little (though, at one point, he did step off to the side of the room with his rosary and mouth his morning prayers).

The Dalai Lama seemed caught in the same river, as if they were boyhood friends on a forbidden rafting adventure. Rosa had dressed him in designer jeans, almost-new running shoes, a collared short-sleeve jersey and a cashmere cardigan the color of the Adriatic—soft gray-green. She was snapping photos, laughing, making jokes about men being forced to wear pants. Mario was sitting in one of his chairs, sipping coffee, flexing his arm muscles, and beaming like the director of a hit play on opening night.

"Marvelous, marvelous!" the Pope said, breaking his silence. When he turned to me, he burst into laughter. "Look at you, cousin! Your wife is a genius! Mario is a genius! No one will ever guess who we are!"

Before I had a chance to say "I hope not, Your Holiness," and to suggest that Rosa wear a disguise as well, she announced: "It's already light. We can stand here congratulating ourselves all day or we can set off."

"Right," the Pope said. "I have some ideas."

"Wherever you'd like, Holy Father."

The Pope met my eyes, then Rosa's, looked at the Dalai Lama, paused for a moment, and then confidently spoke a single word: "East."

12

The makeup made me hot, and psychologically uncomfortable besides. I could feel a rivulet of sweat running down my spine, but Mario had told me not to worry: the tinted skin polish was water-resistant and would last probably a week if I didn't scrub too hard in the shower or if I didn't perspire, as he put it, "like the wild boar." Rosa had what I took to be a victorious smile on her face as she worked the car free of the alley. I tried not to look at her. This, it seems to me, is the way it works between people who've known each other a long time: every gesture and expression is familiar, anticipated. A certain kind of smile is like a spark thrown on dry leaves; in a second you have a bonfire of memories—sweet or acrid. On the negative side, history works against you in those moments: there's no cushion around your patience; one smug smile and you're assaulted by a hundred old, painful scenes.

The first rays of sunlight were enlivening the sky, but Italians like to sleep in, and so we were still early enough that the roads hadn't yet been choked by the usual assortment of delivery trucks, speeding Vespas, and European driving machines. Working the leather steering wheel and the shining stick shift, my wife took us through the heart of Rome's Centro Storico with all the confidence of a veteran taxi driver.

"What is, for me, most interesting," the Dalai Lama said as we swept past the Colosseum, "is that this building—how you say it?" He waved one hand in a circle.

"The Colosseum."

"Yes. I am thinking that, how many years ago—two thousand?—in the West, people could build something so amazing like this. Even now you have the roads, the machines, the medicines, that we don't have. You have used power of the mind to make all these things, yes? In the East we have not so good roads, not so beautiful buildings, not so much medicine like you have." He paused there, sadly, it seemed, but then added, "All those same years we have used power of the mind to go into the deepest parts of meditation, to learn not to be afraid of death and suffering, to learn that we are not really this body, to raise consciousness toward another level of life. Maybe someday the two worlds come together, West and East." He laughed happily, thinking of it. "Good medicine and big buildings, but also the deep meditation. This is my dream."

"A beautiful idea," the Pope told him. "An idea Christ himself would admire."

"Maybe this is why we are together here now," the Dalai Lama suggested. "Why we escaped."

At that moment a delivery truck cut in front of us, and Rosa slammed her hand down on the horn and cursed under her breath in Neapolitan.

We went along those ancient streets through the craziness of Roman traffic. I loved the Eternal City, loved its urban landscape and messy architectural grace. Everywhere you turned you encountered monuments to the early Romans—a people of genius and excess. Here was the Colosseum, there the broken pillars of the Forum, up ahead the Pantheon, where men in robes had argued about which new law to make and which new nation to conquer, then gone off to their feasts and orgies. Modern

Italy had been built on that legacy. There was still a touch of genius to the people, I thought, running my eyes over the Maserati's interior. There was still a lot of eating and sex, too; and though the conquering was long behind us, the robes gone—except in churches—the politicians were still arguing and strutting around. Surrounded as we were by aqueducts and temples, by museums filled with some of the finest art on earth, we Italians lived in a soup of history, the past whispering to us even as we hurried down a city street with a cell phone pressed to one ear, or as we zoomed along in a race car so new and unscratched it felt like a creature from space. We were chained to that history, buoyed by it, the Neros and Caesars and Mussolinis watching us wherever we went.

History had been Rosa's college specialty until she left school to marry me, and I'd always enjoyed listening to her talk about Italy's painful and glorious past.

We needed only a few minutes to work our way free of the historical center. We turned onto Route 533, which carried us due east from the capital, through a stretch of shops, billboards, and cheap hotels—Roman suburbia— and then toward the foothills of the Apennines. I occupied the passenger seat, separated from my wife by the stick shift and an armrest of the finest leather, on which her bare right elbow rested. It might have been the espresso or the lack of sleep, but I felt almost electrified, hyperaware. My eyes and ears and even the artificially tanned skin of my arms and hands had been tuned to some new frequency, and I couldn't help wondering if this was the way the Pope and the Dalai Lama always made people around them feel. I'd seen visitors tremble in the presence of the Holy Father, grown men and women who looked like they were about to faint, simply because he was standing a few feet in front of them, or had reached out to touch their hand or kiss their child. A few, in fact, actually *had* fainted. Much as I admired him, however, much as I enjoyed his company, the Pope was still my cousin; I'd known him when he was a boy in a pair of tattered shorts on the sands of Mar de Ajó. It wasn't exactly a sacred shock to sit down across from him at the breakfast table on a Thursday morning and eat Belgian chocolate and pears.

And yet, I have to say that from the moment I'd seen him together with the Dalai Lama in the Room of the Blessed Mother, something had changed in my perception of our surroundings. There in the front seat of the Maserati, I felt it again. A clarity infused everything, a sense of trembling precariousness, as if the atomic particles around us had been gripped by an electronic excitement and were moving at faster speed. I've been known to babble when I'm in a nervous mood, and I was certainly nervous then. But at the same time, I wanted to bathe in this new feeling, and I worried that breaking the silence would spoil it.

My wife, my good wife, had no such reservations. "If we're going to be traveling together," Rosa said, glancing at the rearview mirror as she shifted into fifth gear, "I should tell you, Holy Father, that I'm no longer a practicing Catholic."

Boom! The glistening air inside the car shattered into a thousand shards. I turned my head to look at her. I thought: Why are you like this?

Rosa paused, as if to let her great revelation sink in, or as if waiting for the Pope's response. When none was forthcoming, she added, like a handful of mud thrown through a window that had just been broken by a stone, "And, Your Other Holiness, I have to tell you that, beyond a few phrases I've heard from our daughter, I know exactly nothing about Buddhism. Zero. *Niente.*"

An extremely awkward silence replaced the sharpness and aliveness that had filled the interior of the car. I was biting down hard on the insides of both cheeks, looking straight ahead. At that point we were climbing steadily, the pavement running between rows of eucalyptus trees with a few villas beyond them, widely spaced. A stream of morning traffic moved downhill in the opposite lane, headed for the capital. I looked at the tops of my hands, at the wedding ring I'd never quite been able to remove. What kind of comedian God, I was thinking, brought together two people as different as Rosa and me? Of all the billions of men on earth she might have married, of all the intelligent, attractive Italian women who might have come through the door of my travel agency on the second day it was in operation . . .

Behind me the Pope coughed. "What does it really mean to be a practicing Catholic?" he asked. His tone was sincere: he really seemed to want an answer, or to be thinking aloud.

"Attending Mass every Sunday," my wife replied in her perfectly doubtless way. "Receiving Holy Communion. Going to confession. Observing the Holy Days of Obligation. Lenten fasts. Saying the Rosary." She laughed—a bit uncomfortably, I thought. Although, in his infrequent visits to our home, she and her cousin-by-marriage had always gotten along splendidly, they'd instinctively steered clear of religious discussion. Now he was Pope and she'd decided not to hold back. "On all those subjects, I receive the failing grade."

"Yes," the Pope said, warming to the conversation, leaning his newly blond head toward the opening between the front seats and putting a hand on Rosa's elbow. He had taken off the expensive suit jacket, folded it carefully in half and laid it across his lap. "But really, on a deeper level, what does it actually mean, this idea of 'being a Catholic'?"

"I just told you," my wife said. Kind and generous as she could be, Rosa was not a woman of deep patience. In that "I just told you" I could hear that she was already close to the bottom of what had always been a shallow well of tolerance for those who didn't understand her—immediately. On occasion she seemed not to grasp the fact that what was obvious to her might not be obvious to everyone else on earth. "Remember who you're speaking to," I wanted to say, but in her next words she seemed to do just that. "I mean, you're the Holy Father now. The Boss of Catholic bosses. A stand-in for Jesus. That's what we heard growing up. You should know what a Catholic is better than anyone, shouldn't you?"

"The question was rhetorical," the Pope told her.

"Fine, but now I want you to answer it, Holy Father."

"Rosa, call me Giorgio, please, as you always did. I beg you. Dalai Lama, Paolo, at least during this trip or adventure or exploration or whatever it is, please call me Giorgio."

"Then I am Tenzin," the Dalai Lama said agreeably. "And this question make me interested very much. What is the Catholic? What is the Buddhist? Is very interesting questions!"

"Right—then answer it!" Rosa said, in an exasperated voice.

"Calm down, Rosa."

"I *am* calm, Paolo. I couldn't be calmer. I'm just dying to know. Here we are with the bosses of two of the biggest religions on earth and I have a million questions for them! Don't you? This isn't just your cousin who used to come visit us, this is the Pope, for God's sake! And the Dalai Lama!"

I nodded, simply for the sake of making peace.

Rosa looked in the mirror again, expectantly.

"I think," the Pope said, "that I'll need more coffee before making you a decent answer."

"Also for me, but tea," the Dalai Lama said.

Rosa laughed, but the edge, the expectation, remained in her face: she wanted an answer! "There's a place up along this road another few minutes. We can stop there."

I felt the Pope squeeze my shoulder warmly, something he'd done a thousand times. "But as a start," he said, "let me just say that I think all those things—the attendance at Mass, the Blessed Sacrament, fasting—don't exist for their own sake. Christ doesn't love you more if you give up wine or chocolate for forty days."

"Exactly," Rosa said. "That's why I stopped doing it."

"But it's possible that if you spend an hour each week at a holy service; if you mark certain days as special, in the religious sense; if you pray; if you give up some earthly pleasure for a period of time—then I think it helps you to feel Christ's love more clearly. To believe that it's there, always, warming you like the sun."

Rosa was pursing her lips and shaking her head in

small movements. "I don't really get that, Giorgio," she said. Her eyes jumped in quick movements from the road to the mirror and back again, and I worried, now that she'd finished offending the holy man behind me, she'd drive the borrowed Maserati into a ditch.

"I have always appreciated your frankness," the Pope said.

"Thanks. But nothing you've said—forgive me, Holy—forgive me, Giorgio—nothing I've heard you say makes me want to go back to the Church."

"I'm not hoping for that, my Rosa."

"You're not?"

I had half-turned so I could watch the Pope. He moved a strand of yellow hair off his forehead. "I want you to be happy and grateful for life, that's all."

"I am, mostly."

"Then I'm at peace in your company."

"And I'm at peace in yours. I always have been. When you were a cardinal and you used to come visit us, I always thought you were a special man. You washed the dishes, for God's sake! What man ever does that? And I loved the way you played with Anna Lisa, like she was as precious to you as she is to us. She's not a churchgoer, either, by the way, just so you know."

"I love her exactly the same as always," the Pope said. He leaned back in his seat.

Rosa swung her eyes to me, once, quickly, then back to the road. "What?" she hissed. "What, Paolo? You're giving me one of your looks."

I tried to hold the words in my mouth, but they pushed their way out, little puffs of old trouble singeing my lips as they escaped. "You're being borderline irreverent," I said quietly. "This is the Pope you're speaking to about your problem with the Church!"

"Who else should I speak to about it?" she said, beneath the noise of the engine. "You? Even now that he's Pope, he likes to be treated like an ordinary human being, can't you see that?"

"I think I know him a little better than you do."

"You think you know everything a little better than I do."

I bit the inside of my cheek again. I heard the Pope and the Dalai Lama making conversation behind us, something about the scenery, the road—a quiet exchange.

"I don't think you get the big picture here, at all!" Rosa went on.

"You must be right. You're always right, so this time can't be an exception."

"Exactly."

" 'Scuse me," the Dalai Lama said from the backseat.

Rosa looked in the mirror again. The car veered into the breakdown lane, then back. "Sorry, Tenzin. You're a man of peace. My husband here is a pain in the royal *culo,* though, so I'm sorry we're fighting in front of you."

"What is this 'royal *culo*'?" he asked innocently.

"*Culo* means 'rear end,' in Italian. But this 'royal' part comes from an American expression. Paolo taught it to me, ironically enough."

"All people argue sometime," he said.

"Thank you." Rosa half-turned to me and whispered, "Another human being!"

"You didn't ask about Buddhism," the Dalai Lama said.

"I'm not a Buddhist, Tenzin. I told you. I don't know the first thing about Buddha except we always see him as a smiling fat guy. I'm sorry if that offends you, I'm just being honest. My daughter dabbles, I think, but I've never asked her about it, because I'm more the ex-Catholic type of person. Not a big believer in God anymore in any case. I've seen too much bad stuff for that."

"A lot of bad stuff, yes. A lot of pain on the royal *culo.*"

"Right. But Buddha seemed—sorry again, no disrespect—I mean he did a lot of sitting around. Not my style one bit."

The Buddhist's famous laugh filled the car. "Sit, sit, a lot of sitting! Yes!"

"Hard way to make a living these days."

Now it was the Dalai Lama's turn to lean forward between the seats. "He was teaching a lot of time, too. Not just sitting."

"Teaching people to sit," Rosa said.

"Ha, yes! But very important thing, this sitting in quiet mind. Can you do it?"

"Not in a million years."

"This sitting brought him to enlightenment. You would say 'to understand God,' or maybe 'to see clearly the true purpose of life.'"

"Another thing I don't exactly get. How does sitting help you understand anything?"

"When you sit in meditation, after some time, the mind become calm. When the mind become calm, you see clearly. When you see clearly, more easy to believe in something larger than you. More easy to love."

"Easier to stop fighting with your husband?"

The Dalai Lama laughed again and patted her on the shoulder. "Yes!"

"And you can feel that God loves you? I mean, really *feel* that?"

"We don't say 'God.' We say sometimes 'Divine Intelligence.'"

"Some people don't see a lot of intelligence up there on certain days."

"Yes, yes. Some days hard to see."

"But the two of you basically believe in something bigger, correct? Kids die, people suffer with cancer, wars, plagues, and still there's a God up there running the show. Jesus or Buddha or whoever, he's up there?"

"Yes," the Pope said.

"Not a man," the Dalai Lama said.

"Something, though. Something or somebody running the show?"

There was a moment of blessed silence, and then the Dalai Lama said, "It would be the big show to have nothing running it."

"Rosa, there's the coffee place."

"I know it, Paolo!" she said angrily, as if she'd seen it. But I knew she hadn't. This was one of Rosa's many quirks. In the days when we were together, we'd be driving along someplace, headed, say, for Bologna. I'd see the sign BOLOGNA; she'd be thinking about her work, admiring the scenery, lost in a memory or a dream. I'd say, "This is our exit," maybe a little too urgently. And she'd say, "I know, Paolo! For God's sake, will you stop? I just like to put on the blinker two seconds later than you do, that's all."

She swerved so fast into the entrance to the roadside bar that, not having the benefit of something to hold on to, her three passengers shifted to the left like stalks of corn leaning in a wind. The people in front of the little place—two young couples standing beside a pair of motorcycles—swiveled their heads to stare.

"Probably we shouldn't all go in," I said. "Their voices are recognizable."

"Oh, let them stretch their legs!" Rosa said.

"I didn't say they shouldn't get out. I said they shouldn't go in, shouldn't speak."

"You implied it."

We all climbed out into the warm morning, an old, bad feeling souring the molecules between Rosa and me. I loved her, really I did. And I knew there would have been no chance of making a successful getaway without her. Left to my own devices, I would have given the Pope and the Dalai Lama a hat, sunglasses, and a set of clothes and driven them off in a rented van. I'd never have thought of the phone GPS, never have arranged for the elaborate disguises. Son of artists though I was, I seemed to be completely missing the gene for creativity. I admired Rosa's business sense, her work ethic, her unfailing optimism in the face of life's many difficulties. She'd been an absolutely spectacular mother—present, attentive, affectionate, supportive. A loving partner in the bedroom. A friend. I thought she was beautiful, still; that she'd always been beautiful. But from almost the hour we'd met, there had been places in which our personalities ground against each other like gears in a ruined transmission. Fighting had become as regular as lovemaking, and then more regular. In time, like some kind of cancer, it took over so many of the cells of our relationship that when Anna Lisa was out of the house and we were left alone with each other, the tension became unbearable. To my last breath

I will remember the night we sat down and, after talking for three and a half hours, decided we should try living separately. The enormous sadness of that, the immense relief. The bitter loneliness.

Since then, we'd made lives for ourselves, buried our sorrows in the routine of work. We met often for a friendly lunch or a walk. But something between us remained wounded, unresolved. And something about the presence of the two holy men—so calm, so at peace with themselves and each other—something about being around them had cast Rosa and me down into this familiar dirt pit, where we snarled and sniped. It was embarrassing, yes, but worse than that. I don't really like the word "sin," though I know sin exists. I just don't like it applied to myself. I was the Pope's First Assistant, after all; I was praying more, in church more; I was bathed in his presence ten or twenty hours every week. Over the past couple of years I'd held on to the hope that those hours had been working like some kind of spiritual antibiotic, eating away at the bad bacteria within me, making me a better man. And now, from literally the minute I'd seen Rosa outside Castel Sant'Angelo, the old disease was flourishing in me, in *us.* With the motorcyclists still watching us, I found myself wondering if that extra prayer had done me any good at all or if it had merely been a silk cloth thrown over the same old scarred and wobbly kitchen table.

We decided, after another quick, nasty exchange between Rosa and me, that we'd all go inside for a snack. Tenzin and Giorgio wouldn't speak, that's all. It would be the first test of their disguises. And mine.

I offered up a silent prayer. I shot a sideways glance at

my wife, held the door open for her as a kind of apology. We stepped into a sparkling-clean bar.

In Italy the word "bar" has a different meaning than it does in some other parts of the world. Coffee, not alcohol, is the specialty of the house. You're more likely to see a customer standing at a granite counter downing sugary shots of espresso than hunched over a table with a glass of beer, though some types of alcohol are served. There are often pastries for sale, too, and sometimes panini or candy, and almost always what we call a *spremuta d'arancia,* a fresh-squeezed orange juice.

Behind the usual polished counter of the bar on Route 533 stood a very short man in a posture of attentive waiting: eyes up, hands clasped in front of him. Beside him was a brass espresso machine. Above it, near the top of the wall, a small TV was showing clips from the previous day's soccer games. One of the teams was from Algeria, and the complexion of those players caused me to realize that I wasn't presenting my usual face to the world. How strange that was: a lifetime of being white, in the majority, easily ignored by police and fellow citizens alike, and here I was suddenly conspicuous, a boat person, an intruder, an alien! The immigrants one typically saw in Italy were selling trinkets on the beach or in the train stations, scraping a semi-illegal living from Italian society as best they could. Some people treated them decently, others did not; some were in fact criminals, others were not. But they had no chance, none, zero, of blending in. Wherever they went, whatever they did, eyes followed them.

The holy ones took a seat at a table farthest from the counter, told us what they wanted—glasses of orange juice, it turned out, instead of tea and coffee—and Rosa and I walked back and ordered *due spremute,* and *due cappuccini* for ourselves. A familiar sheet of ice had formed between us, palpable, translucent, blurring the way we saw each other. The short man glanced at me and began slicing oranges in two and feeding them into a juicer.

"You think I'm stupid," Rosa said, very quietly, without looking at me.

"Never."

"Yes you do. You've always thought I'm stupid, just because you speak English better than I do, because you have a college degree and I never finished. But I know the world of people better than you, and if you can't tell that these two men just want to be ordinary for a while, then you're the stupid one, *amore.*"

"You're irreverent with them, too casual."

"I'm perfectly respectful. They don't want any fuss, can't you see?"

"These are—"

The short man looked up; some piece of the conversation had caught his ear. On the TV over his head, a news update had replaced the soccer match. I watched carefully, but there was no urgent report from Vatican City. It seemed so peculiar: by that point the security people must have realized the Pope and the Dalai Lama were missing. There had been an official breakfast scheduled for seven-thirty. The word certainly would have gotten out by now; there would be alerts, search parties, police vehicles racing across Rome. Something wasn't right.

The man finished making the juices, and Rosa carried them over to the table. When she returned, the espresso machine was giving off its happy shushing sound. We ordered four sweet pastries.

"I know who they are just as well as you do," she whispered hoarsely, keeping her voice beneath the noise. "I
know it perfectly well!"

Another minute and we were fighting about who
should pay. The one thing I'd thought of in advance was
to take a lot of cash with me; I pulled a thick wad of it
from my pants pocket. "I'm rich," she said, pushing the
money away. "I'm paying."

"I'm making a good amount now."

"I don't care. I'm paying."

She slapped two ten-euro notes down on the counter
and, leaving the change for the short man, strode back to
the table. I lagged behind, pulling napkins from a con-
tainer, and in that moment the man said, *"È forte quella
donna."* She's strong, that woman. He was studying me
now, not unkindly.

"Fortissima!" I told him. The strongest.

He raised and lowered his eyebrows as if conveying
the unspoken opinion that being with a strong woman
had certain advantages in this life, and perhaps certain
disadvantages as well.

I nodded as if to say "I know. Exactly." And I *did* know:
before meeting Rosa I'd had a series of docile girlfriends,
so sweet and amenable, so willing to let me lead in all
things, so afraid to say or do anything that might cause
the slightest confrontation, that it had been like walking
around with a puppet. I didn't want a woman like that.
My mother had been strong, daring, brave, full of life and
argument. She'd raised me to want an equal partner, not
a servant.

I joined my traveling companions, and noticed that the
Pope was eyeing the display of candy bars.

"Odd," I said quietly, after making sure the other tables were empty. "No news about you not being there. And there was a formal breakfast scheduled for half an hour ago."

"Not odd at all," the Pope said. He had a crumb of pastry on the new hair near his lower lip. Rosa reached out and brushed it away, and he thanked her. "They'll keep it quiet at first, so as not to create a panic. They'll hope to find us wandering down in the tunnel or something, lost there, passed out from the fumes of methane gas, stuck behind a door that had slammed shut. They'll make it public only when they're truly desperate."

The Dalai Lama was nodding, the large dark glasses sliding down his nose, the hideous wig ruffled. "Hard practice," he said.

"What's that, Tenzin?" Rosa asked. "What do you mean, 'practice'? Our daughter uses the word that way sometimes. 'Love can be a hard practice,' she told me the other day."

The Dalai Lama scratched the top of his forehead, where the toupee had been glued on. "'Practice' is what we call all things. If you have family to be raising, this is practice. If you are married, also practice. If you are sick, old, or rich or poor, have some trouble or pleasure— all practice. So now the people who are worried about us, they have very hard practice. They are maybe afraid. They worry they will have big troubles." He laughed, as if the idea of hard practice amused him.

"Practice for what, though?"

"For the strong mind."

Rosa tore her soft pastry—a *cornetto con crema*—in half. "I like that. I've had a lot of hard practice in my life, being married to this guy." She knocked her forearm sideways against me, gently. This was the part of the pattern I'd almost forgotten. Fight, fight, fight—yes, we were experts at it. But we'd always been able to reconcile. It had made Anna Lisa uncomfortable at first, when she was a little girl. Then, later, it made her laugh. "The two of you," she liked to say, "are better than a circus act."

I tried to smile but couldn't quite manage it.

Rosa noticed. "Oh, stop worrying, *amore,*" she said. "What's the worst that could happen?"

"The worst that could happen is as follows: I lose my job and go to jail for kidnapping."

"Most hardest practice," the Dalai Lama said cheerily.

"The Pope would never allow that," Rosa said. "Would you, Holy Father?"

The Pope shrugged in a noncommittal way, one of his jokes. Everyone but me was grinning. "Many of the great saints spent time as prisoners. Perhaps that, too, would advance your spiritual life, cousin."

More laughter. I couldn't join in. A small smile; a look at the man behind the counter—he seemed to be studying all of us now, watching, wondering. On the screen above him I saw the face of Silvio Berlusconi, embroiled in yet another investigation, a scandal, a scam. Certain people cruised through life leaving a wreckage in their wake but remaining mostly untouched, free, successful. And then there were people like me.

"You were going to tell me," Rosa said to the Holy Father, "what makes a good Catholic."

He looked at her in the tender way he had, pondered a minute, twitched his lips so that the fake goatee jumped sideways. "A good Catholic," he said, "lives so that he or she feels the love of God the way you feel the warmth of the sun on your arm right now."

"I don't qualify," she said.

"Then, in the time God has given you, put your efforts toward that, the way you have put your efforts toward raising your beautiful daughter and building your successful business."

"Which means going back to church every Sunday," she said.

"Not first on the list," the Pope said.

"What, then? Prayer?"

"There are many kinds of prayer. One kind would be simply to allow yourself some quiet time every day to contemplate the mystery of being alive."

"Hard practice," she said, smiling. "For a busy woman like me."

"Yes, but maybe try," the Dalai Lama put in.

At that point more customers came through the door—a man and a woman holding hands—and we fell silent and concentrated on our food until the espresso machine started up again.

The Dalai Lama was gazing at Rosa through the dark glasses—I could just make out his eyes behind the lenses—and you could see the love in the way he was leaning toward her, the intense compassion. "What is more important," he inquired in a low voice, "that you are so busy, that you make lot of money and have many things, or that you move toward enlightenment in this lifetime?"

Just as Rosa started to answer, the loving couple came and sat down close to us, so the issue of enlightenment was set aside for the time being. We finished our food in silence.

The Dalai Lama's question seemed to hover in the air around us as we stepped out into hot sunlight, as we arranged ourselves in the Maserati and headed back onto the road, eastward, and as we began to climb. Thinking about what he'd said, I felt, for a few good minutes, that the world I knew held us in a kind of hypnosis: money, status, things, comfort, so-called security. Somehow we'd made a god of all that. We put all our talents and energies toward worshipping that god. With their questions, hints, speeches, with the way they themselves lived, the Pope and the Dalai Lama kept warning us about the downside of that kind of worship. We half-listened.

13

Italy's spine is a long, crooked band of upthrust stone, a range of mountains—some of them reaching beyond nine thousand feet—that makes any kind of west-east travel complicated or impossible, depending on the season, on where, exactly, you want to go and where you're starting from. I knew this in part because of early travels with my mother and father, and, more recently, because our daughter had moved to Rimini, a city on the Adriatic, some four hours north and east of Rome. In order to visit her there we had to navigate the sometimes treacherous curves of Italy's interior, or, in winter, drive hours out of our way to find a route that hadn't been closed by snow.

But, of course, I loved seeing my daughter, and had loved my childhood travels, and so I associated trips into the high center of my country with pleasant feelings and family warmth, the sense that I belonged on this earth, that good things and good fortune awaited me. During the darkest days, just before and after Rosa and I decided to separate, I'd sometimes get into the car on a Saturday morning and drive into the mountains with no destination in mind. I'd have lunch in some out-of-the-way trattoria, take a walk, and drive back home again. A mountain therapy.

I was hoping for a similarly uplifting feeling on that day, because, as we entered the high country, I realized I was in the grip of a kind of malaise I'd never really known before. Part of it was the worry that we'd get caught and bring a premature end to the Pope's great adventure; part of it was a related worry—I couldn't afford to be fired; part of it was the reawakened troubles between Rosa and me, something I thought I'd pushed far into the past. And part of it was something else, a cold, mysterious river of thought winding through my subconscious, silently eroding the stone of certainty there. I badly wanted to relax, enjoy the scenery, the adventure and good company, the perfect early-July day, but I could feel this chilly, serpentine movement deep inside me, as if I were being carried along toward some encounter or event that would change me forever, and in a way I wasn't sure I wanted to be changed.

For a little while, though, I concentrated on the view and did my best to relax. On either side stretched vineyards and groves of olive trees, and beyond them were small villages, hamlets really, just clusters of brown stucco homes with red-tile roofs, a bridge, a church, a factory chimney. Cottony clouds drifted past above us, and there was a quiet ease to the sunlight, as if the only purpose of being alive on such a day was to enjoy each breath, soak in the beauty, sit around a table drinking wine with friends and feasting on food that tasted the way food tasted nowhere else on earth.

Rosa seemed at peace. Instead of making my wife more energetic and excitable, caffeine always had the opposite effect. Her free hand sat lazily in her lap, not tapping or twisting dials or running like a comb through her long, dark hair. She guided the car with two fingers and went along at a reasonable pace. There was no conversation in the seat behind us. The one time I glanced back, the Pope and the Dalai Lama were gazing out their respective side windows at the view, buried in prayer, perhaps, or just taking refuge in what the Pope had called a "contemplation of the mystery of being alive."

I seemed to be the only one carrying a cargo of worry. Whenever we saw a police vehicle going by in the fast lane, or traveling downhill in the direction of Rome, I half-expected to see the blue lights go on, and hear the klaxon.

But then something occurred to me, a happy thought. "They won't be able to trace the car," I said to Rosa.

"What?"

"They won't be able to trace the car. Even if they suspect me of being the mastermind, and even if they then connect me to you, they'll be looking for your car, not this one."

"You're a little slow catching on, *amore.*"

"You thought of that ahead of time?"

"I thought of it three seconds after I hung up with you."

"Who lent it to you?"

"Carlo Mancini."

"Carlo Mancini! *The* Carlo Mancini! The guy whose picture was on the wall at Mario's shop? The greatest Italian sex symbol since Marcello Mastroianni?!"

"We do his hair."

"His hair is colored?"

"Who said anything about coloring? I never said it."

"Is it colored, though, really? Is he going gray?"

Rosa looked over at me and let out a one-syllable laugh. "If Carlo Mancini gets old it means we're all getting old, right, my love? And we can't have that, can we. Ten million Italian women would be unable to have orgasms beneath their loving husbands."

"Will you please not talk like that on this trip?"

"Why? You used to like it when I talked like that. And, anyway, I'm talking about our obsession with staying young, not sex. But so what if I was? Sex is part of life. And I haven't made love in ... how long since we lived together?"

"Six years."

"In six years, then. Have you?"

"Of course not."

"You haven't cheated on me?"

"No," I said, though the conversation was bringing up another faded memory: my wife's fiery jealousy. Even in my best days I'd never been a particularly handsome man, but, for whatever reason, women seemed to find me attractive. I had many female friends, and Rosa had never appreciated that, or completely trusted me.

In truth, though, I was at least as jealous of her friendships with men, probably more so. It was another of the ways in which our marriage had seemed destined to fail.

"Really? You haven't slept around?"

"No, never."

"We're still young enough, though, aren't we?"

"Stop, Rosa. I'm thinking about Carlo Mancini."

"I can fix you up with him if you'd like. He's been known to—"

"Stop it. Please. You've been keeping company with decadent movie stars. They've poisoned your thoughts."

"You cheated on me," she said. "I can feel it."

"Stop."

"Tell me again that you didn't."

"I didn't."

"Swear on your soul."

"I swear on my soul. You're the one who's lost her faith, not me. You're the one who can't seem to stop talking about sex, no matter who's in the backseat. You're the one who socializes with movie stars and the fabulously rich."

"Some of them are very fine people."

"I'm sure."

"We had fun, though, didn't we? You and I?"

"Stop."

But instead of stopping, Rosa shifted her eyes to the mirror for a second, then back to the road, and said, "I'm sorry if I'm interrupting, Giorgio, but, given what's going on in the front seat here, I'd like to return to our previous conversation, if you don't mind. About being Catholic and so on."

"Of course, Rosa. Please."

"I'm puzzled about the celibacy issue, for example. When I . . . when Paolo and I were living together, I used to enjoy sex very much. *Very* much. You don't mind me saying that, I hope."

"Not at all."

"It made me feel alive. Made me feel loved sometimes, and other times it just relaxed me after a hard day of work or child-rearing."

"It is the act that made your child come into being in the first place."

"Right. Exactly. The love of our lives, a beautiful crea-ture, as you know. So tell me, why would God look down on something like that?"

"He doesn't look down on it at all. Sexual love between husband and wife isn't evil. That's not doctrine."

"Right, but priests have to be celibate. Why is that? It sends a certain message—that in order to be close to God you have to give up sex."

"No, no!" the Pope said with some force. "It's just that the pleasures of this earth—sex, especially—are so intense, so all-consuming, that they leave less space for attention to God."

"But in my case I think it made more space for atten-tion to God. I never felt closer to God than when Paolo and I were making love. Or sometimes after we finished. And yet, if it wasn't intended for a pregnancy, I was made to feel sinful about it. If we hadn't been married, I would have been a condemned woman. That's the kind of thing that pushed me away from the Church."

There was another awkward silence, more biting down on the inside of my cheek. Once she got started, Rosa would go on and on like this, I knew it. I found myself imagining ways I might escape: go into a roadside café . . . sneak out the back door, and hitchhike to Rome; plead carsickness and sit in a field for a few hours; take a ferry to Albania and work in a tavern there, pouring beer; turn us all in.

"I hear these things often," the Pope said, and I could tell from his voice that the conversation was upsetting him.

"You're not a lawyer," I whispered to my wife. "Stop harassing him. He's with us to relax, not to be tormented."

"Nonsense," Rosa whispered back. And then, at normal volume, "It's chasing people away from the Church, if you don't mind my saying so. In the modern world, you know, the birth-control issue, well, it seems like an anti-sex stance. Has anyone else ever said that to you?"

"Not in so many words," the Holy Father told her.

"But you understand, yes?"

"On many issues," the Pope said, after another pause, "I find myself torn between the ancient traditions of the Church I love, and these kinds of modern questions. Maybe God has brought us together in this way to force me to confront them more directly, more personally."

"See," Rosa said across the seat, no longer making any attempt to keep her words only between us. "Maybe God sent me on this trip so I could talk to the Pope in an honest way. What about *that* idea, *amore*?"

"I dream sometimes about women," the Dalai Lama said suddenly from behind her.

"Hallelujah!" Rosa said. "No offense to either of you, but hallelujah! Yes, I remember now. I believe I read that in one of your interviews—that you dream about women. How wonderful is that!"

"And then I say to myself, in the dream, no, Tenzin, you are the monk. The pleasure of being with woman is not for you in this life."

But Rosa would not be deterred. "I just really and truly don't see the point," she persisted. "If something is good, then it must bring you closer to God, or to the Divine Intelligence, or whatever. Either that, or it's not good. Sex is like eating to me. A natural urge, a need even, though I guess some people can live without it."

No response from the backseat. An ecclesiastical silence. Rosa moved her eyes from road to mirror, twice, expectantly.

And then at last the Dalai Lama said—somewhat timidly, I thought, as if he were afraid of causing an argument— "For us, the birth control not something bad."

"Really?"

"For us, family love is very very important part of the spiritual path. When monks asked Buddha if it could be that ordinary people—they called them 'householders'— could be enlightened, the Buddha said, 'Not one householder, not one hundred householders, but an unlimited number of householders are enlightened.'"

"And they have sex," Rosa pressed on triumphantly.

"Buddha, I think, didn't talk too much about sex."

"And neither did Jesus! When I was a teenage girl I looked for it everywhere in the Bible. Other people talked about it, but he didn't. Other people went crazy when they caught the woman having adultery, but he didn't!"

"Calm yourself, Rosa."

"This is important to me, Paolo. I think it's important to Anna Lisa. To about fifty million women in Italy. To about a billion Catholics. If you can't use birth control, and you already have one or two or six children and you don't want any more, then, really, you can't have sex without worrying. I don't get that. Plus, if you want to avoid abortions, isn't birth control the natural first step?"

Another wave of deafening silence from the backseat. In truth, I missed sex at least as much as Rosa did. Gone was the fiery, logic-demolishing urge I remembered from my younger days, but the desire was there—not just for the physical part of it but for something else, for that kind of intimacy with another human being, for that great weapon against loneliness. "Could it be," I said, to no one in particular but hoping my cousin would answer, "that if you're celibate you cultivate a different kind of intimacy? With God?"

"Exactly," the Pope said.

"But can't you have both at the same time?" Rosa asked. "Intimacy with God and that kind of intimacy with another person?"

We stopped at a red light. Two children in the car next to us slapped the windows and made faces. They seemed to be mocking us. The Pope coughed. At last the Dalai Lama said, "Maybe if you have enough lifetimes with sex, there comes to you a lifetime where it doesn't matter so much as before. You feel the way that after big meal the person feels about eating. Maybe then you have the celibate life and you are content. Like me."

"That more-than-one-lifetime idea explains a lot," Rosa said.

"Yes, very much ... And maybe, also, it is true."

The Pope had fallen silent. It felt to me like an uneasy silence, exactly the type of thing I'd hoped to avoid. I waited a full minute, hoping against hope and history that my wife's noble pursuit of Catholic sexual logic had been temporarily exhausted. I agreed with her, of course—it was just her choice of audience, her timing, that troubled me. "Who's hungry?" I asked.

"I am," Rosa said. "The coffee made me hungry."

"I would like to go to where the earthquake was," the Dalai Lama said, rather suddenly. "I have seen this place in my dreams but I do not know the name."

"L'Aquila," the Pope said. "We're close, aren't we, Rosa?"

Rosa nodded. "It's off this road, not too far. Paolo and I had a fantastic meal there on our anniversary, remember, *amore?* I think I could find that trattoria, unless—"

"What is this L'Aquila means?"

"The word means 'eagle' in Italian," the Pope told his new friend. "It's a famous place. Ancient. I've been meaning to go and pray with the suffering souls there. It's curious that you mentioned it, Tenzin."

"No praying in public this time, Your Holiness," I reminded him.

"Call me Giorgio, please. But yes. I understand. I'd like to go, in any case. I can pray in private, but I would like to see it."

"No you wouldn't," Rosa said. "Believe me. I was there recently, on a weekend business trip to the Abruzzo. It's not something anybody would like to see."

14

On April 6th, 2009, four years before my cousin was elected pope, a massive earthquake struck the medieval city of L'Aquila, killing more than three hundred people and leaving sixty thousand without a place to sleep. Our prime minister at the time, the billionaire media magnate Silvio Berlusconi, famously announced that the homeless would be taken care of, they shouldn't worry, they should consider themselves to be on a camping weekend, or just go to the beach for a bit and pretend they were on vacation. The government would put them up in temporary shelters and build them new places to live.

Thousands of families, their homes destroyed or damaged beyond hope of repair, moved to a tent encampment on the northern edge of L'Aquila or abandoned the marvelous medieval city altogether. Thousands of jobs had disappeared overnight; scores of roads had been rendered impassable. Six years later, as we approached the city, only a tiny percentage of the promised homes had been made available to the survivors.

Strange and disturbing events had accompanied the disaster, the kinds of things that made you lose faith for a while in the sanity of the country you loved. For example, a group of six government seismologists were charged with negligence … because they hadn't predicted the quake! They were tried, convicted of manslaughter, and sent to jail, only to have their cases overturned a year later. Official inquiries were started into shabby construction practices and inadequate materials, and there were rumors—probably true—of Mafia involvement in the vast sums of relief money that changed hands. At the same time, though, the Italian public and Italian corporations responded with a magnificent compassion. Berlusconi himself offered survivors shelter in several of his many homes. Mobile-phone companies suspended billing. For many months no tolls were collected on the nearby highways, students were given free railway passes, and Aquileans were exempted from federal taxes and mortgage payments.

In a nation so defined by the rites and practices of Roman Catholicism, it seemed an eerie coincidence that the majority of the dead were buried in a state funeral on Good Friday. There were Protestant, Jewish, and Muslim services, too, and for a little while a sense of national unity triumphed over our petty squabbles.

In short, the L'Aquila quake showed Italy at its very best and very worst, but the horror of it stayed with us, a deep, deep wound.

The four of us drew close to the ruined city in another of our silences—more reverent, less awkward—gliding on serpentine roads through the hills of the Abruzzo region. Things were still so bad that private vehicles weren't allowed into L'Aquila's center. We parked a kilometer away and walked into the city, uphill, in search of the restaurant where, in better days, Rosa and I had eaten a fabulous anniversary meal.

It so happened that, going along the narrow sidewalk there, Rosa walked side by side with the Pope, and the Dalai Lama and I fell into step behind them. I was surprised again at how powerfully built he was, how limber and energetic for a man his age, and I wondered, as I often did in the Pope's presence, if there might be a link between a life of prayer and vibrant health. He was stepping along slowly, trying to get accustomed to being without his robe, and he was working prayer beads through his fingers in a way that made me worry he'd be recognized. Even with the sad spectacle before us, and even with his slightly awkward gait, his body language had a delighted ease about it, a peacefulness that radiated from his hands and arms and shoulders.

I was intimidated by his presence, of course. Who wouldn't be? After trying, for half a block, to find something intelligent to say, I came up with this: "L'Aquila has special memories for me, Your Holiness."

"Tenzin, please."

"Yes, sorry. Tenzin. My father was American—Italian-American—but my mother was Italian, and I was born in this country and raised here. Up north. They took me on a trip to L'Aquila for my sixteenth birthday. And then Rosa and I came here on our wedding anniversary, not long before we had our child."

"Family love," he said.

"I had a great deal of it."

He reached across the distance between us and squeezed my upper arm. It was the gesture of a loving uncle. "We believe family love is most important part of spiritual life!"

"I'm a little surprised to hear you say that. I mean, you're a monk—no offense—I'd expect you to be emphasizing meditation, fasting, the memorization of ancient texts. Things like that."

He turned his head to me but, with the crazily oversized dark glasses covering half his face, it was difficult to guess what he was thinking. He laughed, suddenly. At me, I suppose. "I had the family, too."

"Yes, of course, I didn't—"

"I was oldest one. My mother and father had nine children, and in our home we had great harmony. My mother, especially, was the woman of compassion and warm feelings. A warm mother *very* important to the spiritual life!"

"Rosa was like that. With our daughter. A supermother."

"You and Rosa are married, yes?"

I nodded.

"But something between you now, yes? Some troubles?"

Another nod. "A long history of arguing over nothing, basically."

"Ah," he said. "Stories."

"Pardon?"

"We make up stories about the other person. In our minds we build these stories—she is this way, he is that way; look, she always do this, he always do that—and then these things keep us from seeing this person full as they are in present moment."

Coming, as it did, with the vision of wreckage and disaster looming in front of us, this mini-sermon slipped into my thoughts like a stiletto. I had my old stories about Rosa, of course I did: that she was illogical, careless at times, that she liked to argue, that it was impossible to go on living with her. And I was sure . . . almost sure . . . that they were absolute truths. I didn't really like the idea of trying to see her only in the present moment, cleansed of history. It was too difficult just then. Some petulant little part of me resisted . . . so I convinced myself the Dalai Lama knew next to nothing about being married, and probably shouldn't be giving advice on the subject.

We walked along, slowly, peacefully, the Pope and Rosa pulling farther ahead—he in the elegant business suit, she in a silvery, knee-length dress. Watching the shift and flex of her calf muscles, I wondered if she was talking to the Holy Father about her neurotic husband, complaining, criticizing, telling stories about *me.* The Pope didn't know much about marriage, either, I told myself, but still, there was a knife in my thoughts then, courtesy of my new Tibetan friend, a thin, sharp blade of doubt that couldn't quite be shaken loose. See her in the present moment, I was thinking. See her in the present moment. Had my parents been able to do that during all their long years of marriage? Had they known something about love that Rosa and I never learned?

"I remember how beautiful the center of the city was," I said, "block upon block of five-hundred-year-old buildings, churches, cathedrals, rows of small shops. Now, look." I gestured ahead of us to where, even from a hundred meters away, we could see what was left of L'Aquila: a nightmare landscape of construction cranes looming over piles of rubble. Some of the less severely damaged buildings were held together by steel beams and cables, as if they were Christmas presents wrapped in construction paper and tied in metal ribbons. In places huge banners hung from the scaffolding: "L'AQUILA'S RENAISSANCE" and "A MODERN RESURRECTION" and "WE WILL NEVER SURRENDER."

I rambled on about the charitable efforts—Madonna had raised a huge sum, did he know who Madonna was? He did—and tales of corruption. "But as far as the money goes, who really knows what the truth is? We're a nation of storytellers and rumormongers."

"Very sad," he said. "So much suffering."

We were just then entering the closed-to-traffic center of the city.

"Give me one piece of spiritual advice," I said suddenly, without intending to say it.

The Dalai Lama squeezed my shoulder again, then let go, but he kept his eyes fixed on me. Through the dark lenses I could just make out his irises—steady, untroubled, caring.

"You maybe sometimes get angry, yes?" he said.

"Yes. Sometimes. Not too bad, really, or too often. I'm not—"

"When you get angry, those times, maybe look to see if ego shows up, okay?"

"Okay, sure, but—"

"Lot of times anger grows out from ego like the weed from dirt, okay? Like the snake come out in the sun sometime, the anger come out when the ego working, the hot sun of the ego, see?"

"Yes."

"Snake always hiding, still there, you maybe can't see it. But then"—he shot one arm forward—"comes out with the ego, okay?"

"Yes, thank you."

"Good student." He chuckled, patted me on the shoulder.

We crested a small rise and moved, a few steps behind Rosa and my newly blond cousin, into the sad heart of L'Aquila's ruins, all dust, cranes, dump trucks, and devastation, medieval doorways turned into crooked boxes, ancient walls veined with cracks. All four of us walked in silence, hypnotized. After a few turns—the tortured new face of the city was playing with her memory—my wife pointed in front of her to a head-high pile of rubble and declared that she'd found the place where we'd eaten one of the best meals of our lives. We were celebrating our marriage on that happy afternoon, expecting a child. The food had been magnificent. Now we were staring at a pile of dusty gray stones, bent metal bars, broken glass. As Rosa ran her gaze over the devastation, a tear broke loose and traced a line down one cheek. The Pope, standing close, reached over and wiped it away. I thought she might say something like "Remember how happy we were on that day, *amore*?" Or "This makes me think of our marriage. Glorious once, now in shambles." But she only stood and stared, crying quietly.

15

From the ruined restaurant, hungry now and in need of a respite, we turned, four abreast, onto what had once been a main street but was now a pedestrian walkway smelling of cement dust, diesel exhaust, and garbage. A trattoria perched on one corner like a triumphant survivor. Dark woodwork inside, six tables. To my surprise—and I noticed it the second we stepped through the door—a small brass bust of Benito Mussolini stood on a shelf above the cash register, occupying a place of pride there, the way, in Italy, statues of the Virgin Mary or St. Anthony sometimes do. We had a history, Il Duce and I: any mention of the man gave me a touch of agita. Any image of him immediately caught my eye. I remembered that Rosa, student of history, had planned to write a thesis on what she'd called "Mussolini's Witchcraft," and I remembered my parents' informal history lectures, the pain in their voices, the bitterness, the horror of war.

Wearing a pinched, taciturn expression and seeming less than pleased to see us, the owner, or waitress—a woman of late middle age—moved out from behind the counter and offered a tepid *"Buon giorno."* It was just after eleven a.m., and I wondered if we might be too early for the actual lunch hour, if we'd disturbed her rest or the cook's preparations.

We were shown to a table at the window. Since the holy men had been reminded not to speak, I took the liberty of ordering for all of us: simple dishes—pasta al pomodoro, bread, a salad, a glass of wine for Rosa and me.

"Per un'immigrante, parla abbastanza bene," the woman said. For an immigrant you speak fairly well.

"I'm not—" I started to say, but she rather rudely cut me off.

"Where are you from? Morocco? Syria? We have more and more of you people now."

"Mezzegra," I said, "near Lake Como."

"You're Italian?"

"Sì, sì," I told her, hoping both that her mood might thaw and that my disguise might not be too closely scrutinized. "Do you know Mezzegra?"

"Of course. A famous place. A place of tragedy. You were born there?"

"In a hospital in Milano, but that's where I was raised."

She hmphfed, as if, given my brown skin and plain clothing, my short biography stretched the borders of believability. "And you travel around now with a beautiful Italian woman." We Italians are famous for our compliments—

another manifestation of our generosity—but I can say with complete certainty that this remark, *"Lei va in giro adesso con una bellissima italiana,"* wasn't offered as anything like a compliment. Not to me, at least. Rosa smiled, but I knew she felt the hidden message, too. When the woman turned away, my wife met my eyes and said, quietly, "A little nastiness there, no? Toward my immigrant husband?"

I nodded.

"And what's so famous about Mezzegra?" the Pope asked.

"It's the place where Mussolini was killed."

I watched his face twist into a crooked frown. He started to say something, stopped, and then: "Ah, yes. I remember now. Your mother and my father mentioned it, more than once. I'm getting old, cousin."

"Never," I said. "The two of you look and move like you're in your late thirties. I feel twice your age."

Both holy men let out a modest chuckle. We'd decided it would be best to eat the meal, as much as possible, without conversation, so as to reduce the risk of the Pope or Dalai being recognized by their voices. But there weren't any other diners at that hour, and—perhaps this seems strange, given my earlier bout of nervousness—a kind of ease had come over us then, almost as if we were four longtime friends. The echo of suffering—ruptured walls and piles of debris—had molded us together in that present moment. "Did you notice Mussolini on the counter?" Rosa asked me.

"Instantly."

"A little weird, no?"

The Pope—sitting with the confident posture of a man of wealth and power—brushed at his lapel, tightened the knot of his tie, and craned his neck to see the statue. The woman behind the counter caught him looking and smiled in an evil way. She made a point of going over to the bust and dusting it with a dishrag.

"So strange," the Pope said in a barely audible tone. He hesitated again. Pursed his lips, finally said, "I've been having dreams of him lately. One of our uncles was killed by his thugs, Rosa. I'm sure I told you."

"You did," she replied. "Paolo told me, also, a thousand times. Paolo's father was obsessed with Mussolini. 'The Grand Benito,' he used to call him, in the most sarcastic way. He thought it was ironic that the house he and my mother-in-law bought near Lake Como, the place where Paolo was raised, stood only a few hundred meters from the spot where Mussolini had been executed. Paolo's mother liked to say their happy life there was her brother's posthumous revenge."

"We believe," the Dalai Lama put in quietly, "that people are sometimes drawn to certain places on this earth because of what happened there in previous life, or to those people they love."

The Pope nodded, as if the idea of reincarnation suddenly made sense to him. "I've been trying to understand something, and I will confess it to all of you now, openly, though it's embarrassing to me." He swallowed, looked at each of us in turn. "For the past few months I've been having especially vivid dreams—they are part of the reason I wanted to make this trip, to try to understand the messages in them. Often, Mussolini appears in these dreams. He's pointing or saluting in that strange way he had. He never speaks. There are other people, too, people

I don't know, but they appear and reappear, night after night. Women, men in robes. There are helicopters and police cars and soccer balls, and a feeling—it's difficult to explain—of something blessed in the air. I wake up sensing a powerful spirit in the room. I've been praying and praying, hoping to understand. There are other things, too, strange things. I—"

"We believe dreams have great power," the Dalai Lama said. He stopped there, abruptly, but I had the sense he'd wanted to make a confession, too.

The Pope was nodding at him, and it seemed to me he also wanted to say something more, to elaborate on his revelation. I watched him. I heard him say, as if trying to take the spotlight off himself, "There are so many important dreams in the Bible. Countless dreams. Zechariah dreamed of John the Baptist before that son was born to him, for one example. Joseph had a dream that Mary's child was from God. Pilate's wife had a dream that he should free Jesus."

"These are the mind sending signals," the Dalai Lama said.

The Pope was nodding again, but there was another strange moment then, a pregnant pause, a sudden awkwardness just as we'd been feeling so relaxed. "God," he said at last, "trying to tell us something."

"Yes, we must to pay attention."

"My stomach is sending me signals," Rosa said. "I hope the food is better than the service."

The waitress, or owner, or whatever she was—the Mussolini polisher—brought bread and oil and our salads to the table, then left and returned with two glasses of wine. Rosa offered one of her gorgeous smiles and tried to charm the woman out of her sulk: "We're sad to see the city like this. It used to be such a beautiful place."

"Sure," the woman said. *Certo.* "And what makes it worse is that all the illegals come here now, all the immigrants. They come from Libya. Albania. Ethiopia. Now the Arabs, too. And Syrians. They get free medical care, did you know that? Just like we do. Only they don't work like we work. Free schools for the kids, free doctors, free food. Naturally they come here, because they find out there's free housing in L'Aquila. We're giving everything away in Italy now. We're giving away our country."

"I haven't seen many people who look like illegals," Rosa said pleasantly.

The woman glanced at me pointedly, then turned her eyes back to my wife. "You don't live here, though, do you."

It wasn't a question. She returned to her place behind the counter, leaving us in air that seemed to have been filled with acrid smoke.

"This person, I think," the Dalai Lama said, "holds little bit to being angry."

Rosa broke a slice of bread in half and dipped it into a shallow bowl of oil. "She's angry at immigrants, Tenzin. There's a lot of that in Italy now. First it was the Albanians, after the Soviet Union broke up. Now it's North Africans, and Central Africans, and refugees from the hell in Syria. Sometimes they get tricked into coming by people they pay, people who promise them jobs that don't exist, and then they end up on these boats that capsize off Sicily or Malta and they drown. Those who do arrive safely, a lot of the time they're unwelcome. Most Italians are generous souls, but the job situation isn't exactly wonderful here, so some of us aren't very happy to see thousands of job-seekers coming ashore. There are racists, too, of course. Racists and haters. And some of the immigrants are good people, some aren't. It's not a simple situation."

"I should have said more about this," the Pope told her when she'd finished. "When we get back I'm going to make a point of addressing this issue—the war, the hatred, this economic system that gives us so much comfort and yet carries suffering in its womb."

"It's everywhere," I said. "I've heard that America has the same problem with people coming from the horrors and poverty of Central America. Even China has North Korean refugees trying to sneak in. Turks in Germany. Moroccans in France. Syrians in Hungary and Croatia and Turkey . . . all over Europe, in fact."

"The poor want to eat," the Dalai Lama said.

The poor want to eat, I thought. Such a simple thing. And then, in practice, it became so complicated. "If you have two cloaks, give one away," Jesus had said. Also simple. But who lived like that? What person in one of the world's rich countries, who among the world's billion Catholics, gave away half of what he or she had? Who gave away even a tenth?

The woman brought our pasta and it was, indeed, very well prepared. Out of the tops of my eyes I watched the holy men eat, noticing how they prayed over the meal before lifting a fork, how they chewed slowly, contemplatively, really tasting, really feeling and appreciating the food in their mouths. I found myself wondering what it felt like to be truly hungry, not for an hour, but for days, weeks, a whole life.

Partway through our lunch the front door slammed open. A man, clearly drunk, staggered in. Such a sight is blessedly uncommon in Italy, where children are served wine from the time they're in grade school and teenagers can buy a glass at a restaurant or bar without any questions being asked. My parents had adopted that custom: I'd been drinking alcohol since I was ten. Seeing wine on the dinner table was as natural as seeing water, and so, by the time I reached adolescence, there was no urge to show the world, by drinking to excess, that I'd come of age.

This man, however—square-built, raggedly dressed—seemed never to have gotten the message. I half-expected the owner to chase him out the door. Instead, the man went up and leaned against the counter and the two of them conversed like old friends, glancing at our table once, laughing, muttering.

We finished our pasta and decided to order coffee and a bowl of tiramisu. Why not? We'd been up most of the night. We were on vacation. At that point my lovely wife was kind enough to bring up the story—commonly heard in Italy—that tiramisu (in Italian the word means "pick me up") originated in the bordellos, where the working women needed a dose of espresso and a measure of liqueur in order to make it through the long nights. Rosa went into some detail. Neither the Pope nor the Dalai Lama could think of anything to say in response.

The drunk staggered out. The owner brought our pick-me-up—delicious!—and then took up her post again by the Grand Benito, watching us as if we might run out the door without paying. It was lunch hour now, but no other customers appeared. We finished in a silence painted darkly around the edges by the woman's bitterness. I asked for the check, paid, and, after my three companions had waved to her in thanks or apology or forgiveness and gone out onto the street, the woman handed me the change.

"Homosexual friends?" she asked, raising her chin in the direction of the door. "Another mixed couple?"

It took me several seconds to understand. I held my eyes on her. I'm not one who believes in auras and such things, but there was a kind of vapor surrounding this woman. Her long, thin face, topped with a mop of badly cut gray hair, seemed cloaked in a spiteful mist. She was working her lips as if she might spit. *"Sai,"* I said in Italian, using the informal address, a mild insult in this case. "You know, you should be careful what you think about people. You never know who they might be."

"And that's what?" she spat back. "A threat?"

"Not at all. You just have no idea who they are, or who I am. You should really stop making up stories about people in your mind, and putting human beings into boxes."

"And you and your queer friends should really stop coming in here," she said. "In fact," she punched a button and the cash register door slammed open. She flipped up the metal bracket that held down the bills, removed the three twenty-euro notes I'd just given her, and slapped them down on the counter in front of me. "We're not taking your money."

"Please keep it," I said. "I only meant—"

"No. We don't need your money here. We don't need people like you coming in here. Go back to wherever you came from. Take it now. Leave. *Prendilo e vai via!*"

I took it and left, thinking, as I walked out, that Il Duce

would have been proud of her. Thinking: No wonder your place is empty at lunchtime.

My companions had wandered a few meters down the ravaged street. Broken buildings stood at odd angles to either side of them, forming a valley of devastation. I tried to imagine what it had felt like to be walking here when the earthquake struck, and what it had been like to live through the aftershocks—days of them, buildings breaking apart and crashing to the ground, even as the search for bodies and survivors went on. Rumor had it that bands of kids roamed these streets after dark now, drunk or high, having nothing to do and nothing to hope for. People want to eat, I thought. Yes, and they want to feel they have value in the world. They want to work, or go to school; they want a share of the pleasures they see around them.

Ahead of me Rosa, the Pope, and the Dalai Lama turned a corner, and when I turned the same corner I saw that the two men were leaning down, talking to a woman in filthy clothes. A Gypsy, perhaps. She was sitting with her back against a stone doorjamb, a beggar's bowl on the sidewalk in front of her. The Pope had his hand on the woman's shoulder, and as I drew closer I could see that she was looking at him, surprised, maybe recognizing the voice, maybe not. The Pope turned to me, "Paolo, do you have money?"

"Yes, *Papa*," I said. That is the actual word for "pope" in Italian, and it slipped from my mouth before I could stop it. The angry fascist, the drowning Africans, the homeless woman, L'Aquila's ruination—they had knocked me into a dream space, pushed all my petty worries to the side. I reached into my pocket and handed over those same three twenties. The Pope placed them in the bowl, then bent down and, holding the woman's head in both hands, kissed her on her filthy, matted hair. She stared at the bills as if they were living creatures, then raised her eyes, offered him a toothless smile, and said, *"Dio ti benedica."* God bless you.

And we went on.

16

We toured what was left of the city in a silence so complete it was a kind of Christian-Buddhist-agnostic prayer. At one point we stopped before a series of enormous photographs that had been taped or pinned to the metal staging around a construction project. The photos gave us L'Aquila in the days immediately following the quake—the ruined buildings, streets choked with rubble. One of the photos, the most powerful, showed a whole field of caskets with mourners wandering down the rows, trying to find the wooden boxes that held their dead. It seemed to me that, in those minutes, we were all four of us acknowledging something larger, some power—merciless it seemed—that insisted on forcing upon us what we least wanted to believe: that things were not stable. Even the earth beneath our feet, the stability we most depended on and took for granted, wasn't immune. In truth, we could count on nothing.

"This," the Dalai Lama said, when we'd agreed to head back toward the car, "is why sometimes our monks sit many days only paying the attention on their breath."

He seemed to be speaking to Rosa, seemed to be answering her question about Buddha and the point of all that "sitting," seemed to be telling us that there was nothing we should take for granted, nothing at all, not our breath, not our life, not the next minute of existence, not our ideas about right and wrong, not even the solidity of the ground beneath our feet. A larger intelligence ruled all that, and we'd been given this time on earth, these millions of breaths, to ponder it. We'd been sent teachers—Jesus for me, the Pope, and a billion others; Buddha for the Dalai Lama and his many followers. Socrates. Moses. Mohammed. Einstein. Those teachers pointed us in a certain direction, but we didn't want to go there. We didn't want to worry about breathing, or the earth splitting apart, or a million whirling universes composed of unlocatable electrons. We wanted to think we understood, that we had some control, when in actual fact we made our way through time on the thinnest film of ice over a lake that was unfathomably deep and utterly mysterious, knowing all the while that one day we'd fall through and drown. We'd seen loved ones disappear like that, one after the next, again and again and again. Still, a sly part of us mouthed a proud "Not me!"

The Pope was nodding, pondering, musing. I thought he might add something from the Christian point of view, but he only pressed his lips together and kept his hands in the pockets of his pricey suit coat. I wanted some alone time with my cousin then, wanted to ask him to talk more about the dreams he'd been having. I wanted to suggest that when we were back in Vatican City, when things had settled into their familiar routine, he make a trip here to L'Aquila and pray with the brave survivors and the mourners and the haters and the drunks. But we were at the car by then, and the skin of my neck was itching from the disguise.

Rosa had a hand on my arm. She asked if I wanted to drive—I didn't. Even *sitting* in a borrowed Maserati felt sinful after what we'd seen. She asked if either of the holy men wanted a front seat—no, they were fine. She worked the car free of the tangle of traffic around the closed-off city center, and when our smooth progress was stopped again by a traffic light, she said, "Unless one of you has some place particular in mind, I have an idea about where we could go."

This worried me, I have to admit. Whenever Rosa said, "I have an idea," a nest of wasps stirred and buzzed in my brain. But the Pope leaned forward and told her, "Show us the country, dear Rosa. Let the Lord guide us now. Take us where we wouldn't ordinarily go."

I thought: Yes, exactly. That's what we ask of our teachers and holy ones: take us where we wouldn't ordinarily go. And I had a moment's peace.

Rosa nodded, looked at me as if I could read her mind. I couldn't. Another few blocks and we reached a highway entrance. She turned the car onto it and headed north.

17

We drove along the highway only a short while—fifteen minutes or so—and during that time the memories of what we'd seen in L'Aquila hung across us like a shroud. A series of sorrowful visions played in my mind's eye, but it was the photograph of the caskets that occupied center stage. What if my own daughter had been one of the dead? What if Rosa and I had been one of those couples wandering down the lines of wooden boxes with a bouquet of flowers in hand, looking for the name Anna Lisa dePadova scrawled on a square of cardboard? What would our foolish marital arguments have amounted to then? Our stubbornness and pride? What would have become of my belief in a loving God? And why had those people been there in the photograph, there in that city at that hour on that particular day, and I had been elsewhere? Which great spiritual tradition, which agnostic genius, had an explanation for that?

It was almost two p.m. by then, hot and dry. I was sure all of Vatican City must be in panic mode, Swiss Guards and black-robed monsignors hurrying here and there, sweating through their collars, making urgent phone calls, tourists weeping and reciting the Rosary in St. Peter's Square, security chiefs pouring cups of hemlock for themselves. It was not, I have to say, a pleasant vision, and I rode along in a small cloud of guilt.

Soon enough, Rosa left the highway, made a series of turns onto smaller and smaller roads, following, it seemed to me, either a map that existed only in her mind or signs for the Parco Nazionale d'Abruzzo. I'd never been to a national park—in their postwar lives my parents were artists, not outdoorsmen. They liked museums, not mud. We went past an entrance—unmanned—and then onto a road—unlined—that slanted gently uphill between high, grassy shoulders. My mind was running, running, running, leaping from one image, one hope, one worry to the next, searching, I suppose, at the deepest level, for stable ground, for an absolute sense of meaning that could carry me through my worst fears.

In the midst of all this I began to think about where we'd spend the night. There was one huge problem: as is the case in many countries, hotels in Italy require all guests to present some form of identification. Passports, usually. I hadn't brought mine along. I doubted very much if any of us had brought a passport along. What were we going to do, then, sleep out under the stars? Call friends and say, "I wonder if you might have four extra bedrooms, because we're traveling secretly with the Pope and the Dalai Lama and we need a place to stay"?

I decided to put these thoughts aside for the moment rather than let them touch the air. I knew Rosa would accuse me of overworrying. And I was afraid she'd come up with another of her crazy notions—buying a tent and sleeping bags in the nearest town, driving to the coast, and making camp on a deserted stretch of beach, or going back to L'Aquila and spending the night on the sidewalk there so we'd truly know what that Gypsy woman with her begging bowl felt like. It would be a spiritual lesson, she'd say. I'd resist. The Pope and the Dalai Lama would back her up. Yours truly would end up sleeping on cold concrete and waking to the sight of a policeman and a pair of handcuffs.

The road angled this way and that and then, climbing more steeply, entered a territory of such magnificence I decided that I would, in fact, be perfectly happy to sleep right there, to live and die right there, in the elements. Ahead and to either side of us, stretching as far as we could see in every direction, spread a vast landscape of untouched meadows and stone-pocked, lime-green slopes.

Behind them, gray mountain peaks stood up in the sunlight like sentries guarding a castle we couldn't yet see.

"The miracle of creation," the Holy Father said.

They were the first words anyone had spoken since L'Aquila.

I'd been all over Italy, from the pink-sand beaches of Sardinia to the Dolomites' stony peaks, but I'd never been so moved by a landscape. "Spiritual" is the word that came to mind. It was a quiet, gorgeous emptiness with this thin ribbon of gravel angling back and forth across it like an indirect ascent to heaven. There was no other human footprint to be seen, not even the sense that we were in any kind of park or preserve, that anyone was watching over what happened here. We'd go along for a few minutes, small stones ticking up against the Maserati's underbelly, and then the road would wrap around the base of one of the great, slanting slopes and we'd be presented with an entirely different aspect of the view. Little by little we were gaining altitude, seeing more, breathing thinner air. The broad green valleys dropped farther below us. There were patches of scrub brush but not a single tree, and then we turned another corner and came upon a flock of sheep watched over by a solitary man holding an old-fashioned shepherd's crook in one hand. Behind him stood a tiny metal shed where he must have spent his nights or taken shelter from storms. I wondered if we'd stumbled upon a remake of *The Greatest Story Ever Told*.

"Stop, please!" the Pope called out suddenly.

Rosa pulled the car onto the shoulder. We all got out. The air was at least ten degrees cooler than what we'd felt in L'Aquila, cool, soundless, eerily still. The Pope set off along the stony field and we followed him. The shepherd looked up. Like a single creature, his sheep shifted their heads away from us and trotted off as if we'd come to that place only to turn them into food.

"*Salve!*" the Pope called. A traditional greeting, pronounced "SAHL-vay," equivalent, perhaps, to the English "Greetings."

The shepherd nodded in a puzzled way. Not wary, not in the least concerned, just puzzled, as if he'd stepped out of the world of people so many years ago that he believed he was no longer recognizable as part of the species. As we drew closer I could see that he had only one working eye, and a week's growth of charcoal-colored stubble on his face. But, if the woman in the restaurant had been surrounded by an aura of bitterness, this man was surrounded by the exact opposite. Nothing, it seemed, could upset him, not even the sight of four strangers leaving their Maserati unlocked on the shoulder of the road and marching toward him on a sunny July day. We came up close and stood there; he watched us, waited, unafraid.

"*Ci dispiace disturbarla.*" We're sorry to disturb you, the Pope went on in his accented but capable South American Italian. "We came to pray with you, do you mind?"

I thought it was an odd thing to say, even for a pope. I expected the rough-hewn man to throw back his head and laugh, to ask us who we were, who we thought we were. Rosa turned her head and met my eyes, expecting the same response, I was sure.

"*Va bene,*" the shepherd said. Fine. Okay. From the look on his face, the request had surprised him about as much as the sun coming up that morning had surprised him.

"Shall we kneel?" the Pope asked.

The shepherd shook his head and pointed one finger skyward. "He don't care if you kneel," he said, his tone the very definition of matter-of-fact. "He don't care what clothes you have on." He turned his lonely eye to me. "What color skin you have don't matter to Him."

"You pray, then," the Pope said. "We'll follow."

Another Cyclopean *"Va bene."* The man shifted his crook so that it was leaning against one shoulder and he put his left forearm across his navel and his right hand over his left wrist. Instead of bowing his head, he tilted it slightly upward. "My Mother and my Father," he began. "We are here on the land You gave. We breathe the air You gave. Our heart makes go the blood in us so that we live. We are here. We ask for nothing."

Silence. Ten seconds. Twenty seconds. At last the Pope said, "Amen." He turned to me, his face beaming, lit with joy. "What can we give him, Paolo?"

I shrugged. I had the wad of money in my pocket. Rosa had the keys to the Maserati. What would such things mean to a man like this?

The Pope had left his jacket in the car. I saw him loosen the tie and unbutton his shirt, and I thought for a moment that he'd take it off and hand it over to the man—an absurd gift it would have been, for a person who no doubt hadn't worn a tailored shirt for one hour in his life. But then I saw that the Holy Father was reaching both hands up to the thin silvery chain around his neck, a chain that held a medal of the Virgin Mother. Many years before, his own mother had given it to him to mark his ordination. The Blessed Mother was his patroness, his protectress, and I knew for a fact that the medal meant more to him than any other physical object in all the Vatican museums. Struggling a bit, he lifted the loop of chain up and over his face—I worried it would peel the goatee away—and handed it over.

The shepherd didn't thank him. *If you knew who he was,* I thought. *If you knew what that medal means to him.* For just a second I wanted to say, "This is the Pope of Rome." But of course I didn't. The shepherd took the medal into the coarse palm of one hand and then, in the simplest and most unself-conscious of gestures, brought it to his mouth and kissed it, then put it over his own head and left it hanging outside his sweater.

He made the slightest of bows to us, almost imperceptible, then turned away—not rudely, just simply, as if our business—odd as it was—had been accomplished and now we all needed to go back to our lives.

We turned and hiked toward the car, the Pope and I shoulder to shoulder, Rosa and the Dalai Lama ahead, walking slowly, admiring the view.

"What made you do that?" I asked him.

He hesitated, lost in thought, or reluctant to answer. After a time, he said, "I saw that man in one of my dreams. Saw him exactly the way we saw him as we were driving up the road. Something's happening to me, cousin. Something very strange."

"In the dream did you give him the medal?"

He shook his head. "It just came to me to do that." Another pause. "After his magnificent prayer."

18

Probably, at that point, we should have left the Parco Nazionale d'Abruzzo, carrying away with us the memory of marvelous views and our fine moment with the shepherd. No doubt we should have done that. Instead, we drove farther along the gravel road, and as we went, Rosa had what she would later call "a thought."

I have to say now that if there was one critical lesson I'd taken away from the years of marriage with my fine Neapolitan wife, it was that once she took hold of an idea, it was impossible to dislodge it. Some of these notions were excellent. It was her idea to have a child, for example, a blessing I'll be grateful for until my dying breath. And some of our most enjoyable trips had come about because of her sudden inspirations, her gift for embracing spontaneity.

But this "thought"—the idea that we should show our guests the Italian countryside by sending them up on the *parco*'s rickety ski lift—was, I believed then ... uninspired. We'd gone only a little way past the shepherd's hut, dipping into a valley for a while so that the sloped fields formed a green V in front of us and we seemed to be heading downhill, when she said, "Look, a chairlift. What a great way to reach Campo Imperatore!"

"What's Campo Imperatore?"

"The summit!"

"Not a good idea, Rosa."

She asked me why, as I knew she would, and I couldn't say why, because the reason for my objection had to do with a secret the Pope had shared with me years before.

Though he flew in airplanes when he absolutely had to—and he absolutely had to quite often—the Holy Father was terrified of heights. He always took a seat close to the middle of the plane, always asked that the shades in his row be pulled down so he couldn't look out, even sometimes took a mild sedative if the fear had a particularly strong grip on him or if bad weather was forecast.

I decided I shouldn't reveal that secret in front of the Dalai Lama and Rosa. Behind me, the Pope was holding to an austere silence. I could almost feel his mind working: he was ashamed. Even with all his decades of prayer and meditation, he'd never been able to completely conquer the fear of heights. He was worried, I was sure, about what the Dalai Lama might think of this, as if every holy man worth his robe should long ago have come to terms with his own death. But it wasn't death that frightened my cousin, it was being up high, especially being up high in a place where he didn't have his feet on something solid. (Standing out on the papal balcony seemed not to bother him in the slightest.)

"No reason," I told Rosa. "I just think it's not the best idea right now."

"'No reason' is so typical of you," she said, in a harsh whisper. "It means you can't defend your position, and you know it." She looked in the rearview. "Dalai," she said, "would you like to see all this from a different vantage point?"

It was a trick question. I closed my eyes and waited for the inevitable.

"Yes, yes, very much!"

"Holy Father, okay with you?"

"Of course," the Pope said, but the words came out

sounding like the squeaking door in the tunnel to Castel Sant'Angelo.

A Neapolitan smirk in my direction. A too-quick turn into the chairlift base camp, or whatever it's called. The chairs were running, all of them empty. Typical. Some bureaucrat in the Department of Tourism had quoted a scientific survey claiming that the chairs up to Campo Imperatore would be more efficiently used if they ran summer and winter, not just in ski season. This same bureaucrat owned shares in a company that made the lift cable, and he wanted it to wear out quickly and need replacement, at the cost of a hundred million euro. Or, more likely, some member of parliament or other high official had a troubled nephew who needed a job, and so he had come up with the idea of paying the boy to run the chairlift . . . in early July! Nepotism in the national park! Wait till the newspapers get hold of that story!

As we pulled up close to the whirring machinery and parked, the troubled nephew roused himself from sleep and shuffled over. *"Ai, che macchina!"* he said, in a voice that made me think he'd breakfasted on beer. Ai, what a car!

"Yes," Rosa said. "We'll let you sit in it for a few minutes if you let us ride the lift."

"D'accordo," the man said. Agreed.

He was a lanky thirty-year-old, and, judging by the watery eyes and loose mouth, unemployable in the extreme. But even an unemployable man could sit there and turn the chairs on and off, greet those few visitors who wandered into the enormous *parco* on a day when all of Italy had gone to the beach. He had the habit of swinging his head almost violently to one side so the shock of black hair lifted off his forehead, and now he made a circuit of the Maserati, admiring the silvery swoops and green fenders, swinging his head again and again, then took a seat at Rosa's invitation and moved the steering wheel back and forth like a child.

"Can we ride?" Rosa asked him.

"Certo!" Sure! "I'll give you some blankets, too. Chilly up there."

"I rode one time on this flying chair!" the Dalai Lama said excitedly. "In New Mexico!"

The Pope stood beside him in a terrified silence.

Rosa had the supply of extra clothes in the car's small trunk. She took out four sweaters. The nephew disappeared for a moment into his tiny shed, re-emerged with four wool blankets that dated to World War II, then pulled a lever that slowed the chairs on their cables. The Holy Father had left his suit coat in the car—easy treasure for a thief—and he and the Dalai Lama stood there looking like tourists, fake hair tousled by the breeze, the Pope's goatee wobbling, the Dalai Lama's dark glasses about to blow off. Once we were sweatered and wrapped, the nephew positioned us so the chairs would clip us behind the knees. I could see the look of abject fear on the Pope's face, and moved to accompany him, but "No, no," Rosa insisted. "Let the two of them sit together, Paolo. They need some private time to talk."

I wanted to tell her that, once he was airborne, there was no way the Pope would be able to speak. But things happened too quickly. The chair swung around behind the holy men. *Plop,* they were seated, the Dalai Lama giggling. Off they went, swinging up and away, a well-off businessman and a rock star, friends on vacation. Rosa and I caught the next chair. Once we were safely aboard and once the metal bar was pulled down in front of us, the nephew speeded things up. Almost immediately I realized he'd been right about the chill. With the breeze and the altitude, the temperature started sinking like a gravestone tossed from an ocean liner. Rosa and I wrapped the blankets around us. I looked ahead, but all I could see was the Pope's left hand tightly clasping the edge of the seat. The Dalai Lama was arranging the blanket around his new friend, laughing, talking; I'd been right: Giorgio was frozen in terror.

"Now they'll have a chance to enjoy a real conversation," Rosa said. "A few minutes of privacy. And you with your worries and objections!"

"Yes, I'm a fool," I said.

"At least you've started to be able to admit it."

Up we went, up and up and up, clanging over the iron towers and swinging side to side in the breeze. Below us spread a vista from some painter's idea of paradise: lime-green valleys and sharp gray cliff sides, endless and untouched. "Turn around," Rosa said at one point. "You can see the Adriatic."

It was true. There in the eastern distance lay a sparkling blue bay. Pescara, it must have been, or Giulianova, but as we climbed, that warm, sunny, seaside vision became part of another universe. I said a silent prayer of thanks to the nephew. He'd described the air in the higher elevations as *fresca*—which means "fresh" or "chilly," but the word he should have used was *fredda*—"cold." Or perhaps *frigida*. We wrapped ourselves tighter in the blankets and pushed in close against each other. "This is so romantic," Rosa said.

"Very."

"I wonder if they're skiing, at the top," she added, making a joke, but as the chair bumped over another tower, the hotel at the summit came into view, and it didn't seem totally out of the question that we might see snow there.

"Holy Father!" I yelled out—I wasn't worried about using his title; there was no one around to hear. "Are you and the Dalai okay?"

"Sì, Paolo. Grazie!" he yelled back over his shoulder, the words positively vibrating with fear. Strangely enough—was it payment for the papal fib?—the instant the last word reached my ears our forward movement suddenly stopped. The whirring above our heads went quiet. The chair swung this way and that in smaller and smaller shifts, then came to rest.

"Wonderful," I said. "The nephew has left for the day, hot-wired the Maserati and gone for a joyride. We'll be here all night."

"What nephew?" Rosa asked.

"We could freeze to death up here. What a wonderful idea this was."

"You're looking for a reason to argue," she said. "You've been looking for an argument from the moment you came out of the tunnel at Castel Sant'Angelo."

"I don't look for arguments, Rosa," I said. "I look for logic. Good decision making. Common sense."

"Typical masculine comment."

"Yes. I am, in case you haven't noticed, a man. And proud to be one . . . at this moment, especially."

"You still don't get it," she muttered, and then, after a

minute of icy silence that seemed on the verge of turning into something worse, "Remember when we went to the marriage counselor?"

"I remember how much it cost."

"She told us when we started to have a fight we should stop and think about some good memory we have, as a couple. Remember?"

"Yes, and look how splendidly that worked."

"I want you to try it. Right now. I'll try it, too. Think of something nice."

I turned my face away, staring out over the cold mountains. I took a breath. I could feel—this is such a perverse aspect of being human—a resistance to making peace. Why is that? I wonder. What is the draw of argument and dissension? Simply the urge to win? To blame every hardship on someone else? Surely this magnetism of discord is the root of war. I could feel it almost as if it were a living creature inside me. But then, who can say why, the bad urge slipped away and I did what Rosa had asked me to do: cast my mind back in time in search of something finer. There had been a day—Anna Lisa must have been two or three—when we'd taken her to the beach at Viareggio. A weekend trip, probably just at this time of year. As soon as she saw the water, our little girl ran toward it ecstatically, stopped at the edge, bent over from the waist as toddlers do, and splashed her hands in the sea, then looked back at us as if to say: "A miracle!"

Who knows why such things stick out from the long wash of memory? But we were all three of us linked tight to each other at that moment, so aware of being alive, so grateful, so at peace in each other's company.

"Did you do it?" Rosa asked.

I nodded, grunted.

"And?"

"And what, Rosa?"

"What were you remembering?"

"Anna Lisa on the beach at Viareggio. The first time she touched the sea."

"I was remembering making love with you."

I looked away. I didn't want to remember that. Anna Lisa was still alive; our love for her was still alive. What had once existed between Rosa and me had perished.

"Embarrassed?"

"No," I said. "Sad."

"Well, at least you admit it. I was remembering the way you kiss."

I kept my head turned away from her.

The chair swung gently in the breeze. It dangled there only a few hundred meters from the top of the lift, but we might as well have been light-years away, because we were, at that point, totally at the mercy of the engineers who'd built the highly unnatural structure, or the men who maintained it, or the nephew down below— God only knew what he was doing with the Maserati and the Pope's suit jacket! Calling his friends to come take his photo in the elegant car, searching for the gas pedal or the shift, scratching the fenders with a jackknife to see how many coats of paint had been applied . . . who could guess?

Clasping one hand to the inside of my left thigh, Rosa pulled us even tighter against each other. She left her hand there. "This will be romantic," she said, "if it doesn't last too long."

It lasted too long. Five minutes, ten minutes, twenty,

and nothing but the chair swinging in the cold breeze. *"Aiuto! Aiuto!"* I yelled at one point. Help us! I thought my voice might reach someone in the hotel, but there was no movement there. Blind windows. Deaf walls. We could see, a hundred feet below us, the last stretch of the gravel road—empty of cars—and then nothing but fields of boulders and tall grass. I wondered about the possibility of jumping.

"It reminds me of pictures of Scotland," Rosa said.

"Only colder."

"They'll have to get it going again soon, won't they?"

"Absolutely."

And she said, "I love you when you're optimistic. And I have to say you look good in that disguise. I love the new nose, and the tan is very sexy."

"The polish or cream or whatever it is keeps me two degrees warmer than I would have been."

"Two degrees might be the difference between life and death."

"Funny."

Twenty-five minutes. Thirty minutes. Nothing. I noticed an angry-looking bank of dark clouds moving toward us from the west. Rosa had begun to shiver, so I put an arm around her shoulders. I looked at the chair ahead and wondered how long it would take for the two old bodies there to succumb to hypothermia. I'd survive, go to jail. The other inmates would know me as the pope killer and I'd endure regular beatings. If there happened to be a Buddhist or two among them, it would be even worse: beatings plus the silent treatment.

Then, without warning, the chair bumped forward a

couple of meters . . . stopped . . . and started steadily forward again. "Mary, help us!" I prayed.

"We have to get off," Rosa said, in a tone—very familiar to me—of absolute certainty. She squeezed the inside of my thigh, once, then removed her hand.

"What do you mean? Won't the chairs bring us back down to the car?"

"Sure. If they don't stop again, Paolo. It's too risky. And our guests"—she lifted her chin toward the chair in front of us—"are not as young as you and I. They must be even more frozen than we are. We should get off. We'll have something hot to drink at the hotel and ask someone to drive us back down the road. You were right, this was a foolish idea. I'm sorry."

For two musical beats I sat in stunned silence. "You apologized."

Rosa kept her eyes forward and said nothing.

"You apologized," I said again.

She nodded once, swung her eyes to meet mine, then away. "I've been trying to change. You haven't noticed. You don't notice those things."

"I do, I do . . . Or at least I want to. Apology accepted. Look at that cloud!"

"We might have to jump for it at the top," Rosa said, but to our great relief, as we crested the last rise and drew close to the station at the summit of the lift, a man in a quilted jacket stepped into view and hailed us.

"*Scendete o rimanete?*" he yelled. "Get off or stay on?"

"Off, off, off, off!" Rosa and I yelled back in unison.

"All four of you?"

"*Sì!*" the Pope shouted, in a voice that might be

described as the quintessence of panic. The syllable echoed against the hillsides. *"Sì! Sì! Sì! Sì!"*

The jacketed man pulled a lever and slowed the chairs. I saw the Dalai Lama lift the safety bar, and the worker help him and the Pope make their dismount. Then Rosa and me. We handed over our blankets and thanked him profusely. Rosa planted a kiss on the side of his face.

"Weather coming," he said, pointing with his free hand to the approaching cloud bank, which was the color of eggplant skin, bubbling, swelling, venomous. "Go inside for a while."

We needed no further encouragement. I asked the Pope if he was all right. "Fine, fine," he said, but he was shivering violently. He'd hooked his arm inside the Dalai Lama's and they were walking along like that, practically vibrating, best of frozen friends. I expected to see the aftermath of trauma on his face, but what I saw there, what I sensed, was something very different. Not relief. Not victory, exactly, but a tiny, triumphant smile visible in the blond brush of facial hair. We walked a few more steps toward the hotel before he said, "Rosa," reached out with his other arm and caught her inside the elbow, "what a wonderful idea that was! What a gift! I'll remember it all my days!"

19

In Italian, Campo Imperatore means "the Emperor's Field" or "the Emperor's Camp," but ... well ... the polite way to say this is that the hotel's name conveyed a grandiosity the building itself did not match. Five stories of mud-brown stone with one rounded side, it squatted there on the summit looking more like a place that had once housed the criminally insane than like any kind of emperor's summer residence (though it occurred to me that the two were not mutually exclusive). A handful of parked cars sat in the tar lot behind. We saw a tiny side building with a cross over the door—a chapel, perhaps, where the local nuns gathered on Thursday mornings to pray for the souls of those who had perished on the chairlift—and a pair of hikers, dressed for Everest, making their way along a path. To one flank was the top of the ski lift, to the other the terminus of the gravel road, and, in between, the Imperatore's scarred back door, through which the four of us stepped, still shivering, hoping for nothing more than a cup of hot tea and a ride down the mountain.

But two things happened as we moved across the threshold. First, there was a tremendous crash of thunder over our heads and a sudden burst of rain against the windows. Second, and more peculiar, we found ourselves in a musty, poorly lit foyer of stone and worn linoleum, where the walls were decorated with framed photos of Benito Mussolini and framed newspaper pages bearing his image. Passing us on the way out, a man—unshaven, smelling of the soil—burped loudly.

It seemed to me that we'd wandered into a neo-fascist bunker, one of history's latrines. The Pope and the Dalai Lama were examining the newspaper pages, one translating for the other. Rosa leaned close to me and whispered, "I forgot, Paolo. That was the other reason I thought of coming to this place: the Pope's Mussolini dreams! Il

Duce was held here for a month or two in 1943, after the king kicked him out. It's a long story, but that was in my mind. There was a whole chapter about this place in one of my textbooks."

"It's a fascist nest," I said. "A nightmare for someone of my political persuasion."

"The man behind the desk looks friendly. Let's ask if we can sit and get something hot."

Surrounded though he was by Mussolini memorabilia, the clerk was indeed a friendly and apparently open-minded type (meaning he did not seem upset by two other-than-white-skinned men entering his establishment). He greeted us warmly, saw immediately that we were cold—"You rode the lift? In this weather? It was open?"—and told us to have a seat in the dining area, he'd send someone out with hot tea.

On a decent day, the first-floor dining room with its curved wall of east-facing glass must have offered a fine perspective on the view, but at that moment the windows were obscured by a silvery deluge. Another crash of thunder, great sheets of water coursing down the glass, a shrieking wind. "Imagine if we were still stuck out there," Rosa said.

"I'm trying not to."

There were twenty circular tables, each covered in white cloth and set with silverware for six, but they were empty of patrons at that hour. Still shivering, we chose one near the front wall, all of us turning our chairs so we could watch the storm. After a bit, a waiter with skin almost as brown as my own came out of a back room carrying a tray with a teapot and four cups. He greeted us in solid, if accented, Italian—a southerner, for sure—and set the cups and saucers before us with a practiced dignity that would have been at home in the Vatican dining rooms. He poured the tea and asked us how we'd gotten so cold.

"We rode up on the chairlift," Rosa told him.

"Sta scherzando," he said. You're kidding.

She shook her head.

"The fool! He's not supposed to send people up yet. We're just testing it to make sure it works."

"Well, keep testing," I told him. "We were stuck out there for the better part of an hour."

He shook his head, kept staring at me. "You speak Italian better than I do."

"I've lived here a long time."

"Ah. And your friends?"

"This beautiful woman here is a *napoletana*. The other two are visitors whose Italian embarrasses them . . . hikers from Alsace-Lorraine."

"Well, welcome. Get warm. Say a prayer of thanks to God that you survived." He smiled at Rosa and just before turning away told her, "I'm a southerner, too. Napoli. Here to make money. No jobs where I live. None."

A minute later he returned with a plate of less-than-perfectly-fresh pastries and cookies. We sipped our tea and waited for the rough weather to pass, but it went on and on—rain, booming thunder, then a steady hard ticking against the glass.

"Hail," Rosa said.

"This reminds me of home," the Dalai Lama said quietly. "In the winter, snow. In the summer, sometimes, like this."

"Do you miss Tibet?" Rosa asked him.

"So much!"

"Think you'll ever be allowed to return?"

"I think so, maybe, yes. I want to walk again, one time, into the Potala Palace. I want to see my people again smiling and not afraid. I pray for that, and for Chinese leaders. That they stop bringing so much terrible karma on themselves."

Rosa studied him, squinting her eyes the way she did when something bothered her. I thought it must be the toupee—it resembled the hairdo of a sixties rocker, and His Holiness could not quite pull off the look—but then she said, "Do you really pray for them? I mean, religious people say that all the time, but aren't you angry? Don't you hate them even a small bit?"

What you saw in the flex of the Dalai's big cheeks then was a ripple of the most profound puzzlement. He hesitated a few seconds, watching my wife, waiting, it seemed, for her to amend the question so that it made some sense. "Hate them?" he asked, his voice spiking high into a note of incredulity.

"*I* would. Most people I know would."

"But I see what they are bringing onto themselves in the next many lifetimes."

"You're sure?"

He turned his eyes to me, trying to comprehend. He'd just said that the sun was hot—wasn't it obvious?—but Rosa was resisting. Couldn't it also be cold sometimes?

"Rosa focuses on this life," I said. Generously, I thought, but—

"And you don't, Paolo?"

"Of course. Yes. I just—"

"I want us all to be honest!" Rosa exclaimed, so forcefully that I was grateful for the empty room. She was about to have—I could sense this—one of her moments. These moments weren't always ugly or angry, but they were always intense, a kind of orgasmic explosion, the release of a huge backup of Neapolitan emotion, as natural to people in that part of the world as heated water coming to a boil at the appropriate temperature. She shifted her eyes—once, twice—from one holy man to the other and back again. "I ask that of you both. I ask respectfully—really, I have nothing but the greatest reverence for you both. But please! No pious . . . *stuff!* Excuse me. Forgive me. I wanted to swear but I held myself back. I swear all the time, I admit it. I think swears are just words, that's all. I simply couldn't bear it if I had the gift of this time with you and we wasted it on a kind of phony, pious . . ."

"Yes, good!" the Dalai Lama put in happily when she hesitated. He smiled at her, a beacon of acceptance, and added, "One monk I know—the soldiers were torturing him with the electricity in his teeth, his guns, yes?"

"Gums."

"Yes, and he was all the time praying for them."

Before Rosa's questions had heated up, the Pope had seemed distracted. Now he leaned closer, fully with us again. "On the cross," he told Rosa, "Christ called out, 'Forgive them, Father, for they know not what they do.'"

Rosa was leaning forward now, too, both hands on the tablecloth, fingers spread and pressing down hard, hot southern blood at full boil. "But are those stories real? And if they are real, isn't that level of forgiveness so far beyond the ability of the ordinary person that it's a kind of lie to imitate it?"

"Your husband, maybe hurt you little bit one time?" the Dalai Lama asked in an innocent way.

"Many times. Yes, we both—"

"But you forgive him now, yes?"

"Now I do. But it took a long time ... and he never put electric prods in my mouth or nailed me to a cross!"

"In deep meditation, person can go beyond feelings of pain, do you see?"

"Not really, no. Plus—"

"And we believe that every person has nature of Buddha inside. Very same nature as Buddha. Friends, enemies ... same. So, therefore, we must pray for their liberation, do you see?"

"It doesn't feel that way," Rosa said sulkily.

"You can forgive your daughter all the time, yes?"

"Yes, easily."

"And you can forgive your husband now. So now you have to see daughter and husband in every person! That's all! Very simple!"

"That's what you do?"

"That what I *try* to do. Every day I try this. To see Buddha in everyone."

"And you, Holy Father?" she asked the Pope, pronouncing the last two words quietly.

The Pope turned his eyes to her with a quick movement, as if he'd been snatched from the depths of thought. "Sorry, ask again?"

Rosa repeated the question, and the Pope scratched in an absentminded way at his goatee. By that point I'd already stopped being surprised by his getup, already stopped paying much attention to the strange hair and beard and street clothes. Once, long ago, he'd said to me that we were all in disguise, always. We went through the world as men or women, old or young, rich or poor, good or evil, but beneath all that, beneath the aspects that could be described with words, there lay some "essence," as he'd called it. "That's what is meant by 'the soul,' I think, Paolo," he said. I remembered the conversation so well. We were walking through the Borghese Gardens on a windy fall afternoon. He was in Vatican City for some kind of retreat or colloquium, visiting from his homeland, and he came to see Rosa and me and our beloved daughter on a free Saturday, had lunch at our home, insisted on washing the dishes, played with Anna Lisa until it was time for her afternoon nap, then asked if he and I could take a stroll through the city. "If you think of a loved one who has died," he said, on that walk, "if you close your eyes and think of your mother or father, for instance, you can feel their essence, can't you? Yes, it might be associated with a face, a body, a particular memory, but there's something else, isn't there? There's something that makes them exactly who they are, a conglomeration of memories that goes beyond the looks and personality. Their *energy*, we could say. Their unique spirit in the world. You can feel it, can't you?"

I said that I could, and I had thought about it many times since. The body, the face, the personality ... and then this something else beneath all that. "Buddha nature," the Dalai Lama would probably call it. The soul. The place beyond pain.

I felt it at that moment, too, looking across the table at my cousin in his blond wig and blond mustache and goatee, his white shirt collar sticking up over the neck of the expensive sweater. The disguise changed his appearance, yes, but not his essence. I imagine he felt it, too, looking at the wife of his immigrant cousin. I wondered if he even saw Rosa as a woman, and I mean that in the very best sense: that he saw her as a soul first, and only then filled in the details.

"For me," he answered Rosa, "the question of suffering is constantly in my thoughts. I see Christ in every person, and so the great challenge on this earth is to watch people suffer, to be aware of the massive amount of suffering, and be unable to help."

Rosa was frowning—in a more or less respectful way.

"You're frowning," the Pope told her. He smiled.

"I believe you mean it," she said. "I do. But I want to hear something else. I want to hear the explanation you give to yourself, in your heart of hearts. For torture. For evil. For terrorism. And, forgive me, but if you say 'original sin' I'll never speak to you again!"

The Pope held his eyes on her. "The explanation I give to myself is this, Rosa: *I don't know.*"

"Zen monks also say this," the Dalai Lama put in.

"And that's enough for you both?"

"It has to be, doesn't it?" the Pope said. "I feel very small in God's world. I do what I can and I accept what is."

"Buddhists, same."

"That's where our faiths overlap, Tenzin. One of the places. We accept what is, even as we try to make things better."

"I don't see things changing for the better," Rosa said. "I see no evidence of that at all."

"Mussolini is gone," the Pope said. "Hitler is gone. Stalin."

"North Korea," Rosa countered. "Syria." She looked at the Dalai Lama. "China."

"Should we give up, then, my Rosa?"

"I never give up," she said. "I've never in my life given up on anything."

Your marriage, I thought, but I didn't say it.

At that moment the Dalai Lama pointed to the windows. Rain and hail drummed and ticked there, a meteorological symphony.

"Maybe somebody could give us a ride down to the car," Rosa suggested. She was one degree calmer now, but I knew she'd ponder the discussion for hours. She'd fall asleep thinking about it, searching for an answer that made sense—intellectually—when both of us knew, at some level, that a logical explanation for the mystery of human suffering simply did not exist.

The Pope turned to me as if I were the one making the decisions. "What if we stayed here?"

"In this nest of fascists?"

"It's exceedingly strange, Paolo," he said. "I dream about the man—Mussolini—and then I walk into this place and see his photo everywhere. He was held prisoner here, the newspaper articles said. Rescued by Hitler's commandoes. They crash-landed in gliders and spirited him away in a small plane."

"Too bad the plane didn't crash, too."

"Yes, cousin, but I have to think God is pointing me toward something. I've been having other strange dreams lately. Hidden messages. Faces. I feel I'm being led . . ."

"Women and helicopters," I said. "Lakes and mountains."

"How did you know?"

"You told me . . . But sometimes dreams are just dreams, no?"

"Dreams never accidental," the Dalai Lama put in, but he said it quietly, pronouncing the word "assidental."

I'm ashamed to say now that I basically ignored that remark. I'd remember it later with some poignancy, but a cloud of worry had overtaken me then. "I don't like the looks of this place. I don't like the feel," I said. "I think it has bad karma."

Rosa turned her smirk on me. "How would you like the feel of going all the way back down the mountain in a hurricane on that chairlift, *amore*?"

"It should stop any minute."

"I say we spend the night. You have cash, don't you?"

"Yes. Almost enough to pay Carlo Mancini back if the nephew absconded with the car."

"*What* are you talking about?!"

"Nothing."

"We're all exhausted and this is as safe as anyplace else. We should get rooms and stay."

"And use what for identification, Rosa? They'll never let us check in without passports."

For any ordinary person, that would have been the end of the discussion, a trump card, an insurmountable obstacle. But Rosa, as she accurately claimed, did not give up as easily as most people: it had always been one of the things I admired about her. "Let me see if I can charm the man at the desk," she said. "I'll tell him we left our passports in the hotel, that we would have been able to get back to Rome tonight if it hadn't been for his faulty damn ski lift. And the damn rain. I'll go while the rain is still pounding and see if he'll make an exception."

She stood up, smoothed her dress, put a hand on my right shoulder as if for luck, then strode away.

There is an aspect to Italian life—a beautiful and mad-dening aspect—that isn't always apparent to people who come to my country as tourists: Italians do not like rules. You can see it in the double-parked cars on any Naples side street; in the fact that something like 40 percent of our citizens don't pay taxes; that here, in a supposedly Roman Catholic country, the birth rate is among the lowest in Europe; even in the fact that most small villages put their efforts into worshipping a patron saint instead of the grand figures one finds in the Vatican. You can see it most clearly on the national highways and roads, where the posted speed limit appears to indicate the minimum rate of movement, and where drivers habitually slip deftly into the wrong lane and pass on treacherous curves. Men and women, both, make a game of cutting in line at the train-station ticket windows (there's even a word for such people—*furbi,* the sly ones); waiters forget to charge you for the second and third glasses of Vernaccia; road signs lead you into dead ends, or out into the forest.

It makes us a nation of great artists and less-than-great soldiers, and, ironically enough, given where we were seated, it was the same national trait that had blunted Mussolini's efforts to turn his people into German clones. Most Italians scoffed when he tried to institute a nation-wide exercise routine modeled on Hitler's. Foolishly proud as we were of him at first—his outthrust chest and Roman salute, his promises to bring Italy back to some imagined glory by stunts like invading Ethiopia—once he aligned with the Northern Demon and drew the nation into war, his popularity plummeted. By the time the Allies landed on Sicily in July of 1943, the king and even Mussolini's own Grand Council of Fascism had

had enough of Il Duce. They stripped him of his powers, brought him here to Campo Imperatore for safekeeping because everyone was after him, everyone—the partisans, the Allies, ordinary peasants whose sons had frozen to death on the Russian front. Later, the king would recall Mussolini saying, at their difficult last meeting, "I am the most hated man in all of Italy." And that wasn't far from the truth.

The last thing, the very last thing, I wanted was to spend the night in the place where Mussolini had been rescued by Hitler's thugs. The man had no appeal for me; he'd killed my uncle; my parents had despised him. Rosa, who knew more about his life than most scholars, made a spitting sound whenever she said his name. But I could read the tiredness on the Pope's face, and I sensed the Dalai Lama had enjoyed more than enough adventure for one day. Rosa was right—it wouldn't kill us to spend a night here. Maybe, in the grand Italian tradition, the man at the counter would bend the rules for her. She was, after all, a woman of substantial charm . . . and we were paying in cash.

While we waited for her to return, the Pope chewed absentmindedly on a stale cookie, the Dalai Lama watched it rain, and the unshaven, burping man I'd seen at the entrance, soaked to the skin after his foray into the parking lot, stumbled into the room and stood near the kitchen door, giving me the most malevolent look imaginable. For a minute I thought he'd recognized someone in the group. But no, that wasn't it. I was an unwelcome guest, nonwhite, an intrusion on his imaginary world of fascist homogeneity. Along with Jews, homosexuals, Gypsies, socialists, union organizers, and soft-handed intellectuals,

I carried an imaginary disease diagnosed by Dr. Hitler. Mussolini had given a concurring second opinion . . . and fifty million people perished.

I stared back at him, trying to see Buddha there beneath the confident hatred, to see Christ.

I couldn't manage it.

Rosa returned to the dining room bearing a brilliant grin and a handful of keys. "Four singles on the top floor," she said. "I told him we were hosting foreign tourists and had come on a day trip all the way from Rome to see the place where Il Duce had been rescued. I mentioned the chairlift. The rain. I gave him my best smile. We're all set."

20

The walls of the fourth-floor hallway were painted floury white, the floor covered with chipped linoleum. The rooms themselves seemed to have been designed to replicate a monk's cell, so I supposed the Pope and the Dalai, at least, would be comfortable. Each room had a tiny bath with a shower you could squeeze into as long as you hadn't eaten in the past week, a good, firm bed, and a window looking out on an Italian version of a tropical monsoon. I couldn't remember seeing anything like it, really, and I couldn't stop myself from wondering what would have become of us if we'd been stranded up there on the chairlift in the storm.

The four of us had agreed that we'd allow some time for hot showers, naps, and prayer, then meet at eight-thirty in the dining hall for the evening meal. I shed my clothes, showered carefully so as not to remove Mario's magical polish, then crawled under the cool sheets. Tired from the long day, drifting toward the kingdom of sleep, I found myself going over the unfinished dining-room discussion. "Karma" was the Buddhist term. People tossed the word around carelessly, but the real meaning, as Anna Lisa had explained it to me, was linked to an expression my father had used when he was in a mood to talk like an American: "What goes around comes around."

There were moments when that equation seemed so true. You saw giving, selfless people—the Pope came to mind—and they were happy and at peace, as if all the good they'd put into the world had circled around like some kind of celestial body, a spiritual meteor, and come back to wash them in a soft tail of golden dust. You read about murderers, rapists, and dictators getting their comeuppance: jail, assassination, a black, bloody page in the history books.

But what about the saints who'd been tortured and killed? Drawn and quartered, burned at the stake, shot with arrows, crucified? What about Jesus? What kind of karma was that? Why had someone like Joseph Stalin died a natural death, apparently after living a healthy life with little suffering in it? Why were all those Tibetan monks and nuns tortured by the Chinese heathens? And why were children suffering with cancer, or born deformed, or dropped from heaven into a place ravaged by hunger and disease?

There in the building where Mussolini had slept—had he felt guilty at all? Would he be made to pay for his transgressions?—these questions, unoriginal as they may have been, swirled in gray clouds across the landscape of my thoughts. People were given free will—that was the Catholic explanation. But I knew what Rosa meant about platitudes, because explanations like that weren't enough for me. What kind of free will caused a child to be born with no arms or eyes or lips? What had he or she done to deserve that? What footnote to the law of karma explained it?

Jesus died for our sins—how many thousands of times had I heard that? Then why hadn't sin ceased to exist on the earth after his crucifixion? And why had his Father sent him to die like that? And why hadn't Buddha—or any of the other holy figures I knew about—died like that?

I listened to the rain drumming on the windows and thought of the people still living in tents in L'Aquila. Had they somehow angered God? All of them? Together? The Jews of Europe, the Cambodians and Angolans and innocent North Koreans, the Hutus and Tutsis, the victims of terrorism, all the millions of men and women who'd been tormented and slaughtered over the millennia of human existence, who'd died in horrible ways—were all of them paying for somehow causing pain in a previous life? Or was this God's harsh way of teaching us to go to the place beyond what the Dalai Lama called "bodily sensations"? And if so, where was the road map? Catholicism, with its sacraments and rosaries and rites? Buddhism, with its focus on the interior world? Rosa, with her brand of blunt, loving agnosticism?

I let these questions run back and forth in my mind like frantic zoo animals in a cage; then I surrendered and simply offered up a prayer to the Blessed Mother, one line of hopeful spiritual verse, a petition to mystery.

21

I've had some bad meals in Italy, exceptions that prove the rule. But I don't know that I've ever had a worse meal than the dinner we suffered through in the dining room of Campo Imperatore. Rosa had awakened from her nap before the rest of us and had charmed one of the drier guests into driving her down the mountain so she could bring the Maserati up to the hotel parking lot. At eight-thirty, as agreed, the four of us met in the lobby. We sat around for a few minutes on the couches there, waiting for the dining hall to open. The rain had turned from a driving torrent to a steady drizzle, and the ground-floor lobby was peopled with an esoteric crowd, a recently moistened mix of valiant hikers in outdoor gear, a few ordinary tourists, and what seemed to be an international cadre of fascist sympathizers on pilgrimage. We watched them amble through the door—men, mostly—ogle the Mussolini memorabilia, and buy copies of the books being sold at the registration desk, biographies with titles like *The Late Great Hope of the Italian People* and *The Noble Man*. There was a certain proud, defiant, besieged air about these pilgrims, as if they could barely keep themselves from proclaiming, right there in the puddled lobby, how much better things would have been if the Noble Man had survived to lead Italy toward the twenty-first century. If only the fools had let him live! If only those twin idiots Churchill and Roosevelt had kept their tanks and soldiers off this golden peninsula and let the great social experiment of fascism have time to succeed! If only we had leaders like Il Duce now, men who were truly men, who stuck out their chests and cheated on their wives and sent boys to die in far-off lands.

It turned my stomach, truly it did. The Pope and the Dalai Lama—or the German businessman and the long-haired, casually rich, nicely tanned rock star/tourist—were sitting across from me, dressed in dry clothes Rosa had brought them, refreshed by a shower, solitary prayer, and perhaps a bit of sleep. I watched them watching the other hotel guests and wondered what they thought of it all.

"*Un gruppo strano*"—a strange crowd—I whispered to my wife.

She nodded uneasily.

"What's wrong?"

A shrug, a glance over one shoulder at the desk. "Someone was taking pictures of the Maserati."

"In the parking lot?"

"At the base of the ski lift." She ran her eyes over three men moving toward the bar beside us. A cacophony of loud voices came through the doorway there, a species of hilarity you'd expect from pilsner at midnight, not Campari at the dinner hour. "We drove up and there were two guys out in the rain. One of them had a camera, the other an umbrella."

"Maserati lovers, maybe. Car fanatics."

"Maybe. But when they saw me get out they hurried away."

"I heard a rumor that there's a Mafia capo hiding in this park. Maybe they were federal police who thought they'd found their man."

"Why, Mr. Logical, would policemen run away from me?"

Before I could mount a sarcastic defense—"Because all men find you frightening" or something along those lines—we were summoned to our table. The menu of the evening consisted of three courses—risotto, pasta, and chicken—and there was something wrong with all of them. Sure, it must have been difficult getting provisions to that isolated spot—one didn't expect a garden-fresh salad—but there was no excuse, in Italy, for tomato sauce that tasted like old juice, or for an oily risotto, a tough chicken breast, a glass of white wine that should have been used to lubricate the chairlift.

The holy men ate very little. Rosa tried two bites of everything, then pushed the plates away. I saw her try to take refuge in the wine and bread, but even that wasn't working.

"At home, sometimes," the Dalai Lama said, "monks don't eat after noontime."

"A good strategy, in this case." Rosa fiddled with an earring—a gift from her loving husband, some ten years earlier. "I feel like I should apologize to you all for the food, for taking you here in the first place. I just thought, you know, the historical angle, the natural beauty . . ."

"I hope you're joking, Rosa," the Pope said quietly, when her voice trailed off. "I can't speak for Tenzin or Paolo, but for me this is the adventure of a lifetime. To mix with real people, without having them come up and kiss my ring or otherwise make a fuss. To be able to eat a meal that isn't served on antique silver and the finest porcelain, with someone watching me every second to see if I'll fall ill. To have a day that isn't scheduled to the quarter hour. Up in the room just now I had the most wonderful prayer session. I could truly feel the presence of Christ."

"And you don't feel it at St. Peter's?"

"Of course, of course. But in the Gospels, Christ, the actual Christ, is never seen in a church. There were no churches built in his memory then, obviously. And after his early years, you don't even see him in the synagogue, do you?"

"I don't remember."

"Trust me, you don't see him that way. You see him out among the people, eating and drinking, walking through the crowds, visiting the homes of friends, preaching, healing, rubbing shoulders with saints and thieves and betrayers, with humanity. Churches are fine, of course. We have to remember him, and it's helpful to have a certain organized way of worshipping him—buildings, prayers, sacraments. But, at the same time, with all our rites and symbols, we tend to lose sight of the actual way he lived, a divine spirit among the people, eating with friends, talking with sinners."

"What I wonder," Rosa said, after the same friendly waiter had come and taken away our dishes, "is why, in the Bible, we never see him laughing. I know he was here on serious business, and maybe he knew the fate that awaited him, but you'd have thought that at least once in the Scriptures you'd see him laughing. All of it is so serious. Even the wedding at Cana—it must have been a good time, there must have been music, right? But even there you only see him performing the miracle of turning water into wine. There's no sense of joy, of celebration."

"Buddha, the same," the Dalai Lama said. "Not too many jokes."

I worried that all the talk about Christ and Buddha would give us away—it wasn't exactly the topic of the hour in that place. But our conversation was drowned out by raucous laughter from the nearby tables, talk of days gone by, of what might have been, the word "he" (*lui* in Italian) resonating in the room like a curse word. *He* would have, *he* could have, *he* should have. If *he* were still alive . . .

"Maybe the jokes got edited out," I suggested. "Probably it wasn't Christ and Buddha who were humorless, but the people after them who wrote down what they said. Those people had a message they wanted to get out to the world, an *agenda,* for lack of a better word, and they believed it was a matter of life and death, spiritual life and death at least. Eternal salvation, enlightenment. Maybe they didn't feel it would be right to keep the funny parts in. And humor never gets passed down through history, in any case, does it?"

The Dalai was nodding and smiling, the Pope looking at me with his blond eyebrows lifted, his head tilted a few degrees to one side, as though I'd said something far above my usual level of intelligence. "*I* laugh," he said, somewhat defensively. "Tenzin is always laughing, he's famous for it."

"I know. But I agree with Rosa. Where's the divine humor?"

The question remained unanswered, but it put me in mind of my father in his last days, lying in bed in the house at Lake Como, drifting in and out of consciousness. "My dad laughed when he was dying," I said aloud.

"You never told me that, *amore.*"

"There were moments of struggle and pain, too— discomfort mostly, not agony. But he never seemed afraid, and sometimes at the end, when he was in a coma, he'd chuckle. As if he was watching a comedy or remembering some old joke."

I felt the Dalai Lama looking hard at me across the table. "Dying like this is sign of particular good man," he said. "He was seeing then that life isn't what we think."

"'For now we see through a glass darkly,'" the Holy Father quoted. "'And then we shall see face-to-face.'"

"I've always liked that." Rosa met my eyes and her lips twisted to one side as if in spasm. "I hope I can laugh a little . . . at the end."

"I'll do what I can, if I'm there," I said, watching the emotion play on the muscles of her face and trying, with a bit of awkward humor, to sweep away the sadness. "I'll do my Elvis imitation."

"That should work, *amore*. Thank you."

Our waiter brought plates of sliced pears and gorgonzola to the table, eyed the still-half-full carafe of wine and our still-full glasses. "Coffee?" he inquired, a bit guiltily, it seemed to me. Where he came from, no doubt, only prisoners with no 'Ndrangheta connections were fed meals like this.

Rosa was alone in asking for coffee. To calm her down, I supposed. When the waiter brought the small espresso cup and set it in front of her, she said something to him in what I knew to be the impenetrable dialect of Naples: *uaglione* and *skutchamenza* and *chidrool* and all sorts of *sch* and *aiei* sounds, music of the streets, a rough-and-tumble symphony. The man grinned and answered in kind, ran his eyes across the rest of us, wondering if we'd understood, then went off to attend to his tables of guffawing *fascisti*.

"What did you say to him?"

"I told him the food was good. We just weren't hungry."

"You didn't!"

"I did. Why hurt his feelings? He didn't cook it. And the man who gave me the ride down the mountain said the hotel is owned by the provincial government, and chronically underfunded. They don't know, one year to the next, if it will even survive. That's not his fault, not even the cook's fault. I'm leaving a huge tip."

The Pope reached across and put a hand on Rosa's wrist. "Your kindness makes me miss my sister," he said. "And you are like a sister to me. Thank you for coming with us."

"Paolo invited me," she said shamelessly. "In the way a husband invites a wife. Without words."

The Dalai Lama looked at me and exclaimed, "Good man!"

"The best!" the Pope agreed. "Just like his father!"

In the midst of this charade Rosa's phone rang—she must have changed her ringtone, because usually it was something from Andrea Bocelli and this sounded like Elton John. She took the phone out of her pocket, looked at the screen, at me, said, "It's Anna Lisa—I called her earlier and left a message," then stepped out into the foyer.

"I've never told you this, Paolo," the Pope said, once the company was wholly masculine, "but when I was in the novitiate I had a pet parakeet."

"What is this mean?" the Dalai asked. "Pair of keet?"

"Parakeet. A very small bird. Colorful. Tropical. You can teach them to repeat a few words."

The Dalai flexed his forehead upward so that the toupee shifted like a small tectonic plate. I worried it had come loose during his nap and would now fall off. He wasn't wearing either his regular glasses or the oversized sunglasses, and he was squinting at the world.

"What did you train it to say?" I asked.

"I trained it in both Spanish and English. Several things. *'Buenos días!' 'Buenas noches!' 'Cómo estás?'* 'God loves you, Giorgio.' 'It's time to eat!' I loved that parakeet very much, actually loved it, but the point is, I've wondered since then, very often, if human beings are trained in a similar way. We hear certain things—as a child, perhaps, from our parents; or as an adolescent from our friends, or as an adult from co-workers—and they become etched into the brain. Later, we repeat them, and etch them into the brains of our children, our friends, the people in our parish. 'He who has ears to hear, let him hear,' Christ said, but I wonder sometimes if we actually hear, if we actually see, or if, like my beloved parakeet, someone comes into the room and we say *'Buenos días!'*—even though it's not day at all, but night. I'm thinking about this in regard to Mussolini and the men around him then, and some of these people now. He said things, they repeat them."

"So you've been listening."

"Cousin," he said, "they're shouting like deaf grandfathers."

I laughed. The word "grandfather" made me wonder if, like me, he was secretly sad about not being one. I made a last attempt to drink the horrid wine. No.

"I think," the Holy Father went on, "I think that perhaps it is the practice of regular prayer that erases this old etching from the walls, that lets us use our minds in a fresh way, with a clear awareness."

An explosion of fascist laughter erupted at one of the nearby tables.

When it was finished, the Dalai Lama said, "Our monks, sometimes, they make retreat, three years, no speaking." He reached over to the unoccupied table beside us, where the waiter had left a menu—printed on a single sheet of paper, encased in plastic. The Dalai held it in front of him, printed side up; then he squinted and turned it over so there was only a blank page. "The mind become like this."

"Okay," I said. "But if you clean the mind like that, by meditation or prayer or three years of not speaking, then what do you do with it? You don't want to have nothing on the walls, do you? What new words do you etch there?"

"This my answer for you," the Dalai Lama said. "When Jesus Christ, they ask him which commandment most important, what he say?"

I caught sight of Rosa coming toward us across the room, phone in one hand, a splash of maternal pleasure on her face. I hoped she'd hurry, because I sensed the Dalai Lama was about to instruct me, the Christian, in the scriptures of my own faith. I remembered that Jesus had been asked which commandment was most important, yes. But I'd forgotten his answer. I ran through a list of possibilities: "They're all about the same"? "'Thou shalt not' is the key phrase"? "They were given in order of importance"? "That was the Old Testament, I have some new ideas"?

I turned my eyes to the Pope, sheepishly.

He grinned. "I know you know this, cousin."

"In principle, I know it. At the moment, I seem to have forgotten."

"Matthew has Christ saying: 'Love the Lord with all your heart and with all your soul and with all your mind. This is the first and greatest commandment. And the second is like it: Love your neighbor as yourself' . . . That's all you have to write on the walls of the mind. No other rules, just that."

"Yes," I said "Exactly. I'm glad you remembered."

The Pope and the Dalai Lama both laughed at me. I didn't mind. But I was thinking: No other rules? Really? Divorce? Birth control? Sunday Mass? Premarital intercourse?

Rosa plopped down in her seat and announced, "We're going to see Anna Lisa tomorrow. She's taking the day off. I told her we had two foreign friends traveling with us and she's all excited."

"Their daughter," the Pope explained to the Dalai Lama.

"Oh, very nice," Dalai said. "She has some news about her life."

22

Late that night I was roused from sleep by a quiet tapping on the metal door of my room. In the unfamiliar darkness I thought, at first, that it might be a death dream: God knocking. My time had come. Then, slightly more awake and remembering our moment of intimacy on the chairlift, I thought it could be Rosa wanting to come in and sleep with me. I got up, eagerly, unarmored, pulled on a pair of pants, unlocked the door, opened it. No one. Neither God nor wife nor anyone else. The hall, lit by a bare ceiling bulb at each end, was as silent and still as a monastery at midnight. Rosa had the room next to mine, and for a few seconds I entertained the fantasy of knocking there and asking if I could climb into bed with her. But no, the armor had already slipped back into place. She'd refuse and I'd feel foolish. Or she'd accept and we'd be drawn into an old pattern of argument and turmoil, the hot fires of marital love. Why those fires hadn't burned out over the years, I didn't know. There remained a heated attraction, absolutely, but also a firewall of argument and stubbornness. Something like war and something like love.

I locked the door and went back to bed. There was no longer any sound of rain tapping on the windows, no creak and bang from the elevator well. In the few minutes it took me to settle into sleep, I thought of Anna Lisa, and for that little while there were no complications to the spiritual search, no questions about karma and humor and judgment and sin, or which commandment was most important. Whatever my faults and failings—and they were legion—from the moment of my daughter's appearance on this earth I had loved her with a love so absolute that it washed our small disagreements aside like the sea tossing flotsam onto a jetty. I'd sacrificed for her without complaint, held her continually in my thoughts, done everything in my power to give her a life and a mind that would lead her toward happiness.

Could it be, I wondered, could it really be that we

were loved that way, too? Could there be some Essence, some Father or Mother or Divine Intelligence that felt about me, about us, the way Rosa and I felt about Anna Lisa? Could our love for her be some kind of metaphor for a larger relationship, God to humankind? If that were true, if that were really true, then it would be as the Pope said it was: our sins didn't make God love us less; they only blinded us to that love. Our sufferings were temporary, as puzzling and passing as a twenty-four-hour flu to a toddler. If the metaphor held, then our task would be—as the Dalai Lama had suggested to Rosa—learning to forgive and love the way I forgave and loved Anna Lisa, only more widely.

My mind leapt and sprinted and gradually settled. Just on the rim of sleep I remembered the Dalai Lama saying, "She has some news about her life," and I wondered what it might be—a new job, a lover, a diagnosis—and how he could possibly know.

Day Three

✥

23

I am, as I may have mentioned, a late sleeper. By preference, at least, if not always in practice. But that morning I was awakened at first light by more knocking on
the metal door, louder than what I thought I'd heard
in my sleep: God or Rosa being more insistent, maybe.
I wrapped the thin blanket around myself, mouthed
a prayer, and pulled at the slab of metal that separated
me from the rest of Campo Imperatore. There on the
threshold stood the Holy Father. He looked sleepy and
aged, his blond goatee was pushed to the side as if he'd
taken a long walk with the wind blowing hard off one
shoulder; his hair, real and not real, was matted and tousled. The eyes were alert, though. That was the thing
about this man: the soul or the spirit or the essence or
whatever you want to call it shone out from him like a
lighthouse beacon. I'd seen him angry and calm, joyous
and sad, tired and energized, quiet and voluble, but the
eyes were always the same: milk-chocolate brown with
this beacon of energy and goodwill shining out through
them. That light had been there since boyhood.

The Bearded Blond Pontiff surprised me by stepping
into the room and closing the door behind him. "I rose
early to pray in the chapel," he said excitedly. "Do you

know that it's actually dedicated to John Paul? Do you know he used to come here, regularly, to ski?"

I shook my head no to both questions.

"It was closed—five a.m.—but the kind clerk at the desk unlocked it for me. I told him I was visiting from Honduras—I forgot you'd said Alsace-Lorraine—that my brother was a priest and I wanted to say a few prayers. A fib . . . for a good cause. I disguised my voice, pretty well, I believe, and the accent convinced him. Can you hear an accent when I speak Italian? I've never asked you."

"Absolutely not," I told him. A fib . . . for a good cause. I looked at my watch. "It's six-twenty."

"I'm sorry to wake you, cousin, but the television above the registration counter was on and I happened to see the news. A dramatic headline: Pope kidnapped! Army and police searching everywhere! Interpol notified. The American FBI involved. People were talking about it in the foyer."

"Nothing about the Dalai Lama?"

"Maybe. I don't know. I pretended I wasn't that interested. I just glanced at it and came up here immediately."

"I had a moment of guilt about it yesterday," I told him. "All this worry and trouble, the whole world upset. It seemed reckless and wrong, somehow. I hope you—"

He stopped me by reaching out and putting hands on both my shoulders. The powerful eye contact, the sense of calm. "My good cousin," he said, "blood of my blood. I feel the same reservations, the same doubt, the same concern."

"Then we should turn ourselves in before it goes any farther."

The Pope was shaking his head. "The same concern," he repeated. "But it is overwhelmed by something else, a louder voice. I can't be specific just yet, but I've had a sense from the first that there's something larger involved."

"Larger how?"

"I don't know. It's as we were discussing earlier—a mystery, an intuition I feel I should follow. I was praying for understanding just now, in John Paul's chapel. He seemed to be urging me on."

"Okay," I said, but without much conviction.

"Sometimes we have to listen to such things. Sometimes we have to risk offending, risk hurting someone's feelings, risk allowing them to worry about us if we feel deeply that we are doing the right thing."

"As you wish, Holy Father."

"Stop with the 'Holy Father' nonsense! Please! Now, go and wake Rosa. Never mind, I'll wake her. I'm going to pack up and explain to Tenzin. We're going to see Anna Lisa! I can't wait. And touch up your skin color, it's spotty." He pointed to his own Adam's apple. "Here."

When he was gone I shaved, packed, reapplied the facial color with some of the extra polish Mario had provided us, left a tip for the cleaning people—sufficient for all four rooms—and went next door to consult with my wife. On her face I could see the same excitement I'd heard in the Pope's voice. It was as if the muscles around her lovely mouth were exclaiming: "Yes! First we embarked on an insane adventure, and now the army is searching for us! What could be finer than that!" But my own chorus of doubt sang louder.

"We need to go, Paolo," she said breathlessly. "Right now!"

"What about breakfast?"

"On the road," she said.

"Fine, good. You're right, as usual. Do you mind if I drive? Do you think Mancini would mind?"

"Be my guest. I'm tired of it anyway. And regarding Mancini—there's nothing to worry about."

"Unless the people taking photos yesterday were from the army or the FBI. In which case—"

"I considered that. I don't think so. I don't see how they could have traced the car to me."

"Your cell phone," I said.

She shook her head. "Before I left I traded phones with Mario and told him to tell anyone who asked that I'd gone to Monte Carlo for a week. And besides, the Pope told me they were talking about *you* on the news. Not a word about your wife."

"Me?"

"He didn't tell you?"

"No, I—"

"You were right about that part of it. The news report claimed they'd found a note from you, handwritten, saying you'd taken the Pope and were holding him somewhere in the south, asking a ransom. Five million euro!"

"You're joking. Or the Pope was joking. He—"

"I don't think so, *amore.*"

"But the note . . . I didn't write any note, Rosa. I never would have written such a note."

"Your enemies," she said.

At the sound of those words, the chorus of doubt was replaced by a symphony, a cacophony. A cloud of bad feeling engulfed me. This, then, was the variable I hadn't factored into the equation. This was the ultimate revenge. Instead of hiring from within, appointing one of the horde of cardinals, bishops, monsignors, aides, functionaries, and

ambitious young priests who surrounded him, the Holy
Father had chosen me, his inexperienced younger cousin.
Unordained. An outsider. Feelings had been hurt, egos
bruised, ecclesiastical careers shifted onto a side track. Now,
one or more of the Vaticanites had sensed an opportunity.
I'd been summoned from the caboose to stand beside the
engineer, yes; but now the door of the speeding locomo-
tive had slipped open. Someone had me by the neck, from
behind, and was about to shove me out the door.

I said, "Oh."

Rosa laughed, hugged me. "We'll watch over you,
don't worry, my love. The Holy Father will tell them the
truth and they'll believe it. 'All shall be well and all shall
be well and all manner of thing shall be well.'"

"Julian of Norwich said that."

My wife nodded in a solemn way.

"They burned her at the stake, didn't they?"

"That was someone else. She was the one who believed
God was both man and woman, so the Church refuses to
make her a saint."

24

The ride from Campo Imperatore to Rimini carries
one through the hills of four provinces: Abruzzo, Molise,
briefly into Le Marche, and then to the southernmost
part of Emilia-Romagna. At one time the cities along
this route—Civitanova, Ancona, Pesaro—were Adriatic
ports with a measure of status in the Roman Empire.
Now, Ancona serves mainly as a jumping-off point for

the ferry to the Dalmatian coast, and the cities north of it are famous beach resorts, choked with tourists in summer and all but abandoned the rest of the year. I remembered being at one of Rosa's company Christmas gatherings, just after Anna Lisa told us she was moving to Rimini to take a job there, teaching school. Rosa and I were separated by then, and I'd gone to the party only out of some misplaced holiday spirit. I was standing around awkwardly, drink in hand, chatting with one of Rosa's wealthy clients. The woman looked across the room at our daughter and scoffed. "Rimini," she said, reaching up to finger her pearls. "Rimini is not one of our important cities."

Perhaps not, but it is one of our finer places to live—a long strand of sandy beach, a small but picturesque town two kilometers inland with clothing shops and a pedestrian center, an arch and bridge that date to Roman times. Anna Lisa loved it there, and both Rosa and I loved to visit.

On our way to Rimini on that second morning, Rosa suggested, wisely, that we avoid the Autostrada with its tollbooths and surveillance cameras, in case the man at the base of the ski lift had been someone other than a Maserati lover with a camera. I agreed. It was an exquisite pleasure to drive that four-hundred-horsepower machine along the two-lane back roads, where the insouciant creativity of Italian drivers meant that absolutely any-thing might happen at any moment. Clutching, shifting, accelerating into the turns, watching for espresso-fueled macho men wandering into our lane while passing a bus on a blind corner—it was a whole-body, whole-mind experience, a kind of meditation. An Italian man's prayer.

At one point Rosa turned on the radio. Word of the

Pope's disappearance was not just out, it was being shouted in a chorus of a billion voices all across the world. Every channel had a report about the kidnapping of the Pontiff, and now speculation was rampant that the Dalai Lama had gone missing as well. As was so often the case in the Italian media, exaggeration and rumor were the order of the day. The Holy Father was being held by a Mafia chieftain in Sicily. He was already dead. The government had paid a hefty ransom, and his return was expected at any hour. A band of Chechen separatists had been seen hanging around the Vatican for the past month; they'd spirited him away in a helicopter. "It's the Chinese," one commentator announced with absolute certainty. "The Dalai Lama, not the Pope, was the main target. The Pope was simply in the wrong place at the wrong time." A reward of 5 million euro had been offered for information leading to the kidnapper's arrest.

As Rosa shifted the dial from station to station, from one piece of absurd speculation to the next, I kept waiting for word of the devious First Assistant and, not hearing it, began to think that the story about the ransom note had been the idea of one delusional reporter. But then, a new channel, another voice: "*Quello dePadova . . .* That dePadova, sources tell me, has been trouble from the beginning. He's been the one responsible for leaks of false information from the Vatican halls, for the Pope's supposed sympathy for gays, his supposed respect for Eastern religions. My sources say the Pope felt obliged to bring him on because they're distantly related, third or fourth cousins, but that he's actually a radical Communist—"

"*First* cousins!" I yelled at the radio, idiotically. "Democratic Socialist!"

"Calm yourself, cousin. Let the fools chatter. We know you're providing a holy service. Let faith carry you."

"It's too much. Turn it off, Rosa, please. I can't bear it."

"One more minute, *amore.*"

"Cousin," the Pope said from behind me. "Remember our conversation of this morning. Let faith carry you."

The announcer went on. "Other reports say he's an atheist. Jealous of his third cousin's fame and popularity, desperate for money to pay for his sex addiction. He's been seen frequenting the bordellos in France—"

At that bit of fantastical imagining, Rosa finally snapped the voice into silence. "I always knew you preferred French women," she said. She swiveled in her seat so she was facing back. "Holy Father," she said. "He prefers French women. Their cooking, their sense of style, their lighter coloring. This has been the problem all along."

"There's been no problem all along," the Pope told her. "That's been the problem."

"All along," she agreed.

"Dalai," I said, risking a glance in the mirror on a straight stretch. "Do you see the craziness I have to put up with?"

"We have tradition in Tibet. Sacred craziness. Men and women who act a strange way. People think they are fools, but their wisdom, in fact, is often more than those we call normal."

"The holy fool," the Pope said. "We have the same tradition."

"What about the *un*holy fool?" Rosa asked. "The unholy, foolish husband?" But before anyone could continue the revelry she pointed to the right and practically shouted, "Coffee!"

"I see it. I know," I said, hitting the brakes hard and swinging the Maserati into a parking lot. "I saw it all along."

All the roadside coffee bars in Italy had televisions, it seemed, and on that hot summer morning all the televisions were broadcasting the same basic story we'd just heard. The Pope and his famous guest had disappeared, along with the Pope's First Assistant. Most likely it was a kidnapping. The police, the army, the Vatican guards, every law-enforcement agency in Europe—all were part of the frantic search. The American FBI had been called in to help. People all over the world were praying for the holy pair's safe return, and even confirmed atheists were coming to understand that these men were human treasures. What would life be like without them?

The guilt was upon me again, all tooth and claw. I looked from one kidnap victim to the other. One word then, a single word, and I would have made a phone call and turned us in. "Sometimes we have to risk offending," the Pope had said. But my thoughts swirled and shouted. I did not like upset and confrontation. I did not deal well with guilt. And I did not at all like the idea of going to jail.

We ordered coffee, pastries, orange juice, and, to escape the TV screen, sat outside at a patio table, where the sun was just peeking over the roof of the building.

"Now," Rosa said, "I think we should keep our profile very low. I wonder if it's even wise to visit Anna Lisa. They may be watching her."

"We *have* to see her," I said. "It will mean everything to her to meet the Dalai Lama, and the Pope is practically an uncle."

"I'm actually her father's third cousin," the Pope quipped.

"Still . . ." Rosa said.

"I miss her too much, Rosa. I need to see my daughter. Now, especially, I need to see her."

"You can see her next week, next month. Anytime. Why risk ruining the adventure before we've really gotten started?"

"There might not be a next month for me. I'm the Pope's kidnapper, remember? A Communist radical. The next time I see her might be on visitors' day at the Volterra Prison."

"You're paranoid."

"Two hours ago you said I was right."

"Paolo, seriously. The Pope of Rome is sitting next to you. Do you really believe he'd let you go to prison for kidnapping him, when this was his idea all along?"

"I'm here against my will," the Pope announced. His mood was particularly festive on that morning. "Tenzin, aren't we here against our will?"

"Completely!" the Dalai Lama said, and the two of them went into a fit of laughter that caused people on the sidewalk to turn their heads.

"What kind of ransom are you asking for us, Paolo?" the Pope asked when he'd calmed down a bit.

"Keep joking, cousin. I'm about to leave all of you here and take Carlo Mancini's Maserati for one last, fantastic drive into the Alps before I'm sent to jail."

"I'd also like to see Anna Lisa," the Pope said. "I'd like Tenzin to meet her."

"Rosa, give me your phone," I said. "Or Mario's phone, or whatever."

I dialed my daughter's number and heard her sleepy voice. "Anna, did I wake you?"

"No, Pa. I've been up. I didn't sleep very well."

"You and me both. Listen, have you heard about the kidnapping?"

"You can't *not* hear about it, *babbo.*"

"Have you heard that I'm a suspect?"

"Just now."

"Has anyone tried to contact you?"

"Not yet. Have you . . . did you really kidnap the Pope? Are you having one of your moods?"

"One of my moods?"

"Yeah, you know."

"Do you think I kidnap popes when I have a bad mood?"

"It's weird news, *babbo,* that's all. I mean, the Pope!"

"He's with us. We're in disguise, at least I am, and he is, and the Dalai Lama."

"What?! You're with them now? The Dalai Lama's there with you? Oh my God! Are you in trouble?"

"Yes. No. The whole thing was your mother's idea. Listen, *carissima,* we want to see you. We've done nothing wrong. I'll explain. We'll be in Rimini in an hour and a half. Meet us on the beach, in the forties section someplace. We'll be walking along the edge of the water, south to north. You'll recognize your mother and then there will be three men with her that you won't recognize. But don't let anyone follow you, okay? If someone follows you, call this number and let us know. If anyone asks if I called, I didn't. Say your mother called, from Monte Carlo, worried. Okay?"

"Totally confused, *babbo.*"

"Just meet us at the beach in ninety minutes. In the forties. Take evasive measures."

I hung up and looked across the table.

Rosa was staring at me, twisting up one side of her mouth. "Evasive measures, *amore*?"

25

In order to find a legal parking place along the beach in Rimini in summer, you have to be living the sinless life. Fortunately, two members of our group fell into that category. As we were driving slowly along, with the Adriatic to our right and a long row of restaurants and shops to our left, we saw a car pull out just ahead, a spot opening up not far from where we were to meet Anna Lisa. A miracle. We parked and stood up into the hot sun like some kind of offbeat theater troupe, three odd-looking men and a beautiful woman. Any club owner in need of a warm-up act would have thought we'd arrived in town looking for work. We put coins in the meter and crossed to the beach side unmolested.

Like many beaches in Europe, Rimini's is dotted with thousands of *lettini*—"little beds" in Italian—canvas-and-wood contraptions on which you can lie comfortably enough and read or sunbathe. You pay a small fee to rent these *lettini* by the day, month, or season; they sit in pairs beneath large umbrellas absolutely indistinguishable from the hundreds of thousands of other *umbrelloni* on that strand. With the fee, you get access to the changing rooms and showers at the top of the sand, near the sidewalk. Each sector of beach, probably a hundred meters wide and stretching from sea to changing rooms, is under different management. Each of them is numbered. Rimini's strip of beach—one of the most famous in Europe—is so long that the numbers start at one, near the school where Anna Lisa taught, and stretch into the high nineties, all the way up in North Rimini, some ten kilometers away. When we visited her we always ended up in the forties. We knew and liked one of the caretakers there and, though it probably wasn't, the water seemed a bit cleaner in that section.

The problem, of course, was that none of us were in beach clothes, and we hadn't thought to bring any along. And it was a particularly hot day. We could have purchased what we needed in the endless string of clothing and souvenir shops that stood shoulder to shoulder on the other side of the road, but we weren't planning to stay long, and, as Rosa pointed out, swimming might have caused trouble with the disguises—my untinted chest and legs would look ridiculous.

Still, the thought of being at the beach and not going into the water was almost physically painful for me. I'd grown up, as I mentioned, near Lake Como, and we'd often made trips to Italy's western shore—Genoa or Viareggio. I loved being in the water almost as much as my mother had. It was a baptism for me, a cleansing—another way, perhaps, of erasing some of the mental etching the Pope had talked about. I thought it might be fun for the two holy men to take a dip, too, but Rosa convinced me it was really out of the question. So we walked onto the sand and started north, already sweating and scratching at our toupees, goatees, and painted skin.

We hadn't gone more than half a kilometer when Rosa said, almost in a whisper, "They'll be looking for groups of three men so I'm going to fall back with Tenzin. You and the Pope go forward. When you see Anna, don't wave or anything. Make sure there's no one following her. It'll be a test to see how good the disguises work!"

She and the Dalai fell back. I couldn't resist—I took off my shoes and socks, rolled up my pant legs, and waded along in the shallows. Yes, if someone cared to look, they'd notice that my ankles belonged to a northern Italian, and my face, neck, and hands to a Libyan or Tunisian. So what? Would that mean I had a pope walking beside me and a Dalai Lama behind?

I splashed in the edge of the gentle surf, doing battle with an urge to dive in. The Pope went along on slightly higher ground. Beyond him, milling and strolling, lying and sitting, were thousands of sun worshippers—Italians and Russians (who liked Rimini for its shopping and its menus printed in Cyrillic, and who loved to bake their pale skin in the sun until it was the color of a Siberian beet) and a few English-speakers. The usual mix. The only other nonwhite people on the beach were the African men selling trinkets, but Rimini was an international place; you heard a dozen languages in the space of half an hour's stroll, and I didn't stand out there in my disguise as much as I might have on another Italian beach.

"My cousin," the Pope said quietly, "aren't you having the time of your life?"

"I'm trying. I'm the nervous type, always have been. The news reports about ransom and so on haven't made things easier."

"I disagree," the Pope said.

"What, they've made things easier?"

He shook his head and laughed. "I disagree with the statement that you've always been the nervous type. That wasn't my experience of you in our youth."

"Most youth aren't nervous."

"I disagree again. There's an epidemic of anxiety in the Western world now. Anxiety, depression. In some places, adolescent suicide. It bruises my heart."

"Because so many young people have abandoned religion?"

"I prefer to think, my cousin, not that the young people have failed us, but that we have failed them. They have a nose for hypocrisy—even in matters of the Church. Sometimes *especially* in matters of the Church. We go on and on about the poor; meanwhile we dress in gold vestments, lift golden chalices to the sky, and perform our rites in cathedrals that cost millions of euro to heat and are more splendid than the homes in which the vast majority of the population of the earth will ever set foot. We talk about the love of God, and yet we make too many people feel like sinners, unlovable. Look at your own daughter, raised a good Catholic, with an uncle who was a bishop, an archbishop, a cardinal, and now the Pope, and she thinks of herself as a Buddhist!"

"It embarrasses me in front of you. I apologize."

"Don't waste your energy. Guilt is the last thing Christ wants of us, the very last thing. I'm looking forward to talking to her about it. I want to hear what she has to say. I want her to speak openly."

"No worry there. Anna Lisa has never in her life failed to say what's on her mind. She takes after her mother in that way."

"There she is! Look at the beautiful being she's become. She's positively glowing."

I saw my daughter a hundred meters ahead of us—tall like her mother, dark-haired and dark-eyed and built more like the classic beauties of old than the reed-thin models of modern fashion runways. She was wearing a flowered shirt and loose white pants that reached halfway down her calf. There did seem to be a light to her. She loved the beach as much as I did, maybe that was it, or maybe she was excited about being reunited with her parents, or seeing the Dalai Lama and the Pope on the same day. Who wouldn't be? I thought. And it was that thought, and the sight of my daughter, that knocked a hole in my gray ceiling of worry and let in a bit of sun. "Don't greet her," I said. "Let's see how the disguises work."

From fifty meters away she didn't recognize us. I checked to see if someone was following her. No.

Twenty-five meters, still no reaction.

There were other strollers and bathers between us, a gaggle of loud Russian kids punching each other in the shallows. Anna Lisa was distracted by them, maybe. Ten meters, only open space between us now, and still she didn't recognize us. The disguises worked perfectly, I thought . . . until she said *"Ciao, babbo!"* and ran the last few steps to hug me.

"I knew you by your walk!" She made a sort of half bow, half curtsy in the direction of the Holy Father, then reached out to take his hand.

"None of that!" he said, and he hugged her tightly against him.

"Look at the two of you! No one would know."

"Shh, Anna!"

"Dov'è la mamma?"

I hooked a thumb over my shoulder and she smiled. "We have to go someplace where we can talk, Pa, we have to! There's a morning meditation I go to sometimes. Would you mind?" She leaned in very close to the Pope's ear and said, "Holy Father, would you mind? It's Buddhist, but . . . we could pray together. Would it be wrong?"

Rosa came up and hugged her, and there was another bow from my daughter toward another holy man, more nervous this time, as if she were in awe. She was right: the beach was no place for any kind of open conversation. By unspoken agreement we angled up toward the main road and crossed it, then continued along a side street, shaded by eucalyptus trees and lined on both sides with cars parked so close to one another their bumpers were almost kissing.

"I can't speak," Anna Lisa said. "Really. I'm so excited I can't get words to come out of my mouth. The two holiest men of our time! Four of the five people on earth who mean the most to me, and all together in my city!"

"We are also excited," the Dalai Lama said, but these words came out with all the thrill and spark of someone asking for the olive oil at the dinner table. He was a kind man, kind, wise, exceedingly joyful it seemed to me. But he didn't seem to have a setting for "excited," not in our sense. It was a Buddhist thing, I decided. I'd heard the word "equanimity" thrown around. It wasn't a word you heard very often in Catholic circles, and not a trait that seemed particularly suited to the Italian way of life, with its great sweeps of emotion, effusive warmth, moods of historical despair. All this made me wonder, as we walked along Rimini's quiet side streets, what my daughter saw in the alien faith.

Anna Lisa had always liked to talk. As a little girl she'd sometimes wake up, already babbling in her bed, and go through an entire breakfast with barely a pause for breath, recounting her unbelievably elaborate dreams in unbelievably elaborate detail—"And, Mommy, then an animal, like a giant dog, came out of the trees and the animal came up and sat next to me and *babbo,* and she started brushing my hair with the hairbrush *nonna* gave me, except it tickled so much I started to laugh, and then the animal started to laugh, it was like a big fluffy dog only it had the face of a cat . . ." And so on.

How was a person like that going to make a three-year silent retreat?

As our odd fivesome went along the shaded streets I listened to her, letting the sound of her voice make a warm vapor around my heart.

"I feel like I should get down on my knees or bow or something," she was saying.

"Exactly what we don't want," the Pope told her. "Your father and mother have arranged for us to be ordinary human beings for a few days. No fuss."

"The world is looking for you, frantically."

"We know," the Pope and Dalai said at the same time.

She turned around and glanced at me over her shoulder. "It's freaky seeing you like that, Pa. Not to mention you, Your Holinesses. Did Mom's people do you?"

"Mario."

"I love Mario!"

"Is he the fifth person?" I asked, somewhat surprised that she knew him. "You said you were with four of your five favorite people."

A blush, uncharacteristic.

"A boyfriend?" Rosa guessed.

Anna Lisa nodded.

"Serious?"

"We've been dating for months but I'm private about these things. You know how I am, right, Pa? He's Buddhist, Your Holiness. We met at his meditation center." She turned to the Pope. "I'm sorry, Holy Father. I still pray to Mary, still sometimes go to Mass. I don't find the two faiths contradictory at all."

"I was hoping you'd talk to us about that," the Pope said. "I couldn't possibly have such a conversation with any other young person on earth."

Her beautiful smile shrank almost to a pout. She pursed her lips and squeezed her eyebrows together. "I respect you so much," she said. "I don't want to hurt you."

"You couldn't possibly."

I had the sense of trouble coming, a premonition that I should reach my hand forward and place it on Anna Lisa's shoulder, to calm her, to warn her, or that I should ask how the local soccer team was doing, shift the conversation to lunch, pizza, chicken cacciatore, could we have some wine? But I was preoccupied, turning my head left and right, alert for an army lieutenant or a police captain who was hoping to spot the kidnapped Pope, bring the kidnapper into custody, and take home the reward. It's not the easiest thing, being wanted by an entire nation, by much of the world. Kidnapping a pope in Italy was a capital offense, worse, even, than blowing up a vodka distillery in Belarus or setting off stink bombs in the bordellos of Amsterdam. One might associate those national treasures with sin, but the Pope—Italian or not—carried the lamp of sinlessness through the *bel paese*. This Pope, especially, was beloved. His kidnapper would be seen as a friend of the devil.

"The rules, mainly," Anna Lisa said, unapologetically. "The sexual rules. Birth control, premarital love. But other things as well. Women's roles. I'm sorry."

"You shouldn't be. These are issues that should be discussed openly."

"But it's not just the rules. The Buddhists—" she stopped and glanced at the Dalai Lama—"correct me if I'm wrong, but they have an approach to life that makes sense to me. They believe in reincarnation, for one thing, which explains a lot of the apparent unfairness in the world. But even without that . . . they have techniques for calming the mind, and I know we—you—have prayer and so on, and going to Mass, but that can be like checking off a list to prove you're a good person. People go to Mass and come out and act exactly as bad as they did before they went in."

"Not all people."

"No, of course not. But if you're addicted, say, or if you're prone to anger, or afraid of something, Buddhist meditation seems to get right down into that place and help you fix it. I love that, I love the calm of that kind of prayer."

"We have centering prayer," the Pope said. "The Rosary. In our monasteries we have a long tradition of contemplative prayer, Lectio Divina, and so on."

"I know. Those things are almost the same, and actually I combine aspects of the two faiths all the time. I'll say five Hail Marys and then do a Dzogchen meditation!"

"Ah," the Dalai Lama said, as if that word meant something to him.

"Sounds like you have a bee in your mouth," I said.

"It's Tibetan, Pa. A tradition of Buddhism. Dzogchen. It came from Padmasambhava."

"Yes, of course, Padmasambhava," I said, as if I'd heard of her. One does not want to look stupid in front of one's child.

"Dzogchen means 'the Great Perfection.' It's so wonderful!" She turned and walked backward, facing the Dalai Lama, all reticence gone now. "I was thinking, I'm sorry Your Holiness, when I heard you were here I was thinking you could give me one word of guidance."

I watched my cousin's face, searching amid the blond hair for signs of distress. Here was my daughter, practically a niece to him, raised Catholic, and right in front of him she was praising another faith, and asking for spiritual guidance from an alien master. He'd said it didn't bother him, that he wanted an open conversation. I wondered if he'd expected one this open.

"Why is it so bad to pray both ways?" Rosa asked, when the Dalai Lama seemed to hesitate.

"Not bad!" the Dalai Lama exclaimed. "Buddhism doesn't require you to leave your faith. It does not mean leaving Christ, just the opposite. It means a way to know Christ better!"

"But you would never say something like that, would you, Holy Father? A Catholic couldn't speak that way about another religion."

Now the Pope did shift his gait in an uncomfortable way. I could see the muscles of his face flex—when something was bothering him, he had the habit of puffing a little air into his cheeks, keeping his lips closed tightly and squinting his eyes. It made him look angry, though I'm sure he wasn't. "No," he admitted. "For us, as you know, there was one Son of God sent to earth. Buddha we can acknowledge as a special man, but a man, not a divinity. No offense meant, Tenzin."

The Dalai Lama laughed. "Buddha, I think, does not care too much what we call him. 'Divinity' is not what he could want people to say."

"But *we* care, Tenzin. I'm sorry. I respect every faith, as I've said publicly, and many times. We have complete respect for sincere seekers in all traditions. I'm not in the business of convincing people to become Catholics. I've said that, too. But I'm afraid this is one point where we can't find common ground. In the style of prayer, yes, of course, we can learn from you. I've said as much. And Anna, I understand completely why certain ancient rules would be problematic, and why you'd be drawn to this kind of interior prayer. I pray that way myself, in fact, though in a Christian version. I know the benefits. But Christ's unique divinity—we can't rewrite that. If we believe in the Resurrection, we can't compare him to anyone, not even Buddha."

A difficult silence fell across our little group. I could hear echoes of history's thunderous clashes, the sacred bloodlust, the insistence on victory, not peace. From an early age we pledged ourselves to a certain system of belief—usually because our parents had embraced it—and its codes were then etched into the walls of our brains and hearts. We defended those codes, argued for them, fought for them, devoted ourselves to them. And that led some of us to salvation . . . and others to war.

Anna Lisa made a right turn and stopped in front of a building with maroon-and-gold trim around the door.

From the street we'd just left came the blast of a police klaxon, rising, then fading away—"the song of suffering," my mother had always called it. "When you hear that sound, someone, somewhere, is suffering." She'd encouraged us to say a silent prayer for them, so I did that. But I was wondering, at the same time, how close the police might be to catching us.

The Dalai Lama said, "I say sometimes now, 'My religion is kindness,' because to say other things only divides people. All peoples can be kind. Those who worship Christ, Buddha, Mohammed . . . the Hindus, the atheists. This, I think, makes for less anger. Less hatred."

Anna Lisa, carrying her mother's gene for bluntness, could not be stopped. "You're both so wonderful, so beloved. But, Your Holiness, I have to say that sometimes what's hard for me is that there didn't seem to be much warmth to the Buddha. He was a great teacher, he seemed like he truly cared about people, but I hear a coldness in his words that I don't like. I guess I'd prefer to have a personal figure who went around teaching and hugging."

"Christ wept when his friend died," my cousin put in hopefully.

"He did, yes. That's what I'm saying, I guess, Uncle Giorgio. I like the internal aspects of Buddhism and the external aspects of Christianity. People accuse me of having a 'cafeteria faith,' taking a little of this and a little of that. I guess I don't see what's wrong with the cafeteria idea."

I could sense that the Holy Father wanted to say something else then, but he and the Dalai Lama had learned to keep their voices from being heard, and a few people were coming up the walk and heading for the doorway, so the conversation evaporated. At that moment I wasn't concerned with the religious differences. I was thinking about the siren, about being found and apprehended, and it was casting a shadow across the sunny pleasure of being with my daughter. Something else was on my mind, too: the sense—vague, and oddly disconcerting, spawned by my early-morning conversation with the Pope—that a new spiritual challenge waited for us another few hours down the road. The hand of history, it felt like. The hope for a grand reconciliation, or at least a step into some new territory. Twenty years earlier there had been a Vatican-sponsored colloquium that examined the "shared concerns" of Catholics and Buddhists. But the idea of shared concerns was one thing—dry, intellectual, official. What I was thinking about felt more personal than that, more immediate: if smart, good young people like Anna Lisa were mixing traditions and gaining in peace and faith . . . if the Pope and the Dalai Lama had been brought together for some purpose larger than a simple road trip . . . if Rosa and I had a small role to play in that . . . well, it unnerved me.

"This will be pretty short," Anna Lisa said, opening the gold-trimmed door. "Twenty minutes or so of meditation, then Piero talks for a while. That's it. Can you manage it, Pa?"

"Of course," I said. "I'm insulted that you even have to ask."

"Well, you're not exactly the kind of guy who sits still a lot."

Over the years of being a father it had occurred to me, more than once, that children are mirrors. They show us to ourselves. We go along for two or three decades just being who we are, accustomed to our foibles and quirks, our flaws, blind to them, perhaps arguing about them with a spouse, but basically certain we're okay as is. And then this other being comes into our life. We have ten years or so when they're blind, too, loving, accepting, watching with an uncritical eye, having nothing against which to compare the king and queen who rule over them. And then they break out of the eggshell of family life. They gain their own perspective. They begin to see you critically—too critically at first, perhaps. They shed a light. Until that moment I'd never really thought of myself as being the kind of guy who has trouble sitting still, but as we stepped through the painted door, me with a small sting on the skin of my brain, a tiny emotional concussion, I decided it was probably true.

The interior of the building was composed of a large room with black meditation cushions set in four even rows, a low stage up front with a door behind, and two well-used sofas guarding the back wall. A nice-looking, wide-shouldered young man in a maroon robe sat cross-legged on the stage, one of the black cushions beneath him. Anna Lisa waved to him; she seemed completely at ease. "Sit wherever you're comfortable," she told us. Another few seconds and she'd left us, chosen one of the cushions, and was crossing her legs and settling herself. The Dalai Lama, still wearing the oversized sunglasses, which were even more ridiculous now that we were indoors, walked up and took the cushion next to her. Rosa ventured a step in that direction, then thought better of it, made a U-turn, and sat on one of the couches. The Pope sat to her left. I took my place beside her on the right.

We waited a minute for things to get started. Another handful of people came through the door. No one spoke.

Most of them sat on the cushions, but one rather elderly woman took the last seat on our couch, to my right.

"*Allora,*" the young man up front said, lifting his face to us. This is a commonly used but untranslatable Italian word that means something like "okay" or "all right now" or "here we go" or "so ...," depending on the circumstance, but it always points a short distance into the future. "*Allora,* let's add up your bill." "*Allora,* let's stop talking and get to work." "*Allora,* let me show you something now." The young man's spine was as straight as a streetlight, his hands cupped in his lap, and his Italian bore a slight Romagnolo accent. "*Per quelli che non sanno ...* for those of you who don't know, I'm Piero. Welcome, everybody. We'll sit quietly for twenty minutes and then I'll say a few words, and that's all that goes on here. Our motto is 'No fuss.' We come together like this every day, and twice a day on the weekends, and you're welcome to join us as often or as infrequently as you like."

A little bit different from the Catholic message, I thought. No pressure. It wasn't a mortal sin if you missed services. The whole easygoing feel was slightly awkward and alien for me, however—the robe, the cushions, the cross-legged sitting. Still, it seemed to make my daughter happy, and to a father, what matters more than that?

It soon became apparent that everyone else in the room had closed his or her eyes and was sitting quietly. I looked at the Pope, who seemed comfortable enough. Rosa had her eyes closed, too, and appeared to be mouthing a prayer, or lyrics from a favorite song, so I closed my eyes and listened to Piero giving final instructions, "Just watch your thoughts and find something to come back to—your breath, a mantra, the image of someone you love. Just do that over and over again when your mind wanders, and see if you can allow it to settle. Let's begin."

We began. Or they began. I immediately opened my eyes again and looked around the room. A soccer ball in one corner—that was a bit odd. Curtained windows. A table with a neat stack of books. The Buddha statue behind Piero made me think back to the Mussolini bust in the restaurant in L'Aquila. I don't mean that in an irreverent way; they just seemed to be made of a similar material—brass, or imitation brass, or gold-painted wood—and to be positioned similarly, observing all who entered. I watched my daughter, thought about the "not exactly the kind of guy who sits still" remark. I looked at the Dalai Lama, perched cross-legged on his cushion and apparently not breathing. I glanced again at the Pope, at Rosa. The woman next to me coughed and I wondered if she was upset at me for my lack of stillness, so I closed my eyes, took a breath, and tried to settle my mind.

For a short time when I was a boy—between the ages of eight and ten—my parents owned a dog. The dog was called Pazzo, which, in Italian, means "crazy." Pazzo was appropriately named. He was a small mongrel with curly white hair and a square snout, and he was a prime example of the kind of dog that is constitutionally unable to be still. Pazzo heard noises where no noises existed. He'd rush to the front door and bark, and his bark was the quintessence of annoyance, a high-pitched *yap-yap-yap* that went on and on as if marking the passing half seconds. Then, suddenly, he'd think he heard something at the back door, and he'd race across the tiles, toenails ticking, and put his forelegs up on the screen and yap there, on and on. Then he'd jump up on the couch and look out the window—more yapping. Finally, someone on the verge of a nervous breakdown would let him outside, and he'd race over to the metal fence and yap furiously at the dog next door, an eerily peaceful golden retriever named Cielo, or "sky." Cielo would languidly turn her head, rest her eyes on the yapping Pazzo just long enough to ascertain that the fence between them was intact, the territorial boundary impenetrable, and then she'd set her head peacefully on her forelegs until Pazzo exhausted himself and gave up. But, though he'd stopped barking for a minute, Pazzo hadn't truly given up, and he was far from exhausted. He'd race around to the front gate chasing a real or imaginary bird, or he'd sniff something on the breeze—anything, another dog, a cat, a pasta Bolognese being cooked five blocks away—and bark crazily about that.

We loved Pazzo, in spite of all this. However, one sad day Pazzo's mad curiosity got the best of him. He burrowed under a broken piece of the front gate and raced into the street, where he was immediately crushed by a truck delivering a refrigerator to the house next door. We found the body there, flattened. The driver was inconsolable. We told him not to worry.

My mind, in that twenty-minute meditation, was a Pazzo mind. It leapt and scurried after imaginary worries: How long would it be until we were tracked down? What would happen then? Why wasn't I the kind of man who could just let events unfold without worrying? Why did I spoil things that way? Is that what had ruined our marriage? How long would the Pope be patient with Anna Lisa's Buddhism? From there it flew to totally unconnected ideas: the sound of the breathing of the woman next to me. Was she ill with something I might catch? Had I embarrassed my daughter somehow? Who was this Piero? The boyfriend? What was Rosa thinking right now? We'd have a conversation about it afterward, a debriefing. No doubt, whatever our impressions of the meditation, they would be diametrically opposed. Why couldn't we stop fighting? We were the Palestine and Israel of the married world. It seemed that the brown polish, or whatever it was that Mario had applied to my skin, had started drying out and cracking in a few spots. How much longer would it last? Was Rosa infatuated with Mario? Was something going on? Why did I care so much?

This continued for twenty minutes that seemed like twenty hours. *Yap-yap-yap.* When I heard a tiny bell, a stirring at the front of the room, and then Piero saying, "Okay now, just a last couple of slow breaths and we'll talk a bit," I wanted to jump to my feet and applaud. Instead, a sigh escaped my lips. I felt the woman to my right turn and look at me. Apparently, I'd made a faux pas: one wasn't supposed to sigh in these places. I could already hear Anna Lisa's exasperated *"Pa!"* And I was sure everyone else in the room had a Cielo mind, while I had a Pazzo.

But my introduction to Buddhist meditation was over, and for that I raised a Catholic prayer of thanks.

Piero, I have to say, had a nice way about him, neither pretentious nor apologetic. The robe put me off, as Buddhist robes tended to do. On the Dalai Lama it would have been as natural as a three-hundred-euro silk necktie on Berlusconi, but Piero looked like the kind of young Italian guy you'd see studying in a café outside the University of Bologna, or having a glass of wine and a dish of pasta with his girlfriend in Trastevere.

"*Dirò alcune parole* . . . I'm going to say a few words, food for thought, and then I'll hope to see you tomorrow." Piero took a breath, looked down into his hands, then up again. I saw that my daughter was leaning close and whispering in the Dalai Lama's ear.

Piero began to speak. "I was thinking today, I was wondering how we would act if, for example, the Buddha was in this room right now. If he was walking along with us in our daily life, there when we lay down in bed, when we ate breakfast, when we were at work, making love, taking a swim, paying a bill. Would we act any differently, sensing that presence beside us? And what message would his presence give? I was thinking that the message would be that we should pay careful attention without being too self-conscious about our attentiveness, without thinking all the time, *Now I'm paying attention.* Just fall into the habit of doing that, the way most of us have fallen into the habit of checking our phone every few minutes when we're waiting in a doctor's office."

The Dalai Lama nodded; all was well.

"I've heard the expression 'Make every breath a prayer,'" Piero went on, "and I wonder if we could try doing that even for a few minutes every day outside of this room. A prayer of thanks, maybe. An awareness of the miracle of the breath going into and out of us and keeping us alive. If we could hold on to that kind of awareness, for example, when we're about to have an argument with our lover, or when we're irritated by someone or something. If we could just shift our attention to the bare fact of our anger or irritation and watch what happens . . . I think it's worth a try.

"The same thing with fear. I've heard it said that the Dalai Lama is afraid of water. Maybe that's not true, but I think I heard it or read it someplace."

At that comment I looked at the Dalai, who seemed even stiller than he had been. If it wasn't true, I imagined he'd leap up and complain: "No, no! I love water!" Or, if it was true, he'd be as embarrassed as the Pope on the ski lift.

"He's a human being," Piero went blindly on. "He has fears like the rest of us. But I imagine him being asked to swim. I picture him sometimes—maybe you'll think this is odd—but I picture him at the beach here, in our city, and someone suggests he take a swim. The fear would rise up in him, but he'd be watching that fear, which would be the first step in overcoming it. I imagine it would have a minuscule effect on his life. The fear, the shame of being afraid, maybe a bad history connected to water. From this life or a past life; it wouldn't cripple him.

"We all have such things, don't we? Sources of fear, anger, irritation. Triggers that knock us out of the present moment. Let's try to be aware of them, okay?" Piero ran his eyes around the room in a compassionate circle. "*Va bene.* Okay. Good. Thank you for coming, for listening. I'll hope to see you all again soon."

He made a small bow to the audience and we bowed back. People stood up, gathered their belongings, made for the door. I noticed that the Dalai Lama stayed seated. Anna Lisa turned to us, her face lit up but slightly troubled. "Did you like it?"

"Loved it," I said, drawing on many years of fatherly diplomacy. "Life-changing."

"Really, *babbo?*"

"Absolutely. Seems like a good guy."

"You like it, Mom?"

"Wonderful," Rosa said, in what sounded like a sincere way.

The Pope was silent, either to keep his voice disguised or because he was upset about having attended.

"Piero wants to meet everybody," Anna Lisa bubbled on. "There's a little room in back. He's making tea. He wants us to go back there."

"I'm not sure that's—" I started to say, but I became aware of Rosa shooting me a steely glance. The four of us were alone in the room by then. The Dalai Lama was stretching his legs and getting to his feet. "Holy Father, do you mind?"

"Why would I mind?"

"Dalai?"

"Good, good," he said, but something was wrong. I could sense it. It must have been the fear-of-water comment. The Dalai's ordinarily serene face was crinkled up in an expression of mild irritation—or so it seemed behind the dark glasses. Anna Lisa led her mother and the two disguised holy men to the back room and I brought up the rear, dragging a heavy sack of worries.

Piero, bathed in innocence, had taken off the robe and set a plate of cheese and fruit on a small square table. "Making tea," he said over his shoulder as we walked in. "Please sit."

We sat. With the new awareness I'd gained from the meditation session I sensed a massive discomfort in the room. It was clear to me that Piero had no idea who his guests really were. We heard the tea water hissing. People weren't looking at each other.

"That was really interesting, Anna," I said.

She smiled at me, looked anxiously at the Pope, and completely avoided the shaded eyes of the Dalai Lama.

Piero brought tea to the table and poured five cups, carefully, attentively, gratefully. Despite the mild torment he'd put me through a short while earlier, I found that I liked him. Liked him to such a degree, in fact, that I worried that if he found out who was sitting at the table with him, he'd feel not so much that he'd put his foot in his mouth as that he'd eaten a boot factory.

"*Allora,*" he said cheerily, "Anna, introduce us, please."

Anna Lisa coughed, cleared her throat, looked at her mother in a pleading way.

"Just the truth, I guess," Rosa said.

"Well," my daughter began, "this is my mother, Rosa. And this guy here is my dad, Paolo. In disguise."

"Ah, the kidnapper!" Piero said.

He'd meant it, I could see, as a joke, but it hadn't worked. He was nervous around us for some reason. Just wait, I thought.

"And this," Rosa said, pointing to the Pope, "this is, well, this man is actually the Pope, also in disguise."

"Ha, ha!" Piero said, smiling broadly. I noticed at that moment that he had a pair of eyeglasses hooked over the collar of his shirt. Thick lenses. He must have taken them off for the ceremony, or because of the steam from his tea-making. He moved his eyes, innocently, from Anna Lisa to the Pope to me and then back again. "Thees must mean," he said, playing along like the good guy he was, trying out his English for a few seconds, and then gesturing to the as-yet-unintroduced member of our odd group, "that thees long-haired fellow here is the Dalai Lama! Ha ha ha!"

This remark was greeted by an absolutely brutal silence. Absolutely brutal. Anna Lisa looked down at her pear slices, then up into Piero's face. She reached out, very kindly, I thought, and put a hand on his arm. I watched his eyes and mouth, watched the understanding come over his even features like sunlight brightening a sky at dawn, second by second, centimeter by centimeter. A brutal understanding. He looked, for some reason, at me.

"I don't really look like this," I said.

He glanced at Rosa, wondering, I suppose, what *she* actually looked like. He turned his eyes to the Pope, seemed, at last, to notice the too-even edges of the goatee, the familiar eyes, nose, and facial shape. I could see him working up the courage to look at the Dalai Lama. I watched the movement of his eyes, the hesitation there. He shifted them halfway, then looked fully, checked out the toupee, the oversized glasses, the famous cheeks and mouth. A pause, two seconds, four seconds, and then "Oy . . . as my parents used to said."

I saw Anna Lisa squeeze his arm. "Piero was raised Jewish," she said nervously.

Piero's hand fumbled for the folded eyeglasses. Eventually he lifted them to his face and set them on his nose.

The Dalai Lama was smiling at him, but it was impossible to tell what was behind the smile, because we could barely see his eyes through the tinted lenses. "Little surprise now," he said. He reached up and slowly, dramatically, removed the big sunglasses.

"I feel very, very, very stupid," Piero said. "Eye em sorry, Your Holiness. I didn't mean a disrespect—"

The Dalai Lama held up one hand, palm outward, fingers pressed together, in what was apparently a Tibetan gesture of absolution. "Everything you said was truth," he said.

"Really?"

"We cannot be afraid of truth!" The Dalai Lama made his famous laugh. "Even if truth is about being afraid! Ha! And what you said about Buddha—not so bad teaching. Pretty good. But now you need to come to Dharamsala and study with monks!"

He went on for a minute—giving Piero time to recover, it seemed—talking about the various kinds of instruction Piero might receive, the texts he should memorize, the different visualizations he could try. When he finished, there was a moment of hope-infused silence—I thought all was well—until Anna Lisa slanted her eyes to me and then to her mother and I could feel a new tsunami curling up over us, about to crash ashore. "Piero and I . . ." she began, then she seemed to lose her nerve. I saw a twitch at the corner of her lips. "We're . . . well . . ." She looked at Piero, who looked at me. "We're pregnant. We're lovers. We're the same thing as engaged."

At that point the stress became too much for her and she burst into tears. Rosa stood up and hugged her, giving me the "Say something, Paolo!" evil eye. I was, for an instant, frozen. In shock. And then: "Honey, that's incredible!!" I said. "We're so, so happy to meet him. We're happy that you're happy! It's a beautiful thing and we love you!"

I went over and hugged her, too. I started to reach

out to shake Piero's hand, but that somehow seemed un-Buddhist to me, like the act of a cliché future father-in-law. I thought of bowing, but didn't, and found myself stuck between standing up straight, leaning over and hugging my crying daughter and my wife (now also crying), and shaking hands. "Great! Incredible! We're so happy!" I kept saying, in English and Italian both. *"Siamo felici!"* And then, out of some primeval instinct, I grabbed my wife's shoulders and kissed her hard on the mouth.

Rosa stepped back, an expression of the purest astonishment on her face.

"Do you mean it, Pa?" Anna Lisa asked me. "You're happy?"

"What's not to mean? Of course I'm happy! Are you going to baptize the child?"

It just flew out of my mouth, that phrase, and it was the equivalent of going up onto a stage at my daughter's wedding, where the band was playing a happy dance number, and kicking my polished shoe, full-force, through the skin of the bass drum, then smiling idiotically. I tensed all my muscles, hoping against hope that I might suck the words back into my body, or that someone, one of the kind and holy people in the room, would rescue me by making a joke, or even just saying a single word. Nothing. "I was kidding," I said. "Half kidding. It's up to you, naturally. We don't care." I could feel the Pope looking at me. "I mean, it would be nice, but you two should do what you're comfortable with. You'll be fine. Piero, I'm happy. We're happy!"

This to the background music of weeping. Rosa had both hands on Anna Lisa's shoulders. The Pope and Dalai were smiling, but the smiles seemed strained to me, forced. Piero, who had been so genuinely and humbly confident at the head of the meditation room, now wore the expression of a man with a glass of wine in one hand and the other in a pot of boiling water. He was happy, you could see it. And, at the same time, he must have thought, as recently as half an hour ago, that life was very simple. Now, suddenly, his future father-in-law and the grandfather of his child was a kidnapper disguised as a hungry refugee and spouting *stupidaggini,* and his girlfriend and girlfriend's mother were weeping uncontrollably and holding each other as if they were sliding across the tilted deck of a ship that was sinking off the coast of Greenland. And the Dalai Lama and the Pope of Rome were sitting right there in the room, staring at him.

"You know," the Pope said at last, "I've been having strange dreams lately."

I was terrified, at that moment, that he was going to add Mussolini into the mix. The air in the room could not have carried such a cargo.

"I've been dreaming about a child—not yours, my dear niece—but some special child who has already been born, a holy child, perhaps. One I may never meet. It's very strange. These dreams—" he stopped and glanced uneasily at the Dalai Lama—"are actually what prompted me to ask my dear cousin to help me, us, make this unusual trip."

You're strange, I wanted to say, but, of course, that would have been another faux pas, and disrespectful besides, and not once in my tenure had I been disrespectful to the Pope in any way. But dreams of a child, women, helicopters, soccer balls, the famous dictator? What kind of subconscious was that? What was going on there? And what kind of Dalai Lama was afraid of water?! As far as I

knew there wasn't even any water to be afraid of in Tibet!
I wondered, then, if they were both in on it, two mystical
dreamers who'd tricked me into thinking all they wanted
was a short vacation, a break, some relief from the burden
of fame.

Rosa looked at me. "Go out and buy champagne," she
said, in a tone of voice that did not admit the possibility
of refusal.

"Mamma, I shouldn't drink alcohol."

"You can have half a glass. I drank a little when I was
pregnant with you."

"Yes, and you both turned out fine," I hastened to say.

"The Pope and the Dalai Lama don't drink, do they?
Do you, Your Holinesses?" Anna Lisa raised her head and
looked at them . . . "expectantly" is the word I would use.

"A little wine," the Pope said. The Dalai started to
shake his head, then stopped, shrugged, scratched at his
toupee.

Rosa had her hands on her hips, a danger signal.
"Paolo," she said forcefully, "go get something. I'll drink
it all myself if I have to."

"There's a store not far that sells wine," Piero said, in
Italian now. "May I come along?"

26

Somewhat shaky in the knees, for different but related
reasons, the young Buddhist and I stepped out of the
wreckage of the moment and into the hot noonday sun.

We turned in the direction of the city center, went along
a little way in an uneasy mood, and then he practically
wailed this sentence:"I can't believe I said that in front of
the Dalai Lama!"

"I don't think he minded much."

"You can't tell with him."

"Exactly. Equanimity."

"Still, I feel horrible."

"I'd let it go. I am richly experienced in the art of putting my foot in my mouth, as you might have noticed.
The best strategy is to let it go. Forget it. Don't replay the
moment in your mind," I said, even as I was doing exactly
that with my baptism remark.

"*Va bene, grazie,*" he said. "Fine. Thanks," and then: "I
would like to ask you for your daughter's hand in marriage."

"No," I said, and for a minute I didn't say anything
else. My mind was mainly on other things—my stupidity,
being a grandfather, the wrath of the Catholic and Buddhist worlds, having my daughter and grandchild visit me
in jail, the look on my wife's face when she'd heard Anna
Lisa's news. Our kiss. Equanimity. The divine sense of
humor.

"I think that's unfair," Piero was saying, but I heard those
words as if they were being mumbled in the next province. "I don't think religious differences—not that Anna
Lisa and I have those differences—but I don't think they
should interfere with you giving me permission to—"

"No, no, no!" I said. "I meant no, don't worry about it.
Anna Lisa's my daughter, not my property. You don't have
to ask me. She's the most precious thing in the world to me
and I want her to be happy, that's all. Make her happy, or

keep her happy, or at least try to break her of the habit of talking all the time . . . but don't worry about me."

He went quiet. I glanced over at him. A nice-looking young man. Sincere. On the gentle side, but in a sufficiently manly way. His English rough, his Italian eloquent. I was old enough to wish that he and my daughter had put things in a different order: marriage first, then parenthood. But Rosa and I had put things in that order and look where we'd ended up . . . so I didn't say anything.

"My family's Jewish," he said. "Dad's a rabbi, in fact. In Venice."

"What happened to you, then?"

He made a noise like a laugh, a small, gentle laugh. I was forming and re-forming my opinion of him as we walked, and the laugh made me see that he had a sense of humor about himself. He wouldn't always need to be right, the way I did, the way Rosa sometimes did. In the tumultuous sea of marital life, the hour-by-hour mix of storm and calm, their little vessel of love might actually have a chance to stay afloat. Plus, the Pope's closest childhood friend had become a rabbi, so we had that going for us.

"Penso che . . ." he said. "I think what happened to me is the same thing that happened to Anna Lisa. We respect the faiths we were raised in, but traditional Catholicism and traditional Judaism left too many unanswered questions and had too many rules. For *us*—let me emphasize that part. I don't judge what other people believe or don't believe. I really don't."

"What do the Jews believe, anyway? Other than the fact that Jesus wasn't the Messiah, kosher food, and so on, I haven't the faintest idea where they stand on the spectrum."

"It's not simple," he said.

"Nothing is. Listen, I have no advice to give, about marriage or anything else. Only this: The older you get, the more complicated everything becomes. Marriage is at the top of that list. At least mine was—is. I hope yours works out better."

"Anna Lisa says you still love each other, you and Rosa. I saw the kiss."

I didn't feel I'd known Piero long enough to discuss how much Rosa and I still loved each other, so I grunted in a more or less positive-seeming way and kept my eyes forward.

"The Jews," he said, "believe, basically, that you should pray only to God and that there will be a resurrection. But when and what kind of resurrection—that varies. There are Orthodox Jews, Conservative Jews, Reform Jews, and they all interpret things a bit differently, but basically just try to live a good and decent life. It can get complicated, though. Some people say there are six hundred and thirteen commandments in the Torah."

"Sounds a little extreme."

"The religion goes back at least four thousand years, and has some wonderful traditions. Bat mitzvah and bar mitzvah. The Day of Atonement. Seder."

"What's a seder? I've heard of it."

"A feast."

"Feasts I like. I don't think the Buddhists have them, do they? I'm sorry. This is why I could never convert. No feasts and too much sitting still—it's not going to catch on in Italy, believe me."

I was in a mood to mutter semi-sane statements. Piero didn't seem to mind, or to be paying too close attention. I decided he'd fit in to the family very well.

"There's a large spectrum in Judaism, just like in a lot of faiths," he went on. "My family is on the Reform end. Less strict, more modern. In fact, my parents observe the High Holidays, and the rest of the time they live more or less like everyone else in Italy." Piero pointed to our right; we turned. "One more block," he said.

"I read where only something like 30 percent of Italians attend Mass every Sunday now," I told him. "When I was a boy it used to be 90 percent."

He pondered that for a few steps, then said, "I think most people feel the need for some kind of spiritual practice in their life, spiritual guidance, or at least something larger to believe in. But they're not comfortable with many of the old rules. That you have to go to Mass every Sunday or you'll be condemned to hell. That you have to eat only kosher food, or wear your facial hair a certain way. A lot of people don't see the connection between those kinds of things and the search for spiritual meaning in modern life. What I'm trying to do with the meditation meetings, what Anna Lisa and I hope to do with our child—children, actually—is to make something new, something that draws on and respects the beautiful traditions and disciplines of the past, but also something that gives him or her—and us—some modern center, some core of belief—in goodness or kindness or selflessness or service, a sense of awe before the mystery of creation—and at the same time makes sense to us on the most practical level."

"You might convert me, after all," I said, and we stepped into the wine store.

I told Piero he could pick out the champagne, but

that I was paying—our first gift to him and Anna Lisa. He didn't object. He spent a couple of minutes looking through the offerings, then chose a bottle at the middle-lower end of the price spectrum and carried it to the counter.

"Celebration?" the clerk asked. He had jowls and a big belly, hadn't shaved in a week, but he was one of those people who give off an undeniable sense of being at peace. In their place. Never in my life had I truly felt that, and I had an urge to ask the man where it came from, what was the secret, what kind of religion did he practice? How much of his own product did he consume on any given day?

"This is my future son-in-law," I said. "He and my daughter just told us they're engaged. We're visiting. We wanted to raise a glass with them."

"*Che meraviglia!!*" the man said. How marvelous! He had the bottle in his hand and was examining it. Looking for the price, I thought, but then he said, "This is decent. Drinkable. Not the best we have, but drinkable." He looked up at me, and at that moment I realized—again—that I was not white, which most likely conveyed to this man the idea that my daughter was entering into a mixed marriage. I braced myself for some kind of remark. Was that the way people of color went through their days in this world—bracing for a remark, a nasty look, or worse? Had I never really understood this before Mario applied the polish to my skin? Was this not, truly, a spiritual lesson? But the bristly, jowly cheeks only squeezed up into a smile. "My gift to you, then," he said. *Il mio regalo.* "My gift to the couple. *Prendete!* Take it. Please. I've had a good summer so far, business is good, the Russians are here, and they drink like they've lived their whole life in the desert! So this is my gift."

He placed the bottle lovingly into a paper bag, and, after trying halfheartedly to pay, we thanked him and started back.

"That kind of thing," I said, "happens more in Italy than anyplace I've ever been."

"You've traveled?"

"With the Pope. Some when I was a boy."

"We'd like to travel."

"Well, don't let people tell you it's impossible with a small child. In fact, it's easier with a small child, and then later on it gets . . . challenging. My parents took me everywhere, all around Europe, New York, South America. They were lovable eccentrics, artists, good people."

"We need more eccentrics," Piero said.

I raised him up one more notch on the likability meter.

All of this—Anna Lisa's news, my beginning the process of liking my future son-in-law, the free champagne—would have made for an especially pleasant afternoon if we hadn't stepped through the gold-and-maroon-trimmed door, walked into the back room, and found our four friends there with faces painted in an expression close to shock. I thought, for a moment, that there had been an argument, a schism, or the opposite: a stunning conversion by one of the holy men, or that the Pope had taken my daughter to task for "premarital love," as she called it, a mortal sin in our tradition. Or that the Dalai Lama had let himself get angry about being shown, in front of everyone, to be afraid of water.

But no.

"Anna's roommate, Beatrice, just called her," Rosa said. She was moving me into the main room and toward the front door as she spoke. The rest of the group was following. "The police were at their apartment, asking questions. 'Where is Anna Lisa?' 'Has she heard from her father?' And so on. Beatrice told them she thought Anna Lisa had gone to the beach. Also, apparently someone in L'Aquila thinks he saw the Holy Father in disguise, and that was on the news, too. We have to go, Paolo. Now."

I looked at the Pope, the Dalai Lama, turned to my daughter. "We could just surrender," I started to say, but something on Anna Lisa's face cut the thought off before it could completely form. The expression there was one of admiration. For me. She'd apparently always wanted a criminal for a father.

"I'm proud that you did this, *babbo*," she said. "When you and Piero were gone, the Holinesses were saying how much it means to them to get away like this, in spite of all the uproar. We made a short recording to protect you, and so people wouldn't worry. I'm so proud of you!"

I shrugged manfully, eyed the champagne. "One drink before we depart?"

"We have to go!" Rosa said. "Now!"

"You shouldn't walk back to the car together," Piero advised, "in case the police are at the beach." Up another notch he went. He put his arm around Anna Lisa. Up two more notches. "Your father should go and get the car and bring it here."

"Here's no good," Anna Lisa said. "Here is someplace they'll look. Someone will tell them I come here for services."

"Then they should go in two groups," Piero said. "Rosa—may I call you Rosa?"

"Of course."

"Please put this on over your head. It's my mother's scarf. I keep it here for luck. They'll think you're Jewish, or Muslim. Russian maybe. You and Paolo go together, and the Holy Father and His Holiness a little ways separate."

"People will guess."

"They should speak Russian, then," Piero said.

"We don't know any Russian," the Pope told him.

"I know some words. I wait on tables. There are Russians here every summer. You and the Dalai Lama should keep quiet, but if someone walks by you should say *'Nu, ladna'* and *'Shto?'* And maybe *'Piva!'*"

"What means these things?" Dalai asked. It was easy to hear the amusement in his voice. He'd be in yet another level of disguise. More trickery. What fun! He and the Pope were a pair of jesters. Soul mates.

"'Well, okay,' 'What?' and 'Beer!'" Piero told him. "In that order. Can you say it?"

The Pope and then the Dalai Lama took turns mangling Piero's half-mangled restaurant Russian.

"And here," the young man said, "take this soccer ball and toss it back and forth, so people will pay attention to that and not to you. They'd never expect the Pope and the Dalai Lama to be walking toward the beach with a soccer ball, speaking Russian. Leave it at Beach 45 if you can, I'll get it later. Or keep it as a gift from me."

"Pa, you and Mamma go first."

"Right," Rosa said, draping the black scarf over her head and accepting a pair of sunglasses from her daughter. "Your Holinesses, walk on the other side of the street and keep us in view. We'll meet at the car and get out of here as fast as we can."

Hugs and handshakes all around. Back out into the midday heat we went, separating quickly to opposite sidewalks and going along at a brisk pace. "You know," I said to my wife as we hurried, "I think it's going to be all right. The marriage, I mean."

"Better than us, I hope," she said, and in such a sorrowful voice that I reached out for a moment and put an arm around her shoulder. She didn't try to shrug it away. "You kissed me," she said.

"I did."

"You haven't kissed me in years."

"I wasn't thinking. I apologize."

"Take that back or I'll hit you."

"Take what back?"

"That hideous apology. Don't you dare apologize for kissing me!"

"Okay, *nonna*," I said, and she did hit me then, but it was a fake hit, a slap on my upper arm, a love tap. "And what's this about a recording?"

She held up Mario's phone. "It was Tenzin's idea. He and Cousin Giorgio feel bad about causing so much concern all over the world. So Tenzin suggested we make a short video and send it in to a TV station. Then we realized a video would give away the disguises, so we made just a voice recording instead."

"Like the ones kidnappers make with hostages."

"It was thirty seconds. Just the two of them speaking, saying they're fine, they'll be back soon. They're not being harmed. I e-mailed the file to a friend at a Naples TV station."

"Can't they trace that?"

"To Mario's phone, yes. But that will take a while, because I sent the file to Anna Lisa and she sent it to the TV friend."

"You're a criminal genius," I said.

Just then I heard the Dalai Lama on the other side of the street, saying *"Piva!"* too loudly. *"Nu, ladna,"* the Pope answered. It seemed they might be overdoing it: every time someone passed by they tossed the soccer ball back and forth—dropping it at least once—and threw out a word of Russian. What would happen, I wondered, if one of the other pedestrians was actually a native Russian speaker? And then that was exactly what happened. I heard the Dalai say *"Piva!"*—Beer!—and a man going the other way stopped suddenly and turned and asked a loud question in what must have been the dialect of the steppes. It very well could have been "Where is the beer?" but for all we knew it could also have been "Isn't Putin a god!" or "Where does a fellow get a copy of *The Brothers Karamazov* around here?" The Pope made a lucky guess, or had a moment of divine intuition. I saw him pointing toward the center of town. The man offered what might have been a thank-you and hurried off.

We made it to the beach road without further incident. "No time to bring the ball over there," Rosa said. "We'll keep it. Let's go!" I turned, for just one second, to look at her—I found the sight of her in a head scarf and sunglasses strangely arousing—and then the Pope and the Dalai Lama opened the doors and we were all in the baking-hot Maserati and making our way through Rimini's summer traffic.

"Watch for police cars," Rosa said.

"I'm watching."

"I thought, for a minute, when you and Piero came back with the champagne, that you wanted to give up."

"I did, but I don't."

"You're growing up. You're starting to understand."

"Nice way to say it, Rosa. 'You're growing up.' What kind of thing is that to say to a man?"

"I'm sorry."

"Two apologies in twenty-four hours. A miracle. Two miracles! You'll be eligible for sainthood."

"Now who's being mean?"

The Pope reached forward and put a hand on my right shoulder and Rosa's left. "What a blessing!" he said. "What a wonderful girl! What a fine mother she'll make!"

Nothing, not a word, not a single syllable about pre-marital love, Dzogchen, or the police. What a magnificent pope he is! I thought. What a man! At that moment, comparing myself to him, recognizing my less-than-kind side, I felt like a snake. I couldn't even meet Rosa's eyes.

I was about to apologize when her phone rang. Out of the corner of my eye I watched her put it to her ear; then I heard her say, "Mario? . . . *Cosa?* . . . *Quando?* . . . *Va bene.* What? . . . When? . . . Okay, well, don't worry. Thanks. You're not calling on my phone, I hope! . . . Well, that was probably for the best. It's replaceable. I'll return the favor . . . Okay . . . Yes, a very good time, thank you. The time of my life . . . Excellent. Bye."

She turned to me. "They called the shop—Vatican police, he thought it was. He told them I was in Africa on vacation, but when they asked where in Africa he said Monte Carlo. They sounded skeptical, he said."

"Hard to understand why."

"He says they hinted they were going to stop by for a visit. Last night he got scared and threw my phone in the river. And just now he was watching the news. Someone recognized the Pope. From Mario's description, I think it was the woman on the street in L'Aquila. She must have heard you say 'Holy Father' or something."

"Shit," I said.

Behind me the Dalai said, *"Piva!"*

"So they know we went as far as L'Aquila, and if they trace the e-mail they'll know we headed from there to Rimini to see Anna Lisa, and they'll be all over her. Any ideas now?"

"One," she said, and then there was a thoughtful hesitation. "I have a friend in Padua. Not the first place they'd expect us to go from here, probably. I'm sure he'll have room to put us up."

"Carlo Mancini?"

"No, another famous friend."

"Who?"

"Antonio Mazzo."

"You're kidding. Now you're really kidding, Rosa ... or lying."

She shook her head and began punching numbers into the phone. "Unlike some people I know," she said, "I don't lie."

27

Antonio Mazzo, for those few souls who don't know, was an iconic Italian film star and international sex symbol. Retired by the day of our visit from all but cameo appearances, in his prime Mazzo had acted alongside all the greats—Sophia Loren, Gina Lollobrigida, Marcello Mastroianni, Giancarlo Giannini—and had been close to the famous American stars Marlon Brando, Frank Sinatra, and Marilyn Monroe. He'd had affairs with scores, perhaps hundreds, of glamorous women. It was said that he'd been the person who'd convinced his younger friend George Clooney to take up residence in Italy, but then again, as he himself once noted, "many things are said about me. Ten percent of them may even be true."

I knew, of course, that Rosa had clients among the rich and famous—especially in the film community— but it must have been the case that in the years since we'd stopped living together, she'd actually become friends with these people. Good enough friends that she could borrow Carlo Mancini's new Maserati, that she had Antonio Mazzo's phone number, and felt comfortable calling and asking if she and three "friends" could spend a night at his villa near Padua. I wondered—what estranged husband wouldn't?—if she might be more than friends with some of them. Mazzo, especially, was famous for his decadent lifestyle and bacchanalian parties, and while he was probably too old to be having an affair with Rosa, he could very well have introduced her to the kind of men for whom sex with a stranger wearing a ring was not morally troubling—the equivalent of having lunch with her, of shaking hands, of spooning sugar into her espresso at breakfast.

As she spoke—first to Mazzo's personal assistant and then to the man himself—I listened through the walls of the bad-smelling chamber of jealousy. She'd told me once that she'd been intimate with "a fair number" of boyfriends before we met, and perhaps because of that she was always at ease with men. But, to my ear at least, she always sounded more than merely at ease—not flirtatious exactly, but something that went beyond simple comfort. She'd greet a client at the door of one of her salons, receive a kiss on each cheek, hold on to his hand, stand close, and the simplest remark—"Massimo, it's been too long, really"—would seem to me to carry a note of physical intimacy, even if absolutely nothing of a physical nature had ever taken place between them. This tone, this silky familiarity, was like a lighted match tossed onto the barnful of dry hay that was my insecurity. We'd had a hundred fights about it. I was always wrong, I know that. I admit it. I'd had a number of lovers, too, in my twenties, and probably sounded the same way to her when I spoke to women. And yet, there was always this nagging whisper of doubt—was something going on? Had something gone on? I don't know whose jealousy was more intense, hers or mine.

Try as I did over the years of our marriage, I could never seem to banish it from my thoughts. Now that we were living separately, rather than being easier, it was much worse. Probably other estranged couples slept around and didn't worry about it: that was part of the arrangement. But it had never been part of the arrangement for us. We'd never talked about it directly, but from time to time one of us would say something that suggested we were still faithful, that there might still be hope for a reconciliation, that there were already enough complications between us without adding lovers into the mix. Friends of mine—and friends of Rosa's—found this arrangement strange to the point of impossibility. But, strange though it might have been, it was our reality. We were past our sexual prime; we both worried about upsetting Anna Lisa by bringing lovers into the mix; we'd both been raised old-style Catholics, and both sets of parents—mine and hers—had stayed with each other until death. Maybe those were the reasons, or maybe it was something else, an out-of-date notion of fidelity to a vow. Or an unspoken hope.

Still, as she cooed into the phone with Antonio Mazzo and I piloted the Maserati along the coastal road north, the little snake of jealousy raised its head again and slithered through my thoughts.

"*Caro mio,*" she began, "my dear, my idol, how are you? How have you been? I'm in pain from the fact that I haven't seen you for so long. Actual, physical pain ... Yes, yes, awful, terrible, couldn't be worse ... Exactly. And I have a favor to ask. I'm traveling with three eccentric friends— we're just south of Ravenna, coming up the coast—and I'm wondering if you might be able to let us stay with you for a night? ... Yes?! Oh, you're a saint, an idol. There's no one like you on earth, really! But I should tell you that there's a catch, Antonio. For reasons I'll explain at some later date, we have to have absolute discretion. No one can know about the visit, would that be possible?" At this point Antonio must have said something ironic and humorous, a sexual innuendo probably, because my lovely wife threw back her head and laughed, and the laughter went on and on, followed by a series of aftershock chuckles. I glanced back in the mirror at the Pope. He had his eyes closed and seemed to be praying. Pray for me, Holy Father, I thought. Pray for me now that the heat of jealousy doesn't cause me to burst into flames right here on the seat in front of you. Pray for me that my insecurities don't pollute all the love and dignity in me. Pray that my wife stops talking this way to her men friends.

When Rosa finished with her little symphony of laughter she said, "That complicates things. But it's workable, I think. It might even make it easier. A masked ball, you say? One of your famous parties? You're the Great Gatsby of Italy, *sai?* Do you know that? . . . But are you sure you have room? . . . Oh, you're just the finest man God ever created, truly. I miss you so much! We'll be there in two or three hours, depending on traffic and our need for food . . . Thank you, thank you, my love! *Ciao!*"

She closed the connection and sighed. I went through a yellow light just as it was turning red. "Careful, Paolo!" she said. "The last thing we need now is to be stopped by the police."

I bit down hard on the inside of my cheek. Took a breath. Said, "The call went well?"

She turned and looked at me. I had tried to keep any hint of jealousy out of my voice, but a note had sneaked in; I was sure she detected it. "Perfectly," she said, in an acidic whisper. "Ideally. Magnificently."

"We can stay?" I whispered back.

"He has a massive old villa just outside Padua and he happens to be there this week. I'm so glad I called him. No problem at all, he said."

"No problem to host your 'eccentric friends'?"

"What should I have said, Paolo? What term should I have used?"

"How about 'my husband and some eccentric friends'?"

I could feel her studying me, and not in a sympathetic

way. I tried to keep my eyes on the road. "How about," she said, "'my husband, who, as you know from the recent news, is an internationally wanted kidnapper . . . and our good friends the Pope and the Dalai Lama'? Would that have made you feel better?"

"And what's this about a party?"

"And what's this about changing the subject? Antonio must be ninety. There's nothing sexual between us, never has been and obviously never will be. Your mind is filth."

"You brought up the Parisian bordellos a little while ago."

"A joke."

"Fine, but tell me this: how can we go there if he's hosting one of his parties?"

"It's a costume party, masks, et cetera. It's perfect. And the house is so huge that even if we don't want to party we'll probably have our privacy."

"You're forgetting who we're with."

"Hardly."

"Mazzo is the king of decadence and we're bringing two holy men to his lair. That doesn't strike you as slightly problematic?"

She *tsk*ed impatiently. I knew this sound like I knew the sound of our daughter's voice. It signified many things: impatience, disdain, regret, superiority. I felt guilty, stupid, childish . . . also justified.

"How I love that sound," I said.

"I'm sorry. I know you don't like it. It's a bad habit of mine, but what I don't think you understand is that the two people in the back of this car aren't like you. They aren't corruptible. They've been praying and meditating and fasting for, what? Fifty, sixty, seventy years? Going to one party where there happen to be—God forbid!—actual women, real alcoholic drinks, isn't going to suddenly turn them into sinners. What do I have to do to get you to stop worrying?"

"I don't know," I said. "I'm trying. I was thinking, just before we saw Anna Lisa, that she'd be so happy at the chance to spend an hour with the Pope and the Dalai Lama. It's a rare opportunity, a gift, a great moment in history, something to treasure. I've been trying to tell myself that, too, so I can get past the worry. But I've always had a terrible fear of going to prison. The food. The cramped conditions. The company of violent men."

"The spiders," she said.

"Thanks."

"Sorry, that was mean. But you're being neurotic again. Please stop."

"Fine, okay. I've always wondered why you don't have a fear like that."

"I do," she said. "But it's a secret . . . Someday I'll tell you, but I'm too ashamed right now."

"Tell me."

"Not now. No. I can't."

We went along for a kilometer in a cold silence, and then she said, "The recording will clear you of suspicion."

"As long as people believe it's legitimate. As long as my enemies don't get involved and try to twist it somehow."

"Well, then I'll ask the Pope to sign a written document saying you aren't guilty. Would that make you less anxious?"

"Yes."

"I'll do it," the Pope said from behind me.

"I, too," the Dalai Lama said. And then he added, "For some money," and enjoyed another spasm of laughter.

"I'll try to relax then, much as it goes against my nature."

"Your nature is a Buddha nature," the Dalai said, between chuckles. "Pure as the sky. Rest in that."

"And stop giving your wife so much trouble," the Pope added. "She's gone to great lengths to use her contacts to help us." I felt him put a hand on my shoulder, give me a quick massage. "As have you. Relax, enjoy. Say a prayer and let the worries go. You're going to be a grandfather soon. Think of that gift from God!"

"Rest in that," the Dalai Lama advised.

I tried, really I did. As we crossed the low hills of the Veneto and made our way toward the beautiful city of Padua, a place I've always loved, I made a tremendous interior effort to leave the worries behind. Worrying was a form of control, Rosa had told me after some of our arguments. A desperate attempt to bend reality to fit an imagined picture in our minds. It was, almost without exception, imposing the future on the present. It was an insidious species of fear disguised as logic.

She had a hundred ways of describing it, and over the years I'd marveled at the fact that she seemed immune to it herself. "Whatever happens, we'll figure it out," she liked to say. Or: "Let's think about that tomorrow." Or: "Bad outcomes are almost always worse in your imagination than in reality." From the moment she announced she was pregnant I'd lived in a state of near-constant terror, watching what she ate and drank, anticipating bad news in doctors' offices when we went for her checkups, making sure there was nothing around the house that might cause her to slip and fall, doing research on hair-color chemicals and birth defects. And then, once Rosa actually went into labor, my mind presented me with every awful possibility, every medical disaster and horrible illness. At one point in her long ordeal the fetal heartbeat monitor showed that our baby's pulse was sinking from well over a hundred—normal—down to eighty, then sixty-two, then forty-one, and my own pulse went in the opposite direction. The nurses, calm as meditators on a cushion, readjusted Rosa's position and the pulse went back to normal, but by then I had sweated through my shirt.

In the end, of course, as Rosa had always believed it would, everything turned out fine. Our daughter was born healthy, and had remained healthy throughout her childhood and adolescence and now into her twenties. I was happy about that, naturally, though I couldn't help noticing that Rosa's life moved along with only a minimum of upset. She started a business and it grew like a fern in the rainforest. I started a business, worked hard, did everything I should have done, and it withered and died. "Worry attracts trouble," she liked to say. Which only gave me something else to worry about.

Still, beginning with that conversation on the road to Mazzo's villa, I tried. I told myself I would live to see our grandchild, that Anna Lisa's pregnancy would move forward without incident, that Piero would make a good husband and father, that the recording and letters from the Pope and the Dalai Lama would be a kind of insurance policy against any potential future troubles. That if I lost my position I'd somehow survive. As we passed through a flatter landscape near Forli—Mussolini's birthplace—I thought again of my mother leaping into Lake Como, and my father's ritual of running naked around the house, outdoors, in the dark, whenever he sold a painting. I wanted to be that kind of person—unafraid, a risk taker and celebrator, immune to jealousy.

Instead, I was me.

Avoiding the Autostrada and its surveillance cameras, we stayed on Route S16 through Ravenna, then crossed the rather flat and featureless plain to the east of Bologna, a landscape of sunflower fields, the lazy Reno river, and close-packed tile-roof settlements that consisted of a church, a place to buy gas and pizza, and a few dozen stone-and-stucco homes. I asked Rosa to help me in my battle against anxiety by not turning on the radio, and she kindly agreed. S16 led us through a last tangle of traffic and into Ferrara, a city famous for the high medieval wall that surrounds it, a history of substantial Jewish populations, and for being the birthplace of Girolamo Savonarola, the fifteenth-century Dominican priest who liked to burn books he considered tainted by heresy. Ultimately, Savonarola himself was hanged and a pyre was built under the gallows. (As my father would say: "What goes around . . .")

Despite that sordid history, we decided to stop. We were hungry. "Let's just buy food and eat al fresco someplace," Rosa suggested. "Less chance of being recognized."

I found a parking space opposite Ferrara's white-faced cathedral, and Rosa and I went off in search of food, leaving the holy men in the warm backseat—windows open. Both the Pope and the Dalai Lama told us they'd use the time for prayer, that we shouldn't hurry, shouldn't be too concerned about what we brought back for lunch. A little fruit, some bread, bottles of mineral water—that would more than suffice.

I have a theory—not very original—that certain key moments from our past crouch in the crevices of memory, hidden there, sometimes forever, below our conscious mind. Invisible, yes, but I suspect these memories form the roots of our deepest insecurities and fears.

As Rosa and I hurried along the hot sidewalk in Ferrara, something lifted one of these primal memories into the light. I don't know what it was—a few notes of an old song playing in a second-floor apartment, a voice that sounded like my mother's or my father's, the smell of a particular meal being cooked in the kitchen of a nearby café—but some mysterious trigger unearthed a pottery shard from early childhood, something long buried and nearly forgotten.

I was four years old. It was summer. I must have wandered out the back door in a moment when my mother and father weren't paying attention to my whereabouts—a rare occurrence. Maybe he'd thought of something he wanted to add to one of his paintings and had slipped into his second-floor studio. Maybe she was on the phone with a dealer in Paris or Berlin, focused on the negotiations, dates for a show. In any case, I wandered into the backyard, strolled around there in my shorts and bare feet, and then opened the back gate and toddled along a path that led into a shallow ravine overgrown with bushes and small trees. In spring, a river ran through that low territory, but this was midsummer, the river was a muddy trickle, the foliage thick. I kept going deeper into the brush. After a few minutes I grew tired, found a stone to sit on, and moved my feet back and forth in the warm mud. For God knows what reason I had the idea that I would hide from my parents there. After a short while I became aware of them calling. Even at that age I sensed the change in the tone of their voices, from casual to nervous to panicked. But on purpose, stubbornly, mischievously, I didn't call back to them, didn't move. I suppose this was a kind of sin, or the instinct toward sin: I knew I was causing them distress, but some sly impulse made me stay silent.

It went on for probably ten minutes, no more. Eventually my father came down the path, and eventually he saw my white shorts there near the muddy stream, saw me sitting on the stone. He must also have seen the expression on my face, which, in memory at least, was a species of devilish smile, a small victory over the giants that ruled me.

My parents never hit me, not once. In fact, I could count on the fingers of two hands the number of times they raised their voices to me or to each other. But as Rosa and I walked along in Ferrara's *centro,* looking for a place to buy food, I remembered, with a surreal vividness, the tone of my father's voice after he'd carried me angrily and a bit roughly back into the house. He set me down on both bare, muddy feet on the kitchen floor and he and my mother shouted at me, telling me what an awful thing I'd done. There were tears coursing down my mother's face—I remember that—and I remember how, when they were finished, my father lifted me up in the air so that my mother could rinse my feet in the sink, then he took me by the hand, led me to my room, and slammed the door behind him when he left. I lay facedown on the blanket of my bed and wept. After a little while my mother came in and sat beside me and told me, in a much calmer voice, how terrified they'd been, what a foolish thing it was that I'd done, how I could have been hurt, or worse. She brought me into the kitchen and made me pasta with pesto, and in another few minutes my father came downstairs, calmer by then, and put both hands on my little shoulders, looked into my face, and apologized for yelling but said I was never, ever, ever to do something like that again.

And, of course, I didn't. My childhood memories are full of warm light—the trips we took, the laughter at dinner, the softness and kindness of my mother and the supportive camaraderie of my dad. But that one dark moment had been buried, and when it resurfaced, I suddenly felt that a curtain had been pulled from a tall window, the window had been thrown open, and I was standing there looking down at my younger self. After that summer day, I had been the most obedient of boys, pathologically obedient. I didn't curse or drink or make love until my third year of university. I didn't miss Mass until I was twenty-four, not once.

Later on, naturally enough, there was a period of rebellion, but even that was relatively mild, a bit of carousing, a few casual girlfriends. Really, the only times in my childhood that I went against my parents' wishes were the times we visited Giorgio in South America and slipped away on our adventures. When we returned, he protected me from the chastisement of our parents, taking the responsibility on himself, the older cousin who should have known better.

All this was part of why I'd fallen in love with Rosa, because she wasn't obedient, wasn't mild mannered, wasn't a safe girl who went to Mass wearing a head scarf and kissed on the fifth date with a chaste timidity. She came from a family where people shouted and swore, cursed each other one minute and hugged and kissed each other the next, talked about sex the way other families talk about the weather. The small apartment in Naples where her parents lived with her grandmother and two younger siblings was a three-ring circus of emotion, the farthest thing from sedate.

In the early years I'd loved all that, loved her feistiness, loved taking the train to Naples to be part of that tempest of affection and argument. But then, little by little, and especially after Anna Lisa was born, I began a gradual retreat into my younger, safer self. The small risks Rosa took—riding her Vespa alone after dark, taking Anna out to splash in puddles in the rain—spawned a nest of worry in me. I felt, I supposed, that I might be punished for any lapse of parenting etiquette. In that flash, in that one sweaty epiphany as we turned, side by side, into the *frutti vendolo* store that had boxes of cherries and wild mushrooms for sale out front, I saw that my childhood obedience had metamorphosed into an adult default setting of neurosis. Maybe it was that gnawing fearfulness that had spoiled my business. Maybe I gave my clients the sense that I was nervous—the last thing a traveler needs. Certainly it was part of what had taken the zest out of our marriage.

Something else occurred to me in those seconds—all part of this one flash of understanding: I'd always believed that the Pope's decision to hire me as his assistant had been intended to bring me into a more secure environment, financially, socially, spiritually. But at that moment I wondered if maybe the exact opposite might be true. Maybe the risks he himself took—in a position where the stakes were so high, where the scrutiny was uninterrupted—were meant as a lesson for me. "Break some rules, Paolo," he was trying to tell me. "Blend some risky creativity into your life. God won't punish you for it."

And then I thought: maybe this escape from Vatican propriety and from the expectations of his flock is the biggest lesson of all . . . and here I am spoiling it again with worry and fear.

I took hold of Rosa's elbow, excited to tell her, to make her understand, to apologize, to promise that I'd change. "I've been an ass," I said.

She gave me a strange look—we were in the vegetable aisle and she was feeling up a tomato—and said, "You're just figuring that out?"

"No . . . I mean yes. I mean I've been so nervous about getting caught and getting in trouble that I've been spoiling the whole grand adventure, haven't I?"

"The three of us are way ahead of you, *amore*. That's all I'll say."

"But I did that with our marriage, too, right?"

She put the tomato back in its place and turned down her lips. A woman behind us was listening with great interest. Rosa's smirk, her lifted eyebrows—that was all the response I received.

"I'm going to change," I said. "Starting now."

"Good, great. *Molto bene.*"

"We're going to be grandparents, after all. How awful would it be to have a neurotic grandpa!"

I could see the woman behind Rosa—at the word "grandparents" her face lit up. She was leaning forward.

Any second now she was going to congratulate me, or offer advice.

"Listen," Rosa said, "focus. Go grab a pound of cherries, they look fresh. I'll get the bread and mortadella from next door. You get cherries and something to drink, and if you see something else, just grab it and meet me outside. We don't want to keep them waiting. We'll talk about all this tonight, okay?"

Six minutes later, the food from both stores had been bagged up and paid for, and Rosa and I were on the sidewalk, hurrying toward the car. I felt young, happy, hopeful. I was going to be a grandfather! I was going to change! Then, just at that moment, we passed a corner tobacco shop where newspapers were set on a display rack out front. The headlines read like this:

PAPA RAPITO
ANCHE IL DALAI LAMA SCOMPARSO
SOSPETTO UN CUGINO DEL PAPA

POPE KIDNAPPED
DALAI LAMA ALSO TAKEN
POPE'S COUSIN SUSPECTED

On the left side of *La Gazzetta*'s front page was a photo of my so-called note, the signature looking exactly like mine. On the right side I saw a very small item, apparently unrelated to the big story: Carlo Mancini was suspected of having an affair with a champion female mountain biker, because one of his Maseratis had been photographed near a chairlift in the Abruzzo National Park. Full story on page 6.

A knot of people stood there with newspapers in their hands, arguing the facts of the case: where the Holy Father might be, what the motivation could have been, what this evil cousin looked like. I heard the word "Satan!" I heard someone say there was a photo of the evil cousin on page 2. And then that the radio had just broadcast news of a recording—obviously fake or forced—supposedly made by the captives.

Rosa and I hurried past, but half a block closer to the car was an open-air osteria with a TV playing too loudly. She grabbed my arm and made me stop. I saw Anna Lisa's face on the screen, Piero beside her. "He was here, yes," she was saying into a reporter's microphone, "but now I don't have the faintest idea where my father could be." It was *my* turn to be proud of *her.* Instead of being upset or intimidated, she was looking directly into the camera, a note of defiance in her voice, unmistakable. One day she'd be able to tell her son or daughter that *nonno* had kidnapped the Pope!

The reporter said, "When he's caught, your father will likely go to prison for life. Yet you don't seem worried."

We turned away, but over my shoulder I heard Piero's voice. "A good man. A good Catholic. It will all be explained, I'm sure."

Another notch up the son-in-law scale he went.

We hurried on. The joy of my epiphany had abandoned me as quickly as it had arrived. Yes, the Pope and the Dalai Lama would exonerate me, but what if the mob reached me before the situation could be explained? Look what they'd done to Savonarola, to Mussolini when he was finally caught!

PAPAL COUSIN KILLED BY MOB IN CENTRAL FERRARA

was the headline I imagined.

TORN TO SHREDS, KICKED, SPAT UPON
GRIEVING WIDOW CLAIMS HE WAS INNOCENT,
TAKES REFUGE ON ANTONIO MAZZO'S YACHT

Rosa was silent, atypically. Her heels clicked out an anxious staccato on the concrete. Another block and at last she spoke. "They're gone."

"Who?"

She lifted her chin at the Maserati.

I saw that the backseat was empty. I lost my grip on the bag of food, barely grabbed it before it hit the pavement.

"They've been caught," I said. "Taken to police headquarters."

"I don't think so. The police would have waited here for you."

I swiveled my head in a slow circle. A tour bus letting off its cargo of Asian tourists. Four schoolgirls with backpacks. Buzzing Vespas, cars glinting sunlight, a boy on a bicycle, a carabinieri vehicle. No Pope. No Dalai Lama.

"I'm going to turn myself in," I told Rosa. "There's the carabinieri."

"Don't be ridiculous."

"Before the mob tears me to bloody pieces."

"What mob?" she said. "What's wrong with you?"

"Maybe I *am* a kidnapper. Evil. Maybe I—"

"Paolo, stop it! Look!"

She turned me by the shoulder. Two familiar figures—

a German businessman and his wealthy rock-star friend—had appeared in front of the cathedral's round-topped middle door. They started walking toward us, surrounded by an aura of calm that was almost palpable, almost visible, and exactly the opposite of what I was feeling. That, I thought, is faith.

Unconcerned, unhurried, the two fugitives waited for a gap in the traffic and made their way across the street, conversing in a serious way, nodding in agreement.

"Sorry, sorry!" the Dalai Lama said when they were close. "The car very hot! We saw the beautiful church and I asked that the Pope could take me inside to see, to pray. We're late, yes?"

We all climbed in. "No problem," Rosa said, "but let's take our lunch out into the country, if you don't mind. Something about this city has me worried." She turned all the way around so she was looking at our passengers. "What's wrong?" she asked them. "You both have the same strange expression on your faces. What happened?"

There was a momentary silence, five or six seconds, before the Pope said, "Nothing," in a tone so false and so unlike him that I took my eyes off the road to look in the mirror.

"Were you recognized?"

"No, cousin."

"What, then?" Rosa pressed.

Another silence. At last, as we broke free of Ferrara's outskirts and headed into the fields, the Dalai Lama said, too loudly, "Beautiful, beautiful place, this church! The windows! The paintings! Beautiful!"

I checked the mirror again and saw a fake grin plastered on the Pope's face. He was sweating. "Grace inspired all that," he said. "Even the design of the building. Grace."

"What this word means?" the Dalai Lama asked, but as if he already knew, which I was sure he did. "Exactly what?"

They were putting on some kind of weird act.

"Ah, you tell him, Paolo. You're better with English than I am. Think of a definition."

"Divine inspiration," I said, suspiciously.

"God's creativity," Rosa said. "God's creativity passing through certain special human beings."

"Ah. We have this, too," the Dalai Lama said. "Statues, paintings, temples. Very beautiful. In Buddhist tradition we have this. Buddha said he does not want images of him for worship, but now we have them! Statues, many statues and paintings. Very beautiful!" He launched then into a long speech—almost a lecture—on artists and their place in human society, how they were similar to monks, standing off to one side, observing, not quite caught up in the melee of ordinary life, how they contributed so self-lessly to humanity with their great gifts. And then how true it was that beauty mattered a great deal on this earth, how monasteries all over the world were usually set in beautiful places, how it was believed in some schools of Buddhism that people who were beautiful or handsome in this life were being rewarded for exceptional patience in a past life, how their beauty was a gift to others, but how at the same time it could be a trap, an attachment.

He said more, in that ten-minute oration, than he'd said since he'd told us about Kali when the flashlight died in the tunnel. Interesting though it was, his speech sounded forced to me, as false as the Pope's smile, and as surprising. Something was going on. Something had happened in the cathedral, and I was about to ask what it was when, traveling just under the speed limit along the two-lane country road, we came upon another kind of beauty, one less traditionally associated with the spiritual life.

28

In Italy, where prostitution is of course illegal, and where the laws are of course ignored, one often comes across women standing in provocative poses by the side of roads like the one on which we were driving that day. The women are African, Russian, Eastern European, almost always young and attractive, and very often dressed in short skirts or very short pants, with the skin of their midsections showing and their lips painted in garish shades of purple or red.

"Stop, please," the Pope said.

"Holy Father, she's—"

"I know what she is . . . a child of God."

This particular child of God was sitting on a lawn chair in a gravel turnout large enough for three cars. There was a small camper behind her, clearly the place where she entertained her clients. When I braked to a stop, a puff of dust rose from the tires. The Pope was out of the car before it settled, the Dalai Lama close behind. As the woman stood up to greet them, her large breasts swayed beneath a flimsy half shirt, and the expression on her face metamorphosed into one of professional welcome. After the tiniest hesitation, Rosa and I saw no option but to get out, too, and try to limit the damage.

"All four of you!" the woman exclaimed, in thickly accented Italian. "*Tutti i quattro!* A party! And a foreigner and a woman, too! What fun! But I charge extra for parties!"

What I expected then, what I suppose anyone would have expected in the face of that salacious greeting, was that the Holy Father, in a kind and loving way, would tell the woman that if she accepted Jesus Christ into her heart, she could turn her life around and save her soul. I have to say I even half expected the Pope to do something like offer her employment cleaning the Vatican offices, if only she'd abandon her sinful ways. That type of gesture would have been perfectly in keeping with the man I knew him to be. Compassionate in the extreme, unorthodox on a regular basis, hewing close to the faith that had sustained him his whole life, but nevertheless the Pope of Sacred Surprises, a man who sometimes seemed to want to shock his followers into a deeper understanding of Christ's message. It was what made him so widely admired, so beloved, so special.

He walked up to the woman and held out his hand in greeting. She took it in a languid, flirtatious way, shook it up and down once, then put her other hand over his and held them there.

"We'd like to share our lunch with you," he said.

She looked at him for a moment. Her professional smile wavered, her eyes narrowed, crinkling the mascara there so that it fell in small dried dots on her cheeks. It seemed to me she suspected a trick, or that she was trying to understand what kind of new sexual game might be inferred from an offer to share lunch with another woman and three men. She peered at the Dalai Lama, at me, turned her head to Rosa, and, though she didn't seem the least bit afraid, it was that cautious curiosity that made me understand, in a way I really hadn't before, the risks inherent in a life like hers. Here she stood, alone at the side of the road, ten miles outside Ferrara. Anyone might stop and take her into that camper. Any brute or rapist, any criminal or just-released convict, any man with a knife in his pocket and a burning hatred in his brain. And after a day of that she'd be picked up by her handler, raped again perhaps, or just given food and a place to sleep so she could be used, day after day, like some kind of ATM with breasts and a vagina. This would go on for a year or a few years, and then she'd be discarded or perhaps even killed.

Her hair was dyed a reddish blond, the work poorly done, but even with that, and even with the purplish lipstick and ridiculous outfit, "beauty" was one word that came to mind. "Grace" was another. In my travels around Italy and, indeed, around Europe, I'd seen plenty of roadside prostitutes. Most of them were attractive by one definition or another. How could they earn anything otherwise? It's not at all true that I harbored some kind of sentimental notion about their profession. Theirs was a harsh, brutal life, the free market at its most animalistic; the men who kept women like this were, to my mind, the worst kind of criminal, and the things these women did with their clients could not by any stretch be filed under the heading of "love." But this woman had a measure of grace to her, an obvious bodily dignity, an obvious courage; she was, or seemed, beyond worry. It shamed me.

"I'm not sure what you have on mind," she said to the Pope in a sly voice and poor Italian.

He gestured toward the car. "We've just bought some food for our midday meal. We want to share it with you. Paolo, take the bags from the car, would you?"

"Eh," the woman said, unimpressed. "Thanks for a invitation, but lunch with you people could cost me pay."

"We'll pay you two hours," the Pope said. "How much would that be?"

"You're joking, correct?" the woman said, but some of her edifice of dignity had begun to wobble around the edges. She released the Pope's hand and took half a step back.

"Not at all. Give us a sum. We'll pay. We'll stand near the car. Bring your chair over, and we'll have a meal."

The woman cocked her head to the side, but kept her eyes focused on the man in front of her. "That's a fake beard, isn't it?"

"It is, yes."

"What's your game? Did you all rob the bank or something? And what's for your friend's bad toupee? You guys on the run?"

I tried to quickly think of an answer, and I came up with one: we were a theater troupe, on our way from Rome to Venice to take part in a play there, a play about tolerance and open-mindedness. Before I could get out the first word, however, I heard my cousin say, "I'm the Pope. And this"—he put his hand on his friend's shoulder—"is the Dalai Lama. Have you been listening to the news?"

The woman laughed in an uncomfortable way. "I'm not the big news person," she said, "and not so religious.

But my last guest he said something about that. He said the Pope was kidnapped by Muslims and was being held on a ransom. A inside job. He said the Muslims had a friend who worked in the Vatican. But he thought the other person was President Obama."

"Not President Obama . . . the Dalai Lama," Rosa said. "The Pope of Buddhism. A great man."

"Ho sentito parlare di lui," she said. "I heard of him." The woman looked from one of us to another. "And you're who?" she demanded, pointing at me.

"I'm the kidnapper," I said, in what I hoped was a joking way.

"You look like it. Didn't you come visit me one time before? You seems familiar."

"No, never. This isn't how I really look!" I raised up one pant leg. "It's a disguise."

"What, then? You want me to join you for lunch? To what, convert me?"

"Never," the Holy Father said. "Just lunch. What would your fee be?"

"For two hours," the woman said, "two hundred."

The Pope nodded at me and held up three fingers. I took a wad of bills from my pocket, counted out three hundred euro, and handed it over.

"Now," the Pope said, passing the bills to the woman. "Let us break bread."

We ate on the lime-green hood of the Maserati, the cold cuts, cherries, and bread laid out on wax paper, the five of us forming an uneven crescent around the car. From time to time a vehicle would slow down as it passed—one even made a brief detour through the gravel turnout—but the drivers saw us eating and sped away.

When the Dalai Lama asked the woman her name, she said, "Marta," at first, and then, after a few seconds, in capable English, "Tara, really. Marta is my work name."

"Ah!" the Dalai said happily. "In Tibet, Tara is the name of the female Buddha! We call her the Mother of Liberation. A bodhisattva."

"What's a bodhisattva?" she wanted to know.

So did I.

"The being who lives for others. The person of most greatest compassion!"

"That's me," the woman said ironically, but she was eyeing the Dalai Lama almost gratefully, as if kind words sent in her direction were rare as rubies. She ate some of the food, but tentatively, warily, as if one of us might snatch it away at any minute, or as if she worried it had been treated with a drug that would knock her unconscious. The Pope stood there with half a mortadella panini in one hand and a bottle of water in the other and, like the Dalai Lama, he was absolutely natural and nonchalant about it. He might have been eating with anyone, a queen or a pauper, another cousin, his sister, a nun. We followed his lead, Rosa and I, trying not to look at each other, thinking of what we might say and coming up with nothing.

Tara turned to me again. "Why did you do this? What do you have to win from it? Not stopping for me—I mean the kidnapping. Money? You selling them to somebody?"

"The holy men asked me to do it, as a favor. I work for the Pope in the Vatican and he said he wanted a break, wanted to be treated like an ordinary man for a while. The Dalai Lama was visiting and he felt the same way."

"And you just took off?"

"Rosa here, my wife, has makeup and hair shops. One of her employees did the disguises."

"They're not bad. Now what?"

We looked at each other. "We're going to see a friend tonight," Rosa said, "and then, tomorrow, we don't know."

"I wish *I* didn't know," Tara said, and she laughed in a self-mocking way I found heartbreaking. "I wish more than anything I didn't know what I'm doing tomorrow."

She shifted her eyes back and forth between the two holy men. Most of the food was gone. A red sports car had driven by once, then again, then driven away, and Tara looked after it, not longingly but out of habit, perhaps. She'd tucked the money we'd given her into the top of her shirt, where a black bra was visible under the thin material. She wiped her mouth delicately with a paper napkin. The Dalai Lama asked if she'd like to come along with us, and for just a moment I thought she might say yes and squeeze herself into the small space in the middle of the backseat. "Going with you," she said, then for some reason looked at Rosa, "would be a good way to make me killed."

Hearing those words, the Pope asked me for a pen. He wrote something on one of the unused paper napkins, then handed it to her. "There's a reward for information that leads to us being found. A very large sum. After we're gone, wait a little while, please, until darkness falls, and then call this number and tell them we stopped to ask directions and you recognized me. Say we were headed northwest. Don't tell anyone else, though, or I'm afraid you'll be cheated."

The woman tilted her head to one side and studied him.

"The reward is five million euro," Rosa told her, and Tara's eyes shifted, sharpened.

"Come see me," the Pope told her. "Afterward. After you get the reward. Call that number and say your name and that we met near Ferrara and tell them I told you to come see me. I'll tell the people at that number to expect a call from Tara."

"I don't have no phone now anyway."

"My God! How can you not have a phone?" Rosa said. "Out here. Like this."

"I don't, that's all. I can borrow one, though, probably. Later."

"Take this one, then," Rosa said, handing over Mario's phone.

Tara hesitated.

"Take it, please. Even if you just save it for emergencies. It will work until the end of the month."

The woman accepted it at last and flipped the plastic creature back and forth in her palm. The red sports car cruised past again, and there was nothing left to do but pack away the food, ask Tara again not to tell anyone for a while, then bid her good day.

She was still staring at us as we clicked our seatbelts into place. When we were pulling out of the parking area, I turned around to look. She had the napkin in one hand, flapping in the breeze, Mario's phone clutched in the other. I waved. She only raised her eyebrows and turned to watch the road.

29

From the Alps in the north to Sicily in the south, the Italian countryside is dotted with magnificent old villas. Red-tile-roofed, stucco-walled, sitting amid orchards or vineyards or surrounded by fields of grain and rows of olive trees, these marvelous structures stand as reminders of the not-so-good old days when the noble family lived in luxury while dozens, sometimes hundreds, of peasants worked the land and slept alongside their animals in unheated outbuildings. Great Italian films like Bertolucci's *1900* and Ermanno Olmi's *The Tree of Wooden Clogs* give a good sense of this era, a lesson in history that lingers in the Italian consciousness to this day.

In time, as the peasants' oppression went on and on and their lives became more and more onerous, millions of them immigrated to North and South America. Those who remained grew restive. The old order began to crumble; there was widespread unrest, violence on the streets, strikes, demonstrations, gangs, a tilt toward anarchy. Inspired by the examples of the Bolsheviks in Russia, a workers' movement emerged—Italy would ultimately have the strongest Communist Party in Western Europe— and then, in reaction to the Communists, perhaps, or simply out of a desire for any change at all, anything resembling order, the backlash and chaos brought forth a charismatic egotist named Benito Mussolini. The rest, as they say, is history. Mussolini brought a kind of order, yes, but through violence and the threat of violence, and by appealing to Italians' basest impulses. A few important civic improvements, a number of grandiose debacles. Then military adventurism, Hitler, the war years, and the dire poverty that followed. It's a miracle Italy survived. Even more of a miracle—a Marshall Plan miracle—that the nation found its way back to something like sanity.

Now, some of the old villas are abandoned, rotting by the side of the road with caved-in roofs and tree branches growing through windows. Others are inhabited, in somewhat more humble fashion, by the descendants of the noble families, or by well-off foreigners who want some Italian *dolce vita*. Or by men like Antonio Mazzo, who made fortunes without the help of a peasant underclass, and who keep the fine old estates with a few hundred olive trees or grapevines as a kind of hobby, a place where they can leave behind the stresses of fame and live, without too much guilt, the luxurious life of lord of the manor.

We arrived at Mazzo's villa in late afternoon, just as a golden July sun was touching the old iron gate at the side of the road, and giving a last embrace to the long sweep of his fields. Ocher-washed stucco, three stories, almost as long as a soccer field, the villa looked like nothing so much as a slightly tattered palace. In fact, as we approached, I heard the Dalai Lama, who was sitting behind me, say, "Which kind of king lives here?"

"An old movie star, not a king," Rosa said. She was happy, almost giddy, at the thought of seeing her friend. And I have to admit that, though the party idea concerned me, I was very much looking forward to a comfortable bed, a nice bath, and food with more taste to it than what we'd eaten at Campo Imperatore. There weren't any other cars in the gravel drive, and as my wife pulled the Maserati to a stop I found myself hoping the party had been Mazzo's idea of a practical joke, or that

Rosa had heard wrong and the event would be held on the following evening, long after we'd left town.

The main doors were made of wood, painted green, arched at the top, and guarded to either side by stone lions with open, toothless mouths. As we stepped from the car the left side of the doors opened, and a very old man appeared. He put me in mind of a chestnut—tiny, somewhat lumpy, tightly built. He was dressed in a gorgeous light-brown suit, his white dress shirt open at the collar, his face showing the polished flesh of plastic surgery and his hair as black as the rubber on the Maserati's wheels. Mazzo was so small compared to what I remembered from the silver screen, so old, so harmless-looking, that my smoky vapor of jealousy evaporated instantly. He spread his arms in delighted welcome, said, "The woman of my dreams!" hugged my wife close, and it didn't bother me at all.

I had wondered how Rosa would handle the introductions and was happy when she presented us simply as three good friends, Fabio, Andrea, and Domenico. Mazzo shook our hands with great warmth and style, but he seemed to be living behind a wall of thick glass, the face frozen in what looked like a sincere grin, but eyes that were dull and distant. I guessed he was medicated, ill, or both. "Have you eaten?" he asked, which is the first thing Italians ask their guests after they say hello. "Are you hungry?"

We shook our heads. Rosa said, "No, we had lunch a short while ago," but Mazzo didn't seem to hear her, or to understand. "Something small," he said. "Small, at first, and then, later, *la festa,* the party!"

He ushered us into the building and very slowly up

a sweeping set of white marble stairs to a second-floor dining room that looked out on neat rows of grapevines. He'd clearly made preparations for our visit, and on short notice. The circular table had been elegantly set, and we'd been seated no more than ten seconds when a man and a woman appeared and poured wine and water and another couple carried in silver trays with caviar on crackers, chocolates, grapes, sliced pears, a selection of cheeses, miniature loaves of bread.

"Eat and drink, please, make me happy," Mazzo said. "The wine comes from my own land here, my own vines." Before sitting down with us, he paused a moment with his hands on the back of a chair, still catching his breath. He surveyed the offerings, our faces, the level of water and wine in the glasses, and then, saying, "I'll join you for a moment," he sat, tucked a napkin into his collar, and took a long sip of red.

"How are you?" he asked Rosa after he'd wiped his puffy lips. "Tell me. Provide all details, as long as they are happy ones."

"Well, my daughter just told us she's pregnant with our first grandchild!"

"Aha!" Mazzo exclaimed. He raised his glass again. *"Maschio? Femmina?"* Boy? Girl?

"Not yet known!"

"May it be a beautiful girl," he said. "And may she grow into a lovely woman with fine breasts to which she one day holds children of her own. May she be happy and healthy for a hundred years. May I be allowed, as an honorary godfather, to bequeath one of my homes to her on her wedding day!"

He raised a toast and we joined him—Rosa and I with

wine, and the Dalai and Pope using water. We picked at the food, politely. It was impossible not to like Antonio Mazzo, but the glass wall behind which he lived seemed to have a line of sight only to Rosa. The rest of us might as well have been invisible, which, given the circumstances, was a welcome development.

"As for me," he said, without being asked, "I am not at peace with old age. Not at peace with infirmity. With death. Though I've had many good things in my life— women, wine, food, travel, fame, money—it still seems to me, my Rosa, that something is missing. I reach for that something and I am like a man waving his arms in the air as he falls from the top of a cliff. What is it? I ask myself. Another beautiful woman? Another spectacular meal? Another summer on my yacht at Costa Smeralda? Yes, a part of me answers. Yes and yes and yes, all those things. And then another part speaks words in a language I do not understand, in a voice I cannot quite hear. I strain forward to listen to the voice, and, falling, I wave my arms, I call out in my sleep. But the answer is hidden from me, Rosa. Hidden."

It was almost like a recitation, a soliloquy from an old film role, Shakespeare perhaps, or Fellini. Finished with it, Mazzo swiveled his head and at last seemed to see the men at the table, however vaguely. "This is the human condition, is it not?" he asked me.

"Yes," I said. "We all feel it."

But the words tasted false in my mouth: it wasn't quite true. The Pope and the Dalai Lama didn't seem to feel it at all. In my many years with the Holy Father I'd never heard him say anything remotely like that.

"It doesn't seem fair, does it," Mazzo went on. "I feel sometimes that we're living a cruel puzzle arranged by a spiteful god. We're given these sublime pleasures. We work for them, yes, in part, but in part we are simply fortunate. We spend nights in bed with glamorous lovers, unforgettable nights, we drink wine that tastes as if it were grown in Eden and harvested by angels, we consume meals we remember for twenty or thirty or forty years, and then all this is taken away. Bit by bit, year by year, decade by decade, our ability to enjoy physical love is diminished, and in some cases—not mine—extinguished. Our ability to drink, to digest, to run and swim and climb mountains! To work! All taken away. There's something so tragic about all this, my Rosa, it seems to me now. You're young, still. These pleasures are still available to you. And now, a grandchild, the greatest blessing. For me, however, there is nothing left but the cold grave, the end of things. A vast and inexpressible loneliness takes hold of me on certain evenings. No matter where I go in this beautiful nation—and I have houses everywhere—it takes hold of me and won't release its grip!"

As he spoke, Mazzo took a marking pen from an inside pocket of his jacket, searched briefly for a scrap of paper, and then, not finding one, lifted a white silk napkin from the table and began to scribble on it. I thought for a moment that he'd lost his mind.

"But you have your parties," Rosa said kindly, pretending not to notice the ruined napkin. "Your legions of friends and admirers. Your body of work."

"Yes, yes," Mazzo said, looking at each of us in turn. A self-satisfied smile played along his famous lips for a few seconds, then vanished. "And tonight's party is going to be one of the absolute masterworks of my career. I've secretly been studying all of you since the moment of your arrival, watching you, deciding what costumes will suit you best. I am making notes, you see?" He held up the napkin, which was covered with ink. "Listen to me now." He wet his lips once more with the wine and seemed, momentarily at least, to have forgotten his angst. "We have crates of costumes here, whole rooms full of costumes. I don't want the four of you to merely put on a mask and dance and drink. I want you to dress up! To assume a new identity, the way all actors do! I will hand these notes to my Giacomo and he will instruct you in the correct costumes to choose. And you must do as he asks, you must! Otherwise I shall be gravely offended." He swung his eyes around the table, spraying us with droplets of attention but, it seemed to me, not truly seeing any of us. "Giacomo will show you to your rooms now," he said. "Rest. Use the swimming pool if you like. I must nap in order to have the energy to perform my duties as host, and, who knows, perhaps something more, later. But please, be at home here. Be absolutely free . . . Maria!" he called to one of the serving women. "Call Giacomo. Tell him to take exquisite care of our guests, of my Rosa and her friends!"

Getting to his feet, Mazzo struggled a bit. When he was upright, he took a last sip of wine, nodded to us each in turn, and, like a great stage actor, strode out of the spotlight and through the door. We heard his feet on the hallway tiles, and then he was gone.

30

"An amazing man, isn't he?" Rosa remarked to the Holy Father, when we were alone again.

The Pope was nibbling a cracker with caviar and eyeing a plate of chocolates. He moved his eyes to my wife, chewed, swallowed, wiped the silk napkin carefully across his lips. There was a certain wrinkling around his eyes, a signal that he was about to be diplomatic. "Yes, but I feel there is something sad about him."

"He's been a generous man all his life," Rosa said, somewhat defensively, as if she expected the holy duo might judge Mazzo harshly for his love of excess. "I wonder sometimes, what does God do with a soul like that when it is finished here on earth?"

"His kindness will be remembered," the Pope said. "If he asks, his sins will be forgiven."

My wife pressed her lips downward in the smallest sign of impatience. I hoped the Holy Father didn't notice, because I could see that for Rosa, his explanation hadn't been enough. The Catholic platitudes had stopped working for her many years earlier, stopped working for Anna Lisa, as well. I'd broached that subject with my cousin once, before his election. "Paolo," he said, "they are platitudes, yes, but within them lies a mystical meaning. 'God is love,' for example. Or 'Christ died for our sins.' It takes years of devotion and prayer to penetrate to the heart of that meaning. It's like the parables. Christ told simple stories to reveal the most complex and mysterious of truths. You can ponder them for decades."

But even that hadn't been enough to quiet a certain

restless skeptic who lived in one corner of my house of faith.

Rosa turned to the Dalai Lama and asked, "In your religion, in Buddhism, what happens to a man like my friend after he takes his final breath?"

"His desires and attachments call him back into another body," the Dalai Lama said without the slightest hesitation, as if that conclusion were as obvious as the slices of cheese on his plate, as if this cause-and-effect karmic law were as clear to him as God's love was to my cousin. "Again and again he will be called back. Life after life. Then, one day, he understands that no physical pleasure can satisfy him in deepest place. At that moment, in that life, he turn in the direction of liberation."

"And what does that liberation look like? What does it feel like? Being neutered and dull? Going extinct?"

The Dalai Lama shook his head. "Extinction of ego, of all sense that you are only individual, unconnected to life. Extinction of desire. Buddha said, after the ego is finished, you reach a state that cannot be described, that is not understandable to us in our human minds now."

"Very similar to what we believe," the Pope said. "Though without reincarnation."

"You have purgatory."

"Yes."

"The soul suffer there, yes? Has a glimpse of God but must suffer until purified."

"Exactly."

"For us, this purification take place in many lifetimes. Almost same."

"Speaking of purification," I said. "I would like a swim. As long as we're here, I'd like a good swim."

"Your skin polish, *amore,*" Rosa warned. She gestured to the holy ones, "And their disguises."

Before I could tell her that I didn't care as much about preserving the disguise as I did about not feeling like a sweat-caked mule, the door opened and another man appeared on the threshold. I wondered if the entire staff had been trained to behave as if they were on stage, because after two seconds of posing, this man made three long steps into the room, came to a halt, stood up to his full height in a posture that was almost military, and announced, "*Sono Giacomo!* I am Giacomo! Come with me! Let me show you what you will wear!"

31

There are people to whom you don't say no. I don't understand why that is, but certain people are so persuasive, so determined, so stubborn, or so painfully vulnerable, that refusing them becomes an impossibility, the equivalent of saying no to aging and death. Antonio Mazzo was all of these things and one of these people. Some of the impossibility of refusing him had to do with the fact that he was feeding us and letting us sleep in his grand home. Some of it was a charisma he seemed to have been born with; some of it an entitlement bred of great fame. And some of it—most of it, I believe—came from the fact that, without saying anything, we all agreed that we didn't want to damage his fragile ego, a brittle and priceless parchment held behind glass. When you shook his hand, you could feel how easily the parchment could be torn; you could see it in the watery yellow eyes and hear it in his complaint about the mysterious "something" he was missing. Giacomo—his butler or aide or house manager—had clearly made a career, a life, of protecting this ego. He was the king's valet. I couldn't help realizing, as the valet led us down a long corridor into a large storage room, that the Pope was nothing like this. Yes, there were times when he insisted on having his way. But the root of that was conviction, not ego; certainty, not fragility.

My musings aside, however, one thing was clear from Giacomo's manner: we were going to the party, and in the costumes Mazzo had selected for us. I could already sense the Holy Father's reluctance, but there was simply not going to be any discussion.

Mazzo's storage room resembled a fashion glutton's pantry: Racks and racks and racks of dresses, suits, and coats. Boxes upon cardboard boxes stuffed so full that we could see protruding hats, gloves, belts, lingerie, pajamas. A hundred pairs of shoes were lined up along one wall next to more boxes with socks and leggings. There were slippers and sandals; there were boots in abundance. We stepped farther into the room and saw furs, scarves, swords, helmets, masks of various shapes and sizes, costumes enough to outfit every Bollywood production for the calendar year.

We stood facing Giacomo in a silent—I almost want to say a "cowed"—half circle, as though we were new interns at the palace, being shown the ropes. The chemistry of our little group had turned docile. In his early or mid-seventies, ridiculously tall for an Italian, balding, thin, with a wide jaw that made his face pear-shaped, Giacomo spoke elegant Italian, and in his speech you heard this same incontrovertibility. He might have been announcing a law just passed by the Roman Senate: "Claudius decrees that all slaves must have eight glasses of wine on Sabbath eve . . ."

Who was going to argue?

He motioned for us to come and stand beside a table on which a stack of folded clothing had been neatly arranged. Holding the linen napkin Mazzo had ruined with his notes, Giacomo began to act out what seemed to me another in a series of scenes. *"Lei, carissima,"* he said to Rosa, checking his notes and placing a hand on her shoulder in a way I didn't like. "You, dearest. *Lei andrà alla festa come una suora."* You will be going to the party as a nun.

It had been so decreed.

The smile that broke across Rosa's face lit the room like the flash from a camera. Not worried in the slightest that a certain someone in our company might find a non-nun in a nun's outfit sacrilegious, she glanced at me and erupted in laughter, hair tossing, fine teeth showing, earrings shaking, the veins on her neck throbbing in irreverent ecstasy. The Pope smiled at her, happy that she was happy, but the smile held all sorts of mysteries. Even with all the practice I'd had—a lifetime of practice, really—I couldn't read his emotions at that moment. Behind his glasses the Dalai Lama's mood was even more obscure. He was standing as still as one of the lions at the entrance to Mazzo's villa, the famous face holding an undeniable power, but expressionless. Oblivious to them both, my darling wife took the nun's habit from Giacomo and held it against the front of her body in a pose of absolute delight.

"*Lei.*" Now Giacomo pointed a long, knuckly finger at the Dalai Lama and lifted from the pile the blue, gold-trimmed uniform of a police captain, a carabinieri officer. "You will be a member of the police. But this is not an ordinary party, *signore,*" he added, handing over the uniform with great formality. "This is a Mazzo party! And so"—he reached into a box beneath the table—"we have for you a holster, gun, and nightstick. Authentic, all of them, *tutti,* but the *pistola* is without bullets so we don't risk an accident!"

At that moment I would have checked to see how the Dalai Lama, prince of nonviolence, was reacting to the idea of partying with a pistol on his belt, but my eyes had fastened themselves to the pile of costumes. Diminished now by half, it showed that a plain tweed suit was next, and set beside it were accoutrements—a pipe, a fedora, heavy-framed eyeglasses. For me, I assumed. Beneath the suit, peeking out around the edges of the tweed, was the outfit of a medieval king.

I heard Giacomo say, in his stilted Italian again, and again with the sweeping gestures of a stage actor, "Signor Mazzo has decided that, on account of some craziness we endured in past parties, we need to have a psychoanalyst in residence for one night." He sent an oily smile in my direction and handed the suit to me. It had been folded in half. I held it in my arms like a prison-issue blanket, and I stood there with my eyes on the king outfit. After a moment I shifted them to Rosa. She'd seen what was coming next, too, and even she seemed a bit worried. The Pope as king: it should have felt no more sacrilegious than the businessman's suit he'd been wearing, but somehow it did. If the Pope was to be arrayed in the garb of power, it should be spiritual, not temporal power. Her earlier delight had ebbed like the sea after a huge wave has broken. Her eyes flipped up to the Pope, and that gave me the courage to turn and look at him, too, even while Giacomo was happily handing over the pipe and eyeglasses and I was trying to balance them on the pile of cloth in my arms.

Cheeks tightened, shoulders pushed back, the Holy Father appeared on the verge of balking, of having finally reached the place where he was unable to play along with whatever foolish thing happened. His rather absurd original disguise, applied by the marvelous Mario: no problem. Lunch with a prostitute: absolutely okay—his idea, in fact. His beloved almost-niece dousing him with the benefits of Buddhism and then taking him to a place where rows of strangers sat cross-legged in meditation: perfectly fine. My cousin's deep well of spiritual self-confidence had enabled him calmly—even happily—to go along with all that and stick to his plan of being an ordinary man for a few days. But dressing up as a king in preparation for attending a party that, we could already sense, was going to be a kind of perfection of decadence? You didn't have to be his first cousin to read in his body language and facial expression that such a joke—if "joke" is the word—was simply going to be the pebble that made the heavy load of ordinariness too much for him.

He was going to refuse, I could sense it. And his refusal was going to set up a confrontation between him and the great Mazzo. Giacomo would ask for an explanation, would tell him that Mazzo's guests were duty bound to obey their famous host's instructions: that was simply the way it had always been done; otherwise the actor would take offense, would be injured. I would try to act as peacemaker; it wouldn't work. Rosa would suggest that her friend be given a different costume, or allowed to go as he was; Giacomo would dig in his heels. The Pope's refusal would spark a similar sentiment in the Dalai Lama, and our hope of a comfortable night in the countryside would quickly disintegrate. We'd end up sleeping in the fields, pissing behind trees, taking turns bathing in a fetid roadside canal while the others stood sentry.

I reached out from under my pile of tweed and put one hand on my cousin's shoulder—a movement that caused the pipe to slip and fall to the floor with an ugly cracking sound. Giacomo frowned, bent from his great height to retrieve it. I managed to say the word *"Se"*— *if*—as in "If it makes you uncomfortable, Holy Father, please say so and we'll skip the party altogether. We'll find another place to stay." But before I could get past this "If" I saw a wave of resolve move through the Pope's facial muscles. The moment of resistance passed. He set his lips, he nodded.

Giacomo, smiling victoriously, obnoxiously, as if this were Mazzo's most amazing bit of imagination and creativity, lifted the king's robe with great dignity, and then reached under the table and produced a brass crown. He looked triumphantly upon my cousin and declared, "And you, my good friend, will go to the party as . . . a great king, a leader of his people!"

I bit the inside of my cheeks, hard, because what I wanted to say to Giacomo after this great triumph of his was something like: "You tall idiot! You *cazzo!* You supercilious, pear-faced, *cazzo* idiot!"

But I noticed that my cousin had regained his balance. "*Allora, va bene.* Okay, very well," he said in his slightly accented Italian, and in a slightly forced tone. "A good idea. In fact, many people comment that I do have the bearing of a leader. Only please spare me the crown. I have a scalp condition that prevents me from wearing hats in hot weather. They cause me to perspire there, which makes the condition worse. Do you think Signor Mazzo would allow me to attend in the robe, but without the headpiece?"

Giacomo hesitated, the wide lower half of his face twisted into an exaggerated frown. At that moment I realized I didn't like him. There was something smug about the man. His smugness made me think of some of the Vatican assistants, who seemed to think their closeness to a famous man elevated them above the position of ordinary mortals. I could feel a sly anger stirring inside me. Like most angry swirls, it had less to do with what was happening at the actual moment and more with memory and association: I was thinking of my Vatican colleagues, one or more of whom had clearly used the Pope's disappearance to tarnish my good name. They'd be perfectly happy to see me lose my job, go to jail even, or at least live out my life in disgrace for having abused my office and harmed the reputation of the most beloved Pope in modern history. I was about to say something to our smugly smiling Giacomo, something less than kind, when Rosa saved me.

"I'm a hairdresser by profession, Giacomo," she said. "I've seen these conditions and they can actually be quite dangerous. If the nerves of the scalp become irritated enough, then the inflammation can travel down into the lining of the brain, and we'd have a real problem on our hands. It would ruin the party, wouldn't it, to have to call an ambulance in the middle of the festivities?"

Giacomo was looking down at her from his great height, skeptically, it seemed. "We've had ambulances before," he noted.

But, after two seconds of hesitation, he gave a slow shrug—pretending not to care about the crown—and turned his attention to me. "You will have a table and chair," he said. "You will sit, please, for at least the first half of the party, until the dancing starts. Our guests will come to you for counsel, and Signor Mazzo would like it if you could amuse them with your responses. Make them laugh. Soothe them. Impart some of your immigrant wisdom, your worldliness. Can you do that?"

"Of course," I said, glad to be off the subject of the Pope's crown. "Naturally."

"He has extraordinary wisdom," Rosa put in. "For an immigrant."

Giacomo nodded, eyeing me so carefully I wondered how much of my disguise had worn thin, or if the lack of an accent had given me away. At last he said, "The party begins quite early. It is important to Signor Mazzo that all guests be prompt. You will notice that everyone arrives exactly at eight p.m. We have hired some people to help with the parking. Signor Mazzo asks that one of them be allowed to move your car into the stables to make room. Would you give me the keys?"

I handed them over. More of the smug smile. A semi-sarcastic bow. "Eight p.m.," Giacomo repeated, and then, almost in imitation of his boss, he strode away.

32

At a quarter to eight, after a careful shower and a quick, if amateurish, touch-up of my skin color and hair cream, dressed dutifully in my too-hot tweed suit, carrying my pipe, hat, tortoiseshell glasses, and resentment, and already sweating, I went down the carpeted hall to the Pope's room and found him standing at a window, staring out. He was dressed in the kingly robe, but it fit him badly in the shoulders, as if it had been sewn for a smaller man. The window stretched floor to ceiling and was open, letting a hot breath of air into the room. Through it I could see that the fading daylight lay across the villa's fields a soft, golden sheet that was losing its luster, slowly, slowly, as each second passed. "Holy Father," I said quietly to his back, "if this is too awful for you, we can still decline to go. Probably no one except Giacomo would even notice at this point."

He didn't answer.

"It's so disrespectful, on the one hand," I went on. "Borderline sacrilegious. And risky, on the other. No doubt someone will recognize you and we'll all be sent back to Rome in the morning."

Still nothing.

"Holy Father?"

He turned, and even though I knew the king's vestments were only a cheap replica, there was still something awe-inspiring about seeing him that way. His body language had changed. He was the Pope again—powerful, magisterial, the Vicar of Christ on earth—even with the blond goatee and wig and a bit of color in his face from our time in the sun. It seemed absolutely impossible that the partygoers wouldn't see what I saw—and that one or more of them wouldn't know about the huge reward and turn us in. My only hope—admittedly a frail one—rested in the idea that even if they happened to be sober tonight, the type of people invited to a Mazzo party would be unlikely to have spent a lot of time gazing at the Pope's photo, watching his appearances on TV, or reading about him in their glitzy travel magazines.

"Join me at the table, cousin," he said in a grave tone.

We sat close to each other at a small, lacquered table in two high-backed chairs. My hands were on the table-top, and the Pope reached out and momentarily covered them with his own. I stared into the brown depths of his eyes. "My beloved cousin," he said. There was a TV in the corner, and I assumed he'd been watching it and had felt guilty about causing so much trouble. At the very least I assumed he'd say we were skipping the party. Possibly he was going to ask me to put in a call to the Vatican and have the papal helicopter sent to carry him back to his real life.

"I have something to tell you," he said. "Something important and possibly upsetting."

"I'm at your service, Holy Father." I'd spoken calmly enough, but when he removed his hands I put my own in my lap, squeezed one with the other, and saw that my palms had left sweaty tracks on the lacquered surface.

My cousin made the expression he often made when I addressed him that way: lips twisted to one side, eyes averted, a ripple of impatience crossing the high, freckled forehead.

"The Dalai Lama and I both have something to tell you, actually."

"I'm at your service," I repeated clumsily. This was it, then: our adventure was finished. We'd face the consequences now.

The same expression again. A sigh of impatience.

"Cousin," he said, "please listen closely ... After Tenzin and I had prayed together in the cathedral in Ferrara this afternoon and were sitting in the pew, side by side, we became aware of one of the paintings on the wall there. It was a gorgeous work, elaborately framed, that showed the Blessed Mother holding Jesus. Jesus was very young, an infant, and, as sometimes happens, the painter had made him rather large for his age. The Christ Child was naked, but positioned in a discreet way. None of this is uncommon, as you know. In fact, it's almost a cliché of the genre." He hesitated a moment, scratched at his goatee. "But what was astounding—and Tenzin noticed it first, not I—was that Mary had the tip of one finger in the child's mouth. Her second finger, I believe it was. Just the top, to the knuckle. It was done in something like the way modern mothers use a rubber nipple—what is it called?"

"A binkie."

"Yes." The Pope averted his eyes again and shifted uncomfortably. Through the open window we could hear tires on the gravel drive below, the sound of doors slamming, the lilting voices of the first of Mazzo's arriving guests.

"Tenzin pointed out that detail," my cousin went on, "and together we studied the painting. In fact, both of us left our seats and went to the side aisle and stood before it. I was mesmerized, cousin. Why? Because the genius of that artist was that with one tiny gesture, he had rescued the Blessed Mother and the Baby Jesus from cliché. He had made them real. Human. Alive. Believable. The baby was crying, or fussing; the mother had wanted to soothe him and had used her finger. I can't begin to tell you how moving it was to me. The love between them. The divine humanity!"

Another pause. He fingered the ring—not his own, of course (that one had been left behind in his Vatican office), but a brass band and seal that had come with the outfit. Mazzo, it seemed, had thought of everything. He'd thought of everything, yes, though he seemed blind to the notion that certain objects—a nun's habit, for example— should remain sacred.

Then the blazing eye contact again. "But what I have to tell you goes beyond that. What I've been worried about telling you . . . is . . . at that moment in the cathedral, the Dalai Lama confided in me that he's been having unusual dreams, too."

"Not more Mussolini, I hope."

A shake of the head, a sad smile.

"He's been having dreams, or perhaps we should call them 'visions'—three of them, to be precise—informing him that what he calls 'a great spirit' has been born at some point in the past few years. Here, in Italy, somewhere in the mountains, he said. He was quite sure of that. Naturally enough, he believes it is a great Buddhist spirit. Perhaps the next Dalai Lama, or Panchen Lama, he isn't sure. The dreams are a bit vague."

"As dreams tend to be," I said.

"Yes. He also confided in me that he'd had the first of these dream-visions on the night before he visited the Vatican, and that he agreed to join us on this trip only because he felt it was somehow connected to the appearance of this spirit. He was slightly hesitant, embarrassed even. He said he's been wanting to tell me about this since our first dinner, but he wasn't sure what my reaction would be. When he saw that painting, the Blessed Mother's humanity moved him to the point where he decided he should take me into his confidence."

"Interesting," I said, though I didn't think it was particularly interesting. The Buddhists, it seemed to me, were far too open to the weirder aspects of religious practice. I'd heard, or read, or perhaps Anna Lisa had told me, that in 1959 the young Dalai Lama had consulted an oracle to decide on the optimal day to flee the Potala Palace as the Chinese army approached. I couldn't imagine any Pope doing such a thing. And the way the Dalai Lama himself had been chosen—more dreams, oracles, a kind of test to see if the child knew of his previous incarnation—there was nothing Christian about it. Nothing of the Western world. Not logical, not scientific. In my case, not even believable.

I was on the verge of saying all that, or something like it, to the Holy Father when he coughed, averted and returned his eyes one final time, and spoke these memorable words. "And I told him I've been having almost the identical dream."

"Excuse me?"

"I've been having the same dream, Paolo! I believe now, my dear cousin, that a special spirit has been born to us. Now, at a point when the entire world seems mired in violence and cynicism, when the Church is shrinking, the environment being poisoned, when good souls are giving up hope, when greed and bitterness seem to be gaining at the expense of kindness and compassion—now, I believe, we have been given a bit of divine help. A saint, perhaps. Or perhaps a prophet. For a while today, when Anna Lisa told us her wonderful news, I thought she might be carrying this special being in her womb. But the dreams— mine and Tenzin's both—seem to indicate that the child has already been born. I've been seeing this again and again in dreams—sometimes it's a little boy and sometimes a little girl—and have told no one, because I worried it might be some kind of temptation, a spiritual dead end, an offshoot of my sinfulness. But when the Dalai Lama mentioned it to me, that doubt was washed away."

"I thought you were dreaming about Mussolini, women, helicopters, soccer balls?"

"All those things, yes. And a sacred spirit besides. I was embarrassed to tell you that part, forgive me. I believe now that all those images are somehow connected, strange as that might sound. I've been praying for guidance, and I believe—and Tenzin believes, also—that there is some connection between the two of us, that we were destined to take this trip together, that we are being asked to witness something. Very soon. All four of us are destined for it, perhaps."

I could hear more cars in the driveway below, a drunken curse, and then the kind of laughter that makes a decent person cringe. Through the window floated these words: *"dolce come un sogno impossibile!"*

Sweet as an impossible dream.

The Pope heard that comment, too, and smiled. He

was looking at me with an expression of great compassion. "I can see that I've upset you," he said. "This idea of a sacred child, it bothers you, cousin, I can see it. It will bother a great many other Christians, I'm afraid, as if the era of saints and miracles must belong only to the past."

"It's a lot to digest," I said. "That's all. The false reports we heard about me on the radio, this party, your costume, my daughter the practicing Buddhist, pregnant, engaged . . . Now this dream idea . . . it's been a difficult day."

"*Capito,*" he said kindly. Understood. "But Tenzin put it in a very interesting way during that same conversation. He said, 'All difficulties in this life, every moment of difficulty, come from the distance between what is and what we want to be.'"

"That seems obvious, doesn't it?" I told my cousin a bit crankily. "We don't want to be ill. We don't want to be in pain. We don't want to grow old, or die. We don't want to be accused of something we didn't do, and go to jail for it. We don't want our beloved, pregnant, engaged-to-be-married daughters to embrace a religion that is not our own."

"We want predictability and comfort," he said, as if agreeing with me.

"Exactly."

"And God gives us a world of continual unpredictability and periodic discomfort."

"Precisely."

"Almost as if it were a challenge. A lesson. A puzzle."

"Right. Yes. Exactly."

"A party we're invited to unexpectedly," he went on. "A costume we don't want to put on. Madmen who come to power and poison our nations—Italy, Tibet, Argentina—with violence and hatred. I agree with you, of course. But at the same time, it seems to me that if we somehow find the courage to go directly into that discomfort—even the discomfort of illness, pain, old age and death—we might discover something unexpected there."

"But what?"

"A courage, a resilience. Possibly an identity that transcends that of this painful life. Mary, remember, said, 'Let it be done to me according to thy will,' and it seems to me sometimes that Christ's message, the message of the Cross, was a kind of supreme acceptance of all that it means to be alive in a human body. All of it. The good, the bad, and the hideous. He stretched out his hands for the nails, remember?"

"So we shouldn't take medicine when we're sick? We should find new ways to cause ourselves pain? Like the monks of the Middle Ages who used to flog themselves? We should put on whatever ridiculous costume Giacomo tells us to put on? We should let the Mussolinis of this world take over?"

He shook his head in gentle movements. "We don't abandon our will, cousin," he said after a moment. "We temper it."

"Temper it how?"

"There is an ideal balance between our small will and God's larger will, and it's our task to discover and refine that balance. It is a balance as delicate as the balance of power in a marriage. There are times when we must act to change a situation, yes, of course. But there are also times when we must yield, accept the unexpected, the unwanted, even the apparently unbearable. The world is bursting with neurosis, and it seems to me that the source of this neurosis is a lack of appropriate acceptance, an urge to control everything, to resist God's divine guidance in whatever surprising or difficult form it takes."

"And the form you think his guidance is taking now is your dreams? This party?"

"I don't know," he said, in a tone of such humility that I felt suddenly like an inflated doll there in the room with him. A puffed-up, cranky man. An egotist. A sinner of the first order. "I don't know. I'm not sure. But for another little while, at least, in the time remaining with His Holiness, with you and your blessed wife, I wish to explore that possibility, and I want you to help me explore it, in a spirit of love."

Before I could tell him that I'd help in any way I could, that I was at his service, as always, that I would try with every ounce of courage and strength I possessed to do what he asked me to do, a pair of sharp knocks sounded, the door was thrown open, and Giacomo stood there, pointing impatiently at his watch. In the hallway behind him I could see a nun and a policeman, and for a tenth of a second I had the sense that the forces of this world—spiritual and temporal both—had come to have me arrested for kidnapping on the one hand and moral weakness on the other. Clearly I was being asked to say yes to something I wanted to say no to. Wasn't life always doing that?

The Holy Father stood up, the folds of his purple, red, and white robe falling into place around his ankles. "Come with me, cousin," he said. "If someone does recognize me, then we shall accept that as God's will. Let us go to this party and see what we can learn about ourselves."

Who could say no to that?

33

In my long and varied life I have never seen anything like the party that was held that night at Antonio Mazzo's villa. And I hope I never see anything like it again. Giacomo led the four of us along a carpeted corridor— marble everywhere, side tables holding vases of fresh lilies, expensive-looking oil paintings on the walls—then down a flight of stairs to a marble-floored, high-ceilinged lobby that was crowded with northern Italy's richest, most cele- brated, and, in some cases, most beautiful people. The cos- tumes were beyond elaborate. In one quick sweep of the crowd I saw a man dressed as a medieval knight; he was clanking about—already drunk—in full armor. Another guest had arrived in the costume of an astronaut, complete with space suit and bubble helmet. Two women were dressed up as high-class prostitutes, clad in the flimsiest of short skirts with mouths and eyes made gigantic by an overdose of lipstick and raccoon mascara. Soldiers, pirates, belly dancers, an elderly woman—she must have been eighty—pretending to be pregnant. One Elvis Presley with gray hair. Two Berlusconis. A diminutive Margaret Thatcher. Young, shapely men and women dressed in what appeared to be the outfits of Roman slaves wound their way through the elegant crowd carrying trays of hors d'oeuvres. A bar had been set up at one end of the lobby, and it was presided over by big-breasted females in tight black vests. Already a knot of drinkers had assembled there. And this was just a first glance. A first, quick glance, because Giacomo was pressing forward toward a door covered in shiny gold paper, waving for us to follow in his wake.

Just as we reached it, the door was flung open. Antonio Mazzo stood there in a pale blue tuxedo with dark blue satin trim at the lapels and cuffs, his face partially hidden by one of the white plastic half masks favored by Venetian carnival-goers. A slim woman with gorgeous red hair piled up on her head stood close against him, her left elbow hooked inside his right. She appeared to be in her twenties, and her torso was covered by an exceedingly strange, diamond-shaped light-blue dress, on the fabric of which had been embroidered the name of a medication known to be used primarily by aging men who wish to remain sexually active. Mazzo was holding an ivory-handled cane. He had to tap it against the door frame only once before the crowd's languid babbling was silenced and, as if belonging to one body, the hundred or so guests turned to face him. Our host lifted his chin, ran his glance over the four of us, raised the cane above his head and announced, *"Cari ospiti, s'incomincia la festa!"* Dear guests, let the festivities begin!

He and the woman stepped to either side. The party-goers rushed the door, jostling each other and pushing the four of us into an enormous ballroom with square, gilded columns around its edges, a glistening parquet floor, and red velvet drapes adorning a row of six floor-to-ceiling windows. The air was artificially cooled to a perfect temperature; there were bars at each end, with bare-chested male models serving drinks; and two chandeliers that had been turned on to their lowest setting, so that the ballroom was cast in the light of a bordello. As we entered, a six-piece band launched into a sporty rendition of "I Want to Hold Your Hand."

I felt Rosa squeeze my arm and press herself against

me nervously. I turned to say a word to her, to check on the Pope and the Dalai Lama, to plan our escape at the earliest possible opportunity, to apologize, to beg forgiveness. But it was too late. A couple dressed as Indian rajas pressed between Rosa and me, separating us without the smallest apology, headed for the bar. The holy men had been spirited off, or had drifted off, or had slipped into a side room to hide and pray for this world. Giacomo took hold of my elbow, gently but firmly, and tugged me across the floor. Near the wall on the window side I noticed a simple table and two chairs, and as I drew closer I saw that a neatly lettered sign had been placed on the table. *Terapia Gratuita,* it read. Free Therapy.

"Il suo posto." Giacomo indicated the chair with a sweep of his arm. "Your place, *signore.* At least until the dancing begins, at which point please enjoy yourself with the others. Please put on your glasses and pretend to smoke your pipe, so the effect will be maximized."

And then he was gone, off to other devilish errands in other corners of the grand room.

I sat. A coal-colored cat tiptoed behind me, rubbing its arched back once against my ankles. I put on my tortoise-shell glasses and, through the clear lenses, ran my gaze around the room. Even in their disguises—Cleopatra, Indira Gandhi, Marilyn Monroe—the women were weighed down with strings of pearls and glittering earrings large enough to use in bludgeoning to death any stray snake that might happen to slither into the room. There was an abundance of bare skin. Here and there, on the faces of males and females alike, one could detect the work of cosmetic surgeons—the swollen lips, the shining cheeks—as if age were a disease that, thanks to the miracle of modern medicine, had finally been cured. Among the men we had the following: one Robin Hood complete with bow and arrow; a Gorbachev with a red birthmark on a high, pale forehead; a bare-chested young fellow with taut stomach muscles, boxing gloves on each hand, and a pretend cut on his face. Around them the Roman-slave servants maneuvered like ballet dancers gliding through the crowd *en pointe,* holding trays of what appeared to be oysters, caviar on crackers, cheese, fruit, chocolate, glasses of champagne. In one way, I decided, we were safe: no one in his or her right mind would imagine this as the destination of two holy men.

I sat there, an awkward teenage boy at his first dance, pretending to smoke my pipe and feeling spectacularly ill at ease. In the minutes before anyone sought my professional advice, I could sense the increase in volume against my skin, a raucous hilarity, the onset of mayhem. At least a third of the guests were already drunk, or high, or they'd arrived in that condition and were enhancing it with glasses of champagne from the dancing Roman slaves or harder liquor from the models at the bar. Drinks were spilled as if it were all just part of the fun, and a trio of maids in black mesh stockings hurried around with dainty mops, cleaning up. I looked for Rosa, the Pope, the Dalai Lama, Mazzo and his Viagric girlfriend, and saw none of them.

After ten long minutes a stunningly beautiful woman with medium-brown skin stepped over to the table and pulled out the second chair. "May I?" she asked.

"Absolutely. Please. How can I help you?"

She sat straight-spined, her back not touching the chair, and I realized she was dressed as an African princess, replete with long, flowing orange gown and a flow-ered headdress. She met my eyes so directly that her gaze might have been a laser beam designed to cut through the syrupy excess surrounding us. "I feel alienated," she said, in clipped, perfect Italian. "*Fuori posto.* Out of place, things, the edge of humanity, in fact. I don't know why I came. It's a famous party, you know. It's considered a social honor to be invited. I work in film. I thought I'd enjoy it. But almost from the minute I stepped out of the car I've felt like I'm not just of a different race, but of a different species . . ." She kept her eyes fixed on me, as if looking for someone—an unwelcome Libyan, perhaps—who understood the language she was speaking. "That's how I feel," she said, "and I'd like some advice about what to do with that feeling."

She was a beautiful actress playing a role, I assumed. But just as I was about to spout some stupid joke I thought might fit in with the mood of the evening, she added, almost fiercely, "And I want a real answer from you, *signore,* not a party answer."

For five or six seconds I could only look at her. Next to her naked sincerity I felt ashamed, of course, there in my false skin. I wanted to explain the situation, tell her the truth, but I had the sense that she was looking for guidance, not apologies. Here, of all places, in the midst of this circus of decadence, she wanted a true word. I looked over her head, hoping I might see the Dalai Lama, someone actually qualified to help her, at which point the woman said, "Look at me, please," and I did. "Please give me some actual advice."

"You are," I began, voice wobbling, "you are, in fact, a child of God, an actual child of God. You are a princess, even without the disguise. I can see it in your bearing. Every princess, every great artist, every saint, every person like you, must always feel on the fringes of society, because most people have forgotten the spiritual royalty that was bequeathed to them at birth. The edge of society, in fact, is the place you belong. Especially"—I waved my arm at the people behind her—"in a society like this." I had no idea where these words were coming from. The woman had cast a spell on me; by her simple presence she'd lifted me up and out of myself.

She listened attentively, not blinking, and when no more words were forthcoming, she said, "*Bene,* fine. But the question is: what do I do with that?"

"You serve."

"Fine. How?"

"By example. By being genuine. Simply by being your absolute, most genuine self in every interaction of every hour, you provide a great and rare service on this earth."

She stared, appraising me. She pushed out her closed lips. She nodded, once. "The exact opposite of this, then. No charades. Ever. I mean, in real life, no apologies for who I really am, no games."

"Precisely."

"*Grazie,*" she said, and she stood, fixed a last look on me, turned, and made straight for the golden door. If she had arrived with someone, that someone was now being abandoned. People stepped aside for her. I could see the back of her head, and then only the headdress. I saw the door swing open, glimpsed her bare brown shoulders, and then she was gone and as if by some chemical reaction, the hilarity in the ballroom went up another notch.

Almost immediately two more women approached

the table. They didn't sit, but crouched, so that only the tops of their almost bare breasts and their elegant necks and faces showed. *"Ciao!"* one of them giggled. I saw that they were wearing only lingerie on top, one red, the other black. The black-bra-wearing one handed me a full glass of champagne. I thanked her and gulped eagerly.

"*Ciao, ragazze.* What are you here as?"

"Whores," the second one said. "We're offended you couldn't tell!"

"Yes, we want to take you upstairs to one of the rooms and ravish you, both of us at once."

"I'm afraid I have to remain here until the dancing starts. There are people here who need me."

"We're serious," the first one said, and I could see that she was, and the offer set off a small, vile spark in me.

"Yes, we can't wait until the dancing starts. We'll find someone else if you say no. This is your chance, *signor terapista.*"

"I saw a nun in the crowd," the other one said. "She's our second choice! We'll take the nun upstairs and corrupt her if you say no."

"Yes, brilliant!" her partner added. They saluted each other with a drunken high five.

"The nun has to help me in a bit," I told them. "You'll have to take a knight or an astronaut, or one of the Berlusconis."

They stared at me in tandem, drunkenly. "You're afraid," the first one said. "I can see it. What kind of man is afraid of going to bed with two women?"

At that point no clever remark came to my lips. At that point the resolve I'd carried into the room, the idea that I could somehow play along and learn something about myself, began to desert me. They watched me. One of the women slipped and fell sideways, then righted herself and laughed. It was the laugh I'd heard through the window of the Pope's room. They waited a few more seconds, giving me a chance to change my mind, to go upstairs with them and bury myself in pleasure. The smallest swirl of temptation did indeed spin in the air around me like smoke from a too-strong cigar. "Come on!" the one who'd fallen said. "You look like you could use some fun! That's why we picked you!"

After watching them for another second, I shook my head.

"Let's go find the nun, then," the second one said, and they stood so abruptly that their tiny skirts shifted up to the bottom of their buttocks and had to be tugged back down.

I watched them stumble away, then caught a glimpse of Rosa in the crowd. A very short man, dressed, apparently, as Julius Caesar, was leaning in close to her and shouting something, glass in hand. Another proposition, no doubt, and perhaps some momentary spark was lit in her, as well, to forget herself, forget her past, slip away for an hour from the role she played in the world. I saw the two whores stumbling drunkenly toward my wife, but partygoers moved between us—Elvis and the astronaut holding hands. Another woman approached the desk and sat. Plump, fortyish, with dark brown hair in braids and magnificent, un-made-up eyes, she was dressed like a Swiss milkmaid in a laced bodice, but I could see, a second after she took the chair opposite me, that there were real tears about to spill over.

"Are you all right?"

"No!" she replied, in a voice that was almost a shout. "My husband has already gone off with someone, another man, or a woman, or two women. It's unbearable. Every year it's the same, and I truly, truly, truly don't believe I can bear it any longer!"

"You're not acting, are you."

She shook her head no, and a droplet of misery swung off sideways and landed with a plop in my champagne. She choked out a sob, hideous and real, that was eaten up by the roar of happy voices behind her. A Roman slave, dressed only in a twist of gold cloth, stopped by to offer us oysters from her tray. Both the woman and I shook our heads.

"You should talk to someone who can help, a real someone," I said stupidly.

More head shaking. Tears flying this way and that. "I can't leave him."

"Of course you can. Do you have children?"

"Twins. Eight years old. I'd be condemning them to a life of near-poverty."

"But you're married. You're wearing a ring."

"Married, yes, in the Church." A syllable of horrible laughter burst from her lips.

"There are laws. He'd have to support you."

"Not the way we live now. The children would be devastated."

"You're allowing yourself to be tortured," I blurted out, because by that point there were no more barriers between me and the truth, no more cleverness, no games. I felt like a man whose soul had been cleaned by being scraped with muddy sponges and washed in an ice-cold spray. "Your own need for luxury is torturing you."

A burst of sobbing. She leaned forward and rested her head on the tabletop, one braid flopping there like a wounded snake, the other hanging straight down just beyond the table's edge. I put a hand on the back of her head and held it there while she wept. I could see the top of her backbone, an even line of bumps beneath perfect skin. She was another stunningly beautiful woman, in the heart of middle age, and I couldn't help imagining what she must have looked like, what a rare beauty she must have been, when her rich husband proposed to her.

"Eventually it might pass," was all I could think to say in the face of her suffering. "Eventually he'll probably get tired of it and be faithful again."

She shook her head underneath my hand, and lifted her face to me. *"Mai,"* she said. "Never. He'll go on and on. Like Mazzo. I have to absorb it. I have to bury myself in it for the sake of the children."

The woman stood and hurried away, and I was about to follow to make sure she didn't harm herself. I'd had enough, more than enough, much more than enough, and had already pushed back my chair and was about to stand when a Mussolini stepped out of the crowd, swung one leg over the other chairback, and sat at attention.

Like everyone else in that room, this man wasn't adorned in a cheap, store-bought costume. Some real thought, work, and expertise had gone into his getup. He was wearing what looked to be a precise replica of the uniform Il Duce had ordered tailored specifically for himself, a uniform that corresponded to no known Italian tradition, to no actual branch of the military or government, but that was festooned with medals as a kind of testament to the falseness of the sycophants around him and his own desperate need for approval. I knew these things because of Rosa's studies, and because, in an attempt to soothe her grief, my mother—the resistance-fighter-turned-printmaker—had made herself into an amateur historian, at least as far as Mussolini was concerned. It was, as my father often told her, a morbid fascination: she wanted to know everything she could about the man who'd caused her brother's murder. As I grew older, she'd share some of her knowledge with me. Because of the location of our home, we practically couldn't go out for a walk or take the car into town without passing the small black-and-gold plaque that marked the place where Mussolini had been executed. In my high-school and college years my mother would tell me bits about Il Duce's life: his genuinely heroic World War I service and wound, his early attraction to socialism, a philosophy he'd later denounce; his rise to power via the use of violence, intimidation, threats, treachery, Machiavellian strategies. His mass appeal—a hundred thousand Italians staring up at him as he stood on the balcony at the Palazzo Venezia, promising to remake an Italy that had never in fact existed. There had been, especially in the early going, some mottled good in the man, an inclination toward public service. He'd instituted insurance programs to aid the widows and children of soldiers killed in the First World War; he'd famously made the trains run on time, drained the Pontine Marshes, brought fresh water to impoverished southern hamlets, tried to set up model agricultural communities.

The great tragedy was this: he was, for a stretch of years, almost unimaginably popular in Italy. Wherever he went people lined up to see him. Men and women would have done anything for his approval. And how had he used that power and popularity? For a little while he mocked Hitler, called him a clown, a lunatic. But Hitler wooed him like a lover, kept inviting him to Germany, kept being refused, kept inviting him, until, at last, Mussolini acquiesced, and dressed in this exact uniform—made specially for his visit—traveled to Munich. There, Hitler put on a show for him, a stunning parade of military might and Nazi precision. And the weak little boy inside Mussolini was won over. That moment of power-envy sealed his fate, and Italy's. He went back to Rome and tried to institute racial laws (under his direction and despite many individual acts of Italian heroism, Jews were mercilessly harassed, stripped of savings, property, titles, and jobs, though none were sent to the camps until Mussolini's demise and the full German occupation). He suggested Italians get up early and exercise (people laughed at him). He invaded Albania, then Greece (Hitler had to send troops to rescue the Italian army from complete disaster). By the time the Allies landed on Sicily in July of 1943, Mussolini was broken, despised, physically ill, and often depressed to the point of paralysis.

But the Benito who sat in front of me held himself like the Mussolini of 1932 and 1935 and 1938. The man bore some resemblance to the real Duce—short and powerfully built, with a square face and protruding chin—and he'd obviously spent some time studying the old films, because he'd mastered the body language, the clownishly overdone posture, the flip of a Roman salute, the self-serious gaze . . . with which he now skewered me. Apparently, the fact that I no longer wanted to play along didn't show on my face, or the man was too high or drunk or deep in his role to notice, because the first thing he said after appraising the brown tint of my skin was, "You know, you belong to an inferior people!"

"No, actually, I do not know it," I said. "I belong to the human race."

He shook his head manfully. "If I have to do it single-handedly, I will clean up this great nation!"

"Your kind of cleaning we don't need."

"Therapists will become extinct! Crime will disappear! Religion will disappear! And in its place we will have the worship of the state!"

"Another false god," I said. "The state, the flag, you. All false gods."

"The state," he went on, "the family. Manhood."

"The husband who was famous for cheating on his wife. The valiant leader who promised to fight to his last breath but was caught leaving his beloved country with millions stolen from the national treasury. The little boy who idolized Hitler, sent thousands of Italians to their death on the Russian front, and brought his nation to ruin. And for what? To fatten his own ego! That's manhood?"

By that point I could feel the muscles in my neck. I was leaning across the table at Il Duce, speaking in a loud voice, and it seemed that through the haze of his drunkenness he was actually hearing me.

"You understand nothing," he said weakly. "I shall purify—"

That was as much as I could bear. I stood up: my chair went over backward. The sound of it falling was lost in the general melee. I left Mussolini there, waiting for his therapy, with an old man in line behind him, another actor, eager to play along. I looked for my people in the crowd. Just then the band started playing Michael Jackson's "I Want You Back." It was almost impossible to move in any direction, because at the first note, as if on some invisible signal, people started dancing wildly, throwing their arms about, crashing into one another. I saw a man on the floor on his hands and knees—a heart attack? A woman saw him at the same time; she climbed onto his back and began slapping him as one would slap a reluctant horse. The black cat raced past them. People danced in threes and fours and singly, swirling like mad dervishes. One senior guest, dressed as a sailor, sat on the floor with his back against a column, holding an empty champagne glass in one hand and fingering the toe of his loafer. The Roman-slave servers had ceded the central territory now and skipped along near the walls with trays held high, or tossed what appeared to be actual gold dust into the air. It lay on the shoulders of nearby dancers like pricey dandruff.

A desperate urge for normalcy seized me. I wanted to find my wife. I worried about the holy ones. In the corner farthest from the golden door I saw that two men had started to shove each other and were shouting, and at that point I finally located the Dalai Lama in his police uniform. I worked my way through the crowd, took him by the shoulders, swung him gently around, and headed back toward the door. I would herd them out, I decided, one by one. I would find my three colleagues and bring them and myself to safety. Ahead of me I caught a glimpse of a king's robe. My cousin. I saw Rosa approaching him. The Dalai Lama and I joined in and made a protective circle, and the four of us floated sideways through the crowd like a jellyfish, moving closer and closer to each other so that by the time we reached the golden door we went through it in a tight group, just as we had come.

Except for one young woman vomiting quietly in the corner beneath a large vase, the marble lobby was empty, the bar abandoned. I saw a set of exterior doors and steered us toward them, and in another moment we were all of us out in the warm air. The doors closed behind us and muted music—the Rolling Stones now, "Brown Sugar"—drifted out through the glass.

Full darkness had fallen. In the middle of Mazzo's vast lawn, a hundred meters from the house, we saw the pool—huge and L-shaped, lit at its corners by Japanese lanterns. We made our way toward it through rows of parked Jaguars and Mercedes, black stretch limousines, a sunflower-yellow Lamborghini. At one end of the pool two couples sat talking quietly. We chose the other end, collapsed into four chaise longues there, and let out a collective breath.

"Everyone all right?" Rosa asked wearily.

"Okay." The Dalai Lama set the nightstick down beside him with a small tapping noise. It rolled to the edge of the water, as if trying to drown itself, and stopped.

"Holy Father?"

"Fine," the Pope said in a barely audible voice.

"*Amore?*"

I had shrugged out of my tweed jacket and tossed it aside. The pipe, hat, and glasses had long ago been abandoned and lay somewhere on the lawn. "I'm here," I said. "Present. Breathing. You?"

"I'd like to apologize to all of you—Holy Father, Your

Holiness, Paolo. This was an absolutely stupid idea, and I'm sorry."

"Forgiven," the Pope said instantly. "You were only trying to find us a place to stay."

The Dalai Lama was nodding in a way that made me think he was replaying scenes from the ballroom.

"I need to swim," I said.

"We all need to," Rosa said. "But won't it ruin your disguise? It's already looking a little thin."

"Only if I scrub. I won't scrub."

Rosa stood and took the nun's veil and wimple from her head, shook out her hair. "As part of my penance I volunteer to go back to the costume room for bathing suits and towels, and I'll fetch our own clothes, too. Please wait. We'll change in the cabana. We'll have a group baptism."

"Don't, please, get in fight there," the Dalai Lama said.

The two couples at the far end of the pool followed Rosa back toward the villa at some distance. They were speaking quietly, taking turns, almost like rational human beings. I heard, "That recording was definitely a fake. Heavily edited, you could hear it. They're in trouble, probably dead by now." And then their voices faded away.

"Dalai," I said, "Holy Father, please say something."

The faint strains of music mixed with notes of tinkling laughter from one of the women on the lawn. For a moment those were the only sounds. I could see, around us, the dark shadows of Mazzo's vines and olive trees.

And then I heard a familiar voice say: "Our Father, who art in heaven, hallowed be thy name. Thy kingdom come, thy will be done, on earth as it is in heaven. Give us this day our daily bread, and forgive us our trespasses as we forgive those who trespass against us, and lead us not into temptation, but deliver us from evil. Amen."

"Amen," the Dalai Lama said, and then, "I am hoping those two fighting men not hurt. I could not be able to stop them."

"No one could have stopped them," I told him.

"Is this the typical entertainment?"

"Not even close to typical, Your Holiness."

We sat for a while, looking up at the stars, a great stillness there, a great peace and order, a sanity that was separated from our craziness by millions of miles. When Rosa returned, she had an armful of clothes, and one by one we went into the cabana and changed. The bathing suits didn't fit well. Both the Pope and the Dalai Lama seemed uncomfortable showing that much skin, even in darkness, but I was thinking mainly of myself then, I admit. I felt as though I'd been pushed so close to the edge of a polluted lake that I might have been sucked in and drowned. I wanted my ordinary life, my office, my duties, the simple pleasures of my breakfasts with the Pope, conversation with my daughter. And at that, like a constellation swinging back into view, I remembered she was pregnant, and I said a small prayer for the child in her womb, that he or she would live out its years, not too poor or too rich, surrounded by a hardworking wholesomeness, in a relatively nonviolent period of history. But then I thought: When, really, had we seen such a period? Now, with widespread terrorism and wars in the Middle East? A generation ago, with the hell in Yugoslavia, genocide in Rwanda, torture in Uganda? The generations before that, with apartheid in South Africa, napalm in Vietnam? Korea and World

War II and the Spanish Civil War? The Inquisition? The conquistadors? The Crusades?

"Time for a swim," I said, because when my mind got to working like that, a good cool dip always brought me some peace. I dove in without checking the depth and scraped the tip of my nose on the bottom. "Shallow," I warned, just as Rosa was making an elegant dive in a one-piece bathing suit three sizes too large for her. The Pope held the railing and walked in—knees, waist, chest. Once I saw that he was safe, I flipped onto my back and floated, studying the stars, unworried about the disguise. But in a moment I realized there were only three of us in the pool. I stood and saw the Dalai Lama frozen at the top of the steps, ankle-deep in water. Rosa saw it, too, and climbed up to him. "I'll hold your arm," she said. "Nothing bad will happen."

The Pope and I paddled over to the bottom of the steps, and as the Dalai made his slow, terrified descent, we were both there to meet him, each of us taking hold of an arm. He was tentative at first, a look akin to panic showing in the light from the Japanese lanterns; but once his feet touched bottom he smiled, ducked down unexpectedly, and came up spluttering and laughing. We gave him a quiet round of applause. He glided forward in a dead man's float and windmilled his arms. I thought: Piero should see this.

Just then we heard a klaxon, and then another, the sound and then the sight of two police cars. Lights flashing, they sped in through the gate and glided past the line of parked luxury sedans to the main entrance, where the sirens quieted but the lights still spun. We saw uniformed officers stand up out of the front seats, their silhouettes revealed in blue strobe. "Stay low," Rosa said.

We crouched with just our faces out of the water and waited. The music went silent and I had the sense that the partygoers had been frozen in mid-revelry, or perhaps they'd thought the carabinieri were in disguise, too—there for show, another ingenious Mazzo touch. Maybe he'd arranged for a staged arrest, Gorbachev or Queen Elizabeth taken out of the villa in handcuffs! Pretend paparazzi snapping photos. It was so eerily quiet that we could hear wavelets lapping the edge of the pool. Maybe the officers had already been tempted to go upstairs with the two faux prostitutes, or been offered oysters and cognac by the dancing slaves, or dusted with gold and lured into a fistfight.

"Someone recognized the Pope," Rosa said.

We waited, chilled but wary of climbing out. I looked over at a metal poolside table, our disguises piled there in a haphazard bundle—nun, policeman, therapist, king. Despite the party's sour residue, I suddenly wanted our adventure to go on. After what seemed a very long time the main door opened again, the officers emerged, and we heard Mazzo's crackly voice: *"Ciao, ciao! Ci vediamo!"* he was saying. Bye, see you! Another few seconds and car doors slammed. We watched the flashing blue lights make tight half circles and head back out the gate.

We climbed up into the air, dried ourselves, then took turns changing back into our disguises. In the cabana's lighted mirror I noticed that my newly touched-up artificial coloring had faded badly. I'd ask Rosa for a more professional touch-up. The small scrape on my nose was bleeding.

"Shall we leave?" Rosa asked, when we were sitting on the edge of our chaises. "Shall we surrender?"

"I don't think so," I said. "Not now. The Pope has something to say to you. They both do."

"Was it something I did at the party? He kissed me, *amore*. I didn't kiss back, I swear it."

I said nothing.

"It's not that," the Pope said.

"What, then?"

"Our dreams."

"What dreams?"

The Pope coughed. "Tell her, Tenzin," he said.

"We been having dreams," the Dalai Lama said. "The same dream. Or very almost the same."

"Of women?"

The Holy Father shook his head. "A child. Children."

"In my tradition this is not uncommon, dreams like this," the Dalai Lama said. "When an important lama has been incarnated, we are sometimes made aware by the dream. Now the Pope and I think there is young child, here or near here, in Italy. Important child. Born maybe few years ago."

"Another Dalai Lama?"

"I believe it was a Christian birth," the Pope said.

"And I believe Buddhist."

"And?" Rosa pressed them.

"We have spoken to each other about this, in the cathedral in Ferrara, and now again, here, this afternoon, before the . . . party."

"And?"

"And then, like a figure from my dreams, I saw Mussolini at the party," the Pope went on. "He came up to me and said, 'We have to make the peace, King, you and I.'"

"That's real history," Rosa said. "That actually happened ... The king—Vittorio Emanuele III—had Mussolini arrested in 1943. Most Italians know that. But before the Allies landed on Sicily, both the king and the Church had supported him."

The Pope shifted uncomfortably in his seat. I imagined stinging ants, carrying bits of Vatican history, crawling up his legs. "We have made a god of science now," he said sadly, tugging the conversation away from the Grand Benito. "In Christ's time, before science ascended to the throne, people believed in signs and miracles, in dreams."

"Tibetans still believe those things," the Dalai Lama said.

The Pope scratched at his wet fake hair. "But now they have been relegated to the province of charlatans and fakers."

The Dalai Lama said, "In the West." And I sensed, for the first time, a ripple of disagreement between them.

"In Naples we still believe in those things," Rosa boasted. "And the rest of Italy considers us heathens. My parents talk constantly about their dreams. They carry the medals of saints in their pockets; they can't pass a church without making the sign of the cross; the boys wear gold peppers around their necks to ward off the evil eye."

"Superstitions," I said.

"Sure, *amore,* but Tenzin told us before going to Rimini that Anna Lisa had news. Do you remember? How do you explain that?"

"How did you know, Dalai?"

He shrugged. "There are different ways of knowing. Sometimes if you meditate many years you have kind of—how you say it?—clairnoyance, yes?"

"Clair*voy*ance," Rosa corrected.

For a bit no one said anything else. We could hear

strains of music from the villa, and then a couple arguing on the patio. "Shithead!" the woman was yelling. "*Cazzo!*" And then, when there was no response from the man, she yelled, "You *woman, you!*"

"I have an idea," I said.

"As if 'woman' is an insult!" Rosa muttered. She turned to me. "What idea? Surrender?"

"Not yet, no!" my cousin said, before I could speak. "I feel . . . Both Tenzin and I have come to believe what I've been sensing all along, that this bit of traveling is more than a vacation or an escape. We've come to believe it has a purpose, a spiritual purpose—that there's something we must learn, or see, someone we must meet."

"Yes, maybe, or two someone," the Dalai Lama added— another remark I would later have cause to ponder.

"Here?" Rosa asked.

"It's too late to leave here tonight," the Pope said. "Unfortunately. But I don't think this is the end point, no."

"Where, then?"

"I believe the answer will be shown to us, Rosa. Perhaps as we sleep."

"We should give it one more day," I suggested. "Not here, but somewhere. One more day, and then, I think, if I may say so, we should turn ourselves in."

"Agreed, *amore.*"

"Agreed, cousin."

"Yes, very good," the Dalai Lama said. "We had our vacation now . . . And I have learn to swim."

We retired to our individual guest quarters with strains of music still floating up from the ballroom and through our windows. Exhausted as I felt, more than an hour passed before I was able to sink into sleep. During that hour, images from the party whirling in my head, I thought about the question Rosa had raised: what happened to a soul like Mazzo—a person who lived purely for pleasure—when he left this earth? I wondered if the old Catholic idea of three major options—heaven, purgatory, hell—was actual or metaphorical. Reincarnation by a different name. Good behavior led to a heavenly next life; evil led to trouble. I wondered why I was so reflexively opposed to the idea of being born many times in different bodies when at least a third of the world believed in that model. Why should we be given only one shot to get it right? And why should some of us be born into circumstances that made getting it right so much easier: good parents, good health, a safe bed and a full belly?

Even after those questions had released me into the arms of sleep, it was a sleep battered by scraps of disturbing dream: a cavalcade of faces dancing past; police cars and weeping women; gold dust on the windowsills.

Day Four

34

In the morning I awoke, again, to persistent knocking. I stumbled to the door in a state of weary undress and found Giacomo there. The last thing I wanted at that moment was more orders, or any reminder of my enforced identity of the night before, but this was a different Giacomo, kinder, gentler, more relaxed. Still, there were orders. "I'm sorry to wake you, *signore,*" he said, running his eyes over my pale chest and mottled bronze face and arms, "but I have knocked on the doors of your compatriots and no one answers. *Signor* Mazzo wishes to breakfast with you. He asked me to call all of you to the table as soon as is convenient." From his great height, with a last look at my chest, Giacomo gave me directions to the dining area and left me to wash up, dress, ask Rosa for some makeup assistance, and wake the others.

Half an hour later we walked into the second-floor breakfast room in our original—and somewhat tattered—disguises. Mazzo stood up from the head of the table to greet us, waited until two servants had poured coffee and uncovered silver tureens of pastries and fresh fruit, then sent them away. The Viagra woman was nowhere to be seen, but Mazzo looked as if he hadn't slept at all. You could trace the footprints of a wild night on the skin of his face. The blue tuxedo had been exchanged for a pressed white shirt, open at the collar, and a pair of gray linen pants. His black hair had been combed straight back, and he had water and fruit in front of him. But his eyes said he'd been poisoning himself all night and had barely survived.

As soon as the last servant left the room, closing the door softly behind her, Mazzo walked over to the Pope, took hold of his right hand, and kissed the place where the papal ring would have been. Rosa and I stood just to one side in a little knot of astonishment. "I hope," our host said, "that on top of a lifetime of grievous sins, I have not committed another. I hope my hospitality, such as it is, will to some extent act as a counterweight. Please say you forgive me, Holy Father. Some bizarre intuition must have been acting in me, because when I first met you I thought: He should have been a member of the clergy, a bishop, a cardinal! And then, midway through the party, when I saw you dressed as a king, I suddenly remembered the news stories about your disappearance, and the fact that Rosa had once mentioned something about her husband working at the Vatican, and I realized immediately that you must be—that you *are,* in fact—the Holy Father. Short of ushering you back upstairs and thereby drawing more attention to you, I saw no option but to hope and pray that by some ironic alchemy, the disguise would actually protect you. I spent the rest of the night worrying that someone else would see what I saw ... which, in fact, is precisely what occurred. Clearly," he said, shifting his eyes to me and then back, "you're not being held against your will."

From the moment Mazzo kissed his hand, my cousin had been unfazed. It was almost as if he'd been waiting for the disguise to fail; as if, after years of being instantly recognized, he now simply expected it to happen, goatee and all. "There has been no crime," he said calmly, "no kidnapping. Those reports are false. I simply wanted, for a short while, to experience the delight of being ordinary."

When Mazzo heard that phrase, a youthful smile blossomed on his old man's mouth. The doctored lips stretched tight; the perfect false teeth shone. He seemed less old, less worn, more vibrant. "Those words make me gloriously happy!" he exclaimed. "They confirm my already extremely high opinion of you, Holy Father. When the world learns of this, you'll be even more beloved."

"Or widely hated. I've caused so much worry."

"No, no, you'll be adored, you'll be revered, I'm sure of it," Mazzo beamed. "*The Delight of Being Ordinary!* I can see it as the title of a film made by one of our eminent directors, a film that changes everything, everything! The Pope choosing to act as an ordinary man—it's the height of holiness! In fact, wasn't that Christ's intent, on taking human form? To feel what ordinary people feel? To suffer as we suffer?" Without waiting for an answer, Mazzo turned to Tenzin. "And you, sir, according to the news reports, you must then be His Holiness the Dalai Lama, also partaking in this delight!" He made a deep bow, keeping one spotted hand on the chair for balance. "Didn't Buddha do the same? Wasn't he, in fact, a prince who left his father's palace in order to experience the pains and joys of ordinary life? You see, despite my sins, I know my religious history. How wonderful both of you are! How perfect!"

Mazzo seemed afraid to give either man a chance to speak. He stepped back and motioned to the table. "Sit, please—eat. You must be famished, and annoyed with me. Please sit." He turned. "And you must be Rosa's husband, in a brilliant disguise, absolutely brilliant! A refugee. Homeless. Terrified. Despised. A broken soul—you play the role like a screen icon! Bravo! Of course it's you, a man about whom I've heard so many wonderful things over the years. How fortunate you are to have found such a woman! The Buddha would say it is your excellent karma!" He laughed at himself and shook my hand in a weak grip. "Please, all of you, sit, eat, drink!"

When we were in our places and passing the food, Mazzo joined us at the table and continued his elaborate mea culpa. "One of my more sober guests must have recognized you, Holy Father. I can't guess who it was, but when I saw the police at the door I knew instantly what had happened. I let the officers gaze in at the party for a moment—which, I can assure you, made certain people in that room extremely uncomfortable—and then, when they didn't glimpse their missing Pope, I quickly escorted them back outside, assuring them it would have been absurd for the Pope to visit a tarnished soul like Antonio Mazzo. Why on earth, especially if he'd been abducted, would he come to one of Mazzo's parties—a kind of Sodom and Gomorrah of the Italian countryside? I mounted, if I may say so, a splendid argument . . . it may have been my finest role! The *capitano* in charge—a friend of mine, actually—told me they'd had hundreds of tips just in Padua alone, and that every man and woman on the force was working overtime, all of them hoping to be the hero who finds and rescues our abducted spiritual fathers."

I waited for Mazzo to mention the reward: he could

have made a phone call and collected 5 million euro—no small sum even for a wealthy man. "No one else knows," he went on, "not even Giacomo. But I would advise you all now, with the greatest respect, to leave as soon as you've breakfasted, so that you may continue your adventure undetected. Your car has been brought around front, washed and polished. I've taken the liberty of putting extra clothes in the trunk—bathing suits, hiking gear, something a bit more formal, too. Attire for any possible occasion. For you, Rosa, and for the men. It's the very least I can do to atone for my carelessness. And I've arranged for some fruit and bread and cheese and my own wine to be packaged up in case you fall prey to hunger on the road. If there is anything you need, my Rosa, anything at all, please say the word and I will make it available to you as part of my penance."

Rosa smiled and thanked him profusely. Between bites of food and sips of coffee we all thanked him. I even managed to compliment him on the party.

Mazzo bent his lips inward and lowered his eyes in a gesture of studied modesty. "Besides a week or two on a yacht off Costa Smeralda, these parties are all I have to offer my friends now."

"You have many friends," the Dalai Lama said.

"Yes, Your Holiness, I do. And some of them even like me!" Mazzo laughed at himself, keeping his sad, worn eyes on the Dalai as if asking for a benediction.

The Dalai Lama smiled kindly at him. "To be famous is very hard karma! Many desires will be exhausted in this life for you! You will make great progress!"

"I really hope so, Your Holiness. I hope in my next life I shall be an anonymous monk. A celibate man, fond of fasting and spending long hours in prayer … But not yet!"

Mazzo grinned, stood, wiped his lips delicately with the tips of his fingers, and, leaning with both hands on the back of his chair—a bit unsteadily—addressed the Pope. "Holy Father, tell me, please, that by creating such a spectacle I have not committed another grave sin. I understand the ungodliness of excess, believe me. I have enjoyed decades of such excess, but I meant only to indulge my need to be hospitable. Despite my reputation, I'm actually a reverent man. I—"

"Christians believe," the Pope interrupted him, "that it is the motivation of any particular act that truly matters. Your motivation was generosity, and besides, you did us a great kindness by not turning us in to the police. Say a prayer for yourself, Antonio, and for your guests. And as your penance, make a contribution to the poor equal to the amount spent on your party last night, and I'll leave you with my blessing."

A nod of agreement; another deep bow, to the Pope, to the Dalai Lama; a small wave in my direction; a kiss on both cheeks for my wife; and, repeating aloud the phrase "the delight of being ordinary!" Mazzo turned from us with an elegant spin and performed one last grand exit.

We ate quietly for another few minutes, then gathered things from our rooms and descended the sweeping marble stairs. Giacomo was waiting at the front door with the packages of food. We thanked him. He said, "Signor Mazzo hopes you will be able to attend the winter party, which, if anything, will be even more … elaborate."

With a straight face, Rosa told him we'd be sure to try.

And then we were in our silver-striped Maserati again, heading down the long driveway and out the gates. I glanced in the side mirror, wanting one last glimpse of Mazzo's villa. Beside me, Rosa had a wide grin frozen on her beautiful mouth, and I couldn't hold back any longer. "What's this," I asked quietly across the front seat, "about a kiss?"

My good wife didn't answer that question—not that it deserved an answer. I'm not sure she even heard it, or that anyone else in the car heard it. As we passed through the wrought-iron gates and turned onto a narrow road that was lined on one side by a canal and on the other by a row of eucalyptus trees, I felt a new mood settling around us. Perhaps our immersion in Mazzo's world of artificiality and decadence had worked a kind of magic on the four of us, because there was something different in the air. I'd felt it when I'd gone to awaken them, and now I felt it even more clearly. Antonio Mazzo had earned his fame and fortune by inhabiting roles, by creating a life on the screen that resembled real life but, in fact, wasn't. He understood, in his bones, the reason behind the Pope's and the Dalai Lama's decision to slip away. In the minds of his legions of fans, Mazzo *was* a certain kind of man—a sex symbol, rich, suave, perpetually confident, forever young. But inside that shell of celebrity there lived an actual human being, with actual problems and fears, and it must have been a terrible burden to carry that shell around with him wherever he went. It wasn't so different, in a way, from the celebrity of the Pope and the Dalai Lama. Complete strangers believed they knew who those men were. They felt a kinship, even an intimacy. Maybe the contribution Mazzo was making with his parties, the gift he was giving his friends, was the thing he most desired for himself: the chance to be someone else for a while.

At that moment, the Dalai Lama announced, quietly and almost apologetically, "Today is my birthday."

We cheered at his news and congratulated him, but inside our celebratory voices I sensed another note: we weren't going to be the same when we returned to our places. The Pope would be the Pope and go about his weighty duties, yes; and that would also be true for the Dalai Lama. But I was beginning to see that these few days would leave a mark on them, and also on Rosa and me. Maybe it was the magic of the stage: by pretending for a while, we had learned, at a new and deeper level, how not to pretend.

"I know just the place to celebrate," I said.

"Where?" my famous cousin asked, at first, but then, "No, no, don't say, Paolo. Just take us there. We'll put our fate in God's hands, where it always lies in any case. We'll trust the kidnapper to show you a good birthday, won't we, Tenzin?"

"Yes, yes, of course," the Dalai Lama said. "So far he is been the most excellent kidnapper!"

"I bet I can guess," Rosa told them.

But my cousin said, "No, Rosa. Please don't. Let it be a surprise for my new friend. A birthday gift from our Creator."

35

I'd like to step aside from our story for a short moment here, as we drive away from Mazzo's villa, and explain something that might seem to make little sense to the reader of this account: why Benito Mussolini has found his way so persistently into a story about two holy men.

First of all, I want to make it abundantly clear, if I haven't already, that I do not consider Mussolini in any way a good or admirable man. Because of the cult of violence he fostered in Italy in the 1920s and '30s, my mother's own brother was killed. My father couldn't mention his name without snarling, and their political views—and mine—were, and are, separated from fascism by oceans of compassion and common sense. Nothing would have pleased me more than to be able to write the account of this adventure without once mentioning the name Benito Mussolini. But that would have kept me at arm's length from the truth, and the Pope and the Dalai Lama and Rosa, I know, would not have wanted that.

The truth is that Mussolini's shadow still falls across the people of Italy. Yes, there are some—like the men we saw at Campo Imperatore—who idolize him. That shouldn't be surprising, given the fact that Hitler and Stalin are also still admired in certain small circles. But even many politically moderate Italians will say that before his alliance with Hitler, Il Duce was somewhat of a mixed case. He had his thugs beat, torture, and assassinate opponents, and he instituted insurance programs for widows and orphans. He imposed bitter racial laws but stopped short of sending Jews to the camps. He invaded

Ethiopia—a genocide, really—and brought clean water to Italian towns that hadn't seen it since the Romans. He had his own son-in-law executed for challenging him, and he set up dozens of sanatoria for sick children. He'd throw female admirers to the floor and have sex with them in animalistic fashion, then stand up and serenade them on his violin.

I could go on, but this is a history of four people in the twenty-first century, not all of Italy in the mid-twentieth. Still, Mussolini cast his shadow over those days, that's simply a fact. Part of that shadow had to do with the Pope's bizarre dreams—some sense will be made of them, for some readers at least, a little farther along in this story. Part of it was the fact that before she left college to marry me, Rosa had been majoring in modern Italian history and knew more about Mussolini than about her own grandfathers. Part of it was my own family's sad connections to the war Mussolini had brought to Italy. And part simply the fact that our story involved the Italian countryside, and it's all but impossible to travel in Italy without touching places on the map that were touched by Il Duce during his twenty-two years on the Italian stage.

That was especially true of our last full day of travel, a day that took us past Salò, at the southern tip of Lago di Garda, and then to Mezzegra.

I didn't plan that route because it more or less followed the route of Il Duce's last days. It was merely a coincidence—if coincidences actually exist (and after this trip I'm not so sure). I wanted, for whatever reason, to show the Dalai Lama the beautiful place where I was raised. I wanted to end our adventure there. Yes, I knew my cousin had been dreaming of mountains and Mussolini, and I'm sure that was on my mind at some level as I steered the Maserati north and west. But I wasn't a believer in dreams and signs then. I told myself I was just an Italian Catholic trying to be a good host, hoping to show a visiting Buddhist a place I thought he'd enjoy on his birthday. Consciously or otherwise, I had no idea what awaited us.

36

If you drive the Autostrada—Italy's version of the Autobahn, a three-lane racetrack with exorbitant tolls—you can make it from Padua to Lake Como in under three hours. But with its surveillance cameras and police checkpoints, the Autostrada was a prescription for capture on that day, and we weren't yet ready to be captured. The Pope and the Dalai Lama had their odd dreams to pursue; Rosa loved risk so much that she could have gone on and on for months, spiriting the holy men across Europe, inventing new disguises, calling on wealthy friends to lend us a different sports car or rooms in their various villas for a night. And I didn't want it to end yet, either. I didn't know why. Because I was finally starting to let myself relax and enjoy the company, maybe. Or maybe for more mysterious reasons.

In any case, eschewing the highway, we zigzagged across northern Italy on two-lane back roads—consulting a map we'd purchased when we stopped for gas—following my country's famously misleading signs, and slipping through places like San Bonifacio and San Gioannino, forgotten little hamlets that sleep in ancient pastures far from the world's sophistication and frenzy. Still, even passing through such places, and even traveling on those country roads, it wasn't hard to sense that the search had entered a new and more desperate phase. Accounts of the holy men's disappearance were on the TV when we stopped for coffee, on every single radio station we tried; the gas-station attendant who took our payment—in cash, from Rosa—was talking about it with his other customers, arguing about the authenticity of the recording, speculating on a motive, spreading rumors and half truths that she was in no position to dispute. Twice, when we were close to the Autostrada, we heard army and press helicopters thumping overhead, and it seemed we couldn't go ten minutes without seeing a phalanx of military trucks or police vehicles racing in the other direction. "There are thousands of Maseratis in Italy," Rosa said, with her typical optimism. "Even if Tara did turn us in, and I have my doubts that she did, it will take them a while to find us."

"I hope so," I said. "I hope God gives us a little more time together."

She stared across the leather front seat. "*That's* the man I married."

A glance in the mirror told me that our captives were buried in prayer. Each of them had a string of beads in his hands. Eyes closed. Lips working. It seemed to me that they filled every empty minute that way, checking in with God, or the Divine Intelligence, the way teenagers check in with friends on the newest electronic device. I wondered if the God who presided over the universes would, on Judgment Day, make any distinction at all between our captives. It occurred to me that, before I'd gotten to know the Dalai Lama, he'd been just another figure in the news—kinder and more compassionate than other celebrities, yes, but somehow, for me, not a person who fit in with my view of faith and meaning, not quite on the level of the Pope. Glancing back again at the two of them—so similar in their devotion—I could feel how much of that old prejudice had eroded.

In order not to disturb them, Rosa and I abandoned the radio and spoke in the quietest of tones.

"If we keep going this way, we'll pass right by the southern tip of Lago di Garda," she said, looking down at the map spread across her thighs.

"I know it."

"Close to Salò."

"Right. My parents took me there once. One of our road trips."

"Should we go there for lunch?"

"Too risky."

"Everything's risky now, *amore* . . . unless we go up into the mountains and camp."

"That's not an option, Rosa. I've now officially entered the post-camping stage of my life."

She laughed in a way I remembered from years before: tender and warm, the laugh of a lover.

"I'm a mattress man from here on in."

"Where, then?"

"I want the Dalai to see Lake Como."

"I *knew* that was what you had in mind. I remember the first time you took me there. I remember sitting out on the concrete patio and looking down at the lake at sunset. I remember those beautiful green hills on the far bank, and the mountains behind the hills, the way they went from gray to pink for a few minutes just as the sun was setting. I'll remember it as long as I live. I wish you still owned that house, Paolo. Anna Lisa and Piero could take their child there for vacations."

I grunted, remembering, too.

Rosa was quiet for a bit. We saw a turn for Salò—the town where, after the daring rescue at Campo Imperatore and on Hitler's orders, Mussolini had set up his absurd "Social Republic." He'd presided there for the better part of two years as, death by death, Italy was reclaimed from its Nazi occupiers. Salò was the place from which he fled at the end, in the spring of 1945. His final road trip. He was finished by then, a wounded rabbit chased by hounds. Still, he took his young mistress with him, and millions in cash and gold, as if he actually believed he deserved those things—a younger woman, a lavish life in exile. As if he imagined another chance for himself, a palace in Switzerland, a castle in Bavaria.

"You wanted to be a photographer in those days, remember?" Rosa said.

"Yes."

"What happened to that idea, *amore*?"

"I didn't have my parents' courage or talent. I was afraid. I opted for the security of a travel business. Ha!"

Silence from her side of the car. The stink of old regrets between us. Another few miles and the Dalai Lama opened his eyes and said, in an unusually authoritarian tone, "Go someplace now to rest for lunch, Paolo!" It was the first time he'd called me by name, and the first and only time, in those days together, that he issued what sounded like an order. I pulled into a gravel turnout—

larger, easier to hide in, no prostitute this time—and not a minute later a police car sped past, lights flashing.

"Chasing for us, maybe," the Dalai Lama said.

"Maybe."

"Long time ago the Chinese chasing for me. I'm in disguise then, too."

"The world is grateful they didn't catch you, Tenzin," the Pope said.

But the Dalai Lama didn't seem to hear, which was strange for a man who was always so present. "Going because of a dream that time, too," he said. We'd gotten out of the car by then, and he was staring across the road at an abandoned building—an old stable, it looked like—with vines crisscrossing the brown stone walls.

"Is it true what Mazzo said about the Buddha?" my cousin asked, as we were opening the bottle of wine and the packages of food. It was another al fresco feast. Never in the history of the world had holy men eaten more meals from the polished hood of a Maserati. "Was he really the son of a king? That is so different from Christ's humble origins."

The Dalai Lama nodded, accepted some cheese, shook his head when Rosa offered wine. "The stories say so, yes. His father tried to keep from him the difficult parts in life—to be sick, to be old, to die. But one day the Buddha go out and he see those things, and that day he decide to go into the forest with the ascetics. 'Ascetics' is right word, yes?"

"Yes."

"For a long time he doesn't eat, he doesn't sleep, he almost die. Then he decides for the middle way: enough food and sleep to live, but not too much. In the legends he says is important to be like the string on the lute: too tight, sound no good; too loose, sound no good also. Middle way works."

"I like that man," Rosa said.

"There's a famous passage in Scripture that's similar," the Pope said, "where Jesus is quoted as saying, 'For John the Baptist came neither eating bread nor drinking wine, and you say, "He has a demon." The Son of Man has come eating and drinking and you say, "He is a glutton and a drunkard."'"

"I know this John Baptist?"

"Yes, Jesus's cousin," the Pope said. "A special relationship in Scripture."

We left the discussion there and took our nourishment.

37

Once, in the days when I still had my travel business in Rome, I saw on my office TV an interview with a famous American writer. He was an essayist, primarily, someone who'd traveled to eighty-five countries and all seven continents, and who'd written about everything from cooking classes to correctional facilities. At one point during the interview the host asked, "What's the most beautiful place you've ever been?" (a typically Italian question)— and without having to think about his answer for even a second, the writer said, "Lake Como."

I don't know that it's the most beautiful place on earth. I don't know that a question like that even makes any real sense, other than as a way to fill airtime. But I do know that my parents, who were people with a sensitive aesthetic radar, and widely traveled, chose to buy a house on a hillside overlooking Lake Como's western shore and to spend the last two-thirds of their lives there, when they could have lived and worked almost anywhere on earth. Part of their choice could be attributed to my father's Italian-American heritage, and part to my mother's love of all things European. But the main part was something else—the beauty, yes, but also the feeling evoked by that beauty, a feeling essential to every artist, and every monk, too: the understanding of what a gift it is to be alive.

As we went along, Rosa offered historical commentary. "This route we're taking now," she said over her shoulder, "west from the southern tip of Lake Garda, is close to the route Mussolini took on the last days of his life."

"It's always surprised me, Rosa," the Pope said, "that a gentle soul like you would choose to study such a man."

I coughed.

"It's what brought Paolo and me together. Did we ever tell you that?"

"Never."

"I wanted to take a trip before I started my senior year in college, and I walked into his travel shop. Instead of giving me information on cheap hotels in Switzerland, he started making small talk, asking me what I was studying. 'History,' I told him. 'Really?' he said, 'What kind of history? What era?' 'World War II Italian history,' I said. 'Mussolini, to be exact.' 'Oh,' he said, 'my mother's brother was killed by Mussolini.' I was sure he was making it all up, you know, but I decided he had a cute face, and that he seemed harmless. And believe me, cute and harmless was rare in the men I'd known to that point in my life. So when he asked me to dinner I said yes, and that was the start of things. I never went back to college at all."

"That is love," the Dalai Lama said. "That is small kind of the big love we can have for humanity."

"It wasn't that small, actually," Rosa said.

In the awkward pause that followed, I did what I often do in those situations: I searched for something, anything, that I might say. "Rosa is superstitious," was what emerged, but those words were greeted only by a terrible silence. I wasn't even sure what I'd meant—or what *she'd* meant. The remark had come from the same general part of my brain as the famous "Are you going to baptize the child?" I offer no excuse, only that I was trying, in my own clumsy way, to smooth over an awkward moment. Rosa *was* superstitious, and from a superstitious people. The Pope's dreams, and then the visit to Campo Imperatore, and now the proximity to Salò and the fact that what might be our last day was apparently going to be close to the route of Mussolini's last day . . . well, it wasn't hard for me to see how all that might make for a resonance in my wife's mind. So I'd said "Rosa is superstitious" not to demean her, but just because there was an obvious linkage.

In my mind, at least.

Rosa was squeezing her hands together in the front seat. "What does that have to do with anything, Paolo?" she said, as if she wanted to say something else.

"Nothing. Sorry. I like it when you talk about history. It reminds me of—"

"But what does it have to do with being superstitious?"

"Nothing, Rosa. I'm trying to watch the road now, that's all. I keep looking in the mirror for police cars. I'm a bit on edge. Let's focus on the scenery."

"You were looking for a fight."

"Honestly and truly I was not."

"Yes you were, admit it."

"I was not. I will not. You're too sensitive."

"And you're too insensitive!"

We fell into one of our bad silences. I stared at the scenery, tried to concentrate on the pleasure of coming home. I could hear my wife breathing through her nose.

Lake Como is shaped like a wobbly upside-down Y, with the stem of the letter pointing north. As we drove past the city of Como's small harbor, the lake came into view, its narrow western branch sparkling like sapphire in the warm afternoon. Steep green hills rose to either side of it, folding over and against each other, with shadows in the valleys, and evidence of humanity—stone houses, tile roofs, the bell towers of churches—showing themselves in clusters here and there. In a moment, over the tops of those hills, we saw the faces of much taller mountains to the northeast—the peaks stand at 2,600 meters there— the same stony cliffs Rosa had seen turn pink at sunset so many years before.

"Beyond those mountains is the Valtellina," Rosa said to the men in back. "That was the place Mussolini swore he'd make his last stand. In this city, Como, on his next-to-last day, he waited for the thousands of fascists who were supposed to join him. They were going to fight to the death in the Valtellina, supposedly. But when the courier finally arrived, he had exactly twelve fascists with him, twelve men willing to die for the cause. So Mussolini decided to make a run for the Swiss border . . . which is probably what he intended to do anyway, the *bastardo*." She paused a second or two, and then: "Was that 'superstitious,' Paolo?"

"On his part, probably. On yours, no."

We curled deeper into the city and the view opened up.

"Ah, tremendous!" the Dalai Lama exclaimed. "Ah, very beautiful!"

"Italy's birthday gift to you," I said, rather grandiosely. But I couldn't help myself. Whatever disappointments and sorrows had touched my life since then, my years at Lago di Como had been marked by contentment and warmth. I had been happy there, and loved, and my early life had been rich with promise. The contentment had faded, the promise was never fulfilled; but I still associated this lake with a better Paolo dePadova. As we left the city and followed the *statale*—the state road—that wound through the western shore's small towns, a battalion of pleasant memories slipped out like partisans from the stony alleys and saluted me. On that hot July afternoon, driving along that familiar road, I felt for some reason that I might be given another chance at wholeness.

I'm sure that as we went through the small villages of Cernobbio and Argegno, dodging the tour buses and delivery trucks that roared south in the opposite lane, we all expected, at any moment, to be caught. The view softened that worry. Turn by turn the lake offered different views of itself, hiding behind a hillside tunnel for a kilometer, then bursting into sight again, opening out, glistening its magnificent blue. Two passenger ferries churned across ahead of us, one headed east, one west. Here and there white specks of sailboats bobbed and glided.

"I just opened a new shop near here, in Menaggio," Rosa said as we twisted and turned through the town where George Clooney—another artist who could have lived anywhere on earth—made his home. "We could have another go at fixing the disguises."

But nobody wanted that. My coloring was faded and splotched, the hair losing its curl. The Dalai Lama had kept his toupee and sunglasses in place, and the Pope still wore his facial hair. The holy men weren't recognizable—I was fairly sure of that—but the heat and travel had taken a toll on Mario's work. We were three tattered men, halfway back to our former selves.

Just past Lenno, with the water close by on our right and the lime and emerald hillsides seeming to lift themselves right up from the edges of the road to our left, we came upon the village of Mezzegra. Hardly anything had changed there in the past twenty years, and not so much even since the April day in 1945 when Il Duce had been machine-gunned to death by Communist partisans a few hundred meters up in the hills. The town center was still only a cluster of stucco-sided commercial buildings pressed tight against the two-lane road. A market, a fruit store, a café, two bars. The growl and buzz of *motorini* engines echoed in the alleys. Light-haired, neatly dressed tourists—German or Dutch, I guessed—stepped down from a blue tour bus, single-file, and huddled on a corner, awaiting guidance. A little ways beyond them, opposite the place where my mother used to make her daring leaps, I turned left. The road climbed due west, steep and unlined, modest houses to either side with fenced-in yards, a dog or two, a few chickens and goats. Up and up we went. In front of a brick home with a patio facing the lake, I pulled to the side of the road and idled the car for a minute. A Danish couple had bought it as a vacation place, but there was no sign of life there now, not so much as a shirt drying on the clothesline or a pile of child's toys on the grass. Across my inner eye flashed the image of a man and woman standing there, side by side. They were watching me, it seemed, studying me, seeing me through the curtain of death that separated us. "We raised you to be free," they seemed to be saying. "Are you free, Paolo? Are you happy?"

"Almost," I answered quietly.

I started forward again. Soon we came to a T. I turned left, riding parallel to the shore, and after another minute pulled the Maserati into a four-space parking area next to a church of white stucco with a gray stone bell tower.

"The Church of Sant'Abbondio," I said, in a tour guide's voice. "I was baptized here. I thought we could go in and say a prayer and then find a place to celebrate in earnest."

"A prayer of being grateful to be alive," the Dalai Lama said. "On this day."

As we walked across the gravel, Rosa put her hand on the small of my back for exactly two seconds. I knew it was her way of apologizing for snapping at me in the car, and I was trying to think of a way to explain the "superstitious" remark in ten words or less when I decided it was better, for once, to say nothing, rather than take another bite from my shoe. I'd pray for wisdom and patience. I'd try to be a better man.

The door was unlocked—as is often the case in Italian places of worship—the church's interior lit only by sunlight bleeding through colored glass. The pews were of dark wood—only a few rows of them with folding chairs behind. Those pews and chairs, the square columns along the side aisles and the white arch over the altar, marble floors, marble saints along the walls—all of this was exceedingly humble by the standards of Italian ecclesiastical décor, and all of it completely familiar to me. Freethinkers in most respects, my mother and father had remained devout Catholics until their final hour. This little church had been a way for them—eccentrics and artists—to fit themselves into the community, and the Catholic faith had given them solid footing in a life riven with unpredictability. When would the next print or painting sell? For how much? I had another vision then—of our blessed friend and parish priest, Don Claudio—"Doncla," everyone called him—standing at the altar, raising the host.

Perhaps because we'd spent so much time together, the four of us wandered the side aisles separately, then sat in different pews.

I sent warm thoughts to Anna Lisa and Piero, tried not to worry about our daughter's health, about the kind of world our grandchild would inherit, tried not to think about any disappointment my mother and father might have carried to the grave or be holding on to in some limbo for disgruntled parents. The only son of artists, a failed travel agent now, separated from his wife, rescued from unemployment by his famous older cousin. It wasn't exactly a résumé to make a mother and father proud.

From that happy thought, my mind leapt and skittered. I grew restless. Something was nagging at me, some internal itch. I stood and stepped out quietly into the late-afternoon sun. Just then a very old man walked past, leaning on his cane. Our eyes met, and we held each other's gaze for two seconds before he went on his way. A few steps more and he turned and looked over his shoulder, trying to see backward through time, maybe thinking he recognized the nose and eyes of the boy who used to stand outside this church with his parents on a Sunday morning after Mass, looking down at the lake and imagining a happy future for himself.

38

Among the descriptive terms that should never be applied to me, "athletic" and "coordinated" would be at the very top of the list. I tried as a youth, truly I did. I spent many hours watching soccer on TV, kicking a ball back and forth in our yard, playing informal matches with my school friends. Nothing good ever came of it. I tripped over myself, let easy passes roll by my feet, missed goals from close range, and generally made such a mess of even something as simple as running a lap around the field that, unlike most people I know, I was actually relieved to grow too old to be asked to play. Still, *calcio,* as we call it, is our national sport, and I've always secretly held to the hope that one day, by some miracle, I'll be able to kick a soccer ball in a neat, curving arc into a net. Like Pirlo, like Cannavaro, like the great Roberto Baggio, Italy's most famous Buddhist. Even a net with no goalie defending it would do.

Set at a level a few yards below the Church of Sant'Abbondio was a soccer field where I'd played among friends as a boy. On an optimistic impulse, and hoping to clear my thoughts, I grabbed Piero's black-and-white ball from the Maserati's trunk and walked downhill a few steps to the chain-link gate. Let the others pray, I thought; I'm going to conquer old demons.

It was not to be. The field—cut into the east-facing hillside and surrounded by a tall fence—was empty. Good thing, too. No witnesses. I set the ball on the turf and tried to jog slowly forward, kicking it gently from foot to foot as I'd seen my heroes do. But my first kick was too hard. The ball got away from me, rolled down the slope, and came to rest against the base of the fence. I retrieved it and tried again, but this time I didn't kick hard enough, tripped over the ball, and fell to one knee. I gave up on the dribbling idea and tried a straightforward shot from ten meters in front of the goal. The ball stayed stubbornly on the ground, banged into the goalpost, skipped sideways, and sat there like a disobedient puppy, mocking me. I ran over and blasted it into the net—impossible, even for me, to miss from that distance.

But trying to take the ball out of the back of the net, I somehow became entangled in the ropes. My left shoe had gotten caught. I sat down to free it and heard, *"Amore?"* in a worried voice. "Are you all right?"

"Fine, I'm fine," I called back grimly.

There, walking onto the field, were my three companions, refreshed from their prayers, eager for some exercise.

"Kick it here, cousin!" the Pope yelled. Still entangled, I grabbed the ball with one hand and shoved it out to him.

The Pope tipped it expertly over to the Dalai Lama, who sent a hard shot soaring into the top of the net.

It dropped down beside me. I shoved it back out, managed at last to free myself, stood up, and jogged a few clumsy steps just in time to miss Rosa's pass. The ball rolled down to the fence again. Rosa was laughing, not in a mean way, but still . . .

"Here, to me!" the Dalai called.

"Let's have a two-on-two."

I hustled after the ball, thinking: Let's make it fair, three on my side.

We started up a harmless little game, sweating and laughing in the late-afternoon sun. My cousin Giorgio stood in goal, Tenzin and Rosa took turns shooting. I was the self-appointed fetcher of errant shots, a task I accomplished without falling. I was enjoying myself; we all were. In fact, the truth is that from those days together, the one image I cherish most is a scene of the Pope standing on the goal line in his tattered disguise, wearing loose pants and a short-sleeve shirt from Mazzo's storehouse, hands on knees, awaiting a shot from the Dalai Lama—who had a look of fierce concentration on his face and a striped dress shirt on his upper body—with Rosa clapping happily to one side.

During these festivities I was vaguely aware that a group of other players had taken possession of the goal at the other end of the field. I glanced at them twice as I fetched. For some reason—and this might seem perplexing to non-Italians—I thought they were Gypsies. "Romany" is the polite term; *zingari,* the word in my language. One often saw them in my country—sometimes in large encampments outside cities; more often in less flattering poses, begging in front of churches, or rushing up close to tourists near the Colosseum or Forum and distracting them with a photo or magazine page while a colleague reached for an unguarded wallet.

Our fellow soccer players made an unusual group. One of the men—stout and tanned—wore a maroon robe not unlike the Dalai Lama's and ran around kicking the ball with great gusto and some skill, laughing as if he'd had too much wine at lunch. Another man—taller, with a small pot of belly and very short hair—was playing goal. Though her hair was light-colored, the older of the two women must have been the reason for my first impression, because she wore the type of ankle-length skirt favored by Romany females and had a colorful scarf tied around her hair. There was a black-haired girl, too, and an athletic younger woman about Anna Lisa's age.

I did notice—hard not to—that they were having as much fun as we were. There were shouts and laughter and then, in American English: "And a beautiful corner kick, right on goal! Ringling with the save!"

Ringling, I thought: they were part of a circus act, then. So much for the Romany idea.

Rosa dribbled in and fired a shot off the Pope's right thigh. He made a sound like "Oof!" but seemed unhurt. I trotted over to fetch and, turning, noticed the ball from the other group bounding down the field toward us. My first thought was: Someone else is as inaccurate as I am, but kicks harder.

The young black-haired girl—eight or ten years old, I guessed—came running after the bouncing ball. I went over, expecting only to help her—and after that moment nothing would ever be the same for any of us.

39

Her ball had come to rest a few meters away from us, near one corner of the field. I jogged over and—God knows why I had an urge to show off for a ten-year-old stranger—instead of picking it up and carrying it to her, I tried a deft little kick. My idea was to lead her with a soft pass, something professional players did with a tap of the instep. Miracle of miracles, it actually worked: the ball went skimming across the grass in a neat line aimed just in front of her. The girl saw me kick it, I'm sure she did, and she must have seen the ball coming toward her. But she ignored it. I was mildly offended. As the ball rolled past, she stopped running and walked straight at the long-haired South Asian tourist in the striped shirt, halted just before reaching him, put her hands together palm-to-palm in front of her chest, and bowed deeply from the waist. Reflexively, it seemed, the Dalai Lama bowed back.

My first instinct, also reflexive, was to turn and look up at the street to see if anyone else was watching. No one there. The only people who'd seen the exchange of bows were Rosa and I (the Pope had leaned over and was rubbing his bruised quadriceps). She met my eyes and made a classic Italian expression—lips flexed, ends of the mouth turned down, eyebrows lifted. In English it might be translated as "So there you have it" or "Well, how about that?!" or "Hmm!"

I would have tried to make sense of what I'd seen, but I didn't really have time to process the moment, because the bizarre circus troupe at the other end of the field was coming toward us en masse. For a moment I had the horrible thought that they were going to suggest a pickup game—I was planning to plead a pulled hamstring and offer to referee—but the Dalai Lama and the girl were involved in an animated conversation, in English, and the Pope was walking over to them, curious. The girl's bow seemed to have taken the disparate movements at both ends of the field and united them into one calm group. There was nothing to do but join in and fake some introductions.

They proved, however, unfakeable. Somehow, mysteriously, the girl had known exactly who she was honoring with her bow, and when my cousin held out his hand and introduced himself as "Francis," all hope of throwing up a smoke screen was lost. The Gypsies or the circus troupe or whoever they were, now in the presence of the famously missing holy ones, seemed surprisingly unsurprised. I shook hands all around, forgot every name instantly, and waited for the acrobats to ask for autographs or tell the twenty-five-year-old to get on her cell phone, quick, and turn us in for the reward.

Instead, the bald, stocky, brown-skinned man—why was he dressed like a monk on a soccer field, and why was he so effervescent?—pronounced these memorable words in troubled English: "We been waiting for you three days now! We founded the person you looking for!" And the house of sanity and logic in which I'd lived to that point in my life fell to pieces.

40

Before any other confusing and disturbing things could be said, the black-haired girl took the Dalai Lama by one hand and began leading him, with some urgency and without any resistance from him, back up toward the road. The Pope and the red-robed man fell into step with them, a few paces behind. The three women followed—I could tell they were trying to communicate in at least two languages—and the short-haired man and I, each carrying a soccer ball and a belly, brought up the rear.

"You must be the kidnapper," he said in pure American English, the tone wry and unthreatening.

"Hardly. The Pope's my cousin. He had the completely innocent wish for a few days off, incognito. The Dalai Lama was visiting and came along, that's all. From that one harmless impulse all kinds of trouble seems to have grown. We're not quite ready to go back, but you can turn us in and get the reward if you like."

"Not looking for that," he said. The man had a kind laugh, and seemed genuinely uninterested in money.

"Five million euro?"

He shrugged.

"You're American, aren't you?"

"Yes."

"A circus troupe?"

Another friendly chuckle. "Sometimes I feel like we should be. I have the name for it—Ringling—but it's a common enough name where I come from."

"Where's that?" By this point we'd reached the road and turned left, away from Sant' Abbondio, away from the car.

"North Dakota, originally," he said. And then: "We're here on account of my sister's mystical visions."

This last comment was spoken casually, lightly, in the way someone else might have said, "We're here on vacation," or "We're here for the wedding of a friend's son." But at the sound of the words "mystical visions" I felt as though an ice cube had been placed against the base of my spine. I shook my head to chase away a passing dizziness. I worried I'd caught the flu from one of the guests at Mazzo's party. The fake prostitutes had probably breathed on me. I suddenly wanted to change the subject, to tell my new friend I needed to go and get the car, or put the soccer ball back in the trunk. But the parade had turned left, so I followed dutifully and said nothing.

Ringling pointed ahead of us. "That's my sister there, the middle-aged blond beauty in the long dress. Cecelia. And she's married to Volya Rinpoche—the strong bald guy in the red robe, a famous Buddhist teacher. Have you heard of him?"

"No."

"Well, I'm sure the Dalai Lama knows him, or at least knows of him. Their child is the lovely creature who's holding the Dalai Lama's hand and prancing. Shelsa is her name. My beloved niece. In certain circles, she's thought to be some kind of holy child or prophet, and she was told, by another famous Buddhist teacher, that another special child had been born in the Italian mountains and that we should go find him. Which, at last, after a trip across the Atlantic, a long stretch of searching in various places, and some unbelievably terrifying moments, we have done. It looks like we're taking you to meet him now."

With each sentence in this confounding history I felt

as though another cube of ice had been set in place on my spine, a cold line of influenza moving up the vertebrae one by one, hip to neck. The illness could very well have been psychosomatic, because I didn't like this kind of talk. The Pope's dreams. The Dalai Lama's oracle. Famous Buddhist teachers telling a family to go to Italy and find a "special child." I don't mind saying now that it threatened me at some deep level. Almost repulsed me. It wasn't my cup of tea at all.

"Not your cup of tea, I'm guessing," Ringling said, just as I was thinking that, and a last cube was set at the base of my neck; another shiver went through me. I felt my forehead for a fever. When I didn't answer, he added, "Brace yourself, then. The woman who owns the house we're going to—we've been there four days, welcome guests, it seems, though she didn't know us from Adam—is an interesting old character. Uneducated, half her teeth gone, but very kind and wise, and she seems to know things she shouldn't know."

"For instance?"

"For instance, she set four extra places at the table an hour ago, before we left her to go and kick the soccer ball around. We asked her about it and she wouldn't answer."

"And the boy? Does he seem . . . different?"

Ringling lifted his chin toward the happy dark-haired girl. "He's like Shelsa. Ninety-nine percent of the time just a kid."

"And then?"

"And then, well, and then he'll do something a three-year-old shouldn't be able to do. He'll say, "The bells will ring now, Mommy," ten seconds before the church bells ring. Or he'll look at you in a certain way, it's hard to explain, but it's not a child's look. You'll see. Just watch the two of them carefully, then tell me if you think we're all crazy. Your English is perfect, by the way. Tiny accent but really perfect."

"Thanks," I said, and then, only to be polite in return: "What's the boy's name?" I asked. I thought it was all crazy, of course I did. From the moment I'd heard the Pope tell me about his dreams I'd thought it was crazy, but I'd wanted to humor him; it was a rare vacation for him, after all, and the last thing he needed was cynical commentary from a sinner like me. By that point, a bit out of breath from the climb, I had little faith in Ringling as a rational man, though he was out of breath, too, and seemed to have a sense of humor, so I liked him well enough. In answer to my question about the name, I thought he'd say "Jesus" or "John the Baptist" or maybe "Benito"—to complete the absurdity of the day—but he said, "Tom. His mother's American, father was Italian."

"Opposite of my situation."

"'Tommaso,' I think, is the actual name, but everyone calls him Tom when we're around."

It wasn't until we'd gone another thirty steps, yours truly carrying his disbelief like a fifty-pound stone inside the soccer ball, that I remembered Thomas was the name of the disciple who doubted Christ's resurrection and demanded proof. Christ let him put his fingers into the crucifixion wounds, and only then did his doubts finally disappear. I shivered, thinking of it.

From that moment on I was two people. There was the frozen-spine man, my insides reacting to the things Ringling was telling me as if they might be true. And then there was what I thought of as my "real self" or "regular self," which wanted to get into the car, drive until I found a nice place to have dinner, drink a good bottle of Barolo, and go to bed.

"I know how all this sounds, believe me," Ringling went on. "I'd advise you to withhold judgment for a while. We're past the dangerous part of the trip, I believe."

"That's comforting," I almost said.

As our ragged group turned from the paved road onto a smaller road—little more than a gravel path, really, with a grass stripe down its center, I started to feel slightly unsteady on my feet. I stopped, turned, and gazed below me at the magnificent blue lake set like a gem in its ring of mountains, a sight that had always soothed me.

"There's nothing to be afraid of, now, really," Ringling remarked. "We're basically normal."

"Not afraid," I said. "Just need a minute."

He laughed, said, "I needed about eight years," and we continued along the path to the place where the peculiar dreams of two holy men seemed to have led us.

41

Tucked away at the end of the dirt track, invisible until you were almost upon it, the house was a dignified but weathered structure, something straight out of nineteenth-century rural Italy, with walls of uneven brown stones, a roof of cracked and chipped red tiles, a second-floor turret that—I guessed—offered a view down onto the lake, and a large stone barn behind. Instead of going in through the main door, the black-haired girl led us along one side of the farmhouse and around a corner, past the entrance to the barn, past a grape arbor and a garden with staked tomato and pepper plants, to a flat piece of lawn on the south side of the house. A long table had been set up there—white cloth, wineglasses, flower-patterned ceramic plates—and the apparent hostess, a semi-toothless, short, thickly built woman, introduced herself as Agnese and greeted us as if we were cousins. There was no child that I could see, but from the garden came another woman, thirtyish and very calm, who said a few words of welcome to us in American-accented Italian and then English. She had a pretty, angular face straight out of a painting—Bellini, maybe—that you'd see in the Vatican museums. When I asked her how she'd come to live in Italy, she smiled mysteriously and changed the subject. I was in the grasp of a full chill by then, almost shivering, clearly unwell. Or at least that's what I told myself.

There was an abundance of strangeness to that summer evening in the hills, but the strangest part of all was the absolute matter-of-factness with which the Pope and the Dalai Lama were welcomed. A warm greeting, yes. Friendly. But matter-of-fact in the extreme. Neither of them made any attempt to pretend they were anyone but who they were, and they were treated with the appropriate respect. At the same time, though, no great fuss was made over them, no elaborate bows, no excited gasps or shocked faces. No one mentioned the headlines, the frantic search, or the reward. Agnese offered them cold drinks with a courteous familiarity I'd never quite encountered before, a perfect balance of reverence and ease, as if the Dalai Lama and the Pope of Rome had been guests in her old house scores of times in the years she'd lived there. It seemed that, at last, the two men had gotten what they wanted: they were ordinary.

I could smell food cooking and discovered, suddenly, that the chill I'd felt while Ringling was telling his odd tale had all but disappeared. Not the flu, after all. But I was ravenously hungry. It occurred to me that we hadn't had a true meal, a true Italian feast, for the whole of our trip. How had I allowed that to happen? Agnese guided us into the house to wash up in the bathrooms there. As we emerged and moved, in a loose herd, toward our designated places at the table, Rosa sidled over to me and whispered, "Something's very different here, *amore,* no?"

I answered with a short nod, then, without planning to, held the chair for her as she sat, a gentlemanly gesture she liked, and one I hadn't offered in at least a decade. My eyes swept the scene, looking for I don't know what—angels, demons, a child who resembled Christ—though, really, who knew what Christ had actually looked like? My cousin and the Dalai Lama were seated opposite us, the stocky, red-robed monk between them, the others spread out to either end. I noticed, with a bit of surprise, that the mysterious thirty-year-old American woman was given the seat at the head of the table. Agnese's visiting daughter, I guessed—though they bore no resemblance to each other, and one was clearly a native English speaker, the other Italian.

I heard a screen door slap shut, and saw a light-haired boy come toddling across the grass on chubby legs. He was three or four years old, barefoot, dressed in stained gray shorts and a white T-shirt with *PACE*—peace—written on its front in large letters. He churned his way toward the head of the table and leapt onto the woman's lap like a koala. His blond mane against her long black tresses, his round face against her angular one—it seemed impossible that she could have borne him, but she held him tenderly and smoothed the hair off his face in the way a mother would.

"*Di hello, Tommaso,*" she said. Say hello, Thomas.

The boy refused with a pout and an exaggerated shake of his head. His eyes were coffee brown. They made a slow circuit of the table, then fixed themselves on the Pope with an unblinking intensity you'd expect to see from a champion chess player studying his king. The Pope stared back for a second, then grinned. The boy laughed and was a boy again, and then Agnese carried out a large plate of melon slices wrapped in prosciutto—the opening salvo in a fusillade of food.

Before we started eating, the woman at the head of the table asked us to bow our heads in prayer. I expected the typical Catholic grace—"Bless us, O Lord, and these thy gifts . . ."—but all she said was, "Great Father and Mother who give us life, help us not to be afraid."

"Amen!" Rosa said, with a bit too much exuberance.

"Amen!" the little boy yelled, mimicking her, and then bursting into an infectious laugh. Everyone at the table grinned.

What has happened to me all my life when I've been upset or anxious is that I eat like a man who's been denied food for five days. This gluttony causes my manners to suffer; it isn't a pretty sight. I consume twice or even three times as much food as I should, and I do it with a single-minded ferocity that has something in common with a starving jungle animal over recently killed prey. That was the way I ate at Agnese's house on that hot evening. Whatever was served—the prosciutto and melon, the mozzarella balls rolled in spinach and basil, the sardines lightly dusted in flour and fried, the white beans in oil, the grilled eggplant—I waited to see that those around me had been served, and then I took everything that was left. Everything. All of it. At one point, when the girl about Anna Lisa's age—Ringling's daughter, it appeared—and Agnese had brought to the table platters of fried lake fish in a gorgonzola sauce, I took three of them—they really weren't that large—and happened to look at my wife. She was staring at me, her eyes full of what must be called pity. *"Che cavalo fai?"* she mouthed. What the hell are you doing? I simply turned back to the food. I didn't know what I was doing. It was a reflex, deep beyond subconscious. I would have needed a decade of therapy to answer the question in any truthful way.

I ate, yes. I enjoyed Agnese's food thoroughly—after the fish came squash ravioli in a sage and butter sauce, then pork in a light tomato cream sauce, then a bit of seasoned polenta—small course after small, succulent course. As I ate I watched, and when she wasn't sending her disdain in my direction I could feel Rosa watching, too. If Mazzo's party had been an exercise in ego, then this gathering was humanity's opposite pole. Small conversations flared, merged, and separated again. Ringling filled us in on the circus troupe's strange journey: they'd been led across the ocean (on the *Queen Mary,* no less) by signs, symbols, dreams, visions, wise women speaking vague instructions in four languages—the kinds of things that made me shiver again . . . and want to eat. Someone, he said, had tried to harm his young niece, but he offered no details. His daughter, hearing that Anna Lisa was pregnant, asked how old she was, and when I told her, she said, "See, Dad, I'm ready." The man across from me—"Rinpoche," they called him—laughed and chuckled almost constantly, made goofy faces at the boy and the girl, spooned food onto the Pope's plate as if trying to fatten him. But—how can I describe this?—while there were distinct person-alities at that table, there was also a certain *smallness* to everyone there. Rather than being separate and superior, controllers of all they could see, the humans in that group fit in with the surrounding trees, the farmhouse walls, the grass and grape arbor. No one took over the conversation. No one was obnoxious or loud or hiding behind a fake personality. The boy and girl—Tommaso and Shelsa—were happy and peculiarly well behaved, but otherwise almost ordinary. Almost. At one point between courses Tom left his mother's lap, went over to Shelsa, and they looked at and whispered to each other with a seriousness you'd expect to see from two executives conferring at a board meeting, or two convicts plotting a crime.

As I continued to eat too much of Agnese's food and drink too much of her wine, I observed and studied, and heard two very different voices—I want to say two very different *spirits*—carrying on a running argument in my head. I believe now that it was this interior debate I was trying to suffocate with food. One voice said some-thing like: "There are no accidents here, no coincidences. You were led to this table by the dreams of the two most important holy men on earth, dreams of Mussolini and mountains and a sacred child. If it hadn't been for those dreams, you most likely would have taken them to see Venice, had some pizza and gelato, and driven them back to Rome. Your future son-in-law lent you a soccer ball, and if it hadn't been for that ball, you would have said a prayer in Sant'Abbondio and then treated the Dalai Lama to a birthday dinner in Menaggio and never met this crowd. Something's different here, subtly but clearly different. You feel it. Look at the Pope: he senses it. The Dalai Lama was fingering his beads like mad before the food was served. Rosa noticed. Pay attention, Paolo, this is no ordinary night."

And the other voice went like this: "Paolo, be a grown-up. You were led here by complete accident, by a family you mistook for a Gypsy caravan or a circus act, for God's sake! What's going on here is that you've stumbled onto a household of people who tell themselves how special they are because they can't deal with being an ordinary family up in the Italian mountains. They have their 'visions' because they can't bear the hard truth of reality. The Americans have fallen for it because they want to be special, too. Look at the woman in the long dress: she smiles all the time, as if she's from a planet where nothing bad ever happens!"

I watched and listened and ate, torn between the two voices, aware, even though I tried to embrace it, that the more cynical argument was a weak one, made weaker by the fact that the people seemed so quietly and humbly sure of themselves that "special" was the last adjective you'd apply. Agnese was acting more like a servant than like the owner of the house, hustling back and forth between table and kitchen, ferrying plates and filling glasses. The family asked to hear more about our adventure, and Rosa gave them the details, embellishing a bit, making it sound like we'd traveled from Campo Imperatore to Padua at high speeds, the sound of police sirens shrieking just behind us.

Agnese and the woman at the head of the table—Cynthia was her name, she told us, though she preferred the Italian version, Cinzia—and the Ringling family listened, rapt. For whatever reason, they were particularly interested in the meal at Campo Imperatore and the fascists there. But they also wanted to know more about the roadside prostitute and Piero, the cathedral in Ferrara, Mazzo's party: and, as the sun fell behind the hills to the west of us, on the Swiss border, we took turns enlightening them, Rosa in the lead. In fact, she talked so much, and so excitedly, that she hardly paused to eat. Her stories were interrupted only when Agnese went into the kitchen—Rosa followed her to help—and it seemed even more difficult than usual for her to sit still. All the while, though, an elephant sat silently on the grass beside me, and no amount of wine and pleasantries, no amount of pork and pasta would shoo it away: the fact was that, at the key moment, we'd been drawn to this abundance of food and hospitality by the mysterious intuition of a ten-year-old girl who had somehow seen through the Dalai Lama's disguise. No one was saying a word about that. My cynical side had no comment on the subject.

At one point after the pasta course and before the arrival of the meat, while some of us were quietly belching, little Tommaso grew restless, as little boys are wont to do. He clambered down off his mother's lap and walked around the table, touching each guest with a flat palm to the spine at first, almost ceremoniously, and then wrapping his little arms around our waists. It seemed a peculiar ritual. Given what Ringling had told me, and the young girl's mysterious intuition, I thought I might feel a jolt of spiritual electricity, but it was just a child's game. Tommaso, I was coming to believe, was, as the cynical voice argued, just a child—nothing more or less miraculous than that. And that's what I wanted him to be. I wanted an ordinary, good, festive Italian meal to mark the Dalai Lama's birthday. I wanted to find a place to spend the night—perhaps Agnese had extra rooms—and then, in the morning, to arrange a riskless surrender.

By the time someone said the word "dessert," we'd been at the table two hours and eaten what felt like a hundred kilos of food.

"It's the Dalai Lama's birthday," I announced, because I was quite sure he wouldn't say it.

Ringling's sister—Cecelia of the long skirt—cocked her head and looked at me as if I might have failed ninth grade, twice. "We know," she said. "Rinpoche told us before we went down to the soccer field. He celebrates it every year. The Dalai Lama's birthday, Buddha's birthday, our birthdays—every birthday but his own. Agnese made a delicious cake!"

A chocolate-frosted cake was carried out, rich, in the Italian style: too much whipped cream. We sang the birthday anthem in Italian—*"Tanti auguri . . ."*—and then the same tune in its English version. Ringling sliced, his daughter passed the plates. Agnese, who'd said very little, raised her coffee cup in a classic Italian toast, *"Cent' anni!"* A hundred years! And I can say that if there was one thing both voices in my head and everyone at that table agreed upon, it was that the man with the toupee and oversized glasses should live and live and live. The world would not soon see another like him, I thought. Nor another Pope like my cousin.

The Dalai Lama himself was mildly embarrassed. He nodded and grinned, put his palms together and bowed to each of us, one at a time, but you could see he didn't want a fuss made. We made it anyway. There were more toasts—to a free Tibet, to world peace, to another spontaneous trip—all of them as full of hope and goodwill as they were absent of likelihood.

At last, Tommaso, curled up in Shelsa's lap, yawned and said, in Italian, *"Posso andare a letto, mamma?"* Can I go to bed?

That alone, in my experience, made the boy exceptional. At that age, our Anna Lisa would no more have volunteered for bed than she would have volunteered to drive our Fiat to the market for a half kilo of ricotta while her mother was at the stove making lasagna.

"A kiss first," Cinzia answered quietly.

The boy went tiredly to the head of the table. His mother kissed him on the mouth, held him tight against her for a long moment, whispered something in his ear. "You stay and talk," he said, in a boss's voice, and this, too, made him laugh. At himself, it seemed. Shelsa stood up and took his hand. "Say *'Sim-jah nahng-go,'*" she said.

"Sim-jah nahng-go," the boy replied sleepily.

Only the Dalai Lama and the man they called Rinpoche answered in kind. "Good night" in Tibetan, I supposed.

Tommaso sported a tired pout. "Please, can they sing for me in American?"

In answer, Ringling and his family stood and followed both children into the house, leaving my three traveling companions with Agnese, Cinzia, and me, out under the stars. Abysmal cook that I am, I nevertheless yield to no one in my aptitude for washing dishes. I volunteered; Agnese seemed offended. *"Assolutamente no!"* she said, and she shuffled tiredly inside and reappeared a minute later with a bottle of limoncello and a tray of mismatched small glasses. She poured some for each of us and sat. A difficult silence hovered over the table. I thought Rosa would break it. I could sense from the way she kept tucking her hair behind one ear that she was anxious or irritated and, knowing her as I did, I expected her to say something like "Can we talk about this?" She turned her eyes to me once, then away, a pained expression on her features. The Pope and the Dalai Lama weren't touching their drinks. My chill had disappeared, but my stomach hurt, and I was mildly drunk.

From inside the house came the sound of quiet song, some kind of American lullaby.

It goes without saying, I'm sure, that I know the Pope well. I'd known him since he was a boy, I could almost always read his moods. And what I read on that night, even through the remains of the disguise, was an intense curiosity the likes of which I'd never seen from him. Though he'd eaten well and had a few sips of wine, and though he'd participated in the conversation like the rest of us, I could sense that a piece of his attention had remained, not on the children, but on the woman at the head of the table. I sensed this from the Dalai Lama, too. After the American family and Tommaso went into the house, I could tell beyond any doubt that the Holy Father wanted to engage Cinzia in conversation. It was there in the way he glanced at her, the way he turned his head, lifted his eyebrows, pursed his lips. But then he seemed to be smitten by second thoughts. He was, after all, a man whose every public utterance was parsed and dissected for secret meaning, for indications as to where he might lead his followers. He was accustomed to being attacked from every direction—his actions too conservative, too liberal, too mild, too provocative. Because of that he'd learned to consider his words carefully before putting them out into the air. He was doing that again; I could see it. I waited.

At last he cleared his throat and turned his eyes squarely on the woman from the Bellini painting. "I would like to ask you something, Cinzia," he began. "May I address you by your given name?"

"Of course, Holy Father."

More throat clearing. A flex of his fake goatee. The quickest of glances in my direction. "I don't know why," he began, "but I have the sense that you might be able to shed some light on this question. Please forgive me if it seems odd." He glanced at the Dalai Lama now, for sup-port, then interlaced his fingers as if in prayer and looked back to the head of the table. "I think I won't be breach-ing any confidences if I say that His Holiness and I have been having similar and rather unusual dreams for the past two or three weeks. Let me speak for myself. I'll be frank. I've been dreaming of, among other things, the late Benito Mussolini, the Italian dictator."

Cinzia held the Pope's eyes for a second or two and then laughed. The laughter was quiet and gentle, like everything else about the woman, but at the same time it seemed to me a somewhat less than perfectly respectful response. The Pope had made himself vulnerable, and she was laughing. His face knotted up in small spasms, as if he felt he'd made a mistake. "Is it funny?" he said at last.

"No, no. Forgive me, Holy Father. It's not that you're funny, or that the question is funny, it's just that lately the workings of the world have been so amusing to me. I've finally come to understand that so much of what happens to us has roots in mystery, and yet we go along believing we can think our way to every solution to our own problems, or the world's. Sometimes we can, and we must try, but other times we're moved this way and that by forces so mysterious—I want to say so *sacred*—that it's almost a sin to analyze them."

"I agree," the Pope said. "But I'm not sure how that relates to what I asked you."

"It relates because this is the house where Mussolini spent his last night on earth. Agnese was a little girl; her mother and father were the hosts."

"You're kidding." The Pope glanced at Agnese, then back.

"I wouldn't do that, Holy Father. After his capture—"

"Just up the lake in Dongo," Rosa couldn't keep herself from saying. I gave her a gentle kick under the table, hoping to prevent her from showing off.

"*È vero,*" Agnese said. It's true. "After he was caught, the partisans weren't sure what to do with him. Some wanted to kill him right away. Others wanted him to go on trial, or to be handed over to the Americans. While they were deciding, they needed a place to keep him, so they brought him and his mistress, Clara Petacci, to this house. As you can see, it's a hidden house, and my father was close with those partisans, he'd grown up with many of them. Mussolini and Petacci were given food and beds in one of the upstairs rooms—I was seven years old; I remember hearing her weep from my own room; she wept until very late—and in the morning they were taken a little distance away and shot in the street. My mother and father and I heard the sound of the machine gun."

The Pope sat in a stunned silence. I thought of my

mother telling me almost exactly the same story: Il Duce caught, held for a night not far from our home, then executed in the street, with his lover at his side. I wonder if she'd known Agnese's father, and I stretched my mind into the past, reaching for memories.

"I grew up very close by," I said. "I know the spot, the plaque. I've walked by it hundreds of times. I knew other people who said they'd heard the shots, too."

"You're in disguise now, yes?" Agnese said, peering more closely at my face. *"Sei italiano?"*

I nodded.

"You're a dePadova, yes?"

"Yes, Paolo. Michael and Luisa's son, how did you know?"

Agnese shrugged and waved fingers in front of her face. "The nose, the eyes. I knew your lovely mother. She used to swim in the lake in December. She and my father did some work together, in the war. She brought you to this house once when you were very small. Tommaso's age. Do you remember?"

I shook my head, but there was something, some wisp of memory twisting along the edges of my thoughts and, combined with what Cinzia had just told us, it set another row of ice cubes on my spine.

"I don't know very much about Mussolini," Cinzia admitted. "My father left Italy for America when he was twenty. He'd occasionally talk about Mussolini, but the truth is I don't have much interest in war and the history of war. I just know that he slept here, and since you were dreaming about him, Holy Father, it must be that something, some greater intelligence, was giving you signals in a kind of code. Leading you to us."

"And there are other dreams, too," the Dalai Lama put in. "For me."

"Of children," the Pope said. "Both of us have dreamt of a child, or children."

"I am thinking," Tenzin said, "that maybe one of these children here could be another Dalai Lama. Someone to take my place when I go."

"And I was thinking," the Pope said, "that the child in our dreams could be a saint or some kind of prophet . . . I don't know, I—"

"And you expected Tommaso and Shelsa to perform miracles," Agnese said, with a pleasant bluntness.

"Not really, no," the Pope told her. The Dalai Lama shook his head in small movements, too, but you had the sense, for once, that they weren't being entirely honest.

"The miracles are small," Agnese said. *I miracoli sono piccoli.* "So far. Birds come to them when they sit out in the yard. They are so still, these children, the birds sit on their arms and shoulders. These children wake up early in the morning, before anyone else, and sit in the yard together and pray until the sun comes. They see things before they happen, small things, like a snake in the yard or the arrival of a guest."

Though he'd removed his oversized sunglasses—there seemed no need of disguise now—the Dalai Lama's expression was inscrutable. Perfectly attentive, but impossible to read. I could see that the Pope was uncomfortable. He grasped one hand in the other, and he felt with his fingers for the papal ring—which, of course, wasn't there. Cinzia and Agnese watched them and waited. Rosa met my eyes.

"You know," the Pope said at last. He paused and

manufactured a small cough. Cinzia hadn't yet tasted the limoncello, but she'd kept her long, thin fingers on the glass and was twirling it in front of her, watching my cousin closely. "Some time ago, about a year before I became pope, there was a story circulating in the halls of the Vatican about an unusual American woman. It was said she had come to Rome in order to advocate for the idea that women should be allowed to be ordained." He paused again, waiting for Cinzia to respond, but she only studied him with the same calm attentiveness that had emanated from her all evening. "That in itself isn't so unusual. People come to Vatican City all the time asking for one favor or another. But it was said that this woman had somehow arranged for a private meeting with a veteran member of the College of Cardinals—Cardinal Joseph Rosario—and for a laywoman who wasn't representing any particular group, that was rare indeed. I have no idea why Rosario agreed to meet with her. Apparently, he'd been in communication with her beforehand, but when she appeared at the Office of the Doctrine of the Faith, he spoke with her only for a short bit and then sent her away. Rather brusquely, perhaps. The cardinal's assistant and translator, Father Clement, is a friend of mine, a North American, and he told me in confidence that this woman seemed highly unusual to him, some kind of unrecognized saint, perhaps. He felt somewhat badly at the way the cardinal had treated her."

The Pope coughed, reached for the missing medal that used to hang from his neck, and went on. "Shortly after this meeting, the Cardinal of Genoa, a man named Martino Zossimo, another friend of mine, abandoned his office. This, in my experience, perhaps in the history of the modern Church, was unprecedented. And he was a famous cardinal, a man whose name was often mentioned as a possible successor to Pope Benedict, a very good and holy man. Exceptionally so. In fact, I'm quite sure that if Cardinal Zossimo had stayed in his position, he would have been selected instead of me to be Pope. But he left a note saying he was leaving, for, of all reasons, to be married, and then he simply disappeared! One note left in his office, then nothing. And this from a man who had devoted his life to the Church. And he was seventy years old!"

The Pope looked at me as if I might contribute something, but I had nothing to add. I'd heard the Cardinal Zossimo story only through the Vatican gossip pipeline—it was unprecedented, yes, and bizarre, but apparently true. He turned back to Cinzia and continued.

"Zossimo was famous for working with Genoa's poor and downtrodden, for walking alone in some of the city's most dangerous neighborhoods late at night, counseling, comforting, giving away money and blankets and food. So, naturally, there were those who believed he'd been kidnapped or killed. There were all sorts of stories and hypotheses. The Genoa police searched for him for months without finding a single clue. The harbor was dredged. Eventually they gave up and a new cardinal was appointed."

The Pope paused again, studying the woman at the end of the table. She kept her eyes on his but said nothing. Just as the silence was turning unbearable, he went on, hesitantly, it seemed: "This same friend, Cardinal Rosario's translator, told me that the mysterious American woman had traveled to Genoa and met with Cardinal Zossimo a few days before his disappearance. Some said she was pregnant. There were, as you can imagine, disturbing rumors. Unfortunately, as my cousin Paolo can attest, certain people in Vatican City are not above spreading gossip. It sounds like a mystery novel, I know, or a scandal, and, of course, both the Vatican and the Curia in Genoa went to some lengths to keep the rumors from getting out of hand. But I've been wondering, Cinzia ... all during this meal I've been wondering, if you might know anything about those events."

The woman lifted the shot glass to her lips, but before drinking she made the smallest of smiles and set the glass back down again. "You found me," she said.

"I wasn't looking for you. Frankly speaking, given the way rumors and stories circulate whenever something unusual happens, I wasn't sure you even existed."

"I do."

"And is Tommaso ... the child?"

"Yes, though there are ... complications. The story isn't a simple one, but this much is true: my husband, Martino—the former Cardinal of Genoa—was Agnese's brother. He brought me here so we could live quietly, at least for a time. He passed away in December, two days after Christmas."

"I'm sorry. I knew him to be a good man."

"He was."

"If I had been made aware of this then, if I'd been in a position to do something, I might have been able to keep him in the Church, at least, though not—"

"I don't think so," Cinzia said, and there was suddenly something different in her tone—not coldness, exactly, not disrespect, but an edge. A quiet force. She'd said those four words respectfully, politely, but with such absolute certainty that, given who she was speaking to, it might have been taken as offensive. Impossible as it had previously been, I was suddenly able to envision her traveling from America, arranging a meeting with a cardinal, pleading the case for female priests. It was somewhat more difficult, however, to imagine her marrying a seventy-year-old ex-cardinal on three days' notice, and then bearing his child.

"Maybe meant to be Buddhist child," the Dalai Lama suggested in what sounded like a strained attempt to soften the sting. "Maybe—"

"No, Your Holiness," Cinzia told him in that same tone, interrupting him, too. "I don't mean to seem rude—I have the greatest admiration for you both. But I believe this child, these two children, have been born outside religion for a specific reason."

"Outside religion? But your husband was a devout Catholic, a cardinal, and—"

Cinzia's face hardened slightly. The Pope saw it and stopped in mid-sentence. She smiled then, softening her mouth, but there was still a quiet force to her words when she spoke. "Who am I quoting," she asked, looking at the Pope, "when I say: 'The Lord has redeemed all of us, all of us, with the Blood of Christ, all of us, not just Catholics.'?" She turned to the Dalai Lama. "And who am I quoting when I say, 'My religion is kindness'?"

At that, Rosa downed her limoncello and motioned for me to pass the bottle. Through the house's open windows we heard a burst of laughter, a pause, the start of an Italian song. Rosa waited a moment, then: "Can I say something here?"

"Of course," the Pope told her.

I thought: When have you ever asked?

"Those things you've just quoted are the comments of great men," she said. "Not good men, *great* men. The history of the world is all about separating people. Dark-skinned from light-skinned. Catholic from Protestant. Believers from nonbelievers. Christian from Jew from Muslim from Hindu from Buddhist. Northern Europeans from southern, northern *Italians* from southern. And the result of that isn't godliness, it's murder! Hatred, war, and murder! Finally and at last we have two incredibly coura-geous spiritual leaders, alive on earth at the same time, who try to unite, not divide."

"And we make enemies by doing it, Rosa," the Pope said. "Some Catholics think I'm trying to bring the Church to its knees."

"And also for me," the Dalai Lama said. "Many Tibet-ans want that I should say, 'Make war with China! Throw bombs! Shoot guns! Do more to save Tibetan culture!' Many people upset with me now."

"What I think about," Cinzia said, addressing Rosa in her measured way, in a voice that seemed to hold suf-fering and hope in a delicate balance, "and what my husband and I often spoke of when he was alive, was exactly that divisiveness. We didn't see any exclusivity in Christ's message, except in his condemnation of evil. Christ wasn't Roman Catholic any more than Buddha was Buddhist. He was born to a Jewish family, yes, but in his adult life he attended no services. He had no name for himself. No label. Not even any real title beyond the Son of Man, which, really, could include everyone on earth."

The Pope shifted in his seat. "True, but he also said, 'No one goes to the Father except through me'."

"Yes, Holy Father. I know the Bible well, I grew up reading it, hearing it at Mass. But I believe that his "through me" meant through the place where he was, spiritually. Along the path he had taken, interiorly. Not through him as an individual. Not through one faith. 'The Kingdom of Heaven is within you,' he said, and that comment can be applied to every soul on earth, can't it? ... And those people from parts of the world where they could never be baptized, should they be condemned simply by virtue of where they were born?"

"Buddha was from the Hindu family," the Dalai Lama admitted, and again it seemed to me he was sensing an escalation, an imminent confrontation, and wanted to defuse it. "The last words he said weren't 'Worship me!' They were 'Work hard to attain your own salvation.'"

"Still," the Pope said, turning from the Dalai Lama back to the head of the table, "we can't just dissolve the differences between faiths. They are very real and significant. The Dalai Lama and I have discussed this at some length."

"Important differences in what you *believe,* yes," Cinzia said, moving her eyes from one man to the other. "But in what you *do,* in what you ask people to do—be compassionate, kind, nonviolent, generous—I would say the differences are so small as to be nonexistent. Can't we emphasize that?"

"We try," both men said at once.

"Couldn't we build a common faith from those common ideas and include every good soul on earth?"

The men were silent.

Something had been happening to me over the course of this after-dinner theological debate. A strong emotion was rising up, an urge to come to my Pope's defense, the defense of my faith. If I understood Cinzia correctly she was saying that Jesus Christ was just another Buddha, that there was no difference between the two. Both were sons of God. That was unacceptable to me. It went against everything I'd heard since I was four years old, so in a less than perfectly sober tone I said to her, "What do you suggest, then? A world with no religion? Is that what you believe Tommaso and Shelsa are called to do, bring us into a future like that?"

She turned to me slowly, and I noticed for the first time that there was something almost physical in the force of her eyes. "I don't know," she said. "They're children now. I want Tommaso to have a normal childhood, and I know that Cecelia and Rinpoche have already had big problems with people stalking and trying to harm their daughter. They want, more than anything, for Shelsa to have a normal childhood. In my own prayer life I've been getting what I feel is a consistent message that we must wait. From the other side of the ocean Shelsa found my son, and I knew, from the instant she appeared at this door, that she was supposed to find him. I knew, from the instant I saw the four of you, that you were supposed to be here. I know, in that same way, that there is something these two children are called to do, but that we must all wait and not force them into roles we don't understand. I want, for a time at least, to keep them safe from the eye of the world. Will you all help me?"

"Of course," Rosa said immediately.

The Dalai Lama nodded.

"Yes, fine, yes," the Pope said. He seemed uncomfortable—almost embarrassed that his friend the Cardinal of Genoa had impregnated this young American and disappeared because of it. At the same time, though, I could sense that the woman intrigued him. He couldn't stop looking at her. He seemed angry, or at least upset, but also trying very hard to keep his emotions from showing.

I am not as diplomatic. Over the course of the conversation one of the voices in my head had been steadily gaining ground. By then it had grown too strong to silence. "I'm sorry," I began, and then I couldn't turn off the faucet. "I'm very sorry. They do seem like wonderful children, even special children. Very kind and sweet. But suggesting that they're destined to bring humanity together in some postreligious era . . . simply because his father was a former cardinal and they let birds land on their shoulders? That seems, I'm sorry, like wishful thinking to cover over a difficult circumstance . . . I'm sorry, I—"

"Difficult circumstance?"

"Your pregnancy."

Rosa kicked me under the table. Hard.

Cinzia stared at me for a moment in such a kind and gentle way it made me feel like the demon who'd visited Eve in Eden. She hesitated, weighing her words, deciding on something. At last she said, "I became pregnant with Thomas without being intimate with any man. The cardinal married me and brought me here to protect me. He was not Tommaso's father . . . Those were the 'complications' I mentioned a few minutes ago."

"That," I said, confident by then, sure I was listening to the true voice, "is simply not possible."

"No," the Pope corrected, and then I did hear a stirring of anger. He'd finally been pushed beyond the edge of his legendary patience. "It was possible, but only once. Only for the mother of Christ. To claim otherwise, really, is blasphemy."

Cinzia tried to smile at him, but I saw that her eyes were brimming with tears.

"My husband believed me," she said. She took a breath. "But I don't expect you to, Holy Father. Or you, Paolo. Or anyone, really. It's strange, besides my husband and Agnese, I've never told anyone what I just told you. Not even Rinpoche or Cecelia. I'm sorry I mentioned it." She blinked, wiped a tear, turned to the Dalai Lama. "But tell me something, Your Holiness. Explain something to me. Before we sat down to eat, Rinpoche told me that Shelsa knew it was you, on the soccer field, from a hundred meters away, even though you look . . . like that? Please explain."

"She saw through his disguise," I blurted out, before the Dalai Lama could answer. "It's just a bad wig and dark glasses." Rosa kicked me a second time. I blundered on. "And she'd heard it was his birthday, so naturally he was on her mind."

"Then how was it that she and her family found their way to us here, in the Italian mountains? In this house? All the way from North Dakota?"

"Extrasensory perception."

"How did Agnese know four guests were coming tonight?"

"The same," I said. "Some people are actually psychic. It doesn't prove—"

"And the dreams?" Cinzia said. "The dreams of these two men? Mussolini, of all people! Mere coincidence?"

"No," Rosa said. "No, *amore.*"

I leaned forward and spoke a little too loudly. "Ghosts and dreams and visitors and psychic powers—none of that equals the birth of another savior, another Christ."

"I never said 'savior' or 'another Christ.' I would never say something like that. I'm not worthy of it in the first place, and it's just not what I feel, not at all. But Christ also called himself the Son of God, didn't he? What if God lends pieces of himself—or herself—in different places at different times, when the world requires it? Sons and daughters. Some of them relatively minor—say, a woman whose loving influence extends only to her spouse, her own family. And some more major—a saint, a guru, a king or great leader. And some like Moses or Abraham or Christ or Buddha or Mohammed, spirits who change lives and inspire millions of people over a thousand generations."

"Buddha never used the word 'God,'" the Dalai Lama put in. "We do not see the world this way."

"And Christ was God's *only* son," the Pope said. "To mention him with those others is considerate but incorrect."

Cinzia looked at them as if she were disappointed. "You are the most wonderful and kind men," she told them calmly. "But with those comments I wonder: have you reached the limits of your openness?"

"That's disrespectful," I said, perhaps too forcefully.

"I mean no disrespect at all."

I looked at the Pope. His face was twisted into a tight knot. There was a terrible silence then, broken by my wife. "What should we do?" Rosa asked Cinzia, as if looking for direction from a great spiritual teacher, while sitting at the same table with two real, actual, certified and well-known spiritual teachers.

"I don't know," Cinzia said again. "But I don't believe we have to be condemned to repeat history. I'm not suggesting we'll have some kind of paradise here on earth. But I would ask you to consider the possibility that these two children could bring about a change. Not the end of war and hatred and poverty and hunger, but maybe less of those things. Not the end of our ruining the planet, but maybe the beginning of doing less damage. Maybe they'll continue the unifying process that the two great holy men at this table have begun with their open-mindedness and generosity. Or they'll inspire them to speak out more forcefully or in a new way against unfairness in this world. As I said, I don't know the specifics. I don't feel like I have to know. But I do know that the two of you, His Holiness and the Holy Father, weren't brought to this house deep in the Italian mountains by some purposeless coincidence. I would ask you, even if you find me to be a fool, or a blasphemer and a great sinner, I would ask you to consider that and to give your blessing to Shelsa and Tommaso."

The Pope and the Dalai Lama couldn't look at her, or at each other. They were staring off in different directions. I felt angry at Cinzia, that she would dare challenge them in this way, that she would claim what she seemed to be claiming—another virgin birth, a sacred child. Even if she was simply delusional, I was angry at her. And my anger extended to Rosa as well. I'd been feeling closer and closer to her during the trip, even entertaining thoughts of a reconciliation. But now I understood why we could never be together again: there was a gullibility to my good-hearted wife, a childishness. She wanted the world to be what it was not.

I was host then to a fierce run of thoughts. My mind was a small gas flame burning at that table in the beautiful mountain night. Cinzia, Rosa, Ringling—they were all of them wishful thinkers, illogical, out of touch with scientific reality.

At that precise moment we heard the door open and hushed, grass-softened footsteps. I turned and saw Shelsa coming toward us. She'd changed into a peach-colored nightdress, and it hung like colorful vapor from her small shoulders and floated around her knees. She stopped, as if our silence were a solid creature, a cold wall. Two things happened then. First, I remembered the Dalai Lama telling me, as we walked toward the center of L'Aquila, that anger was a snake brought into view by the ego. And second, I was visited by a terrible memory, a time when Anna Lisa, six years old, had slipped out of her bedroom after overhearing a particularly ugly exchange between Rosa and me. On her face we could see—not fear, but an enormous sadness. I have never in my life felt farther from God than I did at that moment.

Shelsa stood there with a similar expression: sadness, almost pity, as if she knew the adults had been disagreeing, and knew they didn't understand something they should have understood, something she knew, something they'd forgotten.

"Tom wants you to come," she said to Cinzia. The boy's mother hesitated all of one second, then stood, tried to smile at us, said, "Please forgive me if I've upset you.

Agnese will show you all where you can sleep. We have room," and went quietly away.

After we heard the door slap closed, Shelsa stood there for a moment, assessing the situation, studying the bad air. Then she lifted both arms. In the lamplight I could see a string of beads dangling from each hand. "Little Tom took these from your pockets," she said. "He's a funny boy."

I watched the Pope and the Dalai make identical movements, thrusting a hand into jacket and pants, reaching for the missing rosary and prayer beads. The anger just leaked out of me then. I wanted to laugh, in spite of the feelings that had hung around that table and the bitter fire that had been burning in me, because the shock on their faces was something right out of a cartoon. Rosa did laugh, and she had a laugh that could make you fall in love with her all over again. Something broke inside me then. Some hard shell of judgment cracked open. For no good reason at all Agnese reached over and put a hand on my arm like an aunt comforting a grown nephew who'd just realized he'd made a mistake.

Shelsa said, "He told me I should give them back to the special men or they would be mad at him."

42

My cousin and the Dalai Lama were given an upstairs bedroom to share—not Mussolini's, Agnese assured them. (The Pope would tell me later that the room was hot but otherwise comfortable; that he and Tenzin had both been somewhat upset by the things Cinzia said, but that they'd had visitors and enjoyed "a healing conversation, really a remarkable conversation, with the man called Rinpoche" before retiring to their narrow beds. He declined, out of a surprising shyness, it seemed to me, to provide any details.) And then our hostess, full of apology, sent Rosa and me to the barn with an armful of sheets and pillows. *"La casa è piena,"* she told us in a penitential voice, the house is full, and though I assured her it was fine, no problem, we understood, of course, I was sorely tempted to walk back down to the Maserati—less risk of being bitten by spiders—and sleep there, sitting up.

There were no animals in the barn, at least, or none I was aware of. The air was humid and close but sweet-smelling, the darkness broken only by the thinnest film of starlight filtering through one small window in the loft. Rosa and I spread our sheets side by side on a bed of fresh-cut hay, took off most of our clothes in the darkness, and lay down. From far below, near the town, we heard the sound of a police siren, but when that passed there was only a deep country silence in the air, something I remembered from my childhood. A world emptied of noise.

"We should have brought the car up here," she said, after a time. "I feel sweaty and disgusting and I hate to go to bed without brushing my teeth. Plus, the Pope and the Dalai Lama are still in the clothes Antonio gave us at the villa."

I said nothing.

"You're angry, Paolo."

"No. Aside from the fact that I ate and drank too much, and that I think a poisonous spider just crawled into my underwear, I'm fine."

"Stop lying. You're angry at that woman, and you're angry at me for not being angry at her. And you didn't eat 'too much,' you ate like a wild boar!"

I heard her rustling around in the darkness and then a tiny snapping sound. I tried to remember the last time I'd heard a woman take off her bra.

"Don't you dare fall asleep on me," she said.

"I'm not sleepy."

"And tell me what you're thinking. Be honest."

"I *was* angry with her, Rosa. I'm still a practicing Catholic. Maybe not the best Catholic who ever lived, but I'm Catholic, and, besides, I've always felt a particular devotion to Mary."

"I know."

"From the time I was a boy until now I say an Ave Maria every morning when I first wake up, and every night before I go to sleep."

"I know that, too. I lived with you for twenty-one years, remember?"

"So how am I supposed to *not* be angry with a woman who claims she became pregnant and gave birth without having sex?"

"I don't know why, but I believe her. Strange, though, for sure."

"Rosa, listen, please. I have no idea why this happened, but at some point, just when I was really starting to boil over, I remembered that the Dalai Lama told me that 'anger grows out of the ego.' And I saw something in myself."

"That you can be an ass," she said.

"No . . . listen to me. Stop joking."

"I'm not joking."

"Listen, please, for once. Stop giving orders and look-ing for a fight. Simply listen."

"I'm listening, Paolo. I'm trying."

"I believe Jesus Christ is the Son of God. And I believe his birth was miraculous. And I believe he rose from the dead. I've always believed those things, and I still do. But I realized tonight that I don't *know* things happened that way."

"That's why they call it faith."

"And I also realized I don't *know* there can't be other miracles, of every kind, in every era, and in societies that aren't Christian. I don't know that. It suddenly occurred to me to ask myself the question: Why do you think you know everything? For some odd reason, just at that moment, right in the hottest part of my anger, I saw the link between being angry like that and the fact that I just wanted to be right and wanted her to be wrong. I actually *saw* it. It was so simple, so clear, a kind of vision. And then that girl came outside with the beads and I wanted to laugh, and the anger was like a balloon with a hole poked in it. It just shrank away to nothing."

"A miracle," she said.

"Stop being sarcastic."

"I'm not. I thought I saw something change in you, in your face. I was watching you. The old woman—Agnese—saw it, too, and touched you. When Shelsa held up the beads you made a certain expression—you squeezed up the right side of your cheek and the corner of your right eye—that I've never ever seen you make before. I thought you were having a stroke or something."

"I was changing."

"Yes, at last, and it was because of the presence of that

boy and that girl and that strange woman. They worked a kind of magic on you, on all of us."

"I don't believe in magic."

"You don't believe in it because you're the most stubborn man who ever lived. From the second she came up to us on the soccer field I saw something in that girl. It made me think of the old religious paintings where Jesus and Mary and the saints have a circle of light around their heads. I doubt very much that those people had actual circles of light around their heads. Nobody would have crucified Jesus if he was walking around with a circle of light around his head. But I think there was *something* about them that was different, special, and certain people could see it and certain people couldn't, and the people who could see it had no way to describe it, so the painters put these circles of light around them. They were ... what do you call it?"

"Metaphors?"

"Right. Exactly."

"I didn't see any circle of light," I said. "But I've seen some paintings of Buddha in museums and there was that same circle, or a very similar circle. Blue, sometimes. And sometimes red."

"You're completely not understanding me, as usual."

"Fine, I'm sorry. If you want to believe my anger disappeared because of that woman and those two children, I can't stop you. But she seemed a bit too forceful, and they seemed like mainly ordinary kids to me—extra polite, maybe. Smarter than most kids at those ages. More loving, even. But not exactly kids who would invade the dreams of holy men."

"You think it was 'mainly ordinary' that the girl recognized the Dalai Lama when none of the hundred or so other people who've seen him over the last few days recognized him in that same disguise?"

"I don't know. Mazzo recognized the Pope, didn't he?"

"You think it was 'mainly ordinary' that the three-year-old boy could steal the beads out of the pockets of two grown men without them knowing it?"

"Maybe his uncle was a pickpocket and taught him the tricks."

"Be serious, Paolo."

"I don't know. I haven't thought about it enough. It's not easy for me to believe in things like that."

"You? The Christian who believes in the Immaculate Conception and Christ's Resurrection? Not easy to believe in miracles?"

"Those things are different."

"Why?"

"I don't know why, they just are. They're unique. They're what makes Christ special, what makes him God. Or part of God."

"And so Shelsa can't be part of God? Tommaso can't be? We all can't be?"

"Rosa, I'm trying to say one thing and you're talking about something else, as usual. It simply occurred to me that I was so upset at what Cinzia was saying because I wanted to be right. I wanted her to yield to the authority of the Pope, to the holiness of the Dalai Lama."

"She was perfectly respectful."

"She was challenging them."

"And that's what, Paolo? A sin? For a woman to challenge a man?"

"For an ordinary woman to challenge those two holy men. In that way. Yes."

"She's not ordinary."

"Maybe not. But I'm talking about my anger. You're talking about circles of light and people who do strange things."

"You're focusing on yourself, as usual."

"Let me finish, would you kindly?"

"Fine, finish all you want. But you're an ass."

"And you're as bossy and impatient as you ever were, and still *not listening!*"

"Go ahead, then, talk."

"I'm saying I *wanted to be right* and that overwhelmed all other considerations. I recognized that fact. I wanted God and my parents to be looking down on me and saying, 'You're right, Paolo, and she's wrong.' I saw that something like that is how wars start, wanting God to look down on you and think you're right. And then, after I saw it, I realized that all the fights we had, you and I, all those hundreds of thousands of arguments, came about because I wanted to be right, to *know,* and *you* wanted to be right. And neither one of us could simply let go of our ridiculous stubbornness and make a decent peace."

"It's not so simple."

"No, it isn't. But we never tried very hard. Most of the fights we had were about nothing, about who knew the right time to put Anna Lisa to bed, eight or eight-fifteen. About should we spend forty euro on groceries or forty-eight euro."

"It was *lire* then, not euro."

"Stop, Rosa. You know what I mean. I think it was

connected to fear. I didn't want you to take over the relationship and make me see and do everything the way you see and do it. Especially with Anna Lisa."

"We fought before Anna Lisa was born."

"Right, but the same principle applies and if you would listen to me for once instead of thinking you know everything and constantly interrupting me, you'd see what I'm trying to say!"

"Don't yell! I'm trying to listen. I'm trying as hard as I can."

"All those times I got angry and you got angry, on some level we were both minor fascists. Insecure dictators. Minor Mussolinis. There's a little bit, a tiny bit of the tyrant in me. Or the wish to be a tyrant, to be right, to control."

"In *us,* not just in you."

"Thank you. And if you multiply that by seven billion you get the human predicament. I thought about how brave the Pope and the Dalai Lama are. They've let go of so much in the name of unity, of truth. Even this trip . . . for a few days they even let go of being bosses."

"And look at the trouble it caused. People *want* a boss, *amore.* Most people like to have responsibility taken away from them. They might want to control their wife or husband or child in their own home, but in the larger picture they want to be led. All those screaming Italians in Piazza Venezia. They wanted a god up there on the balcony. At the end they hated the Grand Benito with a passion, but for about twenty years they were perfectly happy to consider him a god. And by the way, *amore,* how do you explain the fact that the Pope dreams of Mussolini and we end up sleeping in the house where he spent his last night?"

"I can't."

"Maybe our wicked Benito is trying to atone for his sins from some other plane of existence."

"Sure, maybe."

"Plus, Agnese told me that ever since that fateful night, this place has been haunted by ghosts. Which is why she was so apologetic about putting us in the barn."

"I'm not afraid," I said.

"Yes you are. And I am, too."

We were both quiet for a while. I felt something new between us, though. Something fresh, an underground stream beneath the surface squabbles. It felt as though Rosa and I had been thrashing around in a polluted harbor for two decades, and we'd suddenly realized we could simply swim over to where the water, fed by this stream, was much clearer. The clear water had been there all along but for some reason we'd kept swimming around in circles in the poison. "What's your secret fear?" I asked her. "Yesterday . . . you never told me. Ghosts?"

She hesitated so long I thought she'd fallen asleep. I thought I heard bats flapping about in the loft. Bats or swallows. Or rats fighting, maybe. Or the ghosts of disgraced Italian dictators twisting in the air. I tried to ignore them.

"I'm afraid," Rosa said at last, and then she hesitated again and shifted position, "of growing old alone."

"You never told me that."

"I was ashamed. The successful business owner, the woman of the world. The strong Neapolitan with rich and famous friends. I was embarrassed."

"You'll have a grandchild now, for company."

"That's not what I mean, Paolo."

"You could find somebody. You're beautiful, rich. Some men are attracted to women who yell at them all the time."

Silence.

"That last part was a joke."

"I don't want to find somebody," she said in a voice that was as pure and true as a flute note.

I listened to those words, really listened to them. What I heard there was something that had gotten lost over time, drowned out in the symphony of daily living. I thought of Cinzia telling the holy men that they could open their minds still farther, and I tried to do that. I tried to shove all my old assumptions and resentments and bad memories to one side, my *stories*, as Tenzin had called them, all my old insistence on knowing. After a minute I felt an emptiness there, where that acidic pile had been— not an emptiness, exactly, but an openness. A new plot of land that might be tilled and planted. A clear ocean that might be sailed across. A view of the sky that had been obscured by a mountain of bitterness. I felt words rising up out of that clear place and into my mouth, and when I parted my lips they flew out. "Are you saying we could live together again?"

A long silence. Suddenly the pleasant openness was covered by a cloud of toxic smoke. Rosa could say two words—"No, *amore*"—and crush me forever. I felt the fear around me as if it were a herd of a thousand spiders. They'd realized I was there, in the barn, in my underwear, in the dark. They were marching on me like an army, from all directions.

But then Rosa said, *"Sì,"* and I could hear her crying very quietly. I reached across and took hold of her hand

and she moved it and placed my hand palm-down on her belly and kept it there. She sniffled, took a long breath and let it out. "When you called me from your office that day, about helping the Pope and the Dalai Lama escape . . . I thought you were calling to ask the question you just asked. Could we try living together again. I had a feeling."

"You believe in ghosts now, miracles, special children. *Feelings.*"

"I always believed in those things."

"A true *napoletana.*"

"When we were first together, when you first brought me here to this beautiful place, you used to say you were glad you found a *napoletana,* remember? You said the north-erners were sane and orderly and hardworking and maybe more honest, but that without the south, Italy would have too many brains and not enough heart. It would be like Europe having only Germany and Austria—no Spain, no France, no Italy. It would be a world of scientists without singers. I thought it was romantic. What happened to the man who said those things?"

"His various fears ate him up."

"What fears?"

"Could I make a living? Would Anna Lisa get sick, or hurt? Would you take over the relationship? Would I fail again?"

"What if you let all that go now?"

I couldn't speak.

"What would you say if I told you this trip feels like it was intended by God to bring us together again, Paolo? I even think the Pope might have had that in mind all along. Maybe all this was for *us,* too, *amore,* not only for him and his visions. What if the magic those children are supposed to bring to earth has already touched us?"

"I would say one of two things: either you're completely crazy, or I'm getting a second chance. A reincarnation without dying."

She let go of my hand. For a moment I thought she was angry because I'd mentioned reincarnation. I heard her moving in the darkness, and then she said, "I'm disgusting and sweaty, but I'm taking off my underwear. I want you to make love to me. Now. We'll make peace between us. It will be the start of making peace in the world."

"I'm not sure I remember how to do it."

"I'll remind you," Rosa said.

Day Five

43

After Rosa and I made our beautiful peace—the details of which shall remain private—I slept a sleep of the deepest contentment. I dreamt of nothing, or nothing I can remember, and probably would have remained in that state of perfectly satisfied empty-mindedness until noon if Rosa hadn't awakened me with a gentle shake. *"Amore!"* I heard. I pried my eyes open and saw that the barn's complete darkness had begun to soften in the direction of day. It must have been four-thirty or five in the morning. There was no real light yet, just the hope of light, the suggestion of it, the promise of light sifting down through the loft window and dusting the edge of Rosa's face. She was leaning over me, one hand on my left shoulder, shaking it gently. For some reason her hair was wet. I remember that because a drop of water fell from one dark strand onto my cheek. *"Amore!* Quick! Get up, get up. We have to go! Now! They found the car!"

"Who?" I said. "What car?" But even before she said, "The police! The Maserati!" I was awake enough to know where I was and to remember what had happened. "Come back to bed," I said, which was something I had enjoyed saying to her on certain Saturday mornings in our youth.

Those words did not seem to raise the same good

memories in her that they raised in me. "Get up, Paolo!" she said in a harsh whisper. "Right this second! I'll explain, but get up and get dressed!"

I clambered to my feet, strands of hay caught in my hair and clinging to my sticky disguise. I was naked. My knees and lower back ached badly. I missed my mattress.

Rosa took hold of my shoulders and shook me until I was completely awake. "Look me in the eyes, Paolo. Listen to me! They found the car. Tara must have called them. The police and the army are all over the town, from Sant'Abbondio's down to the lake. Cinzia and Agnese don't want them to come here, because the press is crazy with the story, and if the reporters get word that the Pope and the Dalai Lama came to this house, and if they get a look at Shelsa and Tommaso, and if Rinpoche or Ringling or one of the women tells them the whole story, then the children will be famous, and hounded by every newspaper and TV station on earth. That's already happened to Shelsa once—a newspaper story—and it was awful for them. We have to go. Now!"

"Your hair's wet."

"I took a shower. I smelled like you smell, except you look even worse than I looked. The disguise is ruined. It's all coming off, see." She peeled from my forearm a stamp-size piece of the hardened, faded polish. "Go inside and shower. I'll give you exactly four minutes."

"I'll wake up everybody."

"Everybody's awake. GO!"

I found my clothes and dressed in the half dark, then hurried across to the main house. Agnese was there, holding out a fresh towel. She pointed me toward the downstairs bathroom, and I showered as quickly as I could, given that the color Mario had applied was peeling from my face and arms in large flakes. I tried to scrub it off, but a splotchy film remained. Eight minutes and I was dressed and being hurried out the back door with Agnese's palm against my spine.

There, on a patch of lawn, the entire group from the night before had assembled, the children sleepy-eyed, Rinpoche grinning and holding Piero's soccer ball like he was ready for a game ("Please keep it," I told him), the other adults looking weary, birds chirping in the trees and the first streaks of gray showing in the east. I noticed that the Pope was dressed in a different suit—one of Ring-ling's, it might have been—and that he'd removed his goatee, though there wasn't much he could do about the blond color in what was left of his hair. The Dalai Lama had his regular glasses on and a new pair of pants and a clean shirt, and he seemed, without the long hair and jet-set getup, utterly recognizable. I realized, at that point, that we were going to walk into town and turn ourselves in and be scolded or cheered, hated or loved, and taken back to our ordinary lives.

There were hugs and bows all around, *arrivedercis* and goodbyes. At Cinzia's request—she had tears in her eyes again—the Pope and the Dalai Lama gave a blessing to the assembled group. And then, without being asked, each of them in turn bent over and held Shelsa and Tom-maso for a moment in a warm embrace. I watched them closely, waiting to see if there would be some momentous exchange, some sign from God that this odd encounter was part of his greater plan. But it seemed we'd had all the signs we were going to be given.

We thanked Agnese for the marvelous meal and hospitality. We took a last look at the children, made a final wave to the eccentric Americans. Promised we'd say nothing to the press.

It would have been a fittingly gentle and loving farewell, a kind of ecumenical reconciliation after the previous night's tension, except that, just as the four of us turned and headed onto the dirt road, Tommaso ran over and kicked me in the back of my left calf, fairly hard. His mother gently reprimanded him. Rinpoche's laughter echoed in the hills. Shelsa took him by the hand and pulled him back. I said, "It's fine, not to worry, normal behavior," or something along those lines, but I limped after my traveling companions wondering if it had been meant as some kind of celestial signal. The little angel had picked out the sinner in the group, the doubter; he'd known exactly which one of us needed to be spurred onto the spiritual path. Maybe he *was* special, after all.

There was more light by then; we could see the two dirt tracks clearly. They curved through the dense bushes and trees like a wisp of golden dust leading toward a bright afterlife. The air was cool and fragrant, and if it hadn't been for the thump of helicopters above the town and the *whee-waw* of klaxons on the lakeside road, that last walk would have been a species of perfect meditation. It would have been, for me at least, a quiet little prayer of gratitude for the gift of those days.

The Pope put an arm around my shoulders and stopped walking. We made a small circle there in the cool morning air. He said, "Before we go down into the mad circus—and that's surely what it will be—I want to thank you both from the marrow of my bones." He motioned for Rosa to step closer and he held us tightly. "Few things in my life have been more helpful to me, spiritually, than this brief time as an ordinary man. Whatever happens now with those two children, whatever the consequences or rewards of our adventure, I simply want you to know that I am grateful."

"I also," the Dalai Lama said. He bowed deeply to Rosa and me in turn, and for once neither my wife nor I had anything to say. We bowed awkwardly. Rosa kissed my cousin on the cheek and we started walking again. As we turned left onto the paved street, she took hold of my hand and I squeezed her fingers.

"That boy," the Pope said quietly, when we'd made another left turn onto a road that led steeply downhill and ran parallel to the road my parents had lived on, "was sent upstairs to wake us at four a.m. He came into the room and tickled our feet, Paolo, laughing quietly the whole time."

"At least he didn't kick you."

"Yes, that was strange. And strange, too, that his mother would send him to wake us and not come herself, or send Agnese. I wonder how she knew, at four in the morning, that the car had been found."

"Maybe the boy told her," Rosa said. "Or that wonderful girl."

"Possibly. After he'd finished tickling us he said, 'I'm sorry you ever have to leave us. We like you two guys!' And for some reason I felt he was telling me I was soon to die."

"Me, the same," the Dalai Lama said.

"Don't even think about it," Rosa admonished them. "Either one of you. Don't you ever even begin to consider the possibility of dying ... At least not until those children are grown and we see what becomes of them."

"God's will be done," my cousin said. "God's will be done."

We went along silently after that, the sky over our heads slowly filling with light. The tarred road curved around a hillside; beyond it we could see gold-edged clouds above the mountains of the Valtellina. Below that display, gray cliffs stood like witnesses, then the dark hills, and then the lake itself, almost purple at that hour, and quiet, except for a single ferry making its way toward Menaggio from the east. You could feel the frenzy below, actually *feel* it, but the four of us went along in our little bubble of contentment and gratitude, approaching the end of our great adventure, step by step, half lost in dreams of a finer world, and at the same time at peace with ourselves and each other, and willing, like all the sons and daughters of God, to wait.

Epilogue

Well, the rest of the story—most of it, anyway—is widely known from the massive international press coverage that accompanied the safe return of the two holy men. But allow me to fill in a few blanks.

After we left Agnese's house and that bizarre and remarkable collection of people, we strolled down, in the early-morning Lake Como light, toward the center of the small village of Mezzegra, a place I knew like I knew my own name. It was a wild scene on that day, however, all but unrecognizable. There were police helicopters overhead, army vehicles blocking the streets, crowds of curious locals on the corners even at that early hour, and an abundance of armed men in the uniform of the state. Despite that chaos, or perhaps because of it, the four of us were able to duck into a coffee bar just uphill from the town center. The Pope and the Dalai Lama moved to a table in the back corner, Rosa and I ordered. Rather than wait for them to be recognized and risk inciting a riot about who deserved the reward, we decided to turn ourselves in to the first official-looking person we saw.

Just as our cappuccinos were being placed on the counter, as if on some heavenly cue, a young policeman stepped through the door. I carried the coffees over to the holy men and let Rosa have the pleasure of surrender.

If we could have chosen someone to receive the news that the missing men were safe, we could hardly have done better than this young policeman. Deeply tanned, with an innocent expression in his dark, handsome eyes, and a beak of a nose leading him wherever he went, he looked to have been raised in one of the poor southern provinces—Sicily, Calabria, perhaps Basilicata. My guess was that he felt grateful to have landed a secure, decent-paying job, but that he wasn't so happy to have been pressed into service up north, among a people who didn't speak his dialect, didn't like his accent, and possibly didn't think much of the place where he'd been raised. Even as I sat with the Pope and Dalai and watched my wife speaking to this man, I thought there was a kind of perfection to the moment. Hadn't Christ spoken for the poor and outcast? Wasn't this better than making an army general the hero of the hour?

But the young man's heroism was brief; the generals appeared soon enough. Summoned by radio, one of them strode into the place, a steel rod up his spine, an elaborately decorated uniform covering his broad shoulders, a look of great self-seriousness on his face, while the truly important men in the room sat in a dark corner, spooning steamed milk into their mouths and watching the gathering crowd with quiet amusement.

An argument ensued. The general, soon joined by a regional police commissioner—with members of the press clamoring at the door and the barista and early-morning customers staring—insisted on taking Rosa and me into custody and flying the kidnapped holy men back to Rome in a helicopter. The Pope would have none of it. "There will be no arrests," he said, in the calm voice of authority I'd heard from him many times. "Nothing improper or illegal was done. The four of us will be driving back to Vatican City in our borrowed car. You and your colleagues are perfectly welcome to provide an escort, but we shall be returning by road, not by air."

What a final leg of the journey that was! I'm told the whole seven hours of the trip were broadcast live on televisions around Europe, filmed from the press helicopter that hovered above us, and from the TV trucks that rumbled along behind. I've never watched the video myself, but I can say that, from inside the Maserati, with blue lights and sirens going all around us, that ride felt like a victory parade. Mazzo, it turned out, had been correct: once the true story got out, people loved the idea of the Pope and the Dalai Lama taking a vacation as ordinary men. By the time we reached the outskirts of Rome, thousands of other ordinary men, women, and children were standing along the roadside and crowding the bridges. They waved Italian and Tibetan flags and plastic crucifixes. They cheered. They sang hymns. They wept. Some of them held up signs: THE PEOPLE'S POPE! WE LOVE YOU BOTH! I even saw one that said: WHAT WOULD BUDDHA DO?!

Inside the car, we said little. The Pope and Dalai waved out the windows. Rosa turned on the radio and adjusted the dial. I guided the Maserati along the fast lane of the Autostrada, following a phalanx of police cruisers. My wife and I were happy to hear the news of our exoneration, happy not to have to worry about being torn to shreds by angry mobs, happy at the new feelings between us—spawned, perhaps, by the touch of two miraculous children. Somewhere near Milano, Rosa put her hand on my leg, and, except for one, brief, bathroom-and-espresso stop, she left it there all the way to the gates of Rome.

Preceded by our police escort, we turned into St. Peter's Square. I pulled up near the obelisk, officers forming a perimeter around us, pilgrims shouting welcome in twenty languages. Just before the holy men were taken away by their frowning security forces, Tenzin and Giorgio held Rosa and me in warm embraces and thanked us three more times.

"Cousin," the Pope said, meeting my eyes and keeping his hands on my shoulders, "breakfast in the morning, as always. Bring your beautiful wife."

The only shadow on this happy scene—in addition to the debriefing Rosa and I were forced to undergo before being released (and the fact that Tara, who had, in fact, led police to the car, did not claim the reward and was never heard from again)—occurred in the weeks after our return, when the frenzy had died down, when all of us had gone back to our usual business. My enemies among the Holy Father's advisors had put so much pressure on him during that time, made him so miserable, argued so persistently, so forcefully, that his negligent cousin had put him in danger that at last he was forced to relieve me of my duties as First Assistant. Yes, he apologized profusely. And yes, he seemed genuinely sad and made sure I was given a severance and a pension on which I could live fairly comfortably for the rest of my days. Still, he fired me. Difficult as it is to write those words, my cousin fired me.

It was, of course, another of his tricks, another act of

loving genius—though it took me months to understand that.

Anna Lisa and Piero were soon married (they invited the Pope and the Dalai Lama, but neither man could attend). My so-called firing freed me to move to Rimini and be close to my daughter and son-in-law. At that point, Rosa decided on a major change, too. She shifted most of her responsibilities to trusted associates and moved in with me, in a cozy apartment on a shaded street, three blocks from the beach. She spent a few hours a day on her business, but it seemed to have loosened its hold on her.

Six months later little Giorgio Paolo came into the world, a healthy, bubbly, Jewish/Catholic/Buddhist creature, named for his cousin once removed, the Pope of Rome. It goes without saying, I'm sure, that Anna Lisa and Piero's child became, instantly, the sun around which our lives orbited. Rosa and I were there every day, helping, holding, changing diapers, playing games, singing, adoring.

Still, I had no business to oversee, no office to go to in the morning; the substantial joys of grandfatherhood couldn't completely fill my days. There were long walks on the beach and quiet dinners out with my wonderful wife. There were books to read and symphonies to listen to and soccer matches to watch. Even so, there were too many empty hours.

It was then that my cousin rescued me, yet again. One fine June day, when the Russian tourists were flocking back to Rimini's beach, he summoned me to Vatican City. There, after a night of rest, we enjoyed another of our traditional breakfasts. Over chocolate, fruit, and coffee he said he'd been in regular contact with the Dalai Lama and that the two of them had decided it was important to record the story of their trip. For posterity. For the popes and lamas of the future. For ordinary people.

"You are going to do the job," the Pope said, pointing at me.

"What job, cousin?"

"You are going to write up the whole thing, start to finish. My understanding is that Cinzia and the children have moved to another location, in another land, so there will be no danger to them now."

"Holy Father," I said. "I'm no writer, and it's an important job. You should hire a professional."

He turned down his mouth and made his face into the stern mask his opponents in the bureaucracy had come to know well. "Cousin," he said, in a certain tone, "listen to me now. What Tenzin and I did, what you and Rosa enabled us to do, has been the subject of millions upon millions of words, all of them written by professionals who, frankly, have no idea what they're talking about. They weren't there. They have no inkling as to our true motivation, of God's hand in all this. There is, of course, no mention of our dreams, and none of Shelsa and Tommaso."

"What have you heard about them?"

"That they've moved on, as I said. I do receive the occasional secret note from Agnese, and from the other one—what was his name? The American."

"Ringling."

"Yes. That part must remain in confidence for the time being, subject for another book, perhaps. I only hope I live long enough to see what becomes of them all . . . In the meantime, our story has to be told. And it has to be told with the most rigorous honesty. You are to leave nothing out, avoid nothing. *Niente, capito? Do I make myself clear?*"

"But—"

"I hereby appoint Rosa to assist you—she's more honest—and I require you to present the completed manuscript to me exactly one year from today, in this room, if God grants me that much more time on earth. Typed. Double-spaced. Pages numbered in the upper-right-hand corner. Absent of spelling errors and grammatical slips. Failure to do so will result in your excommunication. Do I make myself clear?"

"Abundantly clear, Holy Father."

"Giorgio."

"Abundantly clear, Giorgio."

"Good. Have yourself a stroll in the Borghese, then take the afternoon train back to Rimini. Get started on the book tomorrow morning. Any questions, my beloved cousin?"

"Yes, one. What would you like as a title?"

The Holy Father pondered a moment, pressing his lips together, slanting his eyes to one side. At last, a small glow of pleasure lit his face. He looked at me and said, "What was that phrase I used, at Mazzo's villa? The one that seemed to make him so happy? Do you remember it, *cugino?*"

"*Sì, me lo ricordo. Me lo ricorderò per sempre.*"

"Yes," I said, "I remember it. I will remember it always."

The End

July 7, 2014 / Cagli, Le Marche, Italy
August 3, 2016 / Conway, Massachusetts, USA

ABOUT THE AUTHOR

Roland Merullo is the acclaimed author of twenty previous books, including *Revere Beach Boulevard, Golfing with God,* and *Breakfast with Buddha.* Merullo's work has been translated into German, Spanish, Korean, Portuguese, Croatian, Chinese, and Turkish, and he has won numerous prizes, including Massachusetts Book Awards in both fiction and nonfiction. He lives in Massachusetts with his wife and two daughters.